Ghost Notes

by

Beth Henderson

Ghost Notes

Cover Art by *Diana Carlile*

The Wild Rose Press, Inc.
PO Box 708
Adams Basin, NY 14410-0708
Visit us at www.thewildrosepress.com

Publishing History
First Edition, 2022
Trade Paperback ISBN 978-1-5092-4179-8
Digital ISBN 978-1-5092-4180-4

Published in the United States of America

Dedication

Dedicated to the Memory of
Andy Henderson
1951 - 2020
A wonderful pianist and composer
who, after an injury to his right hand,
let the music die in him.

"In music, a ghost note is
a musical note with a rhythmic value,
but no discernible pitch when played."
~Wikipedia

Chapter One

"I don't understand."

"What part?"

She sighed, irritated. "Any of it. The man is dead. Has been for nearly ten years."

"Then prove it to the client," the man across the desk from her said. "He believes Hastings is still alive, just in hiding."

"Then he's hiding for a reason. A good reason."

"That's not our call. We're simply being paid to find him."

Her sigh was louder this time. She shifted in her chair. "But he's dead. It was in all the news reports at the time."

"Was it?" He rifled through the papers in a folder on his desk. So old school. But when briefing an investigator, he liked to stab a finger down on each as he laid out the facts already corralled for the job. He never took one on without a bit of personal research into the matter. Though, considering the myriad ways technology had opened sleuthing far beyond the paper trail, he was way behind the times. He left those searches to the minions. Like her.

His index finger poked the printout to her left. "Here's the original report. She was killed outright because she was behind the wheel. *He* was taken to the hospital."

"I remember," she said. "He wasn't expected to live the night."

"But apparently he did. Here's her death certificate. The funeral notice. The media coverage of both the investigation and her funeral. There's a single line about him in one of the tabloids, that he's in intensive care, and that's five days after the accident."

"Which doesn't prove he recovered."

"Doesn't prove he died, either. That's your job. Find him whether he's alive or buried. But…" He paused for effect. Dramatic bastard. "…he's alive. The client is very emphatic that that's the case."

She was silent for a full minute, studying his face, the way his hands shuffled the copies of various reports and tucked them back in the bright red folder. Bright red because he liked color coding, and red not only indicated that he felt this was a high-profile case but that he was gouging the client for big bucks because he scented scandal in everything they'd told him.

"Why me?" she asked.

He leaned back in his chair. The leather groaned beneath his weight. "Not that I want this to sound like it's sexist—"

Which meant it was very sexist.

"—but you've got all the qualifications necessary to draw our man from hiding."

If he was hiding and not dead, which was far more likely.

"Meaning I'm female," she said.

"A female with all the attributes our man was known to appreciate. You turn heads, Gaeley."

She hated when he used the pet name. The one her husband had called her.

"Plus, you've got pipes."

"Pipes! I haven't sung in over five years. I didn't have *pipes* then, so I really don't have 'em now."

"You got 'em," he insisted. "You sang at the Christmas party last year."

"*Holiday* party," she corrected, "and it was a group sing-along."

"Yours was the only voice *I* heard," he said, his grin wide and a bit lascivious.

Pig. "I gave up singing because I was merely passable at it. That means not good enough to make a living from it, in case you need a translation. And besides—"

"Bullshit. You gave it up because you make far more money being one of my hounds. There's no *besides* about it. You know why?"

"I'm on tenterhooks," she said dryly.

"Because I don't want you to follow the money on this one, honey. I want you to follow the music. That's how to find Jace Hastings. Follow the music."

****

"You're killing yourself."

The man once known as Jace Hastings looked up at the woman resting her weight on her forearms atop the baby grand. Her stylishly cropped blonde locks were streaked with attractive silver highlights, and her loosely fitted, cream silk blouse had been accessorized with a black-and-sand figured scarf wrapped to encircle her neck, then spill in two trailing tails down her front. As usual, her makeup gave the illusion of a flawless complexion and directed the attention toward her sage green eyes.

He cleared his throat. She gave him a look he was

quite familiar with, huffed in disgust, and shifted her stance so her hip leaned against the side of the instrument instead, leaving the top once more a smooth sheet of highly polished onyx, free of obstruction.

Except for what he'd placed on the surface, that is. Sheets of wide staff manuscript paper with his sketched-in arrangement notes dancing along the lines were spread before him, a pencil resting atop the partially worked-out score. Next to the grand and within easy reach, a round, ceramic-tile-topped table held a coffee mug. A keyboard and a drink were currently all he required to feel like a whole man.

Or a close replica of one these days.

"You are such a stickler," she grouched. "I do own this thing, so if I want to lean on it, it's my prerogative."

"But *I'm* the one who plays it, tunes it."

"Loves it more than you do your mother," she snapped.

He grinned at her. Ran his fingers over the keys. "You've never admitted to being my mother in thirty-five years, C.C. I believe you've said you were my aunt upon occasion, or a close friend of the family."

"Also, that I was at school with your mother," she admitted. "Which I was, considering I *am* your mother."

When he didn't comment, she sighed. "You hate me for not claiming you as mine all those years, don't you?"

He shook his head slightly, though his eyes were on the piano keys. On the scar that hadn't faded on the back of his left hand. One of the ever-present reminders of the past. "It was a game you played. Or that's what

Dad insisted. You didn't claim him as your husband most of the time, either. Didn't mean you didn't love us."

"You did hate it," she said. "You told me so."

"When I was what…six?"

"Eight," she corrected.

He chuckled.

"Don't laugh, Pel. It's true!"

He played a set of chords, then switched key to play them again. "You didn't come over here just to mar the grand's finish, C.C. Out with it. You want a song. Which one?"

She gave him her frustrated face, the one that made her nose twitch and the lines around her eyes deepen. Cecilia Pelham still looked ten years too young to be his mother, thanks to a fortuitous gene pool and expensive spa visits. Which he paid for. She hadn't after all used her own funds for the baby grand or the building that housed it, though her name was on the bill of sale and the lease. But a man who wished to disappear didn't put his name on things, even if it was his bank account taking the hit.

"Okay," he said, relenting. "In what way am I killing myself? With this?" He tipped his chin to indicate the nearly empty coffee mug on the side table. Nobody messed with the finish on his prized, orchestrally voiced piano. Not even him.

"By cutting yourself off from the only thing that matters," C.C. insisted, ignoring his attempt to divert her. It wasn't coffee in the mug, but something with more of a bite.

"Music."

"Of course, music. You can't just jettison it, Pel.

It's in your blood. Your father's a musician. I'm a singer. You can't help but eat, sleep, and breathe music. It's bred into you."

Pelham Flannery laughed. "Bullshit. Both of your parents are rabid political activists. Do you care a hoot about politics, *any* politics?"

The answer was reluctantly given. "No."

"Dad's entire family are equally rabid when it comes to religion. When's the last time he set foot in a church?"

She wilted further. "The Sunday before he turned eighteen and hightailed it for the bright lights."

"Which means…"

"Oh, go to hell," she snapped.

"Already been there and have the scars to prove it," he said trying for flippant. Just trying for it. Flippant wasn't easy to pull off anymore.

"I'm fine, C.C.," Pel assured. "And you know why?"

She gave him her suspicious look, head turned slightly away, chin cocked at a defiant angle. "Why?" she asked.

He let the keys tell her. Played the chorus of a chart topper decades old.

But he didn't sing the words. Singing is what would kill him. So he simply played the notes to "I've Got the Music in Me."

What was surprising was that C.C. didn't sing them this time either.

****

Gaelen Wyndom hated to admit it, but her boss was right. Nothing anywhere indicated that Jace Hastings, the guy who not only plucked heart strings

When a percussive knock sounded on his open office door, he glanced up. The once soggy guest hovered there, his shirt swamping her upper body, though she'd tied it at her waist. She lifted the carryout bag.

"Just wanted to thank you again," she said.

He wondered what her rendition of "Georgia On My Mind" would sound like. There was simply something in her voice that hinted at the ability to sing. Yet he doubted that was why she had come to the restaurant that day.

"Listen," she said. "While this sounds like a really bad pick-up line, and that's not my intention in the least…"

"No woman's tried to pick me up in a long time," he told her. "Go ahead. Shoot. It'll do my ego wonders."

She grinned at the lie.

"It's the least I can do to show my appreciation over the loan of your spare shirt."

"So, what's the line?" he asked.

She tilted her head to the side. The sweep of chestnut hair swung with the motion. "Have we ever met before? There's something familiar about you, but I can't put my finger on it."

Warning bells clamored in his mind.

with his music but carved his way into millions of women's hearts with his smile, had died of injuries in the traffic accident that had taken the luscious and talented Ashley Hopper's life. A decade ago, they'd been the tabloids' match made in heaven. Hell, they'd gotten stuck with being called Jaceley! Always seen together, his dark hair and sun-warmed skin acting the perfect foil for her surfer-girl hair and lightly toasted complexion. His brilliant emerald eyes drew the attention more than her pale baby blues. Posed next to each other, Jace and Ashley were photographic gold. In every duet they sang, their voices blended as though required ingredients in a song. Then she died and he...vanished.

Gaelen scoured not just the archives of national news reports, the music biz gossip, the fan clubs still in worshipful existence, but watched every online video clip that Jace appeared in. Some were music videos, others guest appearances on late-night talk shows, at music awards ceremonies, movie premiers. Everything she came up with revolved around his public life as an entertainer. Nothing surfaced about his personal life. Which meant Jason Hastings wasn't Jace's real name.

He'd adroitly dodged questions about hometown, family, schools, and anything that would give a glimpse of a private life or who he'd been before forming a band.

No bank accounts. No birth certificate. No driver's license. No passports issued to anyone other than the previously nonexistent Jason Hastings. And definitely no death certificate. Numerous web pages and far more videos than she cared to watch, yet watch them she did. She'd forgotten the soft whisper of his rough voice, one that could take a previously up-tempo love song and turn it into something that left no dry eyes in the audience. Videos that included shots of those audiences showed grown men dashing a tear aside.

Although he composed no songs, Jace rode one reworked standard after another onto the bestselling pop and jazz music lists. That equated to a very healthy bank account.

She'd always followed the money on a case. It's what any investigator worth two cents did, and she was worth at least a dime. Or so Hank Wyndom, her father-in-law and employer, said. Some days he was generous and upped her into the twenty-five-cent category.

Too bad he'd gotten her husband—his son—killed on a case.

Which was only partly true, Gaelen admitted. Luke's damn hero complex was the true murder weapon.

That hero quality had dazzled her enough to put a ring on her finger.

Gaelen realized she had been unconsciously rubbing the spot where the ring had rested though five years had passed since she'd taken it off, placing it in the coffin with Luke. It wasn't memories that haunted her but old habits. They were harder to dismiss. To break.

To kill.

Some, at least, stood her in good stead. Hank might think following the money wouldn't help with this case, but that was no reason not to follow it. Jace Hastings' career had been short but profitable. For a pop star, he'd been rather frugal. He hadn't bought a cliffside villa with spectacular ocean views or a cloud-level condo in

The Big Apple or San Francisco. No downtime spent on Riviera or Acapulco beaches. Never bought a yacht. His only indulgence equated to a lipstick-red electric roadster worth well over $100,000 when new, which he'd bought secondhand, according to all reports. He'd never upgraded to a later model.

Had never let anyone else drive it, according to the tabloid stories and various articles that focused on electric vehicles.

And yet Ashley Hopper had been behind the wheel of the sports car the night it was T-boned by a semi too fired up to stop for a red light.

Perhaps *that* was the first mystery to solve. Jace doing the unexpected and letting his girlfriend drive. None of the articles Hank had handed her or she'd found on her own supplied an answer to that question. While it didn't seem connected, it wasn't unconnected, either.

Gaelen turned back to her computer and fed in *Ashley Hopper*.

****

"I see you've got a new case," Paprika Mendez said before sucking on the straw resting in her Tequila Sunrise.

Gaelen put her own Sunrise down. She hadn't bothered with the straw but had plucked it free to rest on a bar napkin. "Why do you think that?"

Her friend tilted her head, her long bleached-white hair swinging with the motion. The two inches of roots showing were naturally black, as were her brows and lashes. While Gaelen's profession called for her to blend into a crowd, Rika's cultivated drama did the opposite. Gaelen had already counted five men who'd given her companion admiring head-to-toe scans. Of course, Rika had given them each reciprocal summing-ups, too. "You've already sucked down a third of your drink, Gael. You only do that when Hank shuffles a problem off on you. What's it this time?"

"A wild goose chase."

"You're a private detective, and you don't do cheating spouses, and hate security checks, and... Well, I always forget that other thing."

"Skip tracing," Gaelen supplied. She did hate it, although it was frequently the bread and butter of private investigation.

"Yeah, that!" Rika said, using her straw as a pointer to emphasize the comment. "That means you get all the weird jobs."

"Well, this one is weirder than usual," Gaelen said. "Tell me if any of this makes sense."

"Go for it," Rika ordered, snagging the half-moon orange slice from her drink to suck on.

Gaelen re-wet her whistle, then set her glass aside. "First, Hank won't tell me who the client is. Claims it's a need-to-know that I don't need to know. That's hinky to begin with, but I'm supposed to find a guy who's most likely dead."

"Huh."

"Huh," Gaelen repeated. "It gets better. You remember Jace Hastings?"

Rika placed the now crescent of orange peel on the edge of the cocktail napkin. "God, I worshipped him when you and I were dorm mates. But he died—Oh. My. Gosh! Is that who you're supposed to find?"

"So Hank tells me. Doesn't make much sense, does it?"

"I can't remember, but was he from Phoenix? The accident happened in LA, didn't it? Did he live there at the time?"

Gaelen shrugged. Played with the toothpick impaling the maraschino cherry to her own orange slice. "No idea. Not even the usual and dreaded skip trace routes are paying out. I can't find anything about him other than the obvious things. Doesn't sound like he lived in LA at the time. His band was in the middle of a tour, so it was just a stop along the way."

Rika tapped one aqua-lacquered nail against the side of her drink. "There was that girl——"

"Ashley Hopper," Gaelen said.

Her friend frowned. "Was that her name?"

Gaelen shrugged. "It's what they put on her tombstone. You don't remember what happened on stage that night? You were such a fan."

Rika snorted, playing with the straw again. "And you weren't? Seems to me you were the first one to buy each of his CDs—wait! They put a vinyl out, and you bought that, too, even though——"

"Neither of us owned anything to play it on," Gaelen admitted. "The library had a player to use. I had a paper due in one of the music courses, and it was research."

"Sure it was," Rika murmured. "Gael, I was a music major, too, and I didn't buy the research materials required for a paper. You were smitten as much as the rest of us were. You just didn't want to admit it."

"It was the music, Rik. My topic was the arrangements and how he managed to evoke such strong emotions from an audience."

"Uh-huh. I just remember you were really ticked to get a *B* on the paper."

She had been. It was only in retrospect that she realized it hadn't been smart to hand in a paper on a pop musician who rescored jazz and big band tunes for twenty-first-century audiences. Everyone else in the class wrote about Itzhak Perlman, Gyorgy Sandor, Pablo Casals, Yo-Yo Ma, or George Gershwin's classical pieces.

Of course, if she was in that class now, she'd probably pick Lindsey Stirling as her topic and be just as unlucky with the grade.

"To get back to the impossible case—what everyone was talking about, before the accident knocked it from favor, was that on stage that night, after singing a duet with Jace, Ashley got on one knee and asked him to marry her."

The video clip hadn't been keyworded to pop up with Jace's name—which was strange—but it had when she'd sent the search engine looking for tidbits about Ashley. The woman's action had placed all eyes on her, but in rewatching it numerous times, Gaelen noticed that Jace himself had appeared taken aback at the move. It hadn't looked like he'd said anything before Ashley bounced to her feet and threw her arms around him.

It made Gaelen curious about whether he'd said *yes* or not.

Of course, perhaps he had, off stage. There was the oddity of Ashley being the one behind the wheel of his car that night. The vehicle, every article that referred to it claimed, he had never let anyone else drive before.

Rika's expression said it all. She'd forgotten that little incident. Well, getting killed in a traffic accident bare hours later did tend to make people forget what happened to a person earlier.

Gaelen savored her Sunrise, waiting for her friend to lose the stare of a popeyed goldfish.

"I totally forgot that," Rika said. "Does this client expect you to dash about the country looking for a lead on Jace Hastings, then?"

"Nope. That's another of the incomprehensible elements of this case. The mysterious client called Desert Wynd Investigations because he believes Hastings is living in Phoenix."

"You sure the client is a *he*? Could be a woman. Some groupie who after a wild night with the band found she was pregnant and plans to hit Jace with a belated paternity suit."

Gaelen waved her index finger, negating the idea. "Nope. Hank definitely said the client was male."

"The woman's father or brother?"

"Not getting that sort of vibe off this," Gaelen admitted. "No, this guy has got an agenda and is playing those cards close to the chest. He wants to find Jace Hastings so bad, he probably won't believe the man is dead even if I find a memorial plaque with his name on it in a cemetery. In any case, I've spent two days getting nowhere."

"Sounds like you need to get your mind off this for a bit, Gael. Why not come with me? There's this new lounge that opened in Surprise a month ago. My agent says they're looking for a singer. Just a part time gig— Friday and Saturday nights. I've got an appointment to talk to the owner, C.C. Pelham."

Gaelen considered. Maybe Rika was right. She needed to get her mind off this ridiculous case. Well, impossible case.

She rocked her glass back and forth, watching the remnant of her Sunrise wash from left to right. The glass was half full. But then, so was her life. She couldn't even blame that situation on Luke, considering they'd been on the brink of breaking up when he died.

"Out in Surprise? You know the population out that way is skewed toward the retirement communities."

"Which means I cover Sixties and Seventies songs rather than current hits," Rika said. She slipped off the bar stool, extended a hand, wriggled her fingers in invitation.

"Oh, what the hell," Gaelen said. "You driving?"

"Absolutely."

Gaelen tilted her glass, finishing off her drink. "Then lead on, my friend. This girl's mind needs down time bad."

****

"This is without a doubt the worst idea you've ever had," Pel grouched, running a hand back through his hair in frustration. The leather office chair swung to the right as he rocked against the high back. "Hell, C.C., I thought you wanted to run a bar so *you'd* have someplace to sing. Not that you'd go looking for someone else to do so."

She stood in the doorway of the office, her fists resting on her hips. Her expression was one of disgust. "Darling. Why did we pick Surprise, Arizona as the perfect place to live? Because it's basically a retirement community. Lots of golf courses. Lots of people who never heard of or at least paid any attention to—"

"Don't say it," he warned. She knew what he

meant. They'd agreed that his other name would never be spoken, just in case someone overheard. It was too dangerous.

"...to any modern musicians," she finished. Yep, she'd almost said the name and was trying to cover her tracks.

"Considering we don't play country music or what young people listen to, the clientele we cater to is my age or older. Their favorite online stations feature what we Baby Boomers grew up listening to. But they also like jazz. You like jazz. I sing jazz. We can lure more people in on the weekends by having someone *other than me* at the mic."

"Someone younger than you."

"Insults will get—"

"Facts," he countered.

C.C. huffed in disgust. "It will be okay, Pel. You aren't the man you were before."

But he was. He might not look quite the same. Ten years, far too many surgeries, tinted contacts to turn his memorable green eyes to brown, clear-lens dark-framed glasses to further hide them, and a bottle of dye to turn his dark hair to a lighter shade had all contributed to make him look less like he had during the height of his career. Rather than cultivating a scruff of beard, he was clean shaven. Hell, he even pitched his voice an octave lower these days. Had done so long enough that even when talking to either of his parents, he no longer sounded like Jace Hastings. But he was still the same man.

On the inside.

One of these days, someone was going to see beneath the shroud he'd constructed to bury his former persona, and then the jig would be up. And when it was, the guy who'd missed killing him a decade ago would take another shot at making that shroud real.

"I'll stay right where I am while you do the interview. We'll hope your interviewee can accompany themselves on the grand."

"You're being ridiculous, Pel."

"I'm being careful," he countered. "What are they? A Sinatra or a Julie London?"

"Darling. *I'm* not old enough to be a Julie London, so why would I hire one? Think a young Dionne Warwick or…" She paused, running names through her mind, he supposed.

"Mama Cass? Cher?"

She frowned at him. "You're being obnoxious. And I don't know if the girl who's coming plays any instrument. I never did, and it never stopped anyone from hiring me."

"Dad says you got the gigs because you had great legs and weren't shy about flashing cleavage."

"He says that because those are the reasons he married me. I got the gigs because I could sing."

Which, Pel admitted, she indeed could.

"I'm still staying right in this chair," he said. "If you like her and she can't accompany herself, we'll just have to call the musicians' union and hire a combo to back her."

"But *your* playing is—"

"No. When *you're* the one singing, I play, C.C. Not for anyone else."

She huffed. "You're as stubborn as your father."

"Yep," he agreed. "You've always said that. Is he ready to give up the road and join us here? Hold out the lure of his own drummer and bass player to back up his slide. Seduce him here, and you'll have no need of me, because his trio can back you."

"He's not as easily convinced these days," she warned.

"Then mention the magic four-letter word, Cec," Pel suggested.

She laughed, amusement replacing her irritation with him. "That might work," she said.

The magic word was a way of life in Surprise. *Golf.*

****

The building Rika pulled up before had begun life as a Mexican restaurant. It had rounded posts protruding from beneath a wide porch, ochre-tinged stucco, and red half-round tiles on the roof. Landscaping incorporated a couple ocotillos with barrel and prickly pear cacti, and railings that looked like hitching posts. A patio was off to the side and featured mesquite trees in the corners and ranch-style tables with benches. Wide windows on the restaurant's northern exposure led visitors to the outdoor seating area.

There were only a few other vehicles in the parking lot. Those toward the back probably belonged to the staff, Gaelen decided, and those near the door were in handicapped spots, though not all of them.

Rika slipped her metallic orange compact sedan into a slot a row back from the door. Despite having grown up in Phoenix, Gaelen's friend felt whenever possible the goal was to move from air-conditioned building to air-conditioned car and back within the shortest distance.

Rika hadn't dressed for cranked-up cooling,

though. She'd dressed to make an entrance, to be remembered. Her lightweight cotton jade dress complemented the aqua of her painted nails. It sported narrow straps and a skirt that swished around her thighs. Her long strides were unhampered by her high-heeled sandals. Rika's dusky skin and two-toned hair simply made her even more noticeable. By comparison, Gaelen felt her chestnut locks and conservative dove gray business suit indicated a severe lack of fashion sense. Like a well-trained pet, she followed her more vibrant friend through the entrance door.

The interior had been stripped of southwestern touches, leaning more toward urban upscale club. The walls and carpeting were dark, as were the tables and upholstery in the booths. Large modern art paintings done in beige, various grays, blues, and touches of rust made for a relaxing background. Lighting fixtures were chrome with stocky white drum shades that hung above each table or booth. Perhaps because the clientele was largely retired, the lighting was brighter than in many upscale restaurants. Gaelen wondered whether it was adjusted, lowering in intensity after the dinner hour. She had noted the hours on the door when they entered. They opened at 4 p.m. for dinner but switched to drinks only from 10 p.m. to closing at 2 a.m., which implied not all the customers were funded by Social Security. Open seven days a week, C.C.'s Place featured live music every evening.

At this hour, the music was piped-in soft jazz. She recognized a piano number, followed by a sax selection from her own music collection. In a far corner, on a slightly raised stage, a gleaming black baby grand piano and a mic stand waited in the shadows for their turn in the spotlight.

"I already love this place," Rika said. "Even if I don't get the job, I'm coming back just for the ambience."

Gaelen silently agreed with her friend. C.C.'s was worth the drive, and she hadn't even tasted anything from the menu yet.

"That's just the sort of comment we like to hear," an older woman claimed as she ghosted to the black-lacquered maître d' podium. There were smile creases at the corners of her eyes. Her makeup showed the deft hand of a performer, enhancing her best features and downplaying others. In her case, the focus was on her eyes and high cheekbones rather than her mouth. Her hair was a carefully wisped cap of wheat streaked with platinum. She was slim but dressed so that her form blended into rather than stood apart from the dark walls and fixtures, her choices being simple jet slacks and matching button-front silk blouse. An intricate silver-and-turquoise squash blossom necklace peeked from the open neckline. The only element that hinted at her true age were her hands, and she had sensibly done without flashy rings that would have drawn attention to them. "Let me guess which one of you is Rika. I'm C.C., by the way."

Rika grinned at her. "The rather famous C.C. Pelham," she insisted. "Three-time nominee for Best Jazz Vocalist, a long-standing recording contract with Visions Records, and guest spots on late-night talk shows—"

"I think Rika's trying to say she's impressed and envious and honored, Ms. Pelham," Gaelen said, cutting her friend off before Rika could babble her way to embarrassment.

C.C. laughed. "Best to take into consideration the 'almost' elements. Just a nominee for the award, never a winner, and always a couple thousand record sales shy of meriting gold. Didn't get rich but always found a gig, and sometimes that's the hardest part."

"And now you're a restauranteur," Rika said, "and looking for a singer rather than sing yourself?"

"Oh, I still sing. I just need a night or two off. This joint may carry my name, but my son is the brains behind it. Come on back to the bar where we can talk business," she suggested, turning to lead the way farther into the building. Then she glanced over her shoulder at Gaelen. "I'm guessing you're Rika's agent?"

Gaelen started. "Oh, no. Sorry. Gaelen Wyndom, and I'm just her tagalong," she said.

"As an accompanist?"

Gaelen admitted her shortcomings. "I'm even hopeless at 'Chopsticks.' "

"Same here, honey," C.C. said. "You've got a lovely voice. Singer?"

"Not anymore. Just an office pencil pusher these days. Rika's the star."

"I like you both already," C.C. declared, moving behind the bar. "What can I get you?"

Gaelen wasn't surprised that Rika asked for a glass of water. Enough to soothe her throat and counteract the earlier Sunrise. She requested decaf coffee, no special flavoring, but two regular sugars. There were some things she hadn't the courage to down, particularly if the words *diet* or *artificial* appeared on the label. C.C. supplied the java in a stoneware cup-and-saucer set that blended a mushroom gray exterior with a gold-touched crème interior glaze.

Thanking her, Gaelen gave the two songstresses space by moving to a booth, ostensibly to check emails on her cell. Instead, she Googled C.C. Pelham.

C.C. had her own website, she found. Photographs of her on stage with various famous people peeled away on a carousel that imitated a visitor's idle turning of pages. The fact that she could be found at the restaurant, entertaining, most nights was also on the front page. The menu offered a discography of her recordings and a history of the various places she'd played. She'd opened for bigger names numerous times, headlined at intimate lounges in NYC, LA, San Francisco, DC, Chicago, Waikiki, and New Orleans. Had graced the stages of lounges in half the Las Vegas hotel resorts and been the headliner on cruise ships. Every charity event she'd participated in was recorded. Mention was made of regular visits to nursing homes where she urged her audience to sing along with their favorite standards.

Gaelen moved on to the bio page. Here she found every element Rika had babbled was at the top of C.C.'s accomplishments. The fact that she'd married Jay Flannery, a trombone man with one of the first bands she'd joined as vocalist, was oddly nearly a footnote. Their careers took them in different directions via bookings, but they'd managed enough time together to produce a son. A casual snapshot of the family, with the Smithsonian castle in DC in the background, showed a boy around eight years old sandwiched between his fair-haired mother and a much taller dark-haired man. Since the boy wore a baseball cap with the bill tilted forward to shade his face, it was impossible to guess which parent had contributed to his coloring or features the most. From the clothes C.C. wore, and her hairdo in the picture, Gaelen guessed the photo had been taken in the mid Nineties. Whether the boy's name had been left off as unimportant or to protect him was unclear. In any case, since C.C. had said her son ran the restaurant, any tall, thirty-something male who surfaced from the back of the building would likely be the now-grown son. Considering both C.C. and her husband were good-looking, their offspring would likely be the sort of guy Rika always fell for. No doubt Gaelen would learn far more about him than she cared to know when that happened.

Unless Rika didn't get the job.

But she would. Not only was she a talented singer with a well-weighted performance resume, but few local vocalists also specialized in covering older songs. And, considering the titles of songs listed on C.C.'s recordings, plus the likely tastes of the clientele, her friend was practically a shoo-in.

Since Rika and C.C. were still talking, Gaelen unearthed earbuds from her purse and pulled up one of the older woman's performances on a late-night TV show, now immortalized on the Net. The song was one she'd always been fond of. Had frequently sung in her short and uninspiring career as a singer herself. C.C. sang "Misty." Gaelen closed her eyes and silently sang along.

Word for word. Same pauses. Same drawn-out notes. Same breathy delivery.

Her eyes popped open as she realized both she and C.C. had used the same arrangement on the song. Which was impossible. She'd used the arrangement perhaps six years ago. Based on the date shown for C.C.'s performance, she'd used the arrangement twelve years ago.

Eleven years ago, when she'd still been a music major in college, "Misty" was one of the songs she'd concentrated on for that *B* grade paper she'd written about Jace Hastings' arrangements. The song had been among those on the vinyl record she'd bought to use as reference material.

She'd used Jace's arrangement of "Misty" during her short singing career. But C.C. Pelham had used the same arrangement even before Jace had recorded it.

Twelve years ago, Jace Hastings had been playing small clubs with his band. His real success began shortly after the date on the video of C.C. using this specific arrangement.

Which meant either Jace hadn't done the arrangements his musical reputation was based on...

Or C.C. Pelham knew Jace Hastings. Had worked with him as her arranger before anyone knew he existed.

Gaelen replayed the clip, this time with her eyes open, scanning the musicians visible behind C.C. to see if any of them looked like her missing man. The screen on her phone was too small to help, even when she enlarged sections of the video. Once she got home, pulling the clip up on her larger screen could be done. Which meant the visit to C.C.'s was simply a break in what would be a long workday. She could ask about the woman's connection to Jace Hastings before leaving the restaurant, though. Perhaps if she and Rika stayed in the club for dinner, it would make C.C. more inclined to spill anything she knew.

While she'd been engrossed with the recording, Gaelen realized Rika and C.C. had moved to the baby grand and were sorting through sheet music. She bolted from the booth without glancing to the aisle and nearly knocked a waiter off his feet. The tray of drinks he'd been balancing tipped. Gaelen hissed in a breath as a variety of soft drinks and crushed ice soaked the front of her suit jacket and skirt. She staggered back into the table behind her hard enough to have coffee washing over the table—and her cell.

"Oh, sh—sorry," the waiter said. "I didn't realize you were getting up."

"Wasn't your fault. I wasn't looking to see if there was traffic," she insisted. The smile of apology she gave him was probably as soggy as her damp clothes. "Can you direct me to the restroom so I can clean up a bit? And be sure to give me a tab for the spilled drinks."

"We never charge for spilled drinks at C.C.'s," he said. The server's tray was on the table now as he gathered up all the upended glasses. "Mind your step. You don't want to slip on a clump of crushed ice."

Gaelen thanked him when he directed her toward the restrooms and apologized for giving him more work. As he hunkered down to scoop up ice slush with his hands, she noticed he'd received his own baptism in their collision. As another server rushed up with bar rags to help him, Gaelen headed in the direction he'd pointed and belatedly realized she'd left her purse in the booth and the cell on the table. It would be sticky from the soft drinks, if not the sweetened coffee, when she returned. At least there was little chance of the phone being stolen while she was gone, since the dinner crowd was currently thin. Hopefully, no one would notice her black purse where it remained on the dark upholstered banquette seat.

She dripped as she moved down the hall, feeling like a fool. She'd made it partway to the ladies' room when a glob of melting ice slipped from her collar to slide inside the buttoned front of her jacket. Startled, Gaelen gasped and stopped, hoping to...well, she wasn't sure what. She was damp and further chilled by the cranked-up air conditioning. At least the lining of the jacket kept it from clinging as a blouse or dress would have.

It was only when a man asked, "Is there something I can do for you?" that she realized she'd stopped across from an open door. A brief glance inside the room identified it as an office. The man behind the desk had rolled back the cuffs on his dress shirt and loosened the tie at his unbuttoned collar. He wore glasses but seemed to have slid them down his nose to look over the top as he peered at a computer on his right. His hair looked like he might have run his hand through the light brown locks for some reason. She'd done so with her own hair often enough—usually in frustration.

"Oh, no. Sorry. I'm enroute to the...well, to get a little less sticky. Totally fine otherwise." She turned to dash into the washroom, then paused and looked back at him. "I told the waiter to bill me for the drinks that were spilled when I bumped his arm. It wasn't his fault. Wasn't looking where I was going." With that clarified, she hoped, Gaelen nearly ran the rest of the way.

Chapter Two

Pel stared at the spot recently vacated by the attractive brunette in the hallway. Had she been C.C.'s songstress? If so, it appeared from the way she dressed that singing was a sideline for her. The business suit of soft gray, basic black heels, and lack of eye-catching styling for her makeup and collarbone-brushing straight hair, didn't shout professional performer. It yelled chameleon instead. She'd certainly vanish in a crowd of office workers.

Well, that showed he'd been around C.C. too much. Even without carefully crafted costuming, the woman was attractive. He'd heard music in her soft voice, but also a decided helping of determination. Even with her clothing soaked and obviously uncomfortable in the AC, she'd covered for the hired help and offered to pay for her drenching. That indicated a caring person and one who was fair in her dealings with others.

She hadn't been flashy, but she'd definitely intrigued him in their short exchange. If he offered to compensate her with free cleaning for her suit, would she accept? Probably not. However, he could give her something that she'd likely accept the loan of and give her a reason to return. He hoped.

Pel pushed away from the desk, headed to the wardrobe unit that housed his spare clothing and backup apparel for waitstaff in need of immediate replacements—like the one who'd probably got dampened along with the woman in the hall. Rather than a staff shirt, he took one of his own dress shirts from the upper shelf. When she exited the ladies' room, he had a shoulder propped on the doorjamb, his weight on his good leg and the surgically reconstructed one bent at the knee.

She stumbled to a stop when she saw him waiting, folded shirt in hand.

"I can't do anything about your damp skirt, but this might keep you from getting a chill otherwise," he said, holding the folded shirt out to her. "You can return it the next time you visit C.C.'s. It's a spare I keep on hand for when I'm the staff's target."

Her lips twitched in amusement, but her eyes had widened at the offer. They were a lovely shade of blue, as though the Arizona sky at midday had served as tincture in constructing them. There was a touch of embarrassed rose in her cheeks. Her neck was long, pale, and made for a man to taste as he nibbled his way to her delectable and earring-free lobe.

"Thank you," she murmured, accepting the loan.

"I have more, but consider *this* a gift," Pel insisted and reached aside to snag a carryout bag with the C.C.'s Place logo on the side. "Call it luggage for your damp things."

That won him a full smile as she accepted it. "You obviously know the way to a woman's heart," she said, the promise of a laugh in her voice. Then she nipped back into the restroom. Lacking further reason to procrastinate over the stock reports he'd been studying, Pel returned to his desk, though Wall Street lost out to his curiosity about the lovely woman with the blend-into-the-background clothing choices.

Was she the daughter, lawyer, or insurance agent for one of the regulars currently dining in the main room? Not, he decided, the woman C.C. was interviewing and immediately had that guess verified as a lyrical contralto voice drifted down the hall, hitting every note dead on as she crooned "Georgia On My Mind" without accompaniment. He had no idea who the singer was. No idea whether there were other vocalists due to swing by for an audition. If any others sounded like the woman singing out front, C.C. would have a difficult time narrowing in on a choice. This one's performance would be hard to best.

There was no way he could concentrate on his stock portfolio. Between the intriguing woman in the hall and the lyrical sound of C.C.'s auditioning vocalist, his mind wanted to rebel. Considering he hadn't been tempted from a life of celibacy in a long time and had tried to resist music's Lorelei call, both were jostling for his attention now. The pose of being a businessman—though his ability to milk profits through agile dancing with stocks proved he was one—was harder to maintain some days. During the long recovery after nearly dying, he'd not only needed something to keep his mind active, he'd needed a way to reboot his finances. They'd taken severe hits with the series of operations and physical therapy sessions to get him back on his feet. Generous bonuses to the various medical professionals had guaranteed his identity remained a secret throughout that first year. Oddly enough, he'd discovered he had an affinity for stock juggling. It had been a profitable hobby. Money wasn't something he worried about any longer.

Losing his mind by staying under the radar of the man who'd nearly killed him was more difficult to deal with. Some days he entertained fantasies about women he'd known, about women he'd *like* to know. Other times he itched to be back on stage so badly it was like being swarmed by hungry fire ants.

It did not help that C.C. kept finding ways to tempt him back where she felt he belonged, in the thick of the music business.

He gave in to the urge briefly, jotting down song titles that would suit the mystery performer out front. It kept him from making a mad dash to the piano to supply accompaniment. While the public at large could be fooled over his identity, Pel doubted the same could be said about someone from the music community. They'd see past his disguise to the man straining to break free of those self-imposed chains.

When a percussive knock sounded on his open office door, he glanced up. The once soggy guest hovered there, his shirt swamping her upper body, though she'd tied it at her waist. She lifted the carryout bag.

"Just wanted to thank you again," she said.

He wondered what her rendition of "Georgia On My Mind" would sound like. There was simply something in her voice that hinted at the ability to sing. Yet he doubted that was why she had come to the restaurant that day.

"Listen," she said. "While this sounds like a really bad pick-up line, and that's not my intention in the least…"

"No woman's tried to pick me up in a long time,"

he told her. "Go ahead. Shoot. It'll do my ego wonders."

She grinned at the lie.

"It's the least I can do to show my appreciation over the loan of your spare shirt."

"So, what's the line?" he asked.

She tilted her head to the side. The sweep of chestnut hair swung with the motion. "Have we ever met before? There's something familiar about you, but I can't put my finger on it."

Warning bells clamored in his mind.

"Maybe I've got that kind of face," Pel said and hastily attempted to undermine any lingering suspicion she might have. "You know, overburdened with mediocrity. Are you here auditioning for the vocalist job?"

"Oh, no. I just came with my friend. She's the singer. Are you C.C. Pelham's son?"

"Guilty."

Her smile was back. "Then that's probably where the sense of *déjà vu* comes from. You probably have features in common with her."

"Yep, that's probably the case," Pel agreed, though everyone who knew the family said he was his father's clone.

"Sorry to have disturbed you, Mr. Pelham."

"Flannery," he corrected. "Pelham Flannery."

"A man with two last names, huh?"

"Sadly, yes, though Pel will suffice," he allowed, then surprised himself by leaving his chair again and heading around the desk. "What were you drinking before the collision?"

"Coffee," she said. "I'm probably wearing some of

it, too, though the majority washed over my cell when the cup flipped over. I sorta fell against the table when the drenching occurred."

As dangerous as it might be, Pel found he wanted to stay within the range of her smile a bit longer. "Not a water-resistant model?"

"Not much water to avoid in Phoenix, so I skipped that feature. Definitely keeping it in mind when I upgrade in the future."

"Come with me," he said, joining her in the hall and pausing only to close the office door.

"I really should get back to my friend," she insisted.

The auditioning friend had moved into "That's What Love Is All About."

"C.C. will want to hear another two or three songs yet. You've got time."

He took a turn toward the kitchen and held the swinging door open for her to precede him. The scent of steak, ribs, salmon, and chicken grilled over mesquite supplied a sensory slap, one he had stopped appreciating due to over-familiarity. The woman at his side inhaled deeply, though, obviously enjoying the aromas. When the cook and his helpers looked up, expecting to receive a new order, they seemed surprised to find him there. Or perhaps it was that an unknown female wearing one of his shirts was at his side.

"I need a plastic bag filled with uncooked rice," Pel told them. "There's a cell phone that needs to be sucked dry."

The chef turned to one of his minions. "You heard the boss. Get him what he needs," he ordered and went back to supervising the entrees on the grill.

"I am definitely having dinner here before Rika and I leave," the woman next to him said.

Pel laughed. "It wasn't my intention to tempt you with food, but those words are probably music to Tom's ears. You have a preference? We have a small menu but can cater to vegetarian tastes, too."

"I think the decision will be a difficult one," she admitted.

"Let us help you, then. Tom! If you were eating here for the first time, what would you order?"

The chef glanced back over his shoulder. "Tonight, it would be the ribs. They've been marinating in sauce for six hours."

"It's his own barbecue sauce recipe. Has a hefty splash of bourbon in it." Pel added, "You'll want to lick the plate clean."

"Say goodbye to this shirt, if that's the case," she warned.

"Just gives you another reason to visit us again," he said.

When the bag of rice was delivered, Pel led the way back to the dining room. Her friend—Rika, she'd said—was crooning Gershwin's "Someone To Watch Over Me." Although it was one of the songs he'd scored for C.C., the visiting songstress either didn't read sheet music or was playing it safe by belting it out in an arrangement with which she was familiar. It was not only a good decision on her part, he'd emphasize that, in keeping his version to herself, his mother would have different renditions.

In any case, what he'd scored for C.C. recently wouldn't suit a younger, stronger voice. Though she hated to admit it, his talented mother could no longer sing the same way she had in the past. Rather than mention that even Sinatra changed his style as he aged, he'd simply scored things to downplay what had become C.C.'s range handicaps.

The nameless woman wearing his shirt headed to the booth where her phone now lay on a dry table. The cell was dutifully corralled in a cocoon of rice. Once the bag was resealed, she snagged a previously invisible purse from where it rested on the banquette seat and dropped the packaged phone inside.

Pel slipped behind the bar. "Coffee, you said? Are you the one driving?"

She slid onto one of the bar stools. He hoped it was because she was looking for ways to extend the bubble of time they shared. "Not driving," she murmured.

"Planning to stick with coffee or be more adventurous?" he asked.

"Not too adventurous," she said. "I started my downtime with a Tequila Sunrise an hour and a half ago."

"Repeat then?" Without waiting for her answer, he reached for the appropriate barware. "We call them Tequila Surprises here in Surprise, though. Well, we do at C.C.'s. On the drink menu and everything."

"And everything, huh?" she echoed. "I'm game. You joining me?"

His usual choice came straight from a bourbon bottle or in a frosted Coors one. "Absolutely," Pel said and pulled another glass from the rack over the bar top.

"So you're not a singer, but your friend is." He glanced to where C.C. and a beauty of Spanish descent, who'd dressed to steal the spotlight, sat side by side on the piano bench, store-bought sheet music, rather than his arrangements, spread out across the top of the grand. "How'd you meet?"

"The college arranged that. Turned out we'd both requested to have a dorm mate with the same major. The rest is history," she said.

He placed a bar napkin down and set her drink dead center on it. Took his own in hand and, rather than sample it, leaned back against the rear counter, his ankles crossed. "If you're both anything like the people I know were, you didn't stick with that originally chosen major when it came to actually working in the field. What was your choice?"

She removed the straw he'd put in the Sunrise and set it aside on the edge of the napkin before taking a sip straight from the glass. His own preference when downing alcohol, Pel mused.

"You're right. I didn't stick with it, though I saw all four years out with it. Turns out being chock full of the learning experience doesn't mean you're actually good at something."

"So what did you turn out to be lousy at?" he asked, honestly curious. There was something about riding to a damsel's rescue—even if it only required the loan of a shirt and the delivery of a scoop of rice—that appealed to him. It had been a long time since he'd wanted to interact with a woman in his own age bracket.

The still unnamed damsel tilted her head toward the small stage in the corner. "What she's doing right now," she said. "We were both music majors."

The alarm bells screamed to life in his mind, the imagined sound so loud he missed what else she said.

****

Gaelen snapped her fingers. "Ah, I know why you look familiar," she announced. "Before getting drenched, I was cruising your mother's website. There's a lone picture of you and your parents during a visit to DC. You look like your dad!"

She caught Pelham Flannery tipping back his drink. "Hmm. Lot of people tell me that," he murmured, then moved the subject spotlight back on her. "When music didn't work out, what did you find you were good at?"

"Research, trivia compilation, and sorting out puzzles."

"Sounds like you work for a think tank of some sort. Marketing?"

"Nowhere near that. I'm sadly lacking when it comes to a marketing degree," she said. "Sorta married into the job. I work for my father-in-law. It was hands-on training."

He gestured with his glass. "No ring. That a corporate policy or something else?"

"The *else*. He died." No reason to go into further details, though other details were on her mind. "What were you doing twelve years ago?"

"Attempting to find myself," he said. "Hard to do when your parents love the spotlight. Why?"

Gaelen shrugged. "Curiosity. You see, I pulled up a video of C.C. singing 'Misty.' It's one of my favorite classics. In fact, when I attempted to be a singer, it was what I led with in auditions."

"Go on," he urged.

"Well, oddly enough, I recognized the arrangement C.C. used. Recognized it because I used the same one. It was a Jace Hastings' arrangement. Only, twelve years ago no one had heard of him. I wondered whether C.C. had hired him to do arrangements. You have any idea whether she did or not?"

Flannery shook his head slowly. "None at all."

Although there was no hesitation in his deep voice, Gaelen knew a half truth when she heard one.

"You a Hastings fan?" he asked.

She plucked the fruit from the rim of the glass. "Hard to be a fan of someone who's dead."

"I've got no problem with Sinatra being gone," he said, "But then there's a lot more recordings to enjoy Frank's stylings on than there were with Hastings. He was sort of a flash in the pan. Very short career."

"Which is a shame. He was brilliant."

"Brilliant," he repeated, his voice flat and edged with doubt.

"In my modest opinion. You think C.C. still has the score for 'Misty' that he wrote?"

"She probably has a score for it, but whether it's Hastings' work, we'll probably never know. It's not like ASCAP keeps tabs on arrangements, just songs. Chances are it was a one-off, a work-for-hire deal with a guy trying to break into the biz," Flannery said.

"Sounds like you know a lot about how it all works," Gaelen noted.

Flannery gave a wry smile. "Just one of the hassles of running a restaurant that features live music as well as recorded music. I don't have ASCAP on speed dial, but between the two formats, we shell out a lot for ambience at C.C.'s."

"A real pain, isn't it," she suggested.

"A greenbacked bow to the folks who did the real work—writing the music and lyrics," he countered.

She could tell he was sincere in that accolade but felt there was something he danced around, as well. What it could possibly be, she doubted mattered. In any case, C.C. and Rika joined them, and the topic changed to paperwork for Rika to fill out to become an employee.

****

C.C. perched on a corner of his desk, her fingers curved over the edge. "I'm surprised, darling," she said.

"Happily, moderately, or ecstatically surprised?" Pel asked as he retrieved the last of Paprika Mendez's scanned employment documents from the printer tray. He dropped the copies into two waiting generic file folders, one for the accountant, the other for promotion uses by the PR firm. The info was saved on his computer, but delegating things he didn't want to deal with had always been a given.

"Stunned," C.C. clarified. "You gave Gaelen the shirt off your back."

"Shirt from the closet," he corrected. "Is that her name? She didn't supply one."

"Gaelen Wyndom. I liked her. Considering you left your office during daylight hours to socialize in the bar—which is unprecedented—I think you did, too. You should ask her out."

Pel slipped the folders into different manila envelopes and scrawled addresses on each. He recognized the direction his mother's mouth was headed and closed the office door against inadvertent eavesdroppers before asking, "Why would I want to do that?"

"The usual reasons. Pretty eyes to gaze into. A lovely form to hold for a close dance. A mouth made for kissing, and, of course, there is always the opportunity for sex," C.C. said.

"None of which are things a man expects his mother to mention, much less urge him to explore. Next thing I know, you'll begin waxing poetic about wanting grandchildren."

She frowned at him. "Don't be ridiculous. Why would I want to be a grandmother? I was a lousy mother. I will not have improved with age in that category."

"Thank God," he murmured giving the two words an extra dash of theatrics as he regained his chair.

C.C. huffed, probably doubting the sincerity of the exclamation. "Don't give me that," she ordered. "It isn't me who's interested in such things. It's your father. He thinks having a tyke to spoil is a great idea."

"To continue the family name?"

"Darling, to continue the 'family name' you'd need to be a Hastings, not a Flannery, which he chose as a better surname when he escaped his parents."

Pel leaned back and swung his feet to the top of the desk. "My name *is* Hastings," he reminded her. "I couldn't have gotten a passport for gigs outside of the States as my former self if I hadn't legally changed my name. Well, augmented it," he corrected. He'd wanted to have a fallback to anonymity when not on the road, which had come in handy when playing dead had become a sound idea.

Still, officially he'd been Jason Pelham Flannery Hastings for seventeen years already, though few knew that. He'd even had a driver's license under his professional name. Both it and the passport had been left to expire, hopefully serving as proof that he hadn't lived but had died, just at a slower pace than Ash had in the crash. Fortunately, he hadn't changed his name on any other paperwork. It hadn't hurt to have a grandfather who didn't trust the government. Edward Pelham had opened a numbered bank account for Pelham Flannery in the Caymans rather than have funds saved for college at an institution in the States. Every support check either C.C. or Jay Flannery had sent went directly into the foreign account. The bank in the islands didn't care what name he used as long as he got the account number and passwords right. From the start, he'd poured most of what he made as Jace Hastings into the Cayman cache, too.

"Where would be a good place to take Gaelen to dinner?" C.C. asked.

"You're serious?"

"Of course I'm serious, Pel! It isn't natural for a man your age to be alone. You need female companionship."

He grinned across the desk at her.

"You're wasting the best years of your life," she said.

"Just ensuring that I have years of life to waste," he countered. "It's too dangerous to invite someone else into that life."

"But—"

"He's still out there, Cec. Ash was a casualty that he just added to the tally of reasons to want me dead."

"Pel! You didn't do anything to merit this. Why does he want to kill you?"

"Ash, that's why. He was stalking her and sending me threatening notes demanding I get out of her life. Which I would have been delighted to do but for stipulations in the Visions Records contract."

"I argued with them, you know," C.C. said.

"You did? You never told me that."

"Well, it didn't do any good. If I'd had albums that went gold or better, they might have kowtowed, but I didn't. Your godfather could have pulled it off, but he was out of the country most of that year and difficult to find. Visions stonewalled me by insisting that Ashley was good publicity and had a contract for your tour."

"She also had the Visions PR dude in her camp telling her what to do to get notice on her own," Pel reminded. "She didn't want to be part of *my* tour, she wanted one of her own. Wanted a separate recording contract. She was willing to do anything to get Visions onboard for a solo career. I think the stalker was someone she felt was important to that goal, before they dumped her on me. That's probably when she dumped him and inadvertently booked her own death."

C.C. sighed deeply. "I was both proud and fearful during that time. Your performances far surpassed what Jay and I did, but you were in a terrible situation. Not only on the road where security personnel changed with each city, but forced to play the part of a smitten lover. Every time you had to smile while she clung to you before the cameras, then that stupid pairing of your names the media gave you—it all made me furious. I've never felt so helpless, Pel. They were boxing you in, and there was nothing Jay or I could do to help you."

Forget the box, Pel thought. It had felt like chains at the time. He'd already been talking to top office at Visions Records about jettisoning Ashley from any future projects, threatening to take his talent elsewhere. Having a CD go gold in record time had given him some leverage, especially since Ash hadn't been part of the band when they'd recorded it. He'd always suspected that she'd gotten wind of those discussions and had probably seen them as laying waste to the castle of aspirations she'd built. Which they would have been, at Visions, since he had threatened to walk if they took her on. But there were dozens of other recording firms that would have jumped at the chance to get her signature on the dotted line. Which her agent should have told her and hadn't.

So Ash had tried to turn the tables on him. Had proposed to him on stage and made it appear that he'd accepted.

"She was supposed to be just a backup singer," he said. "I still don't remember how I got talked into doing duets with her, which means Ash wormed her way in. It was a grim reality before I realized she was finessing the spotlight. All it took was one duet on stage, and her PR bandwagon began rolling.

"We had a gigantic row backstage that night. She didn't calm down until I offered to buy out her contract. She agreed, with the proviso that I do one nice thing for her—let her drive my car to the hotel. I wouldn't have even had it with me if I hadn't been in LA earlier to harangue Visions."

C.C. was quiet when he finished. "I want you to be happy, Pel. To be safe."

"The two go together, Cec. And while there is a chance that the guy who tried to kill me is still out there, there's no guarantee that I'll ever be safe."

"I should know more about what went on at the time," she said. "I should have followed the case, asked more questions, but I was focused on you. I even slept in a chair at your bedside in the hospital."

"I remember," Pel murmured. "Gram, Gramps, and Dad had to forcefully remove you from the room for your own good."

C. C. waved the reminder aside. "I do know they never arrested anyone for Ashley's death, and I don't know why. There had to be fingerprints all over that semi that rammed you."

"There were, from what the detective on the case told me. Unless that was something I imagined while drugged up," Pel admitted. "But the guy they matched hadn't a scratch on him, and he had an alibi."

"A what!"

He figured his grandfather and dad had done a good job of keeping that from her. His father certainly knew. He'd put his fist through the wall at the hospital and ended up with his slide hand in a cast.

"An alibi. Police arrived at a jewelry store on the other side of town in response to an alarm triggered just before the semi hit the roadster. Display cases were smashed, safe cleaned out, and some very identifiable merchandise taken. Evidence found at the scene sent them hotfooting after Ash's stalker. When they arrested him, he had some of the stolen jewelry in his pocket."

"That's impossible," C.C. said.

"Which is why it is called an alibi, Cec. In any case, there was no one in the cab at the scene. The consensus was that whoever was driving had bailed out before the truck entered the intersection."

"It's like a crime drama on TV. Or that movie."

"What movie?"

"*Strangers on a Train*. It was a Hitchcock thriller. I think I saw it at a Hitchcock retrospective somewhere, but it was a book first."

Pel leaned back in his chair again. "I've seen that one. Two guys agree to kill each other's marks, so nothing points back to them as the killer."

"That's it," she agreed. "Were there other fingerprints in the truck?"

"Not a one," he said. "He went to prison for the B and E. Wasn't his first arrest for it, so he got the maximum, but his time was up years ago now. He's out there. A spider biding his time."

"Did you ever know his name?"

"Oh, yeah," Pel murmured. "Not one I can forget. It's…"

****

Gaelen sat forward in her chair and grabbed a pen, though she kept it hovering over her open notebook. "Rowan McTavish," she repeated back to her caller. "You're sure that's the name, Cliff?"

"Gaeley, would I lie to you? Hell, Luke would haunt me if I did. Guy was nuts about you."

"Liar," she countered. "You're just doing what you always did—covering for him. You got more dirt I can use on this McTavish?"

"It's an old case, Gael, and the guy did his time and got out. I've got no record of him being involved in any crime—not of any sort—since he strolled out of prison four years ago."

While she jotted down the name, Gaelen needed more convincing. "Just no new crimes or no word of him anywhere?"

"Er…well, no new crimes here in California. You didn't mention needing anything else. You just said, and I quote, 'Need the name of the guy Ashley Hopper

43

took out a restraining order on, a decade back.' "

"Yep, that's what I said," she agreed. "Now get me something more, Cliff. I can't work my magic with that crumb, though it does help a bit. You got a picture to share? You know, in case I run into the creep in a dark alley."

"How you going to see in a dark alley?"

"Night-vision goggles," she said. "They came with my dandy superhero crime-solving kit."

"Superheroes don't usually have night-vision goggles," he said. "Unless you're referring to—"

"Don't geek out on me, Cliffy," Gaelen pleaded. "Just find me a mug shot or something."

"Roger wilco," he agreed. "Tell Hank I'd send him my love, but I hate the cuss."

"Don't we all," she said, ended the call to her former colleague, and fed Rowan McTavish into the Web to start a bottom-level search. Half an hour later she switched to the *Los Angeles Times* online archive since the only information the Net search had supplied was that he was from LA. Following his high school sports achievements wasn't where she needed to be. As a juvenile, if he'd had stalker tendencies in high school, they wouldn't show up in anything she could access, but perhaps Ashley hadn't been his only victim in the intervening years.

Instead, brief news stories of his arrest for burglary surfaced. He'd started small and worked his way from convenience stores and housebreaking up to cash machines and jewelry stores. It was very irritating to find he'd been arrested for robbing a jewelry store on the opposite side of town from where the semi had creamed Jace Hastings' sportscar. It had been very fortuitous for him on one hand but not on another. While robbing the jewelry store, he'd inadvertently dropped an appointment reminder card for a tooth cleaning—dropped it near the safe, clearly not a place a customer would have lost it. It had been for the following day. With his background in burglary, officers had headed to where he was expected to be. Gaelen doubted McTavish had gotten his teeth cleaned as planned. He'd had some of the stolen merchandise in his pocket when arrested. Nothing fences liked better than to have a felon with a bright smile visit them, Gaelen snarked to herself.

As that hadn't been the final mention of McTavish to come up, she kept reading and discovered that as a repeat offender he'd gotten six years in prison, and during that time had done what he hadn't bothered to do previously—gotten a college degree. More than one, in fact. Apparently very cognizant of the lack of employment opportunities for ex-cons from previous experience, he'd gone into a field that might give him an edge, based on his background: Criminal Psychology.

Now why hadn't that come up in the Internet search? she wondered. He actually had a Ph.D. in it.

Since no mention of him as part of a practice or in private practice had come up, she tried Dr. R. McTavish and got nothing. Not in the newspaper. Not in any computer resource.

Would he have stayed in LA since that, based on his school sports achievements, was his hometown? She tried the Yellow Pages site. Nil. Searched San Diego as an option. *Nada.* San Francisco. *Niente.* Vegas. *Rien.* Denver. Zilch. Dallas. Zip. Chicago. Nothin'. NYC.

Diddly-squat. DC. Nope. Hell, Seattle? Never heard of him. What happened to McTavish? Get sucked into a black hole?

Gaelen leaned back in her chair. Stared at the ceiling in her office. Took a deep breath and leaned forward again to key in another major city.

P-H-O-E-N-I-X. Closed her eyes. Took another deep breath, hit Enter, and opened them.

****

When Paprika Mendez swung through the front door of C.C.'s Place with a freshly washed and pressed shirt in hand, Pel admitted he'd been lying to himself for a really long time. Yeah, it was safer to restrict his life. To survive, he'd given up performing, given up scoring music for anyone other than his mother, given up socializing with anyone. It meant giving up following through on the attraction he'd felt for Gaelen Wyndom, but he hoped *she* might try to entice him. Once women had been very interested in luring him into their beds. *Those days are long over, Flannery*, he reminded himself. *You're a nobody now, dude. It was your decision to disappear. Live with it.*

Rika's smile was bright as she handed the shirt over. "Gael told me to reiterate her thanks for the loan and hopes the dry cleaners didn't put too much starch in the collar and cuffs, Mr. Flannery."

"Pel," he insisted. To the servers and kitchen staff he was *Mr. Flannery*, but to any of his mother's pets, he was *Pel*. He'd recognized the look in C.C.'s eye the day she'd decided Rika was the singer she wanted sharing her mic and billing.

"Pel," Rika repeated, lingering a bit over the *l*, as she would draw out a note when singing. "C.C. called me. Said you'd hired a trio to back me already, and that I should swing by to work out what we'll be performing."

"Yep," he said. "That's the deal. They should be drifting in shortly. Hope we didn't get you up too early, but rehearsals prior to the restaurant opening work out best."

"Are you part of the backup?" she asked. "C.C. said you're her accompanist."

"Nope. I need a day away from the ivories as much as she does from the mic," Pel insisted. Which was a lie. The moment Rika and the musicians left, he'd either linger on or head home to his other piano and hours of letting music anesthetize his frustration. If he stayed, he'd ask the late-night bartender to follow C.C. on her drive home, something he usually did himself. She might not be singing, but he knew she wouldn't want to miss her current protegee's shows.

He lifted the neatly packaged shirt. "Tell your friend I appreciate getting this back. Will she be joining us on Friday night for your first show?"

"Absolutely. She may have given up on a career in music, but she's very supportive of mine. She rarely misses a performance, and never an opening night."

In his chest, a particle of hope raised its head. There was still a chance. The only question was, would Gaelen Wyndom take the first step in this dance, or should he? Hell, it had been so long since he'd done the pursuing, even contemplating doing so made him as nervous as he'd been the first time he'd asked a girl out when in high school.

Then again, maybe she wasn't interested. *She* had not told him her name. His mother had.

It was barely past noon, and he really needed a drink, the higher proof the better.

"C.C. will be out in a minute. Our deal is she's in charge of entertainment and I run the rest of the place," he said. "If you need anything to drink, just help yourself at the bar."

"Water's all I need," Rika assured. "Not seltzer, but bottled?"

"I'll send some out," Pel promised and made his escape.

C.C. had a stack of sheet music spread across his desk when he entered the office. Regular, purchased sheet music, not his special arrangements, he was relieved to see. Pel headed to the closet and tucked the newly returned shirt onto the shelf, then bent to the dorm-sized mini-fridge to retrieve a bottle of water. "Rika's here."

"Oh, good!" His mother gathered the sheet music into a stack, though not a neat one. She bounded to her feet, excited to be interacting with other musicians again. Perhaps it wasn't just himself he'd been keeping from the music community lately, but C.C. as well. Another sin he could add to his tally, for doing so certainly equated to one.

"She asked for a water," he said, handing it to her.

C.C. looked at him, her expression one of surprise. "Aren't you going back out? You know, give suggestions, point out nuances that could turn a song in a new direction or give it more depth?"

"You have me confused with that other guy," Pel said. "I've got a restaurant to run."

"Don't be ridiculous," she insisted. "You hired people who didn't need supervision. Tom prefers to terrorize his own kitchen and wait staff. Considering he's so picky over the meat and vegetables used, I'm glad he chooses those things. What, I ask you, is wrong with things that come in cans and just need heating up?"

As it was an old refrain, Pel didn't bother answering.

C.C. hadn't finished proving he was superfluous to her club—except at the piano for her own performances, that is.

"Rex keeps the bar well stocked," she said. "We have an advertising agency doing their magic to get people in the door. And the cleaning crew takes care of what they require."

Pel leaned against the bank of four-drawer file cabinets along the wall. "You finished?"

C.C. glared at him. "Men!" she said in a scathing tone and headed for the dining room.

Pel closed the door behind her before settling behind his desk. Wall Street lacked the ability to currently hold his attention. Rather than click the icon that would connect him directly to the hub that made it possible to pay the staff an extravagant wage to remove from his shoulders the day-to-day grind of owning a restaurant, he looked at the listings for other restaurants in the area.

If he took the plunge and asked Gaelen Wyndom out, where could they have dinner and still avoid the chance of his being recognized? Someplace where the likelihood of security cameras was minimal. A man could change the color of his hair and eyes, even the timbre of his voice and the way he held himself, but camera footage made face recognition tricky to avoid.

The Internet supplied the answer—a rustic place in an old bunkhouse outside of Tucson. The drive down would supply a cocoon of time to learn more about her. With luck, the steak joint was the sort of place where no one had ever listened to anything a guy named Jace Hastings played.

Chapter Three

Bingo.

Dr. R. McTavish was listed as a partner at the Hakathi Psychiatric Associates. Their website told her that *Hakathi* was the Yavapai name for the Salt River. Well, didn't they think well of themselves, she thought. Sounded like they were trying to lure the wealthy New Agers in their door. Probably charged some of the highest rates possible, too. And if so, McTavish had simply found a legal way to rob people.

She scrolled through the staff pictures and found that Dr. McTavish was a late thirties man with a shaved head and a close-cut generic brown beard. He'd donned a well-fitted suit with a conservative shirt and tie. The collar didn't disguise the mark of a tattoo on his neck on the left side, though he was turned slightly away from the camera. Probably to downplay its existence. She wondered if he'd gotten it early in his career as an inmate in the prison system. It didn't seem the sort of thing he'd add while working on his plan to beat the system by becoming a psychologist specializing in a field he had personal experience in from the patient's perspective.

A click and the portrait was saved to the separate file she'd created for this case. No need for anyone to know she'd gone off track with the search for Hastings, because there was no way following a trail to the man who likely drove the semi that killed Ashley Hopper, and probably Jace Hastings, was part of what Hank had told her to do, which was to find Jace Hastings.

The incognito mode on her computer hid the evidence of her interest in McTavish. The JPEG of his photo vanished with a single key stroke. As far as the Desert Wynd system was concerned, her only investigation was related to the search for Jace Hastings, and that search was going nowhere.

Although the police had gone with evidence from the jewelry store to charge and convict McTavish of robbery, she couldn't help believing that evidence could have been planted by someone working with McTavish. Even with a history of B and E, the punishment was minimal compared to one for first degree murder, which McTavish wouldn't have been able to shrug off with Ashley's restraining order pointing at him as a viable suspect. The material Cliff unearthed in LA had McTavish insisting the truck had been stolen and he'd passed a lie detector test in relation to it. Like someone couldn't access ways to beat such a test these days, she thought in disgust.

Still, it was handy to have a former colleague to tap for info about a decade-old event on the coast. Cliff and Luke had been her trainers, had quizzed her on everything she needed to qualify for the private detective license long before she'd logged in the three-year apprenticeship required to actually get one in Arizona. Then Cliff had been headhunted by the LA investigation firm, and shortly after he left, Luke had gotten himself killed. Hank had given her a week to grieve—apparently, he hadn't bothered to do so for his son—then dragged her into the field as his own trainee.

Yeah, she knew how Hank worked. How Luke had been a better investigator and Cliff an even better one. One of these days she should take Cliff up on the offer to talk his employers into hiring her. It meant leaving Phoenix, her hometown. Learning to deal with LA freeways, Santa Ana winds, earthquakes, and... Well, the fact that those were the things that she used as her excuses meant she was trying to find reasons to avoid what would be a smart jump up the professional ladder.

Rather than tuck Dr. Rowan McTavish's photograph in her own red file folder, Gaelen slipped it in the manila one in her briefcase. A glance at her watch told her it was time to head to Surprise and C.C.'s Place. But first, she was making a stop at home to change into something less staid. Since she intended to have dinner before Rika went on stage, there was always the chance she'd see Pelham Flannery. He seemed like the sort of manager who cruised the tables to talk to customers. If he did and stopped at her table, she wanted to look like a good reason for the man to linger rather than move on to another table.

It had been a long time since she'd wanted to bask in the glow of a man's smile, and Flannery's grin was the sort to change a woman's mind. Particularly a woman who'd sworn off love.

For all the wrong reasons.

****

Although C.C. usually manned the podium at the front door, seating guests, his mother's mind was all on the entertainment that night. If diners were stunned to have the man they'd only seen seated at the piano serving as C.C.'s accompanist now playing host, none commented on it.

It was easy to spot the regulars. They all commented on the miniscule dance floor that had materialized before the stage since their last visit. As he was the only one who didn't have a specific job at C.C.'s prior to opening, his mother had put him to work rearranging tables. She'd also informed him that she expected him to dance with her. "And anyone else you'd like to rub up against during a romantic song," she'd added.

Yeah, he did have someone in mind to do just that with, though not necessarily while dancing before onlookers.

He seated a retired couple who frequently came for a late dinner and stayed to enjoy C.C.'s vocals. Rika had told C.C., and thus in a roundabout way *him*, that Gaelen planned to get there in time for dinner, so he was on the lookout for her. There was a booth along the far wall that faced the stage. The perfect spot to enjoy the show yet leave closer tables open for the bar crowd, which was usually heavier on Friday night as jazz aficionados drifted in. He'd even dropped a reserved sign on it. Now all he needed was the woman he'd been thinking about all day to show up.

Pel glanced at his watch. It was nearly 8:30. Rika's first set began at 9:00, which was when the kitchen stopped taking orders. Gaelen was cutting it close.

Another guest had come inside while he'd settled the older couple at their table. The man had his back to the dining room, though, his tall, lean form a dark silhouette against the bright sunlight beyond the glass doors.

"Welcome to C.C.'s," Pel greeted. "Table for one?"

"Or more than one if I get lucky," a familiar voice said as the man turned to face him.

"Dad!" Pel barked, startled. "C.C. didn't tell me you were finally joining us." When he offered his hand, Jay Flannery took it and yanked him forward into a fond hug.

"She doesn't know. I wanted it to be a surprise."

"She'll be furious with you," Pel warned.

Jay winked. "Don't I know it. Which definitely means I'll get lucky tonight, son."

Pel wondered whether normal parents alluded to their sex life, or to their offspring's lack of one as C.C. had done. Somehow, he doubted it.

"Have you eaten yet?" he asked.

"Nope. Took a cab straight from the airport, as the items I set off to the side will indicate is the honest truth. At least to your mother."

Now that his father had gestured to them, Pel saw the small, wheeled travel bag and the much larger case that housed his trombone strapped to it. There was also a golf cart with bag and bouquet of clubs sprouting from it.

"I'll lock them away in the office, Dad. I know you don't care about the clothes, but the axe and clubs are sacred."

"Damn straight they are, kid," Jay said, though he grinned.

The same grin Pel had seen in his own mirror that morning. Definitely the grin of a sap thinking about a woman. Or so he'd told the man in the mirror. Who'd only smiled wider in anticipation.

Then the door opened, and Gaelen slipped inside, out of the heat. The business suit was gone, replaced by a knee-length red dress with straps so thin they seemed incapable of supporting the weight of the flowing fabric. The skirt flirted, clinging then swirling about her legs with every step she took. Her hair swung, allowing the lingering sunlight to burnish highlights he hadn't noticed in the dim lighting of the restaurant on her last visit. Rather than the sensible black heels of the workday, lethal red stilettos made it difficult to not drop his gaze to her long, shapely legs. A matching wrap covered her kissable neck and trailed behind her like a veil. Her makeup was that of a woman out for an adventurous evening. Pel hoped she'd decide that adventure included him.

He forgot his father was waiting. Instead, he glanced at his watch. "Cutting it a bit close, aren't you, young lady?" he said.

She smiled at him. No, that was too tame. She *sparkled* in a way he felt was just for him.

"Does that mean I don't get dinner? I did return the shirt you loaned me."

"True. We'll make an exception," Pel said, then remembered his father was watching them, obviously interested in the byplay.

Jay cleared his throat.

"This gentleman was ahead of me," she said.

"He's no gentleman. He's my father. Dad—"

His old man beat him out. "Jay Flannery," he said offering his hand.

Gaelen shook it. Turned that twinkle on the rapscallion. "Gaelen Wyndom."

Pel sighed. "You tell everyone but me your name, don't you?" he grouched theatrically.

His father leaned toward her but cut his eyes back

to Pel. "I don't blame you. I wouldn't give highly confidential information like that to this fella either."

The plan to share the secluded booth with her crumbled to metaphorical ashes. "On that note, you both deserve to share the table we reserved for Gaelen."

Jay's left brow arched. "So you do know her name."

"She told that secrets sieve you married what it was, Dad."

The old man turned back to Gaelen. "Big mistake, honey. C.C. probably blurted it out. You're doomed. Pel's got a mind like a steel trap. He'll never forget you now."

"Damn, you're getting old," Pel declared. "You're falling back on clichés. What happened to the glib guy C.C. claims she fell for?"

"Different guy, obviously," Jay said but his smile hadn't slipped, and the charm was laid on thick enough to drip from every word.

Pel pushed the sleeve of his suit jacket back, ostensibly to check the time again. "Kitchen closes soon. You want a table before then or not?"

The old man offered his arm to Gaelen. "Shall we?"

"By all means," she accepted, grinning up at him.

Pel grabbed his father's luggage before leading the way to the booth. Before he was out of hearing, he heard his father murmur, "Didn't tell him your name, yet he gave you the shirt off his back?"

"Closet," Pel growled to himself, though if anyone heard him, he didn't notice.

****

"...the shirt off his back?" Jay Flannery asked.

"No," Gaelen said. "Considering it was neatly folded and buttoned up, I'm guessing it came off a shelf or out of a file drawer. I'd managed to assist a waiter in drenching me in ice cold tea and soft drinks."

"Understandable then, but not nearly as good a story," he told her. "You come to C.C.'s often?"

She shook her head. "Nope. This is my second visit. My friend's the vocalist tonight. I'm here to support her."

"Just the kind of friend any musician would kill to possess," he said. "You a singer, too?"

Gaelen laughed lightly. "Why does everyone ask me that?"

"Your voice. There's a musical lilt in it."

"Which doesn't equate to having a lick of talent, Mr. Flannery."

"Please, it's Jay. So your friend got all the licks of talent?"

"Yep, but not only can she sing, Rika knew everything there was to know about C.C.'s career highs, and they bonded at the interview."

He chuckled. "That's my honey," he agreed. "Even so, Cec wouldn't have hired her if she wasn't good. So, tell me about my son."

"Pel? I really don't know him. Just a passing acquaintance. We talked briefly while I waited for Rika's audition to end."

"That's it?"

"Yeah. Oh, he did give me a bag of rice to dry my cell out, too. I wouldn't consider that more than two strangers passing the time, though."

"Which is why you dressed to be a standout even though you aren't on the stage."

"No, I didn't. I dressed so that Rika could see—"

Jay indicated the stage at the far side of the room with a tilt of his chin. "Spotlight. She won't be able to see you back here. Plus, I think that interchange at the door was some heavy duty flirting for a woman who's just here for her friend."

Gaelen sighed. "Guilty. There's something about him, something mysterious."

"Mysterious?"

She shrugged. "I thought he looked familiar, not like I'd met him before but that I'd seen him before, but then I realized it was because he looks like you and there was a picture of the three of you on C.C.'s website."

"She's got a website?" He sounded astonished over the news.

"You don't?"

"No need. My reputation precedes me, and my agent flogs it regularly. It means a lot more traveling and shorter gigs these days, but I'll probably die with a slide turning my last breath into a heavenly well-formed note."

A moment later, a waitress arrived with a tumbler of Scotch and a Tequila Sunrise. There were two extra maraschino cherries on toothpicks stabbed through the orange slice perched on the rim. Gaelen laughed at the sight. Plucked one free and savored the bright red fruit. "Maybe your son is flirting with me after all. At least he's turning my head with cocktail hors d'oeuvres."

"It's a specialty of the Flannery men," Jay said. "Give the guy a chance. He's kept to himself for a long time. Hasn't let a pretty face or an intelligent, talented woman turn his head in quite a while."

Gaelen sucked another cherry from impalement. "I'll take the 'pretty' as a compliment, but who says I'm intelligent or talented?"

"I do," he claimed. "I'm a musician. I can hear both in your voice."

She wrinkled her nose. "That's a lot of bull, Jay."

He leaned back against the padded back of the banquette seat. "Well, don't be surprised if Pel tells you the same thing."

"He's a chip off the paternal block? You taught him everything he needs to know about picking up women?"

"No, he had to figure it out for himself. C.C. and I are lousy parents. We left him to be raised by C.C.'s parents. We tried to be there for his birthday and Christmas, but often enough only one of us, or neither of us, managed to make it. Still, he turned out to be a fairly decent guy despite us."

"He's a very nice man," Gaelen murmured. "You can be proud of him."

"Oh, I am. C.C. is too. But I'm curious about why you think he's a nice fella, Gaelen."

She plucked the final maraschino cherry free, held it between her thumb and forefinger. "Because he gave me lots of fruit on my Sunrise. But more importantly, because he gave me the shirt off his back," she declared, gave him a mischievous grin and popped the final cherry in her mouth.

****

Pel had a frosty bottle of beer in his hand and a waitress with a tray of food trailing him when he returned to the booth. It was one of the larger ones, a horseshoe-shaped cocoon of comfort. It was irritating to hear his father and the woman he was interested in laughing when he arrived at the table. Both looked up in surprise as he set the beer on the table next to Gaelen, clearly staking his territory.

"Neither of you get a choice tonight," he announced as he took two dinner plates from the server.

"Punishment for arriving late," Jay said aside to Gaelen.

"Damn right," Pel agreed. "Dad, I asked for a steak for you, close as our chef could get it to walking but crispy on the outside. Gaelen, you're stuck with a grilled chicken breast. House vegetables tonight are candied carrots and scalloped potatoes. You need salads or bread?"

"It wouldn't be a decent punishment if we were allowed any," Gaelen said.

She wasn't successful at sounding serious or contrite, even if it was her goal.

Pel dismissed the waitress with a smiled thank-you and a co-conspirator's wink. She knew there was plenty of bread and salad and other menu items available back in the kitchen. Staff would be taking turns enjoying their favorites from the menu, particularly those due back on the floor to take drink orders. He'd already turned the sign on the front of the podium at the entrance so that it invited guests to find their own seats.

"I didn't mention to C.C. that you're here, Dad. Thought you'd prefer to surprise her. She'll be hovering near the stage and introducing Rika," Pel said. "Of course, if you want to take my place on the dance floor with her, have at it. She ordered me to take a spin with her to get others on their feet, following her lead. I'm willing to delegate the spot to you, though."

"It isn't often a musician gets a chance to dance with his girl," Jay admitted. "Usually, they end up gazing longingly at the guys who are cuddling an armful on the floor."

"Or your girl is attempting to push you out of the spotlight by taking the mic herself," Pel added.

"That's your mother to a tee," Jay agreed.

"Far as I'm concerned, she can hog all the spotlight. I just tickle the ivories in the background."

"At least you do these days."

"These days," Pel echoed. "Spotlight's not my scene."

Jay turned to Gaelen. "See. I told you we were lousy parents. He's years behind on what passes for slang these days."

"It's what you always told Granddad when he asked you to join his latest protest sit-in," Pel said and turned to Gaelen himself. "C.C.'s parents only like protest songs."

"And folk songs," Jay added with a shiver.

"So that's why you both rarely turned up in DC?"

"Pel, if it had been, we would have taken you on the road with us so you wouldn't be tainted," Jay drawled.

Gaelen cleared her throat. "Wasn't the show supposed to start at nine? It's quarter after. Should you check to see if all is well?"

"First show of a new gig. Rarely do they ever start on time," Jay said.

"C.C.'s probably fussing over Rika, giving last instructions, which she doesn't need," Pel added.

"Hard to turn over the reins to a younger performer," Jay murmured. "Even when you know you aren't who you used to be."

Pel frowned. "Your breath control slipping?"

Jay rocked his hand back and forth. "C.C.'s?"

"Volume and high notes. I changed a few keys, chose different songs to counter. Whether she knows I did or not…" Pel rocked his own hand back and forth.

"She knows," Jay said.

Which is when C.C. mounted the stage and took the mic off the stand. The designated staffer turned the house lights down to a more romantic level, and the spotlight slowly brightened. Behind C.C., a drummer slipped into place, and a sax man ducked his head to settle his instrument's support strap around his torso. A guitarist bent to plug his electric into an amp, then pulled up a stool to sit on, his bass resting on a raised thigh.

"Eat up, you two," Pel urged. "The show is about to begin."

****

In the booth in the back—or at least along the wall farthest from the stage—bracketed by two handsome men, Gaelen felt she had the best seat in the house. It was dim in the restaurant now. The wait staff slipped from table to table, lighting candles tucked into clear glass cylinders wrapped in an industrial crosshatch of polished steel. The fixtures, furnishings, and table and barware alone were so upscale, Gaelen wondered if C.C. had sunk her life savings into the place. Perhaps ensuring that she had a place to sing before an audience regularly was all the older woman felt was needed to see out her last decades happily. From Jay's comments, Gaelen had gotten the impression that gigs were not as plentiful as they'd once been, and if C.C.'s pipes were failing her, the restaurant was probably the only way to guarantee nights under a spotlight.

But if Jay was still on the road, and C.C. was settled in an area where the clientele was in her own age bracket, and thus probably musical taste range, why was Pel Flannery managing his mother's club and acting as her accompanist? Everything about him shouted wealth. The same couldn't be said about his parents.

Though she really knew little about him, he seemed an intelligent man. He was too young to have made a killing in the dot-com era. Had he done the twenty-first-century version and created an app that was in great demand? His suits weren't off the rack, and the borrowed shirt had carried a designer label. Out of curiosity, she'd looked the brand up on the Web and found it retailed for nearly a thousand dollars. For one shirt! She hated to think what his highly polished shoes had cost him.

While what he wore put him in an unreachable category, nothing about Pel himself did. He'd simply given her an extremely expensive shirt as though it had run him little more than twenty-five bucks. Since she'd arrived late, she'd had to park farther back in the lot. A metallic beige car from a European firm was parked among the staff's far, far more modest vehicles, yet it wasn't a sports car but an SUV. It had to belong to him, but an SUV for a single man? Weird.

"You'll want to maneuver into position to snag C.C. for a dance, Dad. Next song's perfect for it," Pel told the man opposite him at the table.

"You know the lineup they're doing?" Jay asked.

"Why wouldn't I?" Pel countered.

His father nodded but added a sigh. "Yeah, why wouldn't you? Where's C.C. hiding?"

"Small table near the bar. She wanted to be closer to the stage, but the spot she indicated would have put her too close to the drums and amp. We'd have been shouting at her to hear us all next week if she sat there."

Jay slipped to the end of the seat and stood up. Gaelen noticed he used the flat of his hand against the tabletop to aid himself. C.C. wasn't the only one that time whittled, carving nicks in the person they'd once been. Briefly she thought about visiting her own parents and her remaining grandmother soon.

Before he left to surprise C.C. with a dance, Jay patted Pel's shoulder. "You're taking good care of your mother, Pel. Thank you."

Pel shrugged. "You're welcome to play here any night you want, Dad. All it takes is giving up the road."

"Not an easy thing to do, though I complain about moving from one motel room to another."

That was a telling choice of words, Gaelen decided. Jay had said *motel* not *hotel*. That meant what his gigs paid these days was far from what he might once have received. Had he come to Surprise because his finances were at rock bottom? Even if they were, she doubted he'd actually confess that to either Pel or C.C.

She wasn't surprised when Pel supplied what might sound like a godsend but was simply this son giving his father a way out that wouldn't sound like charity. Wouldn't *be* charity.

"There's a warm bed in a spiffy condo on a golf course already inhabited by a certain lady you're rather fond of," Pel reminded.

Jay chuckled. "Sure you're not in sales, kid?"

"God forbid!" the younger man said.

As his father wove a circuitous path toward C.C., Gaelen found Pel had turned to her, his hand held out. "Care to take a whirl yourself?"

The trio's tempo was guaranteed to lure couples to the floor, particularly once C.C. and Jay started things off. The song had been scored as a cha-cha. Rika stepped back up to the mic. She was dazzling in a silver dress covered in sequins. Polished crystals took the place of diamonds in the bracelets on both wrists. Another, larger one, sparkled on her right hand in an ostentatious ring. Wide hoop earrings moved with each toss of her head. She stretched her arms out toward the audience and begged them flirtatiously to "Come Dance With Me."

"Better to let your parents have the floor for this one," Gaelen said. "Since you already know the lineup, what's the next song that suits a slow dance?"

His grin flashed. "A slow one, huh?"

"I'm not that great a dancer," she confessed.

"With this crowd, we'd try a Twist except too many hip replacements would be put in danger," Pel quipped. "Ditto with about any dance this audience used to boogie to. But somehow I thought you'd be into salsa or Latin dancing."

"You are?"

"There's a lot to be said for an Argentinian tango. All those dips and cheek-to-cheek moves."

"The dragging your partner along the dance floor as she clings to your leg?"

"Definitely that part," he agreed.

"Not in my repertoire, pal," she said.

"I'm crushed," he declared, not sounding as if he was in the least.

"Do you really tango?" Gaelen pressed.

Pel's smile grew even more dangerously attractive than before. "No," he admitted in a growl that drew the word out.

"You had me worried."

"Sure, I did," he said and chuckled. "I'll give you a choice. Rika'll go into 'Something Stupid' after this followed by 'All of Me.' "

"Which would you choose?"

"The one after that."

"Which is?"

"A surprise. Need a refill on the Sunrise in the meantime?"

She shook her head. "No, I'm fine. Have to drive home later, though I do thank you for the extra maraschino cherries on this one." Gaelen tipped the glass. As the level had descended, she'd put the straw back in to reach the dregs below the hill of small ice cubes.

"First thing I always make note of when I meet an attractive woman is whether she likes maraschino cherries," he said.

"And you could tell I like them from the way I inhaled just one the other day?"

"It's a science, though you didn't just *like* it, you *savored* it."

"I did not."

"Call 'em as I see 'em, darlin'," he drawled.

She sort of liked the way he said *darlin'*. Knew her smile told him she did, too.

"You know," Pel said. "If you stay for the jam

session once we close, you'll have plenty of time for a second Sunrise to wear off."

Gaelen knew her eyes had widened. "A jam session?" she breathed.

"Sounds like that might be a yes to staying on. When's the last time you were part of one?"

"Over five, probably six years," she confessed, "but I won't be part of this one. Just an audience for everyone else. Will you be at the piano?"

"Only if I can't think of a way to avoid it."

"Rika told me you play beautifully."

"C.C. claims it comes with the gene pool. But I haven't been in a position to sit in on a jam session for more years than you've been away from one."

Gaelen pushed her now-empty glass aside, put an elbow on the table and propped her chin in the palm of her hand. "Why not?"

Pel shrugged. "Life. Their life—" He gestured to where C.C. and Jay were not doing a proper cha-cha, but a decent fox trot. "—is the one where evening gigs turn into jam sessions. Mine's more surfing cable channels after a day on the computer. This place is a nice change, though I'm still hooked on marathoning."

"You don't look like a couch potato in the least," she said.

His grin flashed again. "Because I start the day in the gym. You?"

"I end the day at the gym…well, more at the dojo," she confessed. "I think I have a secret longing to be an action-adventure star, because the martial art that appealed to me was taekwondo."

"Remind me not to get on your bad side," Pel said. "My ego would suffer a major setback being beat up by a girl. Are you a go on that second drink?"

She glanced toward the stage, at her watch. At him.

"Yeah, why not?" she said. "Three cherries, please."

He returned with a bowl of them.

Chapter Four

C.C. was clinging to Jay's hand when he returned to the table. She scooted into the booth, sliding to the back of the horseshoe where Gaelen was seated. "I'm so glad you came," the songstress gushed, giving her a quick hug. "I hope we can talk you into staying for the jam session later."

Gaelen pointed to the half-empty bowl of maraschino cherries. "Pel already bribed me to stay," she said.

"Ooh, cherries," C.C. gushed. "Mind if I share?"

"Help yourself," Gaelen urged, pushing the bowl her way.

"Giving away your presents, huh?" Pel's voice rumbled in her ear as she moved over to make room for C.C. It did put her nearer him.

"I may have lost my fascination with cherries after so many," she confessed.

"Which means you've got to find another of Gaelen's weaknesses to cater to, Pel," Jay said.

"I was lucky to trip over this one, Dad. Give me a break," Pel returned, but his lips twitched in a grin. Ohh, that devastating grin, Gaelen thought. That could definitely be one of her weaknesses. He could flash it at her for a lifetime and she probably wouldn't get tired of seeing it. Not that she had a lifetime in mind with him. It was just… Well, the grin and that mysterious quality that surrounded him were pretty potent temptations where her heart was concerned.

A heart that had lectured her many times on how rapidly she tended to fall in love and then not stay in love. Among the men she'd known, only Luke had fallen as quickly as she had, which was why they'd gone to Vegas for a long weekend and come back married. Within a year they both knew it had been a mistake. They'd been meant to be friends, colleagues, not lovers.

If she remembered the lessons learned regarding physical attraction, there was no reason not to allow herself to bask in the glow of Pel's smile, though. For a while.

"How come you two weren't on the dance floor with us?" C.C. demanded.

"Had our reasons," Pel said.

Our reasons, Gaelen mused. He'd already confessed to being a loner and out of the dating scene by choice, yet he made it sound as though they were a couple already. Should that be a warning sign or something to enjoy? They *had* been flirting since her arrival.

But then so had his father. She recognized that Jay did it as a reflex—he hadn't been the least bit serious. The man was obviously still in love with his wife. Is that what their frequent long absences in each other's life had done? Made the times they were together all the sweeter?

"What reasons?" C.C. asked.

"The right song, of course," Pel insisted defensively. "Hell, Cec, you're the one who taught me that."

His mother nodded. "I did," she admitted. "What's the song?"

"Not this one," Pel said as Rika crooned "Something Stupid." Gaelen recognized it as a Sinatra hit, which meant it was a favorite of hers. No one could pick a tune like Old Blue Eyes.

Except, perhaps, Jace Hastings.

No thinking about the case, Gaelen told herself. She was off duty. Just enjoying an evening where everything revolved around music. Or would seem to once the customers left, the door was locked, and the musicians let their hair down—metaphorically. She did hope Pel was prevailed upon to play with them in the jam session. She was curious about everything to do with him. Apparently, the one thing they had in common was that they'd both put music aside to follow a different career path.

On the small stage, Rika and her backup rolled into an up-tempo rendition of "All of Me." Each member of the trio did a brief solo, the sax wailing, the guitar riff leaning toward rock rather than jazz, and the drummer turning his sticks into a rapid-fire tattoo that danced from one drum surface to the next and finished with a clash of cymbals. The audience nearly drowned out Rika when she stepped back to the microphone to finish the song.

Pel slid out of the booth and held his hand out. "Show time for your light fantastic, Ms. Wyndom."

Gaelen needed no further urging. "Just don't be surprised when the finish on your shoes is destroyed and you're limping back to the table," she warned.

"Oh, faint heart," Pel murmured and guided her ahead of him as they wove through the dining room to the postage-stamp-sized dance floor.

On stage, Rika was introducing her back-up, cueing the crowd to applaud them each separately again. When she turned back and saw Gaelen with Pel a row back from the open area, she smiled widely, then turned to say something to the sax man. While he passed along what she'd said, Rika leaned into the mic. "This one's by special request," she said.

Pel guided Gaelen to the center of the dance floor. Drew her wrists up to encircle his neck. "Chosen specifically for you," he murmured a moment before Rika went into "Misty."

"This might top the bowl of cherries," she whispered as his arms held her lightly.

"I'm on a roll," he said. "Now shut up and listen to the music. It helps when you're dancing." The warmth in his dark eyes belied the mock complaint. He hadn't been able to keep his lips from twitching into a half grin either. It was as breathtakingly wonderful as its full-sized brother.

She smiled up into his face, totally enchanted. Not that they were actually dancing, merely swaying. The rendition of the song was sultry, slow, and as close as it was possible to get to the Jace Hastings' arrangement she loved without the piano and strings of his recording of the song.

"Is there a reason you're spoiling me tonight?" she asked.

"Yes," he said, drawing her closer.

"Tell me why later," she murmured, her lips nearly brushing his.

"Deal," he breathed.

It was only when they left the dance floor and

stopped by the bar that Pel explained. "I was softening you up, so you'll be more receptive to the idea of having dinner with me but not at C.C.'s."

"That could be fun," she agreed. "You have a favorite restaurant in mind?"

"I have a road trip in mind."

When she cocked her head and gave him a slight frown, he added, "Not an overnighter. Not a weekend away. Just a drive down to the outskirts of Tucson."

"I might be interested," Gaelen allowed.

"Totally casual. Steak place that used to be a working ranch. Or so their website claims. They do have things other than steak, but not a menu like the one here, though we have grilling over a mesquite fire in common. They even have salads."

"So I might get to have one instead of having it withheld?"

"Yep. Is that a yes?"

"Uh-huh."

"What night's good for you?" The bartender set a freshly opened brew near Pel's hand and a fresh Sunrise. Only one cherry was in sight. Not that she really needed further cherries, or more tequila.

"Don't you have a nearly nightly gig playing for C.C.?" she asked, as he picked up the latest Sunrise.

"We have substitutes to call in now," he reminded. "As I don't know what your work schedule is..."

"Nine to six usually, but I can take off early."

"I like the sound of that," he murmured, passing her the drink. "Monday or Tuesday?"

"Monday." She had a feeling she'd go into Pel withdrawal by putting it off any longer. Suddenly, alcohol sounded like a good idea. Something to take the edge off her nervousness. She'd actually accepted a date! Something she hadn't done since meeting Luke Wyndom.

"Pick you up?"

The query offered a slight reprieve. Not that she had any intention of *not* going out with Pel Flannery. "I'll meet you here. That way if I'm running late you won't get stuck in downtown traffic."

"God forbid," he whispered. He was so close she felt his breath stir her hair, brush like a caress along her neck.

The sound of Rika's voice and the trio faded into the background for Gaelen. Who was she kidding? There was nothing she wanted more than to spend time alone with Pelham Flannery.

****

The show ran late. Not just because they had started late, but the audience was so appreciative with applause, C.C. got back on stage and asked why they weren't as enthusiastic when she sang. The guests chuckled, and when she asked if they'd like an encore number, showed the answer was a resounding "yes." This time Rika and the boys did Cole Porter's classic, "Night and Day."

As Pel locked the club's main door behind the last guest to depart, he adjusted the blinds in the door and the side windows that bracketed it, blocking any view to the inside of the restaurant. C.C. was holding court at the bar with the musicians and had roped his father into acting as bartender so the remaining staff could head home. Gaelen was perched on a barstool next to Rika. When Gaelen glanced his way and smiled, it nearly hurt to enjoy the leap in tempo his pulse took. It had been a long time—too long a time?—since he'd allowed himself to feel happy.

It's temporary, Flannery, he reminded himself. Diving into a relationship meant being more visible than he'd been in years. It also might put Gaelen in danger. McTavish was out there somewhere. He knew the man hadn't forgotten him. The note delivered to the hospital ten years ago validated his own trepidation. It had been handled by many people, but none of them had opened the sealed envelope. They'd waited for him to do so, thinking it was just a get-well note from a fan who'd staked out the hospital.

It hadn't been.

Oh, it had been a get-well card, a comedic one, but a message had been added in block letters he recognized from McTavish's previous threat notes. TIED UP FOR A WHILE. CATCH YOU LATER.

Catch you later. The phrase had haunted him for a decade now.

But tonight...tonight he was going to wallow in music, in the companionship of musicians who didn't know who the hell he was. And he intended to keep it that way.

He'd also bathe in the glow of Gaelen Wyndom's lovely smile. Would do so as much as possible for a sadly far too short a time.

"There is only one way to get a brass man away from your door," his father insisted to Rika.

"Yeah," the sax man said. "Pay him for the pizza."

Both Rika and Gaelen snickered at the punchline.

"Careful, Dad. You're dealing with a couple of music majors here," Pel cautioned.

"They can't both be fast-food night managers," Jay

insisted.

"I am neither a fast-food employee nor a musician," Gaelen said.

"Ah, but there's a name for someone who hangs out with musicians, which you are doing right now," Pel said.

"Yeah," Jay agreed. "A vocalist."

His wife slugged him in the shoulder.

"Careful, honey. That's the arm that makes the music."

"If you can call something that was first called a *sackbut* the perfect instrument to *make* music," the sax man said.

"That sounds like a challenge," Jay declared. "Brass instruments at three paces?"

"Hell, no. You'd punch me in the face with that lethal slide!"

Jay grinned. "I'll show you how lethal. Pel. Hit that babied baby grand and give us a song to start things off."

He played often enough for C.C., but this seemed like taking too much of a chance. If he lost himself in the music, Jace Hastings might inadvertently show up.

"Yes, please, Pel. I haven't heard you play, though Rika says you're wasting your time not turning professional," Gaelen said.

"I'm professional enough," he countered. "To be C.C.'s accompanist, I joined the local musicians' union."

Which was when C.C. stepped up, took hold of his sleeve, and tugged him back toward the stage. "So accompany me, dear," she said.

He sighed. There were too many people he cared

about ready to gang up on him and make him play. "Any requests?"

"Your choice, Pel. Surprise us."

He looked back at the group gathered at the bar. At Gaelen. "Please," she mouthed.

"Okay, okay. Challenge accepted. Come on, you lowlifes. Stop drinking the house dry and show your chops."

He waited for them to trail after him before settling behind the piano. When he caught Gaelen's eye, he tipped his head to the side, indicating she should sit next to him on the bench. She hesitated for barely a breath before doing so. It felt good to have her there. To have the heady scent of her perfume surrounding him.

The drummer slid into place. The guitarist, the sax player, and his trombone-playing father arranged themselves either in chairs or perched on a tabletop. Rika and C.C. both kicked off their heels and slid next to each other on a table for four, resting their feet on the seats of chairs.

"Maestro?" C.C. asked.

Pel ran his fingers along the keys. Gave Gaelen a wink and launched into a fast-paced "The Boogie Woogie Bugle Boy of Company B."

****

Dawn was breaking when Gaelen got back to her apartment. It had been a long but invigorating night. The musicians definitely got high on their music, particularly during the jam session.

C.C. had been the first to flag, but not until she'd sung the lyrics to every song, even thrilling Rika with a bit of scat, the improvisation a vocalist would use that contained no actual words. Since Pel kept the tempo fast on every song he guided them into, it was only when his mother requested something less frantic in tempo that things began to wind down.

"Something relaxing but not sad."

"So, no 'Yesterday,' " he'd said and moved into a playful, but much slower "You've Got a Friend in Me." After that, the musicians filed out to catch a few hours of sleep before they needed to return for the Saturday night show.

It took Gaelen forever to fall asleep, and when she did, she wasn't surprised that her dreams were filled with music. Pel's smile danced in as well, and then his hands on the grand's stark white and black keys. Her dream morphed to a concert stage where she was just a member of the audience, but this time it wasn't Pel at the piano but Jace Hastings. She still remembered bits and pieces of the dream when she woke later in the afternoon, but put all the elements down to both a wonderful evening and Rika singing "Misty."

With her physical clock temporarily thrown off schedule, it wasn't until after four that she decided to do what she always recommended in the occasional personal safety talks she gave to women's groups. She sat down at her computer and fed in *Pelham Flannery*. Knowing that he'd grown up in DC under the care of his Pelham grandparents gave her a slight edge for the search. Something that was missing from the search for Jace Hastings. It was time to give herself a breather on that assignment.

There still wasn't much to find. Pel apparently hadn't been interested in sports. At least he hadn't been a member of one in championship playoffs where the masters of whatever ball was used got their names in the paper. He hadn't been valedictorian at any high school, but then, she hadn't been, either. There was a mention of him being the featured pianist in a high school concert his junior year, and again his senior year. She half expected to find a notice that he'd been given a full scholarship or at least a partial one to a music academy or to another university, but nothing surfaced. She did find notices of one or both of his grandparents listed as arrested at political protests and wondered who had taken care of him during their incarcerations, particularly as the dates indicated he'd probably been in elementary school for some of them.

But of the grown Pel Flannery she found nothing. No social media, no newspaper articles, no concert dates as a pianist with a symphony orchestra or as a member of a jazz group. She combed through the compiled list of millionaires and billionaires—no go. Checked success stories in the computer world. The financial world. Even checked politics, though she hadn't gotten the impression he'd been interested in following in his grandparents' footsteps or had appalled them by running for office. Still *nada*. He was nearly as mysterious as Jace Hastings, she thought, resigned to just learn about Pel by spending time with Pel. Not a hardship in the least. She ended the evening by flicking on the television and wondering what shows were among those he might be marathoning right that minute.

And she dreamed of Jace Hastings again that night.

Her work ethic nudged her back to the job the next day, even though it was Sunday. But, since she planned to take off early on Monday, Gaelen decided to go in to the office. There was little chance Hank or anyone else would be in, which meant it was the perfect time to find out the one item of information that her father-in-law had held back.

The name of the client who wanted to find Jace Hastings.

****

Washington, DC, seventeen years earlier

The graduation ceremony had wrapped up hours ago. His fellow students were celebrating the release from governmentally required schooling and were partying. Pel Flannery had no intention of joining any of them. His parents—*both* of them—had arranged their schedules to be with him at this auspicious point in his life, and he had no intention of dissing them in favor of classmates with whom he'd never shared anything in common.

His grandparents had drifted away from the dining table, headed to seats before the television in the front room, primed to discover what the news reported in connection to their latest anti-political stance. It left C.C. and Jay at the table with him, picking over second helpings of the chocolate cake with caramel icing his grandmother had made in celebration of his release from school. It was his favorite.

Or perhaps his grandparents, though fond of him, were celebrating his release from their care. He'd turned eighteen months ago, so with the diploma in hand, he was a free man. Free to choose what he wanted to do with his life.

It hadn't been to toddle off to a university.

"School's behind you, Pel," Jay said. "So, what's ahead?"

"Silly question. Music, of course," C.C. answered.

"That's not for you to say, sweet. We opted out of making decisions for Pel long ago," his father reminded.

"But it is a dumb question, Dad. Music's the only thing I've ever been interested in, and you know it. I even worked my way through various instruments before I found the one that felt right—the piano." Pel didn't mention that his time with the trombone had not been a particularly satisfying experiment. That would feel like he was smacking Jay Flannery with his own instrument of choice. His father could make that slide do wondrous things. His had just collected spit.

"You interested in joining my band or the one backing your mother, then? We've both primed them for the possibility."

Pel reached toward the remaining cake in the center of the table and grabbed another forkful. He'd catch hell from his grandmother for ruining the symmetry of what was left of the treat, but she'd be the only one to gripe about it. Then she'd give him a smacking kiss when he protested that she'd made it especially for him, so...

"I thought about it," he admitted to his parents. "But I think I'd rather distance myself from both of you and make it on my own. Which brings me to the topic I wanted to toss at you. Since I don't want to trade on the successes of either C.C. Pelham or Jay Flannery, I need to change my name."

"You what!" C.C. squeaked.

"Makes sense to me," Jay said. "Who you going to be from now on?"

"Well, that's what I need help on. Nothing I've come up with sounds right for me. I'm looking for suggestions."

Jay gathered up cake crumbs on his forefinger, then licked them off. "You know I wasn't born a Flannery. I changed my name at eighteen. Jaben Hastings became Jay Flannery."

"You stayed close to your first name," Pel noted.

"It was too biblical for me, and the extended Hastings clan were all nuts when it came to religion. They said they'd cut me off if I fell from the fold, so I made sure I was well and truly fallen. My taste has always run to what they termed Devil music."

C.C. leaned over and kissed her husband's cheek. "It's one of the things I like best about you."

"Just *like*?"

"There's plenty of other things I *love* about you, darling," she crooned, borrowing from no tune Pel was familiar with. But then there was an entire world of already written songs that he hadn't gotten overly familiar with. "Familiar" was what taking them apart and putting them back together in a new format was. Or so his godfather, performer and composer Paul Montgomery, claimed. Pel had taken it as his private mantra, if a long one.

"Personally, I think the first name is a given," C.C. said. "You're Jay's son so it should be Jason. Since you could have been born a Hastings, why not use it as your new surname."

"Jason Hastings," Pel mused.

"Oh, we can do better than that. That's too formal for a jazz man. That is what you are?" Jay asked.

"Nothin' else," Pel said.

"Then go with *Jace*. It's more laid-back."

"Jace Hastings. Mmm, I like it," Pel announced.

"You don't mind? I mean, I know I'm named after both of you, otherwise."

"Go by whatever name you wish," C.C. urged. "Just tell us what you want *us* to call you."

"Cec," Pel murmured. "It depends on the venue. In the music world, I'll be Jace, but outside of it, among family, I'll still be Pel."

The same day his parents left, he packed a single bag—because he'd never seen either of his parents arrive with more than a wheeled carry-on bag—and a backpack filled with handwritten sheet music, and left DC on a cross-country bus. Because he wanted to stay as much under the radar as possible, he headed for Charleston, West Virginia, a small enough city to scrape by working a fast-food counter until he could be considered a resident rather than a migrant, then did the official paperwork to legally become Jason Pelham Flannery Hastings. After that, he hitchhiked to LA, joined the musicians' local, and started making contacts. His new life as Jace Hastings had begun.

****

Phoenix, current time

When she arrived at the office building wherein Desert Wynd Investigations was housed, Gaelen figured the only type of P.I. she looked like was one undercover as a jogger.

The parking lot wasn't totally empty, but she knew she wasn't the only person who caught up on backlog on the weekends, and there were plenty of relatively small firms leasing offices in the building to make it normal to have four or five vehicles there on a weekend.

Desert Wynd was on the top floor, but as it was

only three stories up, she rarely took the elevator, preferring the stairs. Her rubber-soled shoes made much less noise than her conservative business heels did against the treads. It seemed appropriate for what she'd come to do to enter silently, though. She intended to break into Hank's files.

Perhaps *break* was an inappropriate word. Yes, they were in locked cabinets, but she knew where he kept the keys in his desk and where he hid the key to his desk. Even the receptionist knew. Not the brightest leaf on the security plant was Hank Wyndom, since he never changed the hiding places. Luke had often wondered how his father had managed to launch the firm on his own and make it a success.

Hers was not to wonder why, Gaelen knew, but her current assignment was enough to make her wonder whether Hank knew what he was doing and what type of clients he was taking on.

To play it safe, she locked the front office door behind her and did a quick look around, making sure she was the only one in on a Sunday. She hadn't recognized any of her co-workers' cars in the lot, but that didn't guarantee they hadn't come in to do paperwork.

It was a relief to find the place empty. In quick order, Gaelen pulled the desk key from hiding behind a framed picture of Hank shaking some politician's hand, liberated the ring of file drawer keys from beneath a box of ammunition and cleaning supplies for his handgun, and turned to the bank of four-drawer cabinets.

Since she had no idea what the client's name was, she would need to go through each drawer. Her father-in-law was methodical in his filing, but rather than use designated case file numbers, he preferred collating them by clients' surnames. It drove the office manager insane since every case was issued a coded combination of numbers that keyed it to the type of assignment, the detective assigned to it or leading it if others were involved as well, and other elements. Her personal choice was the case number simply because it pulled up the documents scanned into the computer automatically without needing to be cross-referenced. If everything on this case had been included in the digitized file—which she knew it hadn't, since she was missing the client information—she could have logged in from home to look at it. But breaking into Hank's outdated system…well, that was going to take a while. At least she only needed to look at things he'd tucked into red file folders.

She started with the *A*s. Since Hank never retired any case file to storage as the firm grew, there were a lot of drawers to sift through. One after another, she pulled files free and flipped them open, using a plastic ruler to hold their place open in the drawer.

Ninety minutes later she had made it to the *M*s and wasn't looking forward to the time yet to be spent on the rest of the alphabet. She was considering stopping for a bit to nip out for a sandwich before continuing. Just considering though. It would be too easy to procrastinate over completing the search if she did, and then it would be another six or seven days before she could finish her secret dig for information.

Gaelen slipped another red folder free. Laid it on the bunched-up files in the open drawer before its specific home. Flipped it open. And nearly yipped aloud in relief.

The first sheet gave the basic details. It was Hank's first contact sheet, the signed contract with agreement upon price and daily operative's expenses spelled out. But she didn't need to scan the contract. The detail sheet gave her all she needed to know.

Assignment: Locate Jace Hastings

She scanned the details, most of which she already knew: what the client knew of the target to locate, appearance, last known address, and what the client wished to do. In this case, the sheet claimed he simply wanted a direction, address, phone, email, to contact Hastings.

A 3" by 5" photograph of the possibly late singer was clipped to the form, a publicity shot of a mid-twenties man in a dark T-shirt and jeans, a stubble of dark beard following his rectangular jaw and painting a faint moustache beneath a Greek nose. His left eyebrow was cocked, and a slight smirk rode otherwise unremarkable lips. He was posed leaning against the side of a grand piano near the keyboard, but there was nothing of the classical musician in his look—it was pure theatrical bad boy.

Which is how she remembered Jace Hastings from the videos she'd watched and the vinyl record and CD packaging of the releases she'd bought when in college.

It was what the back of the form supplied that was her goal, though.

Lines there asked that the full name be printed and then a signature be added. The client's address was given beneath the signature line.

Gaelen recognized the address, but more importantly the name of the client:

Dr. Rowan McTavish.

Her assignment had just taken a different turn, Gaelen decided. She would find Jace Hastings if he was indeed alive, but rather than report where and how he could be found to the man she was quite sure had tried to kill him, she would warn Hastings.

She waited until she was back in her car to call Cliff at his home in LA. "I've got a new request," she warned him. "Can you wile your way into whatever archives are available and find something out for me?"

"If you'd come to LA, even if just for a visit, you could look these things up for yourself, you know, Gaeley," her former associate grouched.

"Believe me, Cliff, I'm very close to taking you up on the suggestion that I apply for a job with that giant firm you work for."

"This case is that bad?"

"Well, it's complicated. But it's also something Hank never should have agreed to take on. It's…"

"Hinky?" he asked, using the word he and Luke had always teased her about, claiming she had to be the only person in the world who used it these days.

"Very hinky."

"Okay. Tell me what you need," Cliff said.

"Something very simple but possibly difficult to unearth," Gaelen warned. "I need the license number and the state that issued the plate on Jace Hastings' red roadster."

****

"I hate Sundays," Pel said. "Actually, I hate weekends. And holidays."

"Why?" Jay demanded as he tipped the chair in C.C.'s miniscule dining area back against the wall.

"Days of rest for most people."

"We aren't *most* people," Pel reminded.

C.C. looked over at them from the stand she'd taken before the coffeemaker, waiting for her morning—although it was just past noon—caramel vanilla crème shot of caffeine to help her wake up. Without taking her eyes off the coffee dripping into her mug with its picture of a chicken playing the accordion, she translated for her husband. "He dislikes such days because the stock market is closed."

Pel and Jay had gone for basic coffee. Jay buried his nose in the coffee mug he'd found in the cupboard. It had the bars of a musical composition with notes dancing along them, but the legend printed on the side claimed, "Vocalists do it in the shower—twice a day!" Pel had pulled his usual choice off the shelf. It said, "I find your lack of pitch disturbing."

"That so goes against the grain," Jay groaned. "Where did we go wrong with him, Cec?"

"Basically, in every way possible," she answered.

Jay turned to where Pel leaned against the patio window frame. "Don't know what to do with yourself, kid? Hell, score some music for us. C.C. says you've got a full-sized grand at your place."

Which he did, but after the high of playing with other musicians again had faded, he wondered if he'd made a big mistake in giving in to everyone's coaxing to not only join the late-night musical free-for-all but lead the way into each new song selection. Was one night of bliss worth destroying everything he'd done to disappear?

Unlike C.C., he hadn't looked for a condo but went farther out of Surprise proper to purchase a recently built custom home that the owners soon found they couldn't afford for some reason. He hadn't asked the real estate person to elaborate. He'd simply walked through the empty, echoing rooms with their high ceilings and wood floors, squinted in the glare off the solar-paneled roof, admired the natural desert landscaping and wide patios both front and back, each covered with trellised wooden canopies. Looked at the emptiness of the desert stretching away in all directions. "How much land is included?" he'd asked and, when they told him, had said, "I'll take it." The four-car garage looked empty even when the SUV was tucked inside. He'd jettisoned the previous owner's plan to build a swimming pool. He'd lived there nearly five months and the rooms still echoed, they were so minimally furnished.

The smallest bedroom served as a backup office since he spent more time at C.C.'s Place than at home. The second largest was turned into his personal gym, though it, too, was sparsely equipped—treadmill, stationary bike, rowing machine, and a bar in the doorway for pullups. He ran every day, staggering the time just in case McTavish ever tracked him down, but it was from the house through the desert to the mailbox on the road and back. And that was just to collect and then jettison ads into a recycle container.

What meals he didn't eat at C.C.'s he ate perched on the lone bar stool at the large kitchen island, all usually reheated delicacies from the C.C.'s menu. When a guy was determined to avoid security cameras, there weren't too many places he could go.

The view he gazed at from his mother's dining nook was all green turf, narrow paved paths for golf carts, and golf foursomes working their way through the course despite glaring sunlight and a temperature registering over a hundred degrees.

"I shouldn't have given in and played the other night," he murmured.

"You not only enjoyed it, Pel, you were nearly yourself again. I wish you'd sung as well as played for us," C.C. said.

"That's the problem," he told her. "I nearly did forget I'm no longer Jace Hastings, and that's too dangerous."

"You don't think McTavish is still out there, do you? That he'd try to find you?" Jay demanded.

"That's exactly what I think. He's been out of prison for four years, and I've been afraid to breathe in all that time. It wasn't Ash he meant to kill that night. He sent me plenty of threatening notes to riddle that out. Everyone knew I never let anyone else drive my car, and it was rare for me to have a passenger with me. I usually slipped out of after-show hoopla when on the road and headed back to the current hotel. I was ticked off at Ash for pulling a publicity stunt and had only let her drive in exchange for her promise to tell the media the next day that she hadn't been serious and I hadn't accepted her proposal.

"So, no, Dad, I don't think he's forgotten. And he probably blames me for him accidentally killing Ash. He's out there. He just doesn't know where, or who, I am these days. I haven't tried to keep tabs on him because I was afraid it would backfire and lead him to me. Staying out of any limelight, away from the public for the most part, is the best solution—hell, the only solution, as far as I can see."

"You could hire a bodyguard. Two bodyguards," Jay suggested.

"That sounds like painting a target on myself, both front and back, Dad."

C.C.'s cup was full. She shuffled over to the table, indicated his father should stop leaning back against the wall, and then perched on his lap once the chair dropped all four legs to the tiled floor once more. Her hair was every which way, her eyes still looked sleep-deprived, and she'd unearthed one of the ankle-length black negligees from the back of her closet but had covered it with a cotton bathrobe. Leopard mules served as slippers. Pel knew most of the ensemble was only donned when his father visited. Only the robe made it appear mismatched.

Jay sighed, nuzzled his wife's neck, and gave up on offering further encouragement. "I suppose that means you aren't interested in letting me beat you in a round on the course," he said.

"Not my preferred choice of exercise," Pel murmured, "so I'll pass."

"It's not my preferred form of exercise either," Jay returned. "In fact, this little lady on my lap looks like she needs to go back to bed. I may as well go with her, since golf is out."

Pel left his parents to their conjugal pursuits and headed home. They'd all be back at C.C.'s Place later that night. It would be his mother's time to shine behind the mic. If he was lucky, they might be able to talk his dad into staying put and forming a combo of his own to back her. Then all temptations to be Jace Hastings would vanish. He could be content just playing the piano at home for his own pleasure, but at that moment he envied his father for having an enthusiastic bed partner that afternoon.

Chapter Five

On Monday, while she waited to hear back from Cliff about the license plate, Gaelen began filling up the Search for Jace Hastings file with trivial things to make it look like she'd hit every possible source, which included running searches for anyone named Jason Hastings and then showing they clearly weren't the man for whom she searched. Any information that might hint at the avenues she was traveling were not included. The 4-in-1 pumped out printout after printout of newspaper clippings dealing with Hastings' concert dates prior to the so-called accident, plus album covers, fan magazine articles, interviews, the first page that came up for the various YouTube videos so that the Internet address was visible for anyone interested enough to go straight to it. The things she'd collected about Ashley Hopper and Rowan McTavish were in her private folder, the one she'd taken out of her briefcase the evening before and hidden in the laundry room in her apartment building behind the middle of three washers. She doubted, should Hank get suspicious and burgle her place looking for the personal file he knew she always made when things began to come together, he'd lack the creativity of thought to investigate other places she might have hidden it. She simply hoped the washing machine didn't break down and require a serviceperson to pull it away from the wall for repair.

They'd find a sandwich-sized, sealed plastic bag with twine sewn through it to allow the packaged-up thumb drive to dangle out of sight, supported by the cord attached via a couple of push pins pressed into the wall.

She was at her desk looking up more file-filling things from the Web when Hank knocked on her office door. "How's the search going?" he asked making himself at home in one of the client chairs before her desk.

"It's a hamster wheel," she said. "Not going anywhere. Even skip tracing hit a wall."

"Did you follow the music like I told you to?"

Gaelen turned away from her keyboard, rested her weight on her forearms on the top of the desk. "Hank. It's been six years since I was part of that world. I don't have contacts in it anymore."

"What about that slinky friend of yours. Cinnamon, Ginger?"

"Paprika."

"She still singing?"

"Yes, but not as often as she'd like. Her network is nearly as meager as mine. She does more event staff and product ambassador stuff these days."

"Damn," he said under his breath. "Well, Gaeley, that just means you need to start hanging out in bars where they have live talent every night."

Gaelen leaned back in her chair. "Then I'll need a hell of a lot more for daily expenses and mornings off to recover from daily hangovers. There's probably live music every night someplace in Phoenix."

"Hang out at the musicians' union. Act like you want to get back into the swing of performing."

"What's the rush? Is the client someone related to

Hastings who's on their deathbed and wants to say *adios* before they kick it?"

"Client confidentiality, sweetheart."

"That would cover anything they tell me, too, Hank, so why don't I get to interview them myself? Maybe I could get a different angle to follow, a tidbit they didn't volunteer because it never crossed their mind."

"Not gonna happen. Creativity in investigation isn't what I taught you."

"True," she agreed. "But Luke did. Are you telling me my husband wasn't right when he urged me to follow any trail, no matter how unlikely it appeared at first glance?"

Hank leaned forward and hit the desk with the flat of his hand for emphasis. "That's exactly what I'm telling you, Gaeley. Thinking that way got Luke killed."

"Not having sufficient backup got Luke killed," she countered.

"He didn't need backup. What he needed to do was get the hell out of the place when he saw a situation developing."

"The police were stymied, and a child had been kidnapped by a mentally unsound neighbor, Hank. It was why the family called private investigators in. Luke was trying to—"

He gave the hand signal to cut the crap. "He wasn't following orders."

"And that's more important?"

"Damn right it is. This is *my* company. You work for me, you do things my way, not your own way."

She met his eyes, the desk serving as a margin of

safety should his temper get the best of him. "Are you telling me that if I run this investigation the way I think it might be possible to actually find our probably dead man, that I'm fired, Mr. Wyndom?"

Hank leaned back in the chair. "Just do the job the way I taught you to."

She stared at him a moment longer, then opened the bottom drawer of her desk and took out the company-issued pistol. Checked to ensure it was empty, which considering she knew it was, was merely a theatrical performance. Pushed it across to him.

"I quit," she said.

"Gaeley! You're a Wyndom. You can't quit Desert Wynd. You own part of the company."

A really *small* part of it. Hank hadn't even given his son equal footing in ownership but a measly fifth of it. The fifth she'd inherited when Luke died on the job. It would all revert to Hank if *she* died on the job. She wouldn't give him the satisfaction of that.

Gaelen pushed to her feet. Held her hand out, palm up. "Give me a dollar."

"Do what?"

"Give me a dollar. You're buying me out, Hank."

"Luke wouldn't do that, and—"

"The dollar," she repeated. When he sighed, fished his wallet out, and handed a buck over, Gaelen took it. Stuffed it in the left-hand pocket of her jacket, then sat back down, turned to the computer, and pulled up the in-progress expenses sheet she'd begun on the Hastings case, and hit print. Pulled her bottom drawer open again and extracted the red file folder, recently packed with paper data, from the equally red hanging folder. Slapped it on the desk before him.

"That's everything I've dug up on Hastings. All ancient history, or might as well be. As I've done most of the research from the office, the expense sheet is minimal. I'll expect to see a separate entry for it in my account. You owe me for the case before this one. I believe there is also the matter of untaken vacation days that the company employment contract says I'll be paid for if I leave Desert Wynd without having taken them. I expect to see everything due deposited in my account by the end of the week."

"Gaeley," he said, getting to his feet.

She gathered up her briefcase-sized purse. If he looked inside it, he'd find nothing dealing with the Hastings case any longer. "Only Luke was allowed to call me that, Mr. Wyndom," she said coolly. Cliff had the cachet to call her by the pet name, but there was no reason to mention it. Cliff had left Desert Wynd shortly before Luke's death five years ago.

"Gaelen, then," Hank growled. "You're forgetting one thing."

"Oh?"

"Your P.I. license. It says you work for Desert Wynd, and you don't anymore, do you?"

"Of course," she said and took a moment to remove it from her purse. Snagged the building and office card keys at the same time. Fortunately, her certification to qualify for the license was in her safe deposit box and made no mention of Desert Wynd Investigations. She placed the card keys and license next to the company-issued gun. She'd never cared for the weapon. Preferred the pistol that rested out of sight in the pancake holster inside the waistband of her skirt on her right. Hank had never known about it.

She was nearly to the door when Hank cleared his throat. "I told Luke he made a mistake in marrying you," he snarled.

"As I did in staying on to work for you," she countered and walked out.

It was a hell of a day. She'd quit her job, and she had a date for the first time in forever. Yep, the day was looking up.

Now all she had to do was find both a new job and Jace Hastings. He needed to be warned that Rowan McTavish was hunting him.

****

It had been the longest day in his life, Pel felt. Well, maybe it simply felt that way because he couldn't concentrate on anything but the coming evening with Gaelen Wyndom. The stock market hadn't held his interest, yet he tried to appear as though it was. Stayed in his office and hoped he didn't look like a man re-experiencing the panic of being fifteen and working up the courage to ask Marney Kinsale to the Homecoming Dance. She'd turned him down because he wasn't a football jock. Wasn't a jock of any kind.

Then success found him, and women had been clamoring for his attention. *Eat your heart out, Marney. You had your chance.* God, he'd been stupid in his early twenties.

Of course, his grandmother, who thought he'd want to know what his old classmates were doing, though he hadn't cared, had told him Marney married a jock, had four kids in quick succession, and was no longer svelte but potato-shaped. *Close call, Pel. Yeah, right.*

It wasn't working up the courage to do the asking. That had been the easy part. It was the anticipation of what he hoped the evening would lead to and the realization that those hopes had probably been sniffing something highly toxic to let such unlikely scenarios dance in his mind.

When Gaelen waltzed in the door at C.C.'s a little after four, he was primed and still dreaming of impossible things. Hell, they'd met exactly a week ago, but a lot had happened in that time. Hiring the combo to back Rika. Choosing music, which shouldn't have been his job, though both C.C. and Rika had asked for suggestions. The rehearsals that he couldn't stop himself from watching and then making a few more suggestions.

The dance with Gaelen.

Having her sit by his side during the jam session and being enthusiastic in her appreciation, even if it had just been applause and words. A kiss would have been nice.

A kiss was on his checklist for the evening ahead. Actually, more than one, and maybe a bit more. Okay, a lot more. Hell, he was thirty-five, not fifteen. His expectations had grown.

"You look a lot different than the last time I saw you," he said when she came through the door.

"Have you been sitting out here waiting to pounce on me?" she asked.

He moved away from the dining table he'd been leaning back against. "I like that idea. Pouncing on you. Hmm."

She laughed and seemed to flow toward him, though who'd have thought *flowing* was a movement carried off by a woman in jeans and Western-tooled boots. She'd topped them off with a scoop-necked, strappy tee that put a delightful amount of lightly tanned skin on display and had added a loose-fitting fringed leather vest. She looked up into his face and went up on her toes to brush a light kiss against his mouth.

"I believe I'd like a second and maybe third helping on that," he said.

Gaelen stepped back, not far enough to be out of reach, though, and grinned. "I'll have to consider that request, Mr. Flannery. Are you ready to leave, or did I get here too early?"

"Perfect timing as far as I'm concerned. Just let me give C.C. a heads-up that she's on door duty. Back in a sec."

But before he could move, his father ambled from the bar area. "Gaelen. You look lovely," Jay said. Then the old scoundrel gave her a hug and kissed her cheek.

"Stop making time with my date," Pel growled in a mock warning.

"Go on," the older man insisted. "Get the hell out of here. Your mother claims I need training in how to seat guests."

"It's pretty easy," Pel told him. "Even *I* can do it without supervision."

"Then it's dead easy," Jay said, following the declaration with a grin. "Have a good time and a safe drive. How far away is Tucson from here?"

"Over a hundred miles," Gaelen answered. "Depending on the destination, maybe a hundred fifty miles. But it's a fairly straight shot down I-10."

Pel pushed the door open for her. "Don't wait up," he said.

Jay laughed, then greeted the couple who slid in

the door as Pel continued to hold it open.

Taking a chance, Pel offered Gaelen his hand and was pleased when she slid hers into it. "My car's parked in the back," he warned. It meant a stroll around the building under glaring sunlight on well-roasted pavement.

She sparkled at him. "So's mine. It's that nondescript silver sedan."

"Very nondescript. For some reason I thought you'd drive something with a bit more flash," he said.

"Says the man with the rather staid-colored import."

"How do you know it's mine?"

"Well, your father seems to think I'm an intelligent woman, and my intelligence says C.C. wouldn't drive an SUV. Plus, few restaurant employees make enough to afford a foreign model. Still, the fact that it's an SUV is surprising. I would have thought a sports car more your style."

"Was once," he admitted as they reached his expensive but far from flashy wheels. "I must be getting old."

Pel leaned on the door, grinning at her as she climbed into the passenger's seat. When he didn't say anything, she frowned at him. "What? Have I got chocolate residue on my face from the candy bar I snagged to sustain me on the drive here?"

"If you did, I'd be tempted to lick it off."

An impish grin curved her lips and lit her eyes, incredibly pretty reflections of the sky overhead. "You know," she said, "I think I've got another one in my purse. Shall I tempt fate?"

What the hell, he thought, pulling her back out and

into his arms. Then he did what he'd been dreaming of doing for days. He kissed her. Quite thoroughly.

A few long kisses later she moved a breath away. "We're getting a late start, then?" Her breath whispered against his mouth, teasingly.

This time he settled his hands at her waist to lift her off her feet and into the seat. "There speaks one hungry woman," he murmured, closing the door.

Although her seatbelt was snapped in place, Gaelen had already turned to face him when he slid behind the wheel. Her right leg was crossed over the left, though both legs angled away, putting her knee next to the gear shift. "Yes, but hungry for what?" she purred.

"I can see you're going to be a handful tonight," he said, turning the engine over. "Does that mean you had a good day at work?"

"Absolutely top drawer," she said. "I quit. Best decision I've ever made. Should have done it long ago, but you know, it's hard to give up a regular paycheck when things are what you expect them to be. It's dead easy when the boss you despise ticks you off, though."

Pel pulled out of the lot. "Then it's job shopping you begin tomorrow?"

Gaelen twisted back into place, facing forward. "Not quite yet. I need to finish the investigation I was doing, though I won't be paid for it. However, there is possibly a man out there somewhere—" She gestured, the wave of her hand seeming to cover not just Surprise or Phoenix or even Arizona, but the entire planet. "—who needs to be warned that there's a man gunning for him."

"Gunning for him! Were you with the police? FBI? US Marshal's Office? Homeland Security?"

She shook her head. "Nothing as protocol-based as any of those. I'm a private investigator. Well, we prefer *professional* investigator these days."

"Never would have suspected," Pel murmured.

"My husband was one. Trained me. Unfortunately, after he got killed on the job, I was working for his father. Not the nicest or most ethical guy you'd want to meet."

"Why'd you choose today to quit?"

She sighed. "Because I snooped in his files yesterday. He wouldn't tell me who the client was, on this job, and I had my suspicions it was a hinky set-up."

"Hinky," he repeated. "In what way? I mean, beyond you not knowing who the client was. I take it that's not usual?" He took the turn onto Route 60, heading southeast toward the connection with Route 101.

"Very *not* usual," she said. "I like to do a face-to-face with the client and ask a few of my own questions. This time, I was totally in the dark. Never saw him, met him, or knew diddly about why he wanted us to find this man. Until I…ah, burgled my way into Hank's office yesterday, I didn't even have the client's name."

"But you do now?"

"Do now."

"And he's looking for someone you've decided needs protecting rather than whatever the client wanted him for? Who is the guy you're looking for? A criminal lowlife or an absconded husband?"

"Nothing so cut and dried," she said. "Before I knew who the client was, his name surfaced in my investigation. The reason I did an earlier bit of investigating on his name was because…"

"He sounded hinky," Pel said, using her connotation.

"Yeah. I'd rather he didn't find the man he hired Desert Wynd to locate. But enough about work...or what was work."

"Still *is* work, since you plan to find and warn the guy the client wants found," Pel pointed out. "I know it's none of my business, but this is like a show on cable or at the movies. I'm hooked now. Can you tell me who you're planning to warn about the hinky dude?"

She sighed. Stared out the front window at the road, though he didn't think she was enjoying the scenery.

"It's this way. Hinky guy wanted us to find someone who is supposed to be dead."

Pel nearly flinched. Too close to home. But what were the chances?

"Probably is dead," Gaelen continued. "But there's this miniscule chance that he isn't. Still, it's probably a wild goose chase."

"Gaelen," he murmured.

"Pel," she returned.

"You're frustrated. How am I supposed to enjoy the evening with you when every time you stare off into space, I know you're thinking about another guy. One that probably doesn't deserve your time and trouble."

"Concentrate on you, huh?"

"Well, I was selfishly hoping for more clinches and kisses," he admitted.

"Okay, I'll tell you and then just shove it all into a mental drawer and slam it shut. You're the only man I need to concentrate on tonight."

"I like the sound of that," he said. "Name, please."

She took a deeper breath. "Okay, this is going to sound really weird, but the man I was supposed to find is…"

"You're going to kill me with drama, aren't you?" Pel demanded when she paused. Probably wondering whether she should tell him the name. One that might be a garden variety Jimmy Hoffa.

"Patience, Pel. I'm only sharing this information because you might have had a connection to him somewhere in the past.

"It's Jace Hastings."

****

He was lucky he hadn't jerked the wheel or driven onto the apron of the road. Or off it.

"Jace Hastings? That goes beyond weird. Hell, he's been dead for…well, a long time," Pel declared, hoping he didn't sound like he'd snarled the words.

"Told you it was weird," Gaelen reminded. "But it's a job for another day. Tonight, my job is to concentrate totally on you."

Which, in a way, was the same thing, Pel decided. What were the chances…

"Pel?" she asked. "You're awfully quiet. Does that mean you *have* met Jace Hastings yourself?"

"Yeah," he said. Saw him every time he looked in a mirror. Recognized him every time he sat down at the piano. "Long time ago. We had similar tastes in compositions, but it was just a passing acquaintance. We went in separate directions."

"You were in LA then?"

"Briefly."

"Well, the music biz is a small community, even in

LA. It's not surprising that you bumped into each other. Seems to me that Jace and C.C. both did recording at the same studio, too."

It would be stupid to pretend he didn't know which one. "Visions. Back then I was just happy to find any gig—studio musician, cocktail party pianist, you name it. Not, I'm sure you know, the way to make a living."

"So you switched to something that suited you so well you got rich," she said.

"What makes you think I'm rich?"

"Ah, the Porsche? The shirt maker to the stars?"

"I got the shirt online," he said, "so, not quite 'shirt maker to the stars.' "

"Pel. I looked the maker up. The thing cost more than I've spent on three suits, and that includes a bit of tailoring magic to hide my gun."

"Your gun? You were suited when you came with Rika for the audition. Were you carrying?"

"Sorry, but yeah."

"Missed the notice on the door that said, 'No firearms'?"

"I've got a permit to carry concealed, and I'm licensed—or was at the time—as a provider of security."

"And now?"

She was quiet before answering. "Yes. It's part of why I'm wearing the vest. The fringe helps to hide it, though it's inside my waistband. And, before you ask, I'm wearing it because I feel naked without it. I'm considering forming my own agency rather than work for someone else, so it's not something I'm likely to stop wearing. If it makes you uncomfortable, I'll be glad to tuck it in the glove box."

Pel glanced over at her. "Which side?" he asked. "You know, so I don't get in the way of a smooth draw if necessary."

Though he'd meant to sound flippant, her answer was serious. "My right."

He nodded, wondering if it looked like acceptance of the weapon or that he'd just been verifying a guess. At dinner on Friday night, the right had been her dominant hand to wield a knife when cutting her chicken.

"What model?"

"Same as the Navy Seals use."

"Huh," he mused, then added casually, as though discussing the weather, "Personally, I carry the Secret Service's lethal choice."

A quick glance to the side showed her lips parted as she stared at him. Pel figured he'd won this "who had stunned who the most" round. She'd no idea she'd knocked him for a loop with the mention of his other name.

"You are a most unusual man," Gaelen said.

"Naw, just your average Joe."

"This is Arizona, Pel. Average Joes drive pickup trucks with rifle racks in the back window."

"Okay, your above-average Joe," he corrected.

"You didn't make your money via an armored truck heist and then elude authorities, leaving your associates to deal with prison, did you?"

"That's very creative thinking," he said. "If the P.I. thing doesn't work out, you might try becoming a novelist."

"Ha-ha," she said, obviously not amused but waiting for an explanation.

"No heist. Found I had a knack for the stock market. Sank a chunk of what I'd made tickling the ivories into a variety of risky choices and lucked out. After that it took no time at all to make even more. The trick is to have enough to bet in the market to make a killing when that bet pays off, but not enough to bankrupt yourself if things go to hell."

"You live dangerously on a different plane, then."

"Yep."

"And are you carrying right now?"

"I'm driving a foreign in redneck territory, Gaelen. Of course, I'm toting it!"

"I'd no idea I should frisk you before getting in this vehicle," she said wryly.

The snark relieved his mind. "If I'd known there was a chance of that earlier, I'd have fessed up immediately," he insisted. "It's a long time since a woman wanted to paw me."

"Seriously, should I turn my P.I. talents back on to protect you?" she asked.

"Were they turned off?"

"Well, no, not exactly."

Via the rearview mirror, he glanced at the traffic strung out behind them. It had become habit to do so years ago. Not to see if someone was about to pass, but whether someone was following him. "We're a pair, aren't we? Both armed with no real reason to be carrying weapons on a dinner date other than it's your professional hardware and I'm paranoid. No one knows either of us in Tucson. Hell, *we* don't know each other beyond a few pleasantries."

"Are you referring to trading information about our professions, or the kisses?"

"The kisses, I think. Who the hell cares about professions when there are kisses in the wind?"

"Somehow, I doubt you bought a gun simply because you drive an expensive car. What's the real reason? I can protect you. I'm trained to do that, Pel."

He sighed. "Lighten up, Gaelen. I don't want you to protect me. I'd rather spend the night *with* you. All the way to breakfast, if you want further clarification."

The connection from 101 to I-10 was approaching. "Now, considering I've confessed to being nothing but a sex-starved nutcase, do you still want to head to Tucson for dinner? If it's a pass, I can take you back to your car," he offered. Sometimes it was a pain in the ass to be a decent guy, but on the other hand, best to declare his probably-not-so-decent intentions.

"I'd like to go back to Surprise," she said.

"Too much honesty too soon, huh?" *You deserve to be a monk, Flannery! Way to kill what began as a really promising evening.*

"We don't really know each other," she explained. "Honestly, I don't want to go to Tucson for dinner anymore. I'm not hungry…"

Nice one, Flannery. Shot yourself down this time.

"…for food, just for you."

For the second time within the short drive, he nearly drove onto the shoulder.

****

Gaelen wasn't surprised that they bypassed C.C.'s but was when Pel headed deep into the desert. The road was narrow, the lack of civilization astounding, this close to Phoenix. But the landscape was beautiful in its wild state, and when a building appeared in the distance, it was a huge place, though the coloring allowed it to blend into the land around it nicely. It was the glint of solar panels catching the sun as it slowly lowered into the western sky that she saw first. The lane back to the house was beaten earth. White, open-slat fencing marched parallel to it on either side. Probably to designate where there *was* a drive, she figured. She had barely taken in the size and minimal landscaping around the house before Pel pushed a button that opened a wide garage door. The SUV slid inside and seemed to sigh with pleasure over being home.

Pel was out of the driver's seat and around to her side before the exterior door had lowered into place. When he pulled the passenger's door open, she'd barely released her seatbelt. He surprised her by bending slightly to sling her over his left shoulder in a fireman's carry. She shrieked, but it dissolved into laughter that echoed in the large and fairly empty garage space.

The door to the house proper led into a massive kitchen. Pel deposited her on the counter-height island in the center. Sitting there, her legs dangling over the side, Gaelen slid her arms around his neck. He shoved his fingers back through her hair, drawing her in for a deep kiss.

Yep, she thought happily. She hadn't been the only one no longer interested in food. She returned his hunger when they parted by planting light kisses on his chin. Worked her way along his jaw to his earlobe and teased it with her teeth.

He caught her hand, raised it to his lips to plant a kiss in the palm. Moved on to the inside of her wrist. "Which side was that weapon on again?" he murmured.

"We wouldn't want it discharging unless there's a purpose, would we," she whispered back.

"We wouldn't want *anything* discharging before intended," Pel said.

"I'll remove it," Gaelen said.

"I think you should remove more than just the gun. It's a scientific fact that wearing clothing for too long a period is detrimental to a healthy lifestyle, Ms. Wyndom."

He'd worn another expensive dress shirt but hadn't fastened all the buttons nor tucked it into the pair of well-worn and faded jeans he wore. Considering she'd always seen him in business apparel, the change was drastic. But she liked it and the fact that *this* was probably the real Pel Flannery. Something about him seemed less rigid, more carefree. Things she would not have thought he could be when first they'd met.

She liked the broad width of his shoulders, the tantalizing glimpse of his sun-warmed chest, the square, solid set of his jaw. It radiated determination, strength. She knew his lips thinned, pressed tightly together when he thought no one was looking, yet when she glimpsed the slightest hint of his grin, the man had the ability to make her stop thinking about anything but kissing him. Touching him. He radiated a power that mesmerized her.

Gaelen slid her hands to the shirt button just below his collarbone, toyed with it. "Really? Then you must be suffocating in this, Mr. Flannery. Could you do something about ridding yourself of it?"

Pel released her long enough to rip his shirt off. Buttons rattled about the kitchen. He ignored them.

She laughed as she pushed the shirt off his shoulders, gathered it up, and tossed it back over her shoulder. Whether it fluttered to the floor or got hung up on another empty counter, Gaelen didn't bother to check. "How much did that one cost you?" she asked.

"It's all in the analysis of the amortized cost to desired function ratio," he said at her ear.

His voice had dropped an octave lower as he pushed her vest off her shoulders. It was a growl, but an extremely pleasant one. It recharged the fire his smile alone had kindled a week ago. She loved the elegant length of his fingers—perfect for a pianist, allowing for a long reach on the keyboard and a light-to-demanding touch on the ivories. The memory of watching his fingers fly, float, and flutter notes to life played in her mind.

Those same fingers brushed her newly bared shoulder. Followed the course of her camisole's scooped neckline. His palm brushed over the tip of her breast. "In this case," he whispered, "the cost was minimized by the prospect of what I hope to gain."

She planted another teasing kiss at the corner of his mouth. "Where's your weapon hiding?" she purred.

"Where I won't inadvertently shoot off something I might want to use," he answered. Then he reached behind his back and pulled the handgun from where it had obviously been tucked in his waistband and hidden by his shirttail. "Yours?" he asked as he placed the pistol in an otherwise empty cabinet drawer.

She scooted a bit on the island's top. "Not as easily removed at the moment."

"What's it take to disarm you, darlin'?" He nuzzled her throat.

The rapid throb of her pulse betrayed the delight everything he did—and said—gave her. "You've sorta done that already, sir. But regarding my handgun, sadly, unless I merely draw it, which I'm sure you don't want—"

"Absolutely. No drawn guns," he agreed.

"—the holster setup requires standing upright and the removal of something that would put me ahead of you in the search for that healthy lifestyle."

Something flickered in his dark chocolate eyes. Mischief, she was sure. "In that case, I'll help," he offered. "It's what a gentleman does."

"Really?" she asked, sliding to her feet. "Did your father or grandfather tell you that?"

"Actually, a girl I met at the musician's union in LA. I was eighteen. She was twenty-one."

"She played the flute?" Gaelen queried in mock innocence.

"Unfortunately, no. The violin."

"Ah, poor Pel."

"Don't feel sorry for me. She liked to fiddle around. Now where was that weapon you needed help removing?"

His hands cruised over her ribcage to the waistband of her jeans. Found and released the button catch and slowly, oh, so slowly, slid the zipper down.

Gaelen found it was difficult to breath.

"Ah, there it is," Pel whispered.

She gasped. "Are you sure that was my weapon you touched?"

"Oh, definitely," he said. "It might not have been the gun, though."

"Pel. If you do that again, I'll—" Her breath shuddered when he did it again.

"Bedroom?" he asked, his tone one he might use at C.C.'s, casually asking if she'd like a menu.

"And if I said no?"

"I'd wish I'd bought a dining table to ravage you on."

She sighed as though resigned. "I sorta noticed there was only a piano in the main room. Maybe you should consider adding something, like a sofa?"

"Gaelen?"

"Hmm?" she murmured.

"You're a terrible tease," he said.

"Then I'll just have to practice more to get it right, won't I, Pel?" She walked her fingers up his bare chest.

"Floor," he growled.

"Floor," she agreed and grinned happily at him.

****

They made it to the bedroom as the last of the brilliant sunset faded to deep purple. The evening was turning out even better than his daydreams had been, Pel admitted. There were still the nightly security features to see to. Gaelen had slipped into an exhausted sleep the moment she slid beneath the sheet. She lay on her side, one hand tucked under the pillow. He wondered whether she'd realized that, as she turned over, the sheet had slipped to leave the soft curve of her spine on display.

They'd left their clothing where it was discarded, which meant a trail led from the kitchen to the main room, stopping just shy of the grand piano. The highly polished flooring had felt hard only after their first nearly frantic coupling. Still, they hadn't moved elsewhere for the second helping. Probably because it had followed rather quickly after the first.

No wonder she was sound asleep. They'd had quite a workout. But it had invigorated him as he hadn't been in years. Considering the last sex he'd enjoyed had been with a physical therapist while relearning to do just about anything physical after the near-death experience, it was good to know he had staying power. Had gone the course. Met and possibly surpassed all expectations.

Yeah, yeah, Flannery. Here's the gold medal. Now stop patting yourself on the back and get on with your life.

Except, of course, he didn't really *have* a life. He had an existence tempered by the need to be invisible.

It was still light outside, but the sun had begun its departure for the day. Soon the sky would be painted in hues from rust to gold to pink and purple. He rarely got to enjoy the sight despite the house's situation on the nearly deserted desert road. He took no chances.

Except he had. He'd let himself follow through on his attraction for a woman who just happened to have been hired to find Jace Hastings.

She was the flame that sparked something in him that he'd buried deep a decade ago. He should trust her. Not enough to tell her his secret. It was too dangerous for anyone but his immediate family to know he had survived. Dangerous for him and dangerous for her now their relationship had changed.

Rather than join Gaelen, he visited each room in the house, ensuring that all solid wood shutters were closed, and the thermal, light-blocking drapes were drawn over them. The set-up wasn't so much to keep light out as to keep that inside from showing outside. From turning a dark form against a bright interior into the perfect target. If he were found and McTavish took a post in the desert and fired on any movement inside the house at night, he wasn't the only one in danger.

Occasionally C.C. came out to visit. As did his tailor. The barber who kept his hair trimmed to business standards and lightened to a mediocre brown. The housekeeper visited twice a week when he was already at C.C.'s, so occasionally she left only as the sun set. They'd all been told the windows should be covered at night, though not why. He paid them all generously to not ask questions and not to mention what they did for the desert recluse he'd become. He didn't want them dying because McTavish just fired, not bothering to verify the identity of the target.

Rather than disturb Gaelen's rest, he headed to the shower just off the gym room at the far end of the hall. Before stepping under the water, he stared at his face in the mirror. *Nope, no Jace Hastings in sight.* Then he removed the tinted contacts and looked again. Eyes of polished emerald looked back at him. *How ya doin', Jace?* he asked the man returning his stare in the glass.

Removing the contacts felt good. So often he wore them for far too many hours, but it was the only way to hide Jace Hastings' most memorable feature. He'd tossed the Clark Kent glasses somewhere between the kitchen and the main room. He'd have to locate them. If they hadn't survived his careless treatment, no problem. There were another half dozen in a drawer, just slight variations on the frames. C.C. hadn't thought a man who dressed as he currently did would own only a single pair of them or duplicate the style. The trick would be to get the contacts back in before Gaelen woke. She had been hired to find him—well, Jace Hastings—and though she now intended to warn and protect the man she didn't know he was, he wasn't convinced that confessing the truth to her was a good idea.

He'd been hunted for too long to trust easily.

Even if she had good intentions and—

And he wanted her again and again. And again.

Pel stepped into the shower, letting the warm water that emerged from even the cold setting sluice over him. He'd just wrapped a towel around his waist and was rubbing his hair dry, when a gasp in the open doorway brought his head up sharply.

Gaelen stood there, the sheet wrapped around her, her chestnut hair spilling in wild abandon. The way his fingers had left it.

Her gaze moved from his water-darkened hair to his eyes.

And he knew the jig was up.

Chapter Six

"You're Jace Hastings."

Gaelen barely believed what she was saying, yet so many things fell into place now. How familiar he'd always seemed. The way his hands danced across the piano keys. Even, though he pitched it deeper, how the tone of his voice was like Jace Hastings'. She'd just watched video after video of Jace on stage, sitting at his ease talking to late night television hosts or to reporters who followed the entertainment world at various affairs. She knew the length of his stride, the way he cocked his head to the side when he grinned. How that smile had always made her knees weak.

Things Pel did. Particularly the effect of his smile when it curved just for her.

She had recognized it all at a gut level but not a conscious one. Geez, what a lousy detective she was. Both Luke and Cliff would have railed at her, then quizzed her on what she should have done to correct such a stupid oversight. Shit, even her dreams had made the connection, but had she? Hell, no!

But Pel was good at hiding. He did enough things differently to allay suspicion. Changing the color of his eyes, lightening the shade of his hair, being clean shaven, deepening his voice, dressing as a corporate honcho rather than the bad boy persona Jace Hastings had cultivated. It was why, though he still drove an expensive vehicle, it was a staid shade of metallic beige and an SUV rather than a lipstick-red sports car. Though now that she considered things, she had noted the word "hybrid" next to the model style near the manufacturer's logo on the import, and Jace Hastings had driven an electric sportscar because he was vocally adamant—a trait Pel picked up from his political protesting grandparents?—about using alternative, renewable, less harmful power sources. Even the house he lived in now used solar energy.

Pel's tossed-off comment about carrying a handgun because he was paranoid was a lie. He wasn't paranoid. He knew he was being hunted.

The lack of information she could find about him as Pel Flannery should have rung a bell in her investigative mind. It had barely been more than she'd found on Jace Hastings, and it was because where one left off, the other began.

Pelham Flannery grew up in Washington, DC, but she hadn't been able to find anything about him after high school graduation. And even what she'd found about his early life made no mention of C.C. Pelham or Jay Flannery as his parents. He'd already mentioned that he'd headed to LA, had been eighteen when he joined the musicians' union there. Yet he disappeared from documentation after leaving DC.

Jace Hastings' career began to take off when he was twenty-two, though as no birth date was ever given for him, or parents named, everyone simply had to take what he told them as gospel. However, Jace Hastings surfaced in LA at eighteen. She'd been able to find enough documentation to prove that. He'd been a card-carrying member of the musicians' union in the City of

Angels.

She hadn't looked to see if Pelham Flannery had been one as well.

And she knew from having run her fingers lightly over the scars on Pel's body not long ago, that something horrendous had happened to him. When she asked, he said he didn't want to talk about it. She'd thought perhaps he'd been in the military, had been injured in an incident in the Middle East while serving. That sort of thing many men didn't want to talk about.

But it had been a semi ploughing into Jace Hastings' sportscar that had given him the wounds.

"Why couldn't you tell me?"

"Gaelen. I don't tell anyone. It's too dangerous."

"I know it is, Pel. Or is your name really Jace?"

"It's Pel. Always has been. Jace was invented, though Jason Hastings is legally part of my name. Has been for seventeen years."

"I didn't find that in my search for you under either name."

"You looked for Pelham Flannery?"

He sounded angry over that revelation. "Of course I did. I don't go out with someone I haven't checked out. If Jason Hastings is your legal—"

"*Part* of my legal name," he corrected. "I changed it, to tack Jason ahead of it and Hastings behind, when I was eighteen."

"I didn't find—"

"You didn't comb the records in Charleston, West Virginia. Even back then I didn't want anyone to know who I really was, though that was to avoid trading on C.C. and Dad's reputations. I need you to promise to keep my secret, Gaelen."

"Pel. I know the name of the man who tried to kill you. He's the client Hank was hiding from me. Rowan McTavish."

Pel tossed the damp towel in his hand aside. "Let me get some clothes on."

"He's here in Phoenix."

"Then all I need to do is lie low until he does something stupid again. Robs another jewelry store or kills someone in a bar fight," he said as he pushed past her.

Gaelen trailed him down the hall. "Neither of those is going to happen. He went legit. Got a degree while he was in prison. He's a psychiatrist now, Pel. A doctor with a shingle hanging at one of the most distinguished psychiatric firms in Phoenix. His specialty is criminal behavior."

Pel stretched his arm out, his palm against the wall, leaning into it. Dropped his head. Took a deep breath, then turned to look at her. "Well, it's been nice knowing you, Ms. Wyndom, but it's time I grabbed a bag and ran for my life again, if that's the case. I kept on the move in the past, always expecting to find one of McTavish's buddies breathing down my neck. That feeling began to subside when nothing happened in the last two places I stopped. I thought the search had been called off. Hoped something dire had happened to him. After a while it felt almost safe to settle in one spot. I've gotten better at hiding, over the years. Thought here in Surprise there would be no more surprises. How'd he find me this time?"

She paused. Bit her lip in thought. "He didn't. It's why he hired Desert Wynd to look for you—well, the other you. But he did know Jace Hastings was in the

Phoenix area. At a guess, I'd say that means whoever he's had keeping track of your whereabouts since Ashley's death lost you or something happened to them that left McTavish with only part of the information he needed. How long have you been Pel Flannery again?"

"Far longer than even Jace Hastings existed. C.C. and Dad got me transferred to a rehabilitation clinic far from California. I left LA as Jace Hastings and arrived at the new place as Pel Flannery. Cost a hell of a lot to get my name altered on the hospital records. It nearly bankrupted Jace Hastings. It didn't do Pel Flannery's separate account much good either. Get out of my way, Gaelen. I need to leave Arizona before your father-in-law manages to hand me over to McTavish," he growled and headed back to the master bedroom.

She trailed him through the open door. "Maybe it's time to stop running."

"Oh, and let him find me?" He pulled a distressed gym bag from the closet. It was already packed, though barely big enough to hold changes of clothing for a layover. His movements were so economic and purposeful, she knew this wasn't the first time he'd left somewhere at a moment's notice. He did a quick check, as though mentally ticking off things on a list. She saw that the items were varied when he tossed them onto the bed. Things that would easily change his appearance. Two ball caps, each a different color and lacking a manufacturer or team logo. They'd hide the color of his hair. Dark glasses styled from wireframed specs to Secret Service agent to race car driver to hide his eyes, and not in cases to protect them so all sported a scratch or two, probably to further sell the drifter he'd appear to be. A generic hoodie. A windbreaker that was navy with a light gray interior, obviously reversible. A trio of T-shirts, black, white, and heathered gray. Two pair of jeans in various stages of fading. A couple pairs of socks. He shoved all but a pair of jeans and the gray tee back inside the bag, then pulled the pants on while still standing. When he tossed a pair of scuffed brown work boots out of the closet, Gaelen realized he was nearly ready to run.

"Pel. Listen to me," she pleaded. "If you don't stop running, you'll never…"

"What? Have a life? It almost felt like I had one again. Now…" The sheets whispered when he dropped to the mattress to pull on socks, then boots.

"It will crush C.C. to lose you again. Jay, too."

Pell didn't look up at her but concentrated on tying each boot in turn. "Crush my parents. Like my death wouldn't do that in any case?"

"Then think about me," she urged.

"You?" He raised his head, closed his eyes. Those gloriously brilliant emerald eyes. Took a deep breath, steeling himself, she guessed. "Honey, we barely know each other. I can't even tell you which man had sex with you. Was it Jace Hastings or Pel Flannery? Hell, I don't know who I am most of the time. It was a hell of a sendoff, Gaelen. Thanks," he said and stood up to shrug the gray tee on.

The fabric clung to his shoulders, hugged his pecs when he tugged it in place. It fit loosely enough at his waist that, once he reclaimed it from the kitchen drawer, the pistol would be hidden. Scooping up the nearly filled and still open bag, he was out of the room, headed for…a linen cupboard?

Pel dropped the bag at his feet and pulled the door

of the narrow hall closet open. Scooped up the tall stack of fluffy cobalt blue towels and dropped them on the hall floor. The shelf came next. His fingers probed the back edge of the one above and the wall panel he'd exposed dropped open.

A wall safe! His fingertips danced over the electronic keypad, and then he opened the door and grabbed stacks of bills. Not newly issued but well used, aged from handling by thousands of strangers. He tossed them toward the waiting bag and hunkered down to peel a selection of different denominations from the cache.

"I'm going to need you to drop me at the bus station. You can ditch the SUV afterwards. Don't take it back to C.C.'s. Nothing about me can lead back there. When you've abandoned the car, take a cab back to the club for your sedan. Don't go back to the club after that. Let Rika tell C.C. and Dad that I'm gone and why. You'd better get dressed, slick. Looking like that, you'll draw a crowd."

When he stood up again, she trailed him back to the main room. "Pel," she said quietly and let the sheet slip to the floor. He glanced at her and, temporarily distracted by her unclothed form, was easy prey for the roundhouse kick she delivered. Taken totally unaware, he fell back against the wall near the grand piano and crashed to the floor. By the time he shook off the disorientation from the blow, she had his arms pinned with her knees as she straddled his body. "I have a counter suggestion, Pel. Spare me the time to hear it?"

She knew he could easily escape her hold. He was larger, stronger than she. And she was at a disadvantage, considering she was naked.

A fact that at least had him pausing, though whether in thought or freshly rising interest was debatable. If the two avenues were warring, her current position gave her clear proof that one side had a better chance of winning the argument than the other.

"I doubt thinking clearly is possible with you sitting on my chest, Gaelen. I certainly can't keep my eyes on your face, considering the options available, so don't expect it," he said. But the panic in his voice had subsided, she was relieved to note.

Then he moved, slipping free of her restraining position. Cupping her head with one hand at her nape, he drew her down to him and rolled quickly, reversing their positions. Now solidly situated between her thighs, he pinned her arms above her head and gave her the half smirk. "I'm not helpless, sweetheart. I've got a few tricks of my own."

"I still have an idea on how to end this, and not with your death, Pel. I have ulterior motives for keeping you around. And before you ask, they have nothing to do with you being two men in one."

He didn't move. Didn't release her. "So, tell me this idea," he suggested.

"Can you ease up? I'm have a little problem with breathing in this position," she said.

"Not falling for that lie, darlin'. I already know from our earlier sessions tonight that you've got wonderful breath control."

Damn it.

"I think you should come out of hiding, Pel. Or rather, Jace Hastings should. And do it in a big way. Contact the people you trust most in LA or elsewhere in the music world. Invite them to a special show at

C.C.'s. The return of Jace Hastings to the spotlight. I can call in people I trust to do security. It will be a private show, only by invitation, but those invitations will be to other performers, perhaps your old producer at Visions, select media reporters. So that it doesn't leak out, we don't tell them who's headlining, and we collect all cell phones and tablets at the door. That way no tweets or other social media-linked posts can occur during the show. Once the last note is sung, and the last bottle of champagne emptied in an after-the-show reception—where you'll give interviews, answer questions—then we give the electronics back. You'll be away from C.C.'s before McTavish is alerted by the first media posting, and my team will stick with you from then until he's been trapped."

Pel rolled to the side, though he simply stretched out on the floor next to her. "Trapped may not be enough, Gaelen. If he's now a hot-shot psychiatrist, in addition to being a vengeful psychopath, he either has the funds or friends with funds to hire the slipperiest lawyer in the nation to get him off."

"Knowing that's a possible eventuality, we can plan for it. Have a way to neutralize him."

"A bullet's the only way to do that, honey. Don't think I haven't thought about it. I'm a damn good shot on the course, but against another human being? I've always known I'd be the one with top billing at the funeral, not McTavish, if it came down to the two of us with weapons drawn. And don't tell me you'll take care of it. I doubt you've ever killed a man either."

She hadn't and doubted she could do it in normal circumstances. But to protect Pel...maybe she could. But maybe she'd freeze, unable to take McTavish down.

"We won't let it come to that. Are you willing to consider it?"

He was quiet, staring at the ceiling for far longer than her nerves could stand the silence. "That's a lot of details worked out already. How long have you been considering this? Certainly not during the brief time since you found out who I was."

"Who you *are*—at least part of the time. And, no, I didn't come up with this off the top of my head. I'm good at my job, but not that fast at spinning alternative solutions. Once I realized that the client who wanted Desert Wynd to find Jace Hastings was likely the man who had nearly killed him, and did kill Ashley Hopper, ten years ago, my allegiance took a sharp turn. McTavish needs to be stopped and tried for the real crime he committed, not the one he had a buddy do, leaving evidence behind at the jewelry store that pointed to McTavish. Now that I know you're Jace Hastings, more of this possible plan has fallen into place."

Pel got to his feet. Offered Gaelen a hand to help her up. "You want to put Jace Hastings in a position that will lure McTavish into making a mistake. One he will immediately suspect that your plan is tuned to do. He's probably already thought of ways to avoid being caught in such a situation. He's had the same ten years I have to consider things. Maybe we need something to eat while pondering this in more detail."

"Back to C.C.'s, then?"

"To the refrigerator. Tom packs up meals for the staff to take home when he's made too much of something. There's a variety from Sunday to choose from. But first…" He peeled the gray T-shirt over his head and pulled it down over hers. "I'm really going to give you the shirt off my back this time, because a lot less distraction is called for right now."

She shimmied the shirt into place. It barely reached to mid-thigh on her. "Better?" she asked, holding her arms out and doing a quick spin around.

"Hardly," Pel murmured, but as he pulled her in for a deep kiss, Gaelen had no complaints. He was already leaning toward her plan. Which meant it was time to marshal her troops. First item: Call Cliff.

****

"Where have you been?" Cliff snarled at her through the phone. "I've been trying to get hold of you."

"The cell was in my purse, and I'd switched it to vibrate rather than the ring tone for reasons that if you thought about it would have been obvious," Gaelen said. "It wasn't convenient to take calls."

"Other than if you're on a stakeout, what obvious reasons would require that while you're on a case?"

"I was on a date, Cliff. It's been a long time since I was even tempted to make another foray into that world. Besides, I resigned from Desert Wynd earlier today."

"Hank finally crossed the line, huh?"

"He crossed it long ago, which I think you knew and didn't tell me because you thought I was staying because of Luke."

"You weren't?"

"Maybe at first. In any case, I'm unemployed now but thinking of opening my own agency. Just a minute. I'm putting you on speaker." She set the cell on the counter near where she perched on the lone bar stool. It was the total extent of furnishings in the kitchen, other than those built in. She'd swooped up the fairly buttonless dress shirt Pel had discarded earlier. Mostly because it covered more of her than his T-shirt did and downgraded the hunger in his eyes every time he looked at her, though not by much.

Allowing Pel and Cliff to hear each other would make the information-sharing session conducive to questions, answers, and suggestions being batted about. If nothing else, Cliff needed to know everything that was going on and Pel needed convincing that Cliff was on his side.

"Pel!" she said.

He turned from arranging a wealth of what she considered leftovers in a variety of takeout containers on the counter next to the refrigerator. Each carried the C.C.'s logo on the side. Naturally, they'd have containers made of paper rather than aluminum foil, Styrofoam, or thin plastic, she thought. Jace Hastings was a crusader for saving the planet. The fact that even when in hiding Pel continued it on a smaller scale was something she found endearing about him.

But since he hadn't pulled on a shirt after tugging his tee off and over her head, which left him in a pair of jeans, a state that emphasized his bare chest, she wasn't tempted by any of the food. Gazing at him was like looking at a masterpiece. The scars that crisscrossed his torso could never be considered flaws. She had traced each one with her fingers, learning a different facet of this man since every marring line had left more than a brand on his skin. They were mile markers documenting the trials that had made him the man he now was. It didn't hurt that he was both lean and muscled, or that when he moved it was like music that could be watched rather than heard.

"Hmm?" he mumbled around something he'd just popped in his mouth.

"Give me a dollar," she said. "I know you've got one in your pocket because I watched you peel a batch from that hoard earlier."

"Where are you going to put it if I give it to you?" he asked. "You don't exactly have pockets at the moment."

"I'll hold it," she insisted. "You're officially hiring me. This is the surety fee."

"You work really cheap," he said, putting down the makeshift meal to fish out a buck.

Gaelen turned back to the phone once she had it in hand. "Okay, I'm officially on the clock with a new client."

"Then you don't need the information you asked me for?" Cliff demanded. "Thanks a lot, Gaeley. You know how many favors I pulled in to find this?"

"I'm sure you'll tell me."

"What did you ask him to find?" Pel asked.

"The state and possibly license number on the plate issued to Jace Hastings' roadster."

"Huh." Pel reclaimed the carton from C.C.'s. "It's CPJF-1S, a vanity plate issued by the Commonwealth of Virginia."

"How the hell did he know that?" Cliff sputtered. "Who the hell is he?"

"The guy who bought the roadster," Pel said.

"From the junk yard for parts?"

"Because it was a beautiful machine and a dream to

drive," Pel claimed and popped another morsel in his mouth.

Cliff was silent for the space of two heartbeats. Then he breathed, "You found him."

Gaelen grinned across the kitchen island at Pel. "I found him. Now we need to keep him alive."

"We?" Cliff repeated.

"Who else would I trust to have my back on this?" she asked. "You currently working anything that can't be shifted to another investigator?"

"Not anymore. I've got a family emergency to see to in Phoenix, don't I?"

"Yeah, you do," Gaelen said softly. "You really are my family."

"I'll leave at dawn. Should be at your place around—"

"Not my place," she interrupted. "I don't trust Hank. Could be he found my timing for quitting hinky. If so, I'll bet he's got someone watching the apartment."

"Probably has your car bugged, too," Cliff offered.

"I hadn't thought of that." A touch of panic fluttered in her ribcage. She had gone home to change for her date with Pel. Hank could have followed and put a transmitter in place during that time. If he hadn't bugged it previously. She wouldn't put it past him to have a device in all the Desert Wynd employees' vehicles. But *her* car was currently parked at C.C.'s. If Hank homed in on it... "Pel, it's—"

"We'll have it towed. The owner apparently forgot they'd parked it on private property," he said. "Still ditching the import, just in case."

"Ditch an imported vehicle!" Cliff exclaimed.

"You wouldn't like it. It's an SUV," Gaelen soothed.

"Could always replace it with an electric sport," Pel said. "I sorta liked the model I saw online. Copper with frozen gray accents. Too flashy for Pel Flannery to drive, but just right for Jace Hastings if we can safely bring him back to life."

"Two electric sportscars plus an import?" Cliff groaned. "Buddy, I love you."

Gaelen cleared her throat. "Back to the task at hand, gentlemen. We'll shelve the car situation for later. Pel, should we send Cliff to C.C.'s? Or is that a bad idea?"

He grinned across the counter at her. "I think the Flannery family should adopt him. I never met any of my cousins. I think it's about time I did. Cousin Cliff can stay with Mom and Dad at the condo. You play golf, Cliff?"

"Hell, yes."

"Bring your clubs. That's your reason for hanging around. My dad's been looking for someone to beat on the course."

"Well, that gives you a reason to hang out with Cliff, but not me. Maybe we cou—"

Pel cut her off. "You'll come along with me, of course."

"As your recently hired assistant?" she asked.

"Gaelen. You're wearing my shirt. I think that qualifies you for the role of my lover," he said.

"Oh, I may start out immediately," Cliff announced. "This is too good a story to get secondhand."

"Just stay away from anywhere Hank is likely to

be," Gaelen warned. "You know his habits. They haven't changed since you were part of Desert Wynd."

"Understood. Now all I need is an address and the names of the people I'll be calling family," Cliff said.

Pel supplied both, but before Gaelen could cut the connection, Cliff cleared his throat in a way she remembered of old.

"Okay, I know that fake cough. What is it?" she demanded.

"Just wondering whether you ever went through Luke's things," Cliff queried.

"Well, that's really off the wall," Gaelen muttered. "What brought that on?"

"Hank."

She sighed. Looked across the island to where Pel lounged, leaning back against the closed double door of a humongous refrigerator that suited the house but not a man who lived alone. He was eating out of one of the containers, skewering bits of grilled carrot with an extra-long bamboo fruit kabob pick like those C.C.'s used at the bar. His mouth full, he gestured with the mini pike to find out what her old friend was implying with that one loaded word.

"There wasn't much to be kept. Some photo albums from when Luke was a boy. Sports trophies, his high school and college diplomas. His P.I. license and gun. A couple of really well-thumbed old noir detective novels. I only kept them because they were his favorites, so battered that the pages were only intact because he'd wrapped a wide rubber band around them. It's a short list, and they've been in a box in the closet only because I felt required to keep them," she admitted. "No reason to go through them, Cliff. It only took one time through the small archive to memorize what was in it."

"How many detective novels?" he asked. "And is one of them Raymond Chandler's *Farewell, My Lovely*?"

Although he couldn't see her through the phone, Gaelen blinked. Stared at the cell resting on the counter. "Yeah, it is. Why is that important? Because I can tell from the casual way you dropped that into the conversation that it *is* important, buddy."

Cliff had the nerve to chuckle. "Hell, Gaeley, I thought you knew Luke inside and out. You didn't just finish each other's sentences, you could exchange information with just a look between the two of you. Pull the damn box out and open the books. I think you'll find Luke Wyndom left you something with which to fight his father if you ever needed to."

And with that cryptically tantalizing suggestion hanging in the air, Cliff wished her a successful treasure hunt and said he'd see her the next day. But before he ended the call, he dropped one last suggestion. "There's one more thing I think you should do, honey. Clean Luke's gun, load it, and carry it with you as well as your own weapon. I've a feeling, you might need more than just me as backup in the coming days."

****

"I've got a present for you," Pel said after calling C.C.'s to relay the news to his parents that his cousin Cliff would be arriving for a visit after discovering that he was an old friend of Gaelen's. He hoped it was enough to clue them in. If it wasn't, Gaelen's former colleague could explain things to them.

Since he lacked furniture beyond a piano, a bed, a

single bar stool, and a computer desk built to stand at, they'd returned to the bedroom. Both had plumped pillows behind their backs as they reclined against the headboard. Gaelen had grabbed blank music manuscript sheets from his stash and was making notes above and below the staff lines. Pel had opted to stare at the ceiling. Now he leaned over, reaching under the bed to access the shirt gift box stored there. A moment later, he had palmed two prepaid disposable flip cellphones and handed them to her.

Gaelen stared at the simple generic devices. "Oh, so we're going to have matching cells now? Are coordinated outfits next? A tee that says, 'I'm with Stupid'?"

"Tempting," Pel murmured, "but if your father-in-law is likely to put a transmitter in your car, how likely is he to have a similar feature on your phone? Or to have bugged your home?"

She groaned. "You're right. It's all quite possible."

"Which is why I am offering not one but two of the verified effectively untraceable Jace Hastings use-'em-and-toss-'em devices."

"Toss 'em," she repeated.

"Actually, take them apart and stomp the separate electronic parts to hell-and-gone and *then* toss 'em. Preferably in separate dumpsters behind businesses on opposite sides of town."

"That does not sound like the Jace Hastings I remember being quite vocal about tossing plastic and electronics hither and yon."

"As you aren't attempting to disappear, just not be tracked on your home ground, you could follow the Hastings guidelines if you choose. There are recyclable places that deal with electronics and the plastic that houses them. You don't even have to go to them, just mail the damn thing. These two phones are already fully charged and have sixty minutes of airtime pre-loaded. Each has a different randomly generated number. Wyndom won't be able run a trace if you use one of these."

Gaelen sighed deeply, put her list aside, and tossed back the sheet. She was still wearing his T-shirt, but that left her long legs visible. A bit more of her went on display when she bent over to grab her cell phone from the purse she'd left with the pile of clothes on the floor. In quick order she had the back off, the battery out, and was picking at the SIM card to physically neuter the device completely. She left the pieces next to her things and returned to the bed. "There. I am totally unreachable for any of my near and dear. Happy?"

Pel rolled over on his side. Propped his head on his hand. "I could be made extremely happy," he said.

She slipped under the sheet, totally ignoring the sheets of paper as some of them slipped to the floor and she assumed a similar position. "I may be totally exercised out, Mr. Flannery. You are a very demanding client."

He leaned toward her. Brushed a light kiss over her lips. "I like working close with some of those I hire," he murmured.

"*Some*?" she echoed.

"I don't have a lot of experience in dealing with a staff, and I've always been a rather selective fellow."

"The story about the violin girl in LA didn't sound all that selective," Gaelen purred. "In fact, it sounded rather—"

"Rambunctious? Extemporaneous?"

"Desperate. Possibly fumbling. Thrilled," she countered.

Pel grinned. "All of that and more. Hey, I was eighteen. There was definitely fumbling involved. I hope the earlier demonstration this evening proved that fumbling has fallen from the lists."

"Then the remaining 'slightly desperate, though thrilled, rambunctious, and extemporaneous' remain things to keep in mind for future reference."

"Glad you noticed. Please tick off the appropriate boxes on the customer satisfaction survey when you receive it, Ms. Wyndom."

When he leaned in for a longer, more thorough kiss, she met it with a touch of desperation herself. When they parted, she brushed her free hand through his tousled hair. "What are we doing, Pel? Just grabbing the gold ring while it's in reach? Or something more? Once you get Jace Hastings' life back, what happens then? Back to a life lived under the eyes of cameras and reporters? Back on the road for concert tours? You'll be so surrounded with women eager to get a piece of you, you won't need me in your life any longer."

"Gael—"

She pressed a finger to his lips. "Don't say anything, Pel. No promises that will likely be broken. Even if you're serious now, the future will change things."

"The future," he said. "I haven't had a future for years, slick. I live in the now, not in the what-might-be, because the might-be hasn't changed. McTavish could still get lucky. Besides, I gave groupies a wide margin back when there were crowds of them. And that's when

I was young and stupid. Now I'm older and—"

"Just as stupid, if you think I'll let McTavish kill you, Pel."

"You can't guarantee that, Gael."

"And you can't expect it to happen, either, Pelham Flannery."

He was silent, simply watching her, searching her face. Memorizing every lovely angle of it. "Here's the deal then," he whispered. "You let me make love to you, *with you*, from now until things change, no matter in which direction they change, and we don't talk about any tomorrows. No futures extrapolated from the here and now. We simply live every minute as it happens, but we do it together."

"For now," she said.

"That's the deal. For now," he agreed. "What's your answer, Ms. Wyndom?"

"All right," she murmured, "but the name is Shaw. I think it's time I stopped being a Wyndom. I hope you don't mind that Gaelen Shaw had a hopeless crush on Jace Hastings."

"Actually, as long as she develops one for the guy answering to Flannery, it suits me fine," Pel said gathering her close. This time it wasn't hunger-fueled sex. It was slow, leisurely, tender. This time they made love.

Chapter Seven

Despite a night where sleep was considered an option rather than a requirement, Gaelen felt rejuvenated when the sun crested. Not that she could see it. The windows in the room were heavily draped, keeping any light from seeking entry. Pel missed a lot of sunrises because of his security precautions. Not that she could blame him. In his place, would she have turned and fought McTavish's cohorts? Or would she too have run?

She turned over, expecting to find him next to her, sleeping soundly, considering the amount of exercise they'd enjoyed since arriving at the desert house, but she was alone in the bed, in the room.

Gaelen jolted from beneath the light blanket, fearing that, although he'd said he wasn't going to run, that both habit and fear had won out. That he'd bolted.

Then she heard him swear in a distant room. The curse was quiet but frustrated. She smiled and reached for something to wear.

She found him seated at the piano, music scores spread across the top. He was frowning, but when he heard her arrive, Pel glanced up, a smile curving his lips. Oh, if the man could patent it, he'd make a further fortune in royalty rights. Or perhaps it was that the wattage of his grin was topped off with the hungry look in his beautiful green eyes.

"Good morning, gorgeous. Did I wake you with my profane soliloquy?"

"Not in the least. It was the dire need to brush morning breath away. You don't happen to have a spare toothbrush?"

"'Fraid not. You're my first sleepover in a long while. No, I take that back. You *are* my first sleepover. The other times I was the one sleeping over. Would coffee help?"

She took a seat next to him on the piano bench. "No. Orange juice wakes me up."

"Sorry, no orange juice. I'm sadly ill equipped to have overnight visitors. However, there's a carton of pineapple chunks and orange slices from the bar in the fridge you can have to tide you over. Water will have to do until we get to C.C.'s, where there is both orange juice and coffee. This early we won't even run into the kitchen staff. All we need is clothes."

Rather than pull her own things on yet, Gaelen had grabbed another of his shirts, this one with buttons, but she hadn't done them all up, just those deemed most important. He wore the jeans he'd dropped alongside the bed the night before. Yep, neither of them was dressed for an outing, particularly one where an employee arriving early might catch them.

She rested her head on his bare shoulder, the one on his right that bore fainter scars. Those likely incurred as the roadster's passenger-side window shattered when the semi not only flipped the roadster on its side but shoved it down the cross street. She'd found newspaper articles with pictures of the scene, had watched a video a fan had shot at the crash site that ended abruptly when police uniforms filled the screen. Gaelen wondered whether Pel had been conscious or not when the emergency vehicles arrived. Mention was made of a security camera mounted on a building nearby catching everything except an image of the man bailing from the semi before it entered the intersection and creamed Jace Hastings' sports car, but she hadn't been able to find it anywhere online. Obviously, it was buried in the police files stored where all the cold cases went to collect dust.

There was one good thing Gaelen could say about his many scars. They'd given her a myriad of places to stroke him as she charted each of the souvenirs. Including one he dismissed as a flesh wound acquired later. A bullet had etched this mar along his rib cage seven years ago when McTavish's man nearly caught him. He said a waitress patched him up that time. Hospitals created documents that left a paper or electronic trail.

"I almost hate to have to return to reality," she murmured, then raised her head. "However, if we don't get moving soon, Cliff will have beat us to C.C.'s condo."

"Not *us,* sweetheart. Me. Your job is to keep your father-in-law from getting suspicious. Do you think he'll assign a different detective to McTavish's case or take what you collected and work it himself?"

"Actually, I'm not sure what he'll do, though Hank hasn't worked a case himself in years. Staff does the legwork. He just takes the accolades his satisfied clients rain on him."

"Can you find out?"

She knew the grin she gave him sparkled with devious intent. "In a roundabout way. I thought I'd reach out to the detective he's most likely to give the assignment to, Akane Fujihara, the other female licensed investigator at Desert Wynd. When he put me on the case, Hank seemed to think a detective with curves would have a better chance of luring Jace Hastings out."

"He wasn't entirely wrong on that," Pel admitted.

"Yes, he was. I had no idea I was rubbing shoulders with Jace Hastings until last night," she insisted. "My only intentions in regard to you were to bask in the beauty of your smile."

"Uh-huh," he murmured. "Mine in regard to you were a bit more hands on."

"I noticed that," Gaelen said. "But back to Akane... My excuse will be to offer her a job with my new firm."

"So when you mentioned that to Cliff, you weren't just considering it. You'd already decided."

She shrugged. "I guess so. The more I think about it, the sounder the idea is. My finances wouldn't cover overhead for an office, so it will be a P.O. box I use for my business address while working out of my car. There will be enough expenses ahead with footing the bill for a new P.I. license and a business one, plus the bond investigators need to post...and, well, probably more things than I've considered yet. The disposable phones will just be personal ones, since I'll need an unchanging number for a business, so a new provider cell needs to be on the shopping list. I haven't thought it all out yet. Last night I was focusing on security for you while making Jace Hastings a star again, not on starting my own agency."

He laughed. "A star, huh? Not so sure on that, slick. I'm a has-been. There won't be much interest in music circles, and—"

"A *star*," she insisted. "Your talent is far too wonderful to waste."

"As I haven't sung in a decade, you must be referring to the talents I demonstrated last night," Pel said.

"Hardly."

"Well, I'll admit *you* were the one singing."

Gaelen slugged his shoulder. "I've heard you play, and your piano skills and arrangements haven't suffered over the years, even if you weren't using them until C.C.'s opened. We're bringing Jace Hastings back in top form."

"Maybe," Pel said, not sounding convinced. "Let's turn the topic to your plans. When you touch bases with this possible informant at Desert Wynd, will it be a real job offer you use as bait, or—?"

"Of course a real offer. Now if it were one of the men Hank hired when Cliff left and Luke died, I wouldn't actually follow through with hiring them. They're marginally competent, in my opinion, but then they're basically Hank's goons. They'd head directly to his office to tell him I was attempting to poach them. So, nope, giving them a wide berth."

"But Ms. Fujihara won't mention you've contacted her?"

"There's a slight chance, but she knows Hank didn't hire her because she'd be an investigative asset to the company. As an Asian-American as well as a woman, hiring her was a double tick on his diversity-in-the-workplace list. I think she'll be interested. Now I just have to figure out how to afford the paycheck to dangle before her eyes."

"You need an angel investor fronting the money for your start-up," Pel said. "Just so happens I know a guy—"

"You know a guy," she repeated flatly.

"Know a guy," Pel repeated. "He runs B. Cristofori Investments."

"You know him well?"

"I do electronic transfers on all the funds for BCI," he admitted.

"Are you telling me you have a third name?" Gaelen demanded.

"Naw. Bartolomeo di Francesco Cristofori was a harpsicord maker. He invented the piano over three hundred years ago. Now he funds deserving musicians with scholarships and instruments, and he recently branched out with a start-up restaurant for a waning diva."

"C.C."

"He's a really generous guy and interested in funding a security firm with a pistol-packing P.I. to head it," Pel assured her. "Now if I only had a name to give him for this new firm in need of angel financing…"

Gaelen leaned back slightly. Stared at him. "I'll bet that Mr. Cristofori's company has funded windfarms," she said.

"Might have," he murmured. "Though he'd do it through Blue Marble Aid, the non-profit set up by Jace Hastings back in rising-star days. There are some water-purifying setups in Africa and India, too."

She propped her arm up, elbow barely resting on the rim above the keys, her jaw cupped in her hand. "Do you ever spend money on yourself, Pel?"

He laughed. "Shirt maker to the stars. Custom suits and shoes. Giant house for one guy. Expensive cars. Expensive pianos."

"But not when you're on the run. How long have you kept Jace Hastings on the move?"

He ran his hand through his mussed hair. She doubted he knew it gave evidence she'd done a lot of burying her own hands in it the evening before.

"Until C.C. and I rendezvoused in Surprise six months ago, for what felt like forever. I hadn't stayed anywhere for longer than two months since being released from rehab nine years ago. A pickup barreled straight for me the next day."

Gaelen's spine straightened as she gasped. "But McTavish was in prison."

"His friends weren't, slick. They've been tracking me for years."

"Oh, Pel."

His name was a whisper that trembled on her lips. He slipped an arm around her waist, pulled her close. Kissed the concern into submission. At least temporarily. "It stops here, Gaelen. I agree with you. No more running. That's been my default switch for too long. I think I'm ready to live again."

****

Considering her old associate and friend was due to arrive from California, the planned early start was delayed by a shared shower and what came after. Which ended up requiring another shower, though Gaelen insisted on separate ones or they'd never leave the house. Which suited him fine on one hand but not when it came to her determination to get him back on stage.

And keep him alive while doing it.

Although he'd resisted the call of music for years, Pel recognized the enticing Lorelei hadn't forgotten him. Since Gaelen had suggested shoving Jace Hastings back in front of an audience, his mind had been running through every song he'd ever fancied singing and never had. It was the fact that he hadn't sung in all those years that haunted him now. Gaelen didn't need to know how concerned he was in that regard, though. He needed her totally focused on things that weren't in his control but were in hers.

"Your father-in-law will expect you to be looking for a new job, won't he?" he asked as he backed the Porsche out of the garage. This, Gaelen had argued, was not the time for him to do without wheels. He wasn't running. He was turning and standing his ground. "You said he has no idea you were looking into McTavish, and considering you hadn't made the connection between Jace Hastings and me—"

"Not until I saw your hair darkened by water and your beautiful eyes," she agreed. "I love your eyes. I liked the brown ones, too, but the green…"

"Are too recognizable," Pel reminded. They were hidden behind the dual blind of tinted contacts and clear lens glasses once more, and he'd pulled on another business suit to put Pelham Flannery the one in any limelight. "Green eyes are only for after hours, Ms. Shaw."

"Until the show."

"Until the show," he agreed. "Stop trying to sidetrack me. Will Wyndom be surprised that you're going into business as his competition?"

"He'll be amused and sure that I'll be begging for

my old job back within six months if not sooner.""

"Then when we get back to C.C.'s, pick your car up and head home. If it indeed has a tracker attached, you can do exactly what he'd expect you to be doing. Don one of those chameleon suits and head to city hall to do paperwork for your own agency. Refile your P.I. license under your own business name. From there you can contact a leasing agent and look for an office. In fact, I'll make an appointment for you with the one we used to find the C.C.'s location."

"In other words, appear to have dropped all interest in the assignment I walked out on."

"Yep. Except for excursions to support Rika when she's performing, you won't be leading him anywhere but back and forth from your own home to the various places required to get your own firm up and running."

She mused on the suggestion, then nodded. "I do try to make it to most of her performances. That makes sense to me, although I'll miss our time together."

"You aren't the only one," he said, "but I'm sure if we put our heads together, we can come up with a way to put more than just our heads together."

She gave him a fond swat on his arm again. "I'll let you sort out how to arrange canoodling time."

"Canoodling, huh?"

She smiled, but he figured it was because he hadn't been able to keep amusement over her word choice from his voice.

"You're awfully pushy for an angel investor, Mr. Flannery. But I am limited in what I can do about the new agency. Even if you wrote a check today, it wouldn't clear today, so looking at office space can be shelved for next week."

"That's heavy-duty procrastination, darlin'. All I need is your bank account numbers and through the miracle of electronic transfer, the money from BCI can be available this afternoon. No waiting period required if you've got the chops to pull it off."

"And you do?"

Pel flashed her a grin. "You doubt me, Ms. Shaw?"

Gaelen sighed. "They don't call it angel investing without the investor being capable of working miracles?"

"Occasionally," he murmured.

"And what will you be doing, Mr. Flannery, while I'm engaged in spending your money?"

If Jace Hastings was about to make a comeback, there was a lot of rehearsal time in his immediate future. "Practicing," he admitted, "but only at home. First, I have to spend some time with my long-lost cousin Cliff, take care of a few things at the club that can't be handed off without some explanation. Then it will be back to my desert fortress. I'll call you on the currently designated replacement cell when I'm ready to leave C.C.'s."

"Don't forget you need to make a list of people you trust to invite to the show. Cliff can check everyone on it before we move forward."

"My guest list is mentally aligned," he assured her. "However, I have a suggestion to make."

Her head cocked to the side, curious.

"It's about your part in all this," he said.

"You're not talking me out of protecting you, Pelham Flannery," she said. It sounded like a snarl. He decided it was part of what he liked about her. Her ferocity when she made up her mind about something.

And that *he* was something she'd made her mind up about.

"Then you need more than just a role as a lover to stay as glued to my side as you intend to be when we really get this lost legend visible again."

"Oh, so now you're ready to admit you're a legend?"

"Just using your phraseology, slick."

"What role do you have in mind for me? Personal assistant? Very personal bodyguard?"

Pel shook his head but kept his eyes on the road ahead. "Neither are as groupie hindering as you seem to think, Gael. I believe a different title will suit better. It might even lure McTavish into tossing caution to the winds and make himself more vulnerable, though it could put you in more danger. However, after our discussion with Cliff last night, I think he'll agree with this idea because it not only forces McTavish into responding quickly, but the man'll see it as an opportunity to do unto me differently than he did unto me before."

"Okay, I'll bite. What is my role to be?"

He glanced over at her but didn't grin this time. "It makes you a target, Gael, because it's an upgrade. You'd be my fiancée."

****

A bare sixteen hours had passed since she left her apartment. It seemed impossible so little time had actually gone by. She'd gone from a woman on her first dinner date in five years—though she'd never actually gotten dinner, just leftovers from Pel's refrigerator—to having sex with a man she found fascinating, to finding he was the man she had been assigned to find, to pulling in reinforcements to protect him, and now was his fake fiancée!

Shrugging on one of the blasé suits, she exited an exciting world to return to her existence in a rather staid one. So much had happened since her arrival at C.C.'s Place the evening before. It was time to return to reality, though. There was a partial plan in process. Cliff would be able to round out any rough edges on it while she temporarily distanced herself from Pel and did what Hank Wyndom would expect her to do. Before leaving C.C.'s, she'd done as detailed a search of her car for unwanted electronic devices as possible without putting it on a lift. Making sure it went up on one shortly was on her list to accomplish very soon. Her father-in-law might expect her to do that. She did know his business practices very well. He wouldn't be the least surprised that she instigated a thorough combing for bugs on her vehicle.

Her immediate job entailed getting her own business ready to roll. The mock engagement wouldn't be announced until the evening of the show. At the cocktail party afterwards, she'd be glued to Pel's side as he introduced her as Jace Hastings' bride-to-be. The journalists invited to attend that night would distribute the news. Pel claimed it was an odds-on bet. Not only had Jace Hastings survived the accident all those years ago, he'd found a lucrative hobby in juggling Wall Street stocks. The increased bank account funded Blue Marble Aid projects: solar power, wind farms, and other Earth-friendly projects. And, if that wasn't enough to get Rowan McTavish's attention, he'd also acquired a fiancée since vanishing from sight.

Within an hour of Pel getting the number, her bank

account filled with angel funding. But before changing into a suit from the jeans and fringed vest worn for their date, she opened her closet and stared at the storage boxes piled in the back corner.

It was only one box, she told herself. It had been five years, yet she was reluctant to drag the scant collection that represented Luke Wyndom's entire life from where it rested beneath the tall stack that held the holiday decorations she drenched her home in every December. *Drenched.* That's what Luke had laughingly called it when she roped him into untangling what he claimed were miles of twinkle lights.

She could almost feel him standing next to her as she contemplated invading what she now thought of as his private place.

Yet she could almost hear the echo of his voice in the room, too. *Cliff's right, Gaeley. I was investigating my own father. And you* will *need two weapons to make it through this case. Open the box.*

She took a deep breath and began dragging boxes from the closet, off the one that held Luke's collected life.

****

Satisfied that Gaelen would be kept too busy to do something stupid like beard McTavish in his office at the psychiatric practice—which he feared she was of a mind to do—Pel settled in his office at C.C.'s to begin his own Internet search. He needed visual data to tell him what the murderous stalker had been up to since being released from prison.

While Gaelen hadn't supplied the name of the group McTavish had joined, it took no time at all to find the Hakathi Psychiatric Associates website. While he'd only seen the man a time or two a decade ago, the only thing the professional photograph on the site told him about the stalker was that he now patronized an expensive tailor and a barber regularly. Although McTavish was smiling in the shot, it was an emotionless expression.

The bio that went with the photo freely admitted that the man had a record for burglary and drug possession before turning his life around by working on his degree while incarcerated, and how he'd completed his doctorate after being released. It was written to play up the things he had in common with those the court system directed into his hands now and why he was qualified to counsel them.

To Pel, that said McTavish was collecting a private army of people likely to do whatever he asked them to do. Be it finish off the pesky musician he'd missed killing in the past or supplying an alibi while McTavish savored the kill himself. The man hadn't changed, he'd merely become as good at acting as Pel had become in erasing Jace Hastings from everything but people's memories. The psychiatric firm's website also supplied the date the man had joined them: a date barely a month after Pel had moved into the house surrounded by desert. Had McTavish been haunting places where live music was a feature in Phoenix proper, hoping to find him, and only put Desert Wynd on Jace Hastings' trail in frustration? Or because he'd become impatient?

When the kitchen staff began drifting in around eleven, he turned to dealing with BCI's stock portfolio. But the thing that had kept him sane and financially secure for years held no allure that day. Every stock feeding Blue Marble's and BCI's projects could have tanked, and he doubted he'd notice. His mind—hell, his feet—wanted to send him after McTavish. It didn't matter that it was the stupidest step he could make.

Besides, with his parents due to arrive with Gaelen's old friend, Cliff, in tow, he needed to stay right where he was. Or so his father had said Cliff suggested when he'd called to say the P.I. from LA had arrived.

Unable to concentrate on Wall Street, Pel moved to the piano to work through songs for Jace Hastings' comeback. Yeah, it was as bait to draw McTavish out, but now that the seed of returning to the stage was planted, he wanted to water it, prune it, finesse it with a fervor it felt suicidal even to consider. He'd sold the idea of posing as his fiancée to Gaelen as a way of personally protecting him, but it had actually been to keep her within whatever close circle of surveillance Cliff set up.

What he couldn't let himself think about was the sorry-ass shape his pipes were in after a decade of not singing. His sole consolation with music had been an easily carried harmonica that he'd taught himself to play. Maybe it could be worked into the coming show…

He was still musing on it when C.C., his dad, and a lean, sandy-haired beanstalk of a man arrived. Other than his height, there was nothing memorable about the guy, and in jeans and a pastel green golf shirt, he would melt into Surprise society much like a chameleon. Cliff, no doubt, but Cliff what? Somehow that detail had been overlooked during Gaelen's call to her former colleague the evening before. For all he knew, the man could be using either Pelham or Flannery to further sell the story that Cliff was family.

He was slipping, to miss when small things were left in the wind. A very dangerous thing to do now he knew McTavish had arrived only weeks after he himself had first visited the restaurant property in Surprise.

Then again, he wasn't in his right mind around Gaelen. They'd spent a total of three days together…no, just hours within those three days…and she'd already become an important part of his life. If he was honest with himself, the reason he'd agreed to become the staked goat to draw McTavish out wasn't because proving the man had killed Ashley and tried to kill him would remove the target he'd felt drawn on his back for ten long years. It was to have a future. Any type of future with Gaelen Shaw Wyndom. It was ridiculous to feel so sure she was the missing part of his life already, but only people who threw a wide net when looking for mates would think so. While he hadn't made a list of ideal requirements, damned if she didn't fit them all.

"There he is!" greeted the man he suspected was Cliff, his arms flung wide as he wove through the tables to where the piano was backed into a windowless corner.

Pel got to his feet and stuck his hand out in greeting. "Geez, how long has it been since we saw each other?"

"Feels long enough that we might as well be strangers," the stranger said, closing his own mitt around Pel's. The guy could break bones with that grip. "But when I heard C.C. had moved to golfer's heaven, I had to work in a visit."

"I thought Scotland was golfer's heaven," Pel said,

resisting the urge to shake feeling back into his hand when Cliff released it. He felt a warning had been given that it wasn't just his back Cliff would be watching, but also his intentions when it came to Gaelen.

"Florida," Jay countered, joining them. "That's golfer's heaven as far as I'm concerned. Always plenty of sunny days to play a round."

Pel gestured toward the bright day visible at both the glass entrance doors and the trio of double patio doors that led to an outdoor eating area. "Sunny. What the hell is all that out there, Dad? Stage lighting?"

Jay turned to Cliff, shaking his head. "Your cousin didn't inherit the golf gene, Cliff. I'm psyched to have a partner on the greens. Where's Gaelen? I thought we'd find her here," he asked, changing the topic.

Pel was glad he had. The only small talk he had was about music. As a drifter for nearly a full decade, he'd had to fall back on the weather and asking about local employment opportunities he had no intention of following through on.

"Off getting ducks in a row to open her own agency," he said. "She quit her job yesterday."

"Huh," Jay murmured. "That why she seemed really up when I saw her yesterday?"

"I was hoping that had something to do with going out with me, Dad. She'll probably surface later. She was looking forward to seeing Cliff again, since they're old friends."

"Funny how that worked out, isn't it? That she'd start dating my cousin?" Cliff said.

"Small world," Jay mused. "What happened to C.C.? I'd better find her. You two catch up."

As his father walked off, Pel breathed a mental

sigh of relief. The playacting to convince any staffer who overheard them that Cliff was a relative was behind them.

"Get you a drink?" he asked Gaelen's former associate.

"Too early in the day, and I've had my fill of coffee. How about you tell me what Gaeley's got in mind to do."

"Then pick a table. Security wise, which is the best choice? Personally, I've been taking my lessons from Bill Hickok," Pel said.

Cliff smiled. "Yeah, I noticed when you're at the piano your back is to the wall. A corner, too."

"View of the entire room, all entrances and exits, and an option on the direction to escape if needed."

Cliff nodded and pulled a chair back from a table that would have had Wild Bill's approval, too. "You've been doing this a while, I understand."

Pel took the seat adjacent to the P.I. "Feels like a lifetime. I take it you're up to par on the situation here?"

"As much as possible. I still had the stuff Gaeley asked me to dig up in LA, so I went over things again. That was a hell of a setup McTavish pulled off. You're lucky to be alive."

"Which I wouldn't be if I'd been in the driver's seat. If I had, I'd be dead, and Ashley's career would have folded. She was the type of woman who liked to flash a lot of skin. Heavily scarred skin and a limp like I was awarded would probably have killed her too, just in a different way." He often felt Ash had gotten the end she would have preferred. A quick death with no pain involved and lots of publicity afterwards.

"So tell me what we're doing here," Cliff urged. "If I know our girl, she's talked you into something already."

"Yeah, she did. I feel like I'm stealing a line from one of those old movies, one of the musicals from the Thirties, saying this, but we're going to put on a show," Pel said.

"You watch really old movies," Cliff murmured, sounding surprised.

"When you're in rehab for months upon months, you get to the point where you'll watch anything to distract yourself from the aches and pain. Gaelen seems to think the fastest way to end this is to bring Jace Hastings back to the stage. Fortunately, the small stage. The one here at C.C.'s. Which reminds me of something I haven't done yet." Rather than leave the table, Pel pulled his phone from his suit jacket and punched in a number. He could hear the ring echo out from the kitchen where his parents had apparently drifted in search of lunch, which currently wasn't on the menu at C.C.'s Place.

"Why are you calling me from another room, dear?" C.C. asked when she answered.

"I need you to do me a favor. Call Paul and ask him if he'd like to vacation in a really empty house in the middle of the desert. I need his help on something."

"You could call him yourself, Pel," she insisted. "You've gotten too used to delegating things you don't want to do. Why do you want to talk to your godfather but not make the call yourself?"

"Cec," he said on a sigh. "I'm still in hiding."

She tutted at the mere idea. "Then why do you need Paul's help on something?"

"I can hear you're in the kitchen—"

"I'll go out into the hall," she offered.

"Office would be better," Pel suggested. Mostly because he knew what her reaction would be—a scream of delight where his other name might tumble out. And that was the one thing that he and Gaelen agreed on—very few people should know who he was until he actually took the stage. There was no guarantee that any of the staff who might recognize it yet would be able to keep the secret.

"Fine. I'm dragging Jay along so we can both hear the reason." He could hear her footsteps ring on the tiled floor of the service area. Heard his father asking what was up and his mother's shushed response.

He felt like he should provide a soundtrack for their short journey. The theme to *Jeopardy* seemed appropriate.

"Okay, we're here. We even closed the door. I'm putting you on speaker, Pel," C.C. said.

His mother hadn't the least idea of what security measures were. But then, she hadn't had to live with a target on her back, thank goodness. That wouldn't have been the case if he'd spilled even basic details about Jace Hastings' past life and family connections during his rather brief career. He'd been the bane of the Visions Records promotion department for avoiding answering such questions back then.

"What's up, kid?" Jay asked.

"Maybe you'd better sit down. At least, C.C.," Pel suggested.

"I'm already in the chair," she announced.

"Okay, this is top secret, but Gaelen has convinced me to let my alternate self come out of hiding."

C.C. did indeed squeal with excitement.

"But I've been out of the loop a long time and need you to call Paul and lure him over to coach me back into shape."

"Oh, darling, I'm so thrilled you're doing this. You told her who you were last night, didn't you?"

He let her rattle on about how wonderful it would be to have him back on stage properly, what a wonderful girl Gaelen was, and then ended with words that sent a chill up his spine.

"I can't wait to tell everyone!"

"*Mom*!" Since he rarely called her that, she'd know he was serious. "What part of *top secret* do you not understand? You tell Paul and *no one* else!"

"But—"

It was a relief to hear his father's voice override hers. "Don't worry, son. I won't leave her side and will personally strangle her if she slips."

"Thanks, Dad."

When he ended the call and looked over at Cliff, it was to find the man choking down a laugh.

"Will she slip up?" he asked.

"Oh, yeah," Pel admitted. "Which means we need to keep her busy and away from everyone. Any suggestions?"

"Nope, but I bet Gaeley will. Where is she, by the way?"

"Hopefully staying away from Rowan McTavish," Pel said, though he'd bet his Visa Infinite card that she wasn't.

****

The woman seated in the passenger's seat of the silver sedan was exotic in a different way from Rika's

Latin looks. Akane Fujihara's hair was a silken black, cut in an all-business bob that barely reached her shoulders and brushed from a side part across her fair-skinned brow. Her skirt suit leaned toward dove gray. Gaelen's leaned more toward aged concrete in tone. While Akane's features evoked a delicate oriental flower, her voice rang of a childhood in Texas.

"When you called and asked if I'd like to meet you for lunch, I didn't expect it to be a takeout salad eaten while on a stakeout," Akane said as she opened the plastic-topped box on her lap.

Pel would probably frown if he saw the containers—not the sort that environmentalist Jace Hastings would condone, but a P.I. grabbed what was handy.

"It's just getting the lay of the land," she assured her guest as she pried her own salad container open.

"One that we could probably get from a combination of satellite images and street views off the Internet, since you haven't been interested in anyone who entered the building," Akane reminded. "So, why'd you call me?"

"The reason is twofold," Gaelen said. "You heard I quit yesterday?"

"You would be surprised at the number of derogatory names Hank has used in reference to you since you strolled out the door. I'm pretty sure this isn't the first time he's used them in relation to you—and probably to me as well when I was out of the office."

"He's not the most PC-minded boss," Gaelen agreed as she dropped the package of croutons back in the carryout bag. "How'd you like to leave Desert Wynd and work with me?"

Akane's eyes went wide with surprise. "You've already got a new job?"

"No, an agency of my own, in the making. I've got an angel investor footing the startup. I'd like to offer you first dibs on joining me."

Akane studied her a moment, then turned her gaze to the plastic bowl in her lap and squeezed dressing on the contents from a plastic packet. She stared out the front window as she chewed a forkful of salad thoughtfully. "I might lose my license," she said at last. "Hank didn't sign off on my three-year training period that long ago. It has Desert Wynd's name on it. Hank owns my gun, too. There's health insurance to think of, and I haven't been there long enough to get the nod on the 501(k). Would you be picking up the required $2,500 bond's expense like Desert Wynd does? Or not?"

Damn. More expenses. She'd remembered her own bond requirement but had forgotten other agents might expect theirs to be picked up as well. Thank goodness Pel was an extremely generous angel investor. She'd been stunned at the amount waiting in her personal bank account when she swung by to open a business one. As he'd promised, there hadn't been a hold on the funds. They were available immediately. That had to cost him something other than good will.

"We can work all that out to your satisfaction," Gaelen assured, "including the license fee and bond. And I can get you a gun that suits you better than the one Hank supplied. Even let you pick it out. If you've got the time to look over the suite I have an appointment to see in—" She glanced at her watch. "—an hour, maybe the size of the office that would be yours will be the lure."

"But why *me* in particular, Gael? You barely know me since we haven't worked together on a case, so why offer me a job?"

That was the easiest question to answer. "I read your file when you joined Desert Wynd three and a half years ago. I was impressed. Hank has only given you the crap assignments, yet expected you to do all the computer searches for those two goons he hired. I'm offering you a chance to spread your wings and actually use your brains."

"Why the rush, then?" the other woman asked.

"Because I've apparently caught the instant gratification bug from the investor. He's pushing me to get things up and going as fast as possible. I've already had quite a busy day. Gained a PR firm that's working on a logo, a business bank account, filed for a new investigator's license and a business license today. I'm anxious to actually be *in* business now, and I know your strengths already. I couldn't say that about anyone else. I also think Hank gives you those really crap cases to handle because you're a woman. Oh, he might use the excuse that you're fairly new on the job, but it's a lie. He tried the same ploy with me, but my husband had trained me to stand up to his father. Like he did."

As she'd most likely end up doing to Hank Wyndom with the tantalizing surprise she'd found hidden among Luke's mementos. Before she did, a meeting with Cliff about the mysterious gift was on her To Do List. Timing and backup would be required. Whether that backup was the police department or Cliff needed to be determined.

The woman next to her chewed another mouthful

of lettuce thoughtfully. "You've been with Desert Wynd since before your husband was killed," she said. "I thought you inherited part of the firm."

"Hank bought me out for a dollar."

"Well, that was really cheap of him." Akane sounded affronted for her.

Ahh, she *was* ready to leave Hank's company. The mention of the expenses and 501(k) were a smoke screen.

"It's what I said the buyout would cost him," Gaelen admitted. "Want to see the bill? I'm thinking of framing it. It represents freedom from him. Hey, I even called a lawyer for an appointment to change my name back to Shaw. I'm totally divorcing myself from the Wyndom name. In case you haven't noticed, Hank isn't a trustworthy individual."

Akane chuckled. "That's probably being kind, Gael. Okay, I'll go with you to look at the office on one condition."

"Which is?"

"You tell me what we're doing parked in a lot adjacent to a medical building that you haven't taken your eyes off of."

She wondered about that herself but justified it by studying every visitor who had entered the building. Certainly, there were other medical offices besides Hakathi Associates at the address, but this was a high-class business neighborhood, and she doubted the type of patients sent to McTavish's psych couch by the court system would melt into the landscape. They'd stand out as clearly as if under a penitentiary's searchlight glare. *Which is profiling, Gaelen Ellen Shaw. Shame on you.* But she knew what McTavish looked like. His shaved head would stand out should he exit or re-enter the building.

All things she needed to keep to herself.

"Can't tell you until you sign on and officially report for work with Firebird Investigations. That's what I'm calling my firm," Gaelen said, then gestured toward the buildings around them. "This has to do with a new case I caught, thanks to that angel investor. I meant to ask whether you ended up with the case I was on before I quit."

Akane's hair flowed as though brushed by a breeze as she shook her head. "No, I got the impression Hank decided to finish it himself."

Gaelen wasn't sure that was something to put in the plus or minus column. She hadn't left a trail to Jace Hastings because until Pel had stepped out of the shower, she hadn't realized he was the man she'd been hired to find. That didn't mean Hank wouldn't suspect she might be on to something, though. All he had to do was follow her to Surprise and the ruse might fall through. Something she couldn't let happen.

"This does get more intriguing by the moment," Akane admitted. "And I'm a sucker for a mystery."

Gaelen laughed. "Aren't we all, in this business? But I can't tell you anything until you sign the usual nondisclosure statement. Have I lured you into accepting the position, then?"

Akane stabbed the fork into her salad again. "Let me see the size of that office *and* the neighborhood it's in. I'd hate for it to resemble one like those seedy old gumshoes worked from."

"Done," Gaelen agreed and offered her hand.

Chapter Eight

The office suite was a giant step up in class from the one in which Desert Wynd was housed. It was ground level, with broad windows in the reception area that offered a view of a lushly landscaped patio area. The place echoed with no furnishings—neither furniture, carpeting, nor drapes—to blunt the racket of women's heels on the tile. Akane had taken it all in, then offered her hand. "Contingent on you taking this place and those other little items, you've got a deal," she said. "Should I give Hank my resignation or wait a week or more?"

Good question. It would take a while to get the new office ready to move into, but it would also be handy to have a mole at Desert Wynd.

"Once the PR company has the logo finalized, I'll paint the walls to match the colors in the design and order business cards for us both. Let's set opening day for three weeks—maybe four—away, and you make no mention of any of this to Hank just yet. If you don't mind taking a taxi back to Desert Wynd, I'll go find an office furniture store and take another big chunk out of the angel fund. I seem to be going through it rather fast today."

As she hadn't seen McTavish leave or enter the building where Hakathi's offices were but had seen at least one man who might be one of his patients, she briefly wondered whether McTavish knew what *she* looked like, too. Hank did keep everyone's images and the investigator's names off their official website, the idea being that it made the person sent to tail someone safer when on a case. Slightly safer. Very *slightly* safer. The only way a client knew the assigned P.I.'s name was when a business card exchanged hands at an interview. That didn't mean Hank wouldn't have flashed a picture of her taken back when Luke was alive. He did maintain a front that he had a family he was fond of by having framed photos among those taken of him with local political or media figures on the wall behind his desk. If McTavish had made arrangements with Hank while sitting in his office, he might have seen one of them. Still, she had no idea what she had expected to be able to pick up by haunting the area near Hakathi to begin with. Probably just that she was driven to bring this case to a satisfactory conclusion and even staring at the building where McTavish saw patients acted like calamine on the itch to be doing more right now.

She not only wanted to give Pel his life back, she wanted McTavish convicted of Ashley Hopper's murder and the attempted murder of Jace Hastings ten years ago.

She waved Akane off from her new office space when the taxi arrived, then filled out the leasing agreements before heading out to shop for things with which to fill the empty rooms.

Even though she'd always been quick to make decisions, it still took two stops, one for desks and file cabinets, and the next for comfortable but minimalist items for the entry. She wanted visitors to feel they were entering a home. Delivery day was set for three weeks out.

If only her living room would look as good as she pictured the finished project for Firebird Investigations. Even empty, it was still night and day from Hank's miniscule mock doctor's waiting room with the worn chairs, though he lacked out-of-date magazines. Mostly because there were no magazines. She supposed he thought gazing at the blonde receptionist in the one-size-too-small wardrobe choices sufficed.

That left someone to paint the company name on the door and electronic acquisitions on her Yet To Do List. Luke had had a friend in IT. She still had his address book somewhere in the apartment. Having a physical one, rather than an electronic version as she did, had been a quirk she'd teased him about inheriting from his father, who preferred the same systems he'd used when starting Desert Wynd. Back then, supplying desktop computers for employees' use hadn't been in his budget.

The address book was the only thing of Luke's that hadn't gone into the box she'd stored away and only opened that morning. His clothing had been donated to charity shops when she stopped expecting him to walk in the door every evening. But the box had held high school yearbooks, sports trophies, and albums with photos of his mother who had passed away suddenly shortly after Luke had introduced her as his done-deal wife. Funny that she'd nearly forgotten he'd called her that. The *done deal*. Now it rang like a warning—or a challenge—to his father, who only accepted her into the family—and the firm—grudgingly.

The tattered, rubber-band-wrapped copy of Luke's

favorite novel had given her pause before she opened it. The bands had dried over the years and practically crumbled when she touched them. But they'd sealed the paperback closed over the secret within in the intervening years.

A librarian or bookdealer would have paled at the damage Luke had done to the book. He'd carved a covert cache from the middle of it. Probably with the craft knife he always used to open plastic packaging. The niche was a ragged-edged square fashioned to hold two generic, chrome-encased flash drives.

It made her wonder if Hank had kept her on at Desert Wynd after Luke was gone because he suspected his son of collecting evidence against him for some reason. He would suspect her of being Luke's weak link if, that is, Luke had told her what he was compiling. Not that she would have been. But had her father-in-law kept her close and as much under his thumb as she let him on the off chance that she'd find Luke had left accusing data behind? Unfortunately, she hadn't suspected her husband had left a dangerous legacy, so continuing to work at Desert Wynd had become the status quo for far too long.

Would it have if she'd found the thumb drives and plugged them in years ago? Found out why Luke didn't trust his own father? Not that there had been time to look at them that morning. There was always the chance that Luke had security measures to limit who could access the information. She wouldn't know until she plugged each into a computer. One that couldn't have been tampered with by Hank Wyndom's minions, which meant either she bought a new laptop immediately, hoped Cliff had brought his own along, or used the one Pel kept at the house in the desert. None of those would have something that let Hank see what was on her screen as her home one might.

Gaelen left the furniture store just as rush hour traffic reached its peak, her mind on what to wear when she returned to C.C.'s that night, and whether she should search her car again for tracking gear when the unnerving sense that she was being watched nearly brought her to a halt.

She slipped between two parked cars and fiddled with her purse, pulling out a tissue to pretend to blow her nose. With the action sheltering most of her face, she gazed around the area. The store was part of a shopping mall complex, though a separate building. Plenty of shoppers hustled in and out, some headed to the Mexican restaurant nearby. No one looked familiar.

Then, a row over in the parking lot, she spotted her watcher as he shut the door on his vehicle, settled a straw cowboy hat over mousey brown hair, then paused to cup his hands around a cigarette as he lit it. The act covered his face as well as her tissue ploy had hers. But she knew him immediately. Had watched him light up in the office despite the legal ruling against smoking in public buildings. Hank just laughed about it, called Zeke Nagel a devil for tempting him to take up his own nicotine habit again.

Nagel knew he'd been rumbled, too. Possibly had let her spot him on purpose. He gave her a smirk, a nod, and strolled away as though it were a coincidence that they happened to be in the same mall lot at this time of day. Not likely, considering Hank had one rule. If you weren't out of the office for a reason he sanctioned, the hours were nine to six at your desk. It was just past five, and Nagel was far from Desert Wynd.

Gaelen watched Hank's man stroll down toward a sports bar where he crushed the butt of his smoke out, twisting the toe of his western-tooled boot over the remains. Then, without a glance back at her, he went inside the bar.

****

It took repeating all the coaching Cliff and Luke had given her in what felt like an ancient past to stay calm. Fear argued that she should press her foot flat to the floor in the Chevy and barrel out of the parking lot. Luke's voice in her head told her to take shallow breaths rather than deep revealing ones, to assume a mask of indifference—of disdain, the echo of Cliff's added admonition reminded. *Remember you are playing a part*, the two of them insisted in her memory. *Give nothing away.*

Gaelen exhaled slowly. Felt some of the panic slip away. It was the same thing she'd counseled Pel to do the evening before. Don't run. Don't walk. Saunter, to put those following her off their game.

And think.

She'd checked the car for bugs earlier and found nothing. However, her day had been full of visits to government offices, the bank, the PR firm, and shopping to fill the newly taken office quickly. All things that took her away from her car and offered anyone following her the opportunity to put a new one in place if Hank was suspicious of her sudden resignation. She needed to swing by her dad's mechanic friend's shop to get the car on a lift for a more thorough inspection for transmitters. There was only one other way Hank could figure out where she was, and she'd destroyed it, at Pel's the night before, by tearing down the provided cellphone with all the app upgrades.

Just as she was ready to pull out of the parking place, though, her newly acquired disposable phone rang. No one knew the number yet except Pel. Anxious to hear his voice again, she answered.

But it was Rika, not Pel.

"Hi!" her friend's voice chirped. "Don't be surprised that I have this number. Pel gave it to me. They're calling me in to sing tonight in C.C.'s place. The trio's back, too, so Pel's taking the night off from the grand as well. Surprise company from family arrived for a visit, they told me. However, he asked me to swing by your place and pick you up before I headed to the club. Sounded mysterious as all-get-out, but this gives us time for you to tell me how the big date went last night. Warning you, girl—I expect details!"

"Then I'll save them all for when you get to my place," Gaelen said.

"Ooh, that's torture! But okay. Where are you?"

"Around half an hour away from the apartment if the traffic doesn't hold me up more. Are you at home? If so, can I borrow something of yours to wear? The stuff you wear to the clubs when trawling for men. Possible?"

"Just name the color and number of sequins you want," Rika said.

"Sequins! Rik! I'm thirty and not going on stage. A bit subtler, huh? The skirt can't be too tight or short, either. You know I feel half naked without my gun."

"Spoil sport," her friend countered. "You aren't really going to wear that thigh holster, are you?"

Gaelen forced a chuckle, already falling into her

act. Just a woman with early-stage intoxication where a man was concerned. That was her cover.

Though the truth as well, if she was honest with herself.

"Always a chance," she chirped brightly.

"Then my choice will be a real surprise. I'll be waiting in the parking lot at your apartment."

"Deal," Gaelen agreed as she ended the call. Silently she congratulated herself on a performance well done. If she could fool Rika into thinking she was cool and collected, she could fool anyone. Well, anyone but Cliff—and probably Pel, considering how in sync he was with her. Still, she was glad that, rather than leave them in her apartment, she'd tucked the thumb drives with Luke's supposedly damning evidence against his father into the inner pocket of her jacket.

And her late husband's gun in her back waistband.

She put the car in gear and made her way back to the street at a pace that qualified as a *mosey*. With drive time traffic beginning to jam the roadways, even if she spotted Nagel's vehicle a few car lengths back, she could disappear from his sight much more easily than he could from hers. He drove a pickup of sun-faded red that sported a black license plate with the distinctive gold trident logo of Arizona State University emblazoned on it. Her silver vehicle was a chameleon in traffic.

To be on the safe side, she took a few quick turns, not signaling the action, making it look spur of the moment, a diversion in her route to escape a traffic tie-up. She doubled back, then headed in a different direction twice. When the sign for a national pharmacy chain appeared on the right ahead, she turned the corner, zipped into the parking lot, and slid into a sheltered place between two large SUVs. Satisfied that her car was hidden for the moment, Gael stripped off her gray suit jacket and removed the thumb drives from hiding, tucking them into her bra for safe keeping. Stuck Luke's gun in the glove compartment. Pulled her blouse loose enough to cover the holstered weapon. Then she grabbed an elastic fastener from her purse, swept her hair into a messy bun. Satisfied that she'd changed her appearance sufficiently, she took credit card and keys in hand and left her briefcase-sized purse hidden beneath the discarded jacket, which was now turned cream lining side out, on the passenger's seat before slipping hastily from the car. The dart she made from the lot through the store's automatic doors was no different than many others made, anxious to get back into an air-conditioned atmosphere.

She grabbed a plastic basket and pulled items at random from the shelves as she strolled the aisles, ensuring that her reason for visiting the store was unclear to anyone else Hank might still have tailing her. But when Gaelen left the building, she'd not only acquired a new toothbrush to leave at Pel's, but a variety of items she didn't need—all to cover the now very necessary trio of backup disposable cell phones.

****

It had been a very depressing afternoon, Pel decided. After talking to his godfather, a superstar among superstars in the music business, he'd headed back to the full-sized grand at the house to do the ultimate test. He attempted to sing for the first time in a decade. *Attempted* being the key word, he felt, considering what he sounded like. He used the laptop from the token home office, recording the separate efforts, each one seeming worse than the last when he played them back. Finally, he gave "Misty" a try. The song many called his trump card. It was one of his own favorites, and it was the song for which Gaelen had used his arrangement during what she called her "brief fling with a microphone"—the phrase had led his brain to picture quite a variety of things that could be done with one. Maybe for those reasons the playback hadn't sounded as pitiful as some of the other songs he'd essayed.

While he'd already put out the call for Rika and the local trio to entertain the customers, using Cliff's arrival and his godfather's the next day as excuses for bowing out of accompanist duty for the next few days, the plan had still been to rendezvous with Gaelen's friend Cliff and his parents for dinner at C.C.'s. Rather than have her possibly bugged vehicle broadcasting a location in Surprise, he roped Rika in as her chauffeur. It was already an established fact that Gaelen attended as many of Rika's gigs as possible. Hank Wyndom was unlikely to follow her if her college roommate picked her up.

At least he hoped that would be the case.

When he arrived at the restaurant and slipped his SUV into its usual spot, the front of the lot was pleasantly half filled. For a non-franchise establishment that had only been open a month, it was a very decent showing. The food, if not the musical entertainment offered later in the evenings, was slowly finding appreciative clientele. Hopefully, when he came out of hiding and the PR firm discovered they had a Jace Hastings' link to flog, custom would pick up even more.

That is, if Jace Hastings could make the transition from being quietly invisible to being very visible again. Paul Montgomery, his godfather, insisted that Jace Hastings' could and would make the comeback that Gaelen insisted was a shoo-in. If they'd heard the pathetic sounds he'd made that afternoon, they both would likely reverse those opinions.

Which meant he had to push through. Find a way to be Jace Hastings again without being quite the *same* Jace Hastings that he'd been. He'd adapted songs for C.C.'s failing pipes. He could do the same for his own pathetic croaking. Well, pathetic in his own opinion. He'd always been his own worst critic. Apparently, time hadn't changed that.

Although he entered through the rear employee and delivery door, Pel bypassed his office and headed out to see if the couple who dined at the club regularly had come to enjoy something from the C.C.'s menu that evening. He had a big and immediate job for them to handle: add more furnishings to his desert escape before the expected visitors from LA arrived the next day— Paul would no doubt have his wife, Aurora, with him. Lacking even a sofa to crash on himself to give them the master suite for their use meant the place couldn't really call itself a home.

Bradley and Tina Kavanaugh were exactly where he had hoped to find them. He made a stop at the bar, snagging a tumbler of Brad's favorite rum and a fresh margarita for Tina. They looked up, surprised when he set the refills before them.

"Pel!" Tina gulped in surprise then leaned across the table toward her husband. "Watch it, Brad. I smell a favor hovering. Why else would this lovely bribe appear?"

"Better join us and get this over with, Flannery. I notice *you* don't have a drink of your own," Kavanaugh said.

Pel pulled a chair out and dropped into it. "That's because I've only got two hands. But Tina's right. I've got a favor to ask."

"Considering you already made our profits very comfortable for the year by hiring us to do the décor here, you don't have to ask for anything, buddy. Make a wish and it shall be yours," Brad offered.

"Beware of what you offer, Kavanaugh," Pel warned as a cold bottle of beer appeared before him, courtesy of the ever-diligent staff. He grinned a thank-you at the waitress, then turned back to business. "I need my house filled with furniture immediately."

"How immediately?" Tina asked.

"Yesterday."

"And the reason?" Brad pushed.

"Previously unplanned out-of-town company arriving sometime in the morning."

Tina pulled a cellphone from the large purse on the floor next to her and brought up a notebook feature. "What do you have so far?"

Pel confessed to the bed, grand piano, exercise equipment, token standup desk, and lone bar stool.

"And how many rooms?"

He recognized dollar signs ringing up for both of them when he supplied the number and square footage.

"How many guests are arriving?" Brad asked.

He hadn't thought beyond the Montgomerys, but superstars didn't travel without an entourage.

Particularly when a performance was in the wind, whether it was for himself or another artist, Paul came prepared.

"I'd better check," Pel said as he pulled his cellphone from an inner pocket of his suit coat. Paul answered on the second ring.

"I need a head count so there are enough beds," Pel confessed. "I'm guessing Rory is coming with you?"

"Absolutely," Montgomery said of his lovely wife. "But I also called Scott—"

Montgomery's nephew and the Visions Records producer on all the songs Jace Hastings had recorded. In a way, that made sense.

"Nan—"

Scott's adopted sister and a superstar in her own right. But the reason Nan Rawlins was being included eluded Pel.

"And guys to run the recording equipment," his godfather added.

"What recording equipment?" Pel demanded.

"The *Jace Hastings Alive and Kickin', Recorded Live at C.C.'s Place* engineers. You think I'd go to all this trouble and not come away from it without a guarantee of something to go platinum?" Montgomery countered. "Well, think again, kid. There will be at least seven of us. Two females and five guys, if you include me in the count. I'd say putting the others up at a hotel would work, but it won't if we want to keep this under wraps.

"We should arrive at the Phoenix Goodyear Airport just up the road from Surprise by noon if not before. I'll call a heads up when we leave Bob Hope over here." If Pel knew his godfather, mentioning the Bob Hope

Municipal meant a private plane was already booked.

He sighed when he disconnected. Took a long slug of beer before giving the Kavanaughs the number of expected guests. He was nearly relieved when they suggested renting extra beds rather than turn his home into what would feel like a fully operational hotel.

Arrangements made for the emergency décor—one that would lean heavily on floor stock from the Kavanaughs' shop—Pel headed back to his office. The only guideline he'd given the couple was to use desert colors rather than the cave ones featured at C.C.'s. It would be interesting to see what they came up with. At any rate, the Kavanaughs told him they'd be at the house by ten the next morning with a full van to make the place homey.

When he settled behind his desk with the door closed once more, it wasn't to check how his portfolio had done that day. It was to stare at the sleeping monitor without seeing it.

Jace Hastings Alive and Kickin'.

While he'd been considering songs to use for his return from the dead since Gaelen had urged him to do so, it hadn't actually been with a complete reboot to his career in mind. Well, not seriously. He'd been out of the music business for ten long years already. His audience had moved on to other performers, hadn't they? He was a has-been. Nearly forgotten by everyone. When he'd suggested that Rika sing "Misty" Friday night, it had been because Gaelen mentioned the Hastings' arrangement on it was a favorite of hers, although she hadn't known he was Jace Hastings at the time. Rika had chuckled and told him about Gaelen being irate at getting a B on the paper she'd written about Jace Hastings' arrangements, and "Misty" in particular. It made him wonder which one of him Gaelen had had sex with. Had she recognized him on a gut level before seeing him unmasked, his eyes no longer the brown she'd been staring into earlier in the day?

Was she asking him to become Jace Hastings again because she still had a crush on the man he'd been, rather than an attraction to the man he was now? Except, Pel admitted, he still *was* Jace Hastings. He felt the morph every time he sat down at the piano. He'd simply been the instrumental version, not the vocal one. Even that distinction was about to be ripped away.

Jace Hastings Alive and Kickin'.

Damn.

****

Rika had arrived and was waiting as promised when Gaelen pulled into the parking lot behind her apartment building. The garment bag slung over her shoulder, dangling from the crook of the hanger hooked over her fingers, allowed no hint as to color or styling on the borrowed costume. For costume it would be. Something so far removed from the items in her own closet that she'd feel like a different person in the outfit.

"Do I have time for a quick shower?" she asked, retrieving the second weapon from the glovebox, gathering the bags of recent acquisitions.

"Absolutely," Rika promised. "The guys and I don't go on stage until ten, but Pel said you were required at the dinner table and that included your chauffeur—me—so it's like cake with a side of ice cream."

"Nothing's ever simple with you. Things aren't just

fine or copacetic, they're dessert."

"Best part of any meal, though having eaten the delicacies that come off Tom's grill more than once now, that gap is closing," Rika confessed as she followed Gaelen across the lot and into the building.

Gaelen led the way up to her second-floor home. Inserting her key in the lock, she glanced back at Rika. "Did Pel tell you I resigned from Desert Wynd yesterday?"

"No! But if Pel knows and you couldn't be bothered to call and tell your best friend in the entire world..."

"In Phoenix," Gaelen countered, waving her friend into the apartment, "Cliff might beat you out on the 'entire world' category."

"Never!" Rika declared, dropping dramatically onto the sofa. "Unless Cliff knows you quit—"

"He does. Told him last night."

"Get out of town! Oh, wait, does that mean you'll be leaving Phoenix to go work with him in LA?"

Gaelen breezed into her bedroom, shedding clothes, en route to the shower. It didn't matter how much air conditioning you enjoyed, dashing from building to car and back again throughout the day, the Phoenix heat made feeling fresh for long next to impossible. "No, I'm starting my own agency. Cliff should already be in Surprise, so you can arm wrestle him for that 'Gael's best friend' title."

"He'd cheat," Rika said. "You know he always does. Gets me flustered by maintaining eye contact and then flashing that tantalizing smirk. It's a good thing he's married, or—"

"Divorced," Gaelen called back as she turned the

shower on. "Didn't I tell you?"

Even over the sound of the water she heard her friend groan. "We may have to circle Surprise just so you can catch me up on what you've been holding back, girl. Next, you'll tell me you flew off to Vegas and married Pel like you did Luke. You do know I haven't forgiven you for eloping, right?"

"It wasn't an official elopement. It was a spur of the moment thing, and my mother hasn't forgiven me either. But I didn't marry Pel." Gaelen paused for drama's sake, then added as she stepped into the shower, "I just woke up next to him. Find me some shoes to go with the dress, would you?"

****

Rika was waiting, sitting complacently on the bed, when Gaelen exited the bath. She held her left hand up. A bracelet of mock rubies danced in the sun streaming through the window, seeming to spark off the matching ring on her middle finger. The color was the perfect foil for the body-hugging dress Rika wore, its fabric moving from one shade of red to the next, all a bit reminiscent of tones that showed up in desert sunsets. Large golden hoop earrings swung from hiding in her platinum blonde locks. Rika's long, sleek legs were crossed, her right foot twitching in irritation as Gaelen dried off.

"Let me get this straight," the vocalist insisted. "*You*, the woman who has avoided making any changes in her life in five years, in the span of a single day not only quit your job, but you went on a dinner date with a very attractive man, and then slept with him?"

Holding a damp towel around herself with one hand, Gaelen rifled through her dresser for fresh underwear with the other, only briefly glancing at Rika in the mirror above it. "Well, I wouldn't say there was much *sleep* involved," she answered, though couldn't keep a smile from forming when she did so.

Rika leapt up and swept her into a fond hug. "Thank God! You've decided to live again!" she gushed and hugged Gaelen again, putting the towel wrapped around her torso in serious danger of parting company with her.

It felt like they had both regressed to the giggly eighteen-year-olds who'd met for the first time in the dorm room they would share. "I'm so happy for you, Gael! And you couldn't find a better guy than the boss to hook up with."

"The *boss*?"

Rika regained her seat on the bed, turning slightly away to give Gaelen privacy to dress. "It's what the guys who back me call him, and what the C.C.'s staff calls him. As I work there…"

"The boss," Gaelen agreed as she slipped the borrowed dress from hiding. The back was cut so low it made wearing a bra impossible. She pitched the one she'd gotten out back in the still-open dresser drawer, then shut it. "Yeah, he is pretty special, isn't he?"

"And mysterious," her friend added. "Can that man ever play the piano! Well, you heard him at the jam session. But those were all fast, upbeat songs. The few times I've caught him playing sad love songs, it nearly took me back to those nights when we sat around listening to Jace Hastings' recordings. I guess since you left Desert Wynd, someone else will have to go looking for Jace Hastings now."

"If he actually survived," Gaelen cautioned as she

stepped into the dress. It wouldn't do to give the secret away to Rika. At least not until Pel was ready to come out of hiding.

"Yeah, *if.* I'll bet Pel could have given him a run for his money," Rika surmised, her shot in the dark getting far too close to the truth for Gaelen's peace of mind.

She moved to where Rika waited and turned her back to her friend, silently giving the message to zip her up, though the zipper was barely four inches long. "Yeah, "I'll bet he could," she agreed, then caught a glimpse of herself in the dresser mirror.

The woman who faced her was nearly unrecognizable. At least the skirt wasn't too short, and there weren't any sequins in sight. "Shoes?"

But when Rika held the chosen pair up, Gaelen nixed them immediately. "Three-inch stiletto sandals? I don't think so." No one could run in those, and she was on self-assigned secret bodyguard duty where Pel was concerned. Rika groaned when a pair of two-inch heeled basic black pumps replaced them. The groan was louder when Gaelen pulled open the drawer of the bedside table and tossed her thigh holster and the smaller pistol that fit in it onto the bed.

Chapter Nine

When Cliff knocked lightly on Pel's office door, he had a laptop tucked beneath his arm. "I hate to bother you, but I could use a place from which to do some Net searching. Although there is wi-fi available, I'd rather not do it anywhere someone might stand behind me."

"You do know that makes it sound like you're pulling up porn, don't you?" Pel asked as he vacated his desk.

"Sadly, this will be related to your case, rather than voyeur fare on a divorce or personal injury case. I've been estimating where we need to beef up security both here and where you live. Anything I need to know about?" Cliff asked.

Pel relayed the number of people inbound from LA the next morning. He added in the Kavanaughs' visit prior to their arrival to transform his home. When Cliff frowned over having no names for the recording crew, Pel wasn't surprised. "I'm guessing, from what I know of Gaelen, that despite his fame, she already checked out Montgomery. Here's a list of the names I do know will show up, and two of them are high-profile types, as well." He handed over a tally that could pose as part of the invitation list for a soirée. At least to a guy who'd been going the loner route for a decade. "We can print off a basic nondisclosure contract for everyone to sign when they arrive. If collecting cells and anything else not used for recording purposes will make your job easier, do it. Think this will keep you off the streets and confined to this bar for the night?"

"Can't think of a better place to be sequestered," Cliff said, slipping into Pel's spot at the desk. "I'll be back out front when Gaeley arrives. Just give me a heads up, would ya?"

Having been evicted, Pel grabbed a couple sheets of printer paper and a pen before closing the door behind him.

The crowd might be light by some standards, but he doubted other restaurants had people waiting for a table on Tuesday evenings. Only a couple booths were occupied and less than half a dozen tables. The Kavanaughs had left rather than stay for the live music, he noticed. They were probably stripping their showroom for the instant décor he needed installed.

He stopped at the bar for a coffee before taking over the booth closest to the kitchen—always the last place they ever sat guests. He had lists of his own to make.

There were projects to oversee first thing in the morning—and a very early morning, considering he'd reacquired the night-owl hours of Jace Hastings' lifestyle again. Mostly because C.C.'s Place didn't close until two a.m., and it was often three when he returned home. If sleep evaded him, he sat at the piano until dawn was history. If Gaelen was agreeable to the highly erotic proposal he planned to make her, after dinner the two of them would head back to the desert house. With furniture arriving as well as company before noon, the time they could grab to be together was subminimal.

They would have until it was time to lock the doors at C.C.'s Place. It needed to look like Gaelen and Rika had simply been out for a night on the town together, even if Rika was singing that evening.

And whether Gaelen agreed to his planned evening of bedroom aerobics or not, once she left, the house was going to feel very empty. Which, considering she'd only spent one night with him there, was asinine.

That didn't change things, though. He'd never felt this way about a woman so quickly before. Either that meant he'd been lonely and celibate for far too long, or he was programmed by his family's past to recognize the right mate when she waltzed into his life.

Deciding which of those things was on the nose was not what he needed to concentrate on. There was a show to plan, and he knew what all the people about to arrive would tell him in respect to it. "It's Jace Hastings' show, so only Jace Hastings can pick the numbers and the order in which to play them." Hell, it had been far too long since he'd done any of it other than for C.C. If thoughts of Gaelen didn't keep him awake after she left, then the damn show would. Chances were he'd still be wide awake when the Kavanaugh Interiors' van showed up the next morning.

Montgomery would want a theme running through the songs chosen for the show even if the working title for the recording might change. Yet it probably wouldn't if Paul had his way. What he was calling it was exactly what this was—Jace Hastings' rising from the obscurity he'd forced on himself and performing once more, *Live at C.C.'s Place*.

The piped-in recorded music held sway currently in the C.C.'s dining room. All soft jazz with a sprinkling of retrospective pop, the kind of stuff Bublé was crooning. Jace Hastings' preferences in the past—and the present as well.

Maybe it was time to shift his focus. Not as many Great American Songbook tunes but still things he could make his own. Paul would expect a list before the luggage had even been brought into the house the next day. He'd been playing with ideas, but now none of the titles he'd jotted down early that morning suited what was needed.

He needed a song to hang a theme on. Question was, which one of the thousands of songs he knew, and had already scored to keep his sanity over the past decade, suited that requirement? Something like…

The sound system shifted to a new song, a recording of the enticing "I'll Still be Loving You"—a song he hadn't worked out an arrangement on, which meant it hadn't landed on his mental tally of possibilities.

But, as the melody and the softly sung lyrics wrapped around him, it all came crashing together in an instant. Just as it had many times more than a decade ago. A theme bound around a single song. How reassuring it was that *that* hadn't changed when it came to Jace Hastings' repertoire.

The catch was ensuring no one thought he was singing about Ashley Hopper. He'd already espoused a ploy that would work. The ante just had to be upped and costuming acquired to sell it. All he needed was an agent to work through.

Pel scanned through the contacts on his phone and called California again.

****

When she came through the restaurant's front door behind Rika, Pel felt as if all the air in his lungs had been sucked out. Gaelen Shaw…Wyndom…was stunning. The dress was a close match to her blue eyes and hugged her torso at the same time it appeared to drip from her shoulders. But when she turned slightly, a vast amount of bare skin was on display for the appreciation of every man in the joint. From the delectable nape of her neck to the supple curve of her waist, pale creamy skin begged to have him touch her. At the first sign of a shiver in the cranked-up AC, he would be stripping off his suit jacket to drape around her. Keeping her comfortable and marking his territory in one fell swoop. God! Had he ever felt this Neanderthal in respect to another woman? *Ease up, Flannery, 'cause if you don't, she'll do the martial arts thing on you again.* Which was no help in stomping the caveman tendency down, since the view he'd had when she'd pinned him to the floor had been even more enticing.

The sound of the restaurant clientele's conversations, the movements of the waitstaff, the background of recorded soft jazz, and the rush of the air conditioner through vents had faded from his universe. It wasn't until Cliff pounded him on the back and gave a chuckled admonition to breathe, that he came to his senses. The P.I. further turned attention away from him by swooping Paprika Mendez into his arms and swinging her around.

Rika squealed, though whether in surprise or delight, or possibly a mix of the two, she gleaned all the attention in the room. Her arms wreathed Cliff's neck as he literally swept her off her feet. When her back was firmly turned toward Pel, the P.I. let her slide back to her feet.

"Cliff Quinnlan?" Rika breathed reverently as though afraid to believe her eyes, though her hands still rested on his broad shoulders.

So that was the man's surname: Quinnlan.

Cliff grinned. "Is that surprise I hear in those dulcet tones, Mendez? Or is it shock?"

"A bit of both. Gael told me you'd be here, but there was a chance she was fibbing," Rika admitted, then turned her head toward Gaelen. "Are you sure he didn't come to recruit you to work with him in LA, thus leaving me alone to fend off the coyotes prowling Phoenix bars?"

"Nope. Turns out he's Pel's cousin," Gaelen said, keeping to their story, though Pel noticed she turned away as though looking for either C.C. or Jay. Was she afraid Rika knew her so well it would be easy to catch her out in a lie?

"Haven't seen each other since we were kids, and with Uncle Jay nearly always on the road to or from a gig, we aren't exactly a close family," Cliff explained.

The detective gave Gaelen a quick peck on the cheek in greeting and immediately turned back to Rika, leading her off to the table already set up for six.

Pel jerked his head toward the departing couple. Rika was demanding to know everything that Cliff had been up to since abandoning Phoenix more than five years ago. "I haven't seen you since Luke's funeral," Pel heard her say before they moved farther away.

"I like the dress," he told Gaelen.

"Borrowed from Rika. She chose it, probably from her stage wardrobe, so you can thank her later," she said. "The only direction I gave was that it lack sequins. I should have added more cloth be involved in the construction."

He closed in on her. "Not to fear. I'll keep you warm. That was some greeting Cliff gave her. You interested in a similar greeting? I'm up for it if you are."

Her smile was more quirk of amusement than encouragement. "Something a bit less public for me, pal," she said.

He slipped an arm around her shoulders. Delightfully near-bare shoulders, just the long, tightly fitted sleeves of the dress keeping wardrobe mishaps at bay. "Good, because I have a bit of blank wall in my office that is just asking to have a more amorous greeting employed against it."

She leaned away from him slightly. Gave him a flirtatious grin as she gazed up at his face. "You have a fairly one-track mind of late, Mr. Flannery," she teased.

"You're very addicting, Ms. Shaw. Interested?"

"Hmm. Yes, but I'm also interested in your computer."

Pel put a hand to his chest and staggered theatrically. "A wound to the heart. My computer, huh?"

"If you are willing to disconnect from the Internet. Remember how Cliff suggested I look though what I still had of Luke's possessions?"

Pel dropped his arm from around her and acquired her hand instead, immediately leading her through the maze of tables toward his office. "Best keep the rest of that for a different setting, love."

The word slipped out before he realized it.

Mentally he waited for her to catch the slip, for a *slip* it most definitely was at this stage.

Either her mind hadn't been on the specific endearment he'd used, or she didn't mind it.

"You're right. The fewer ears, the better."

Pel didn't know if he should be relieved that she hadn't registered it—which seemed the more likely case, her mind on something to do with her late husband's things—or be disappointed.

Just so he got in his suggestion for the evening ahead, the moment they entered the office, he closed the door, and pressed her back to the blank wall behind it. "First things first, Gael."

Her arms glided over his shoulders. "Absolutely," she agreed, then her mouth met his. Turned out, she was as hungry for him as he was for her.

When they came up for air, he didn't move away, enjoying the way her body fit against his. "I had ulterior motives in calling Rika and the trio in. With company descending on me tomorrow, this is the last night we can grab to be together for…well, until they all leave.

"Care to come home with me…at least until nearly two o'clock, when I'll return you to Rika's chauffeur service and lock the club up for the night?"

She kissed the tip of his chin lightly. "I'd love to."

He was ready to resume testing their breath control when she shot the effort down. "Now, about that computer…"

Pel sighed deeply but stepped aside, gesturing that she should head over to the desk. "It's already Net free. I disconnect from both the Worldwide and power sources the moment I log out rather than tempt a hacker, plus Cliff was using the link earlier. He was right, then? Your husband did leave you something to hold his father at arm's length?"

"I think Luke left me two vials of poison, if you consider damaging evidence of wrongdoing saved to thumb drives the tech equivalent. Of course, I'm just guessing that's what's on these. I didn't want to open them at home since my computer is probably still linked to Desert Wynd's despite my severing the connection. But considering Luke hid them, I think they are damaging enough to move Hank into penitentiary housing. Cliff will need to see these, but that can wait until after dinner. I'll hand them to him to peruse. Then we can move on to those other discussions you have in mind regarding bedding." The glance she flicked at him as she settled in his desk chair was pure vixen.

Pel blocked her in place by leaning on the chair arms. "This doesn't mean you have a preference for silk sheets, does it?"

"Hate 'em," she crooned softly. "If you get too close to the edge, you slip right off the bed."

"If I had any, be assured I'd anchor you in place," he promised. "As I don't, one hundred percent organic cotton will have to suffice. Now, let's see what kind of dirt Luke Wyndom dug up on his dad."

"These aren't numbered, so things may be out of order," Gaelen warned, giving him a quick show as she slid the right side of her skirt up to display a black lace thigh holster held securely in place with a garter strap. When she caught him staring, she slipped the mini automatic free and offered it to him to admire. "Nice, huh? Carries eleven plus one rounds."

"Definitely nice. Oh, did you mean the gun?" Flirty as the comment was, she noticed he did give the weapon a thorough appraisement.

Gaelen resisted rolling her eyes as she retrieved a small plastic zip-locked bag from the wide band of lace, a bag that held two generic flash drives.

"And you're carrying the pistol tonight because…?"

"Taking no chances with my new client's life expectancy. Plus, you might have noticed, Rika's borrowed dress has no place to hide my larger handgun."

"I particularly like the garters," Pel said. "Nice touch. Once the gun is out of that lacy holster for the night, I fully intend to investigate them more thoroughly."

"Not in the least surprised on that, Mr. Flannery. You have a very investigative mind when it comes to certain topics."

"I read a lot of detective fiction while in rehab."

"Uh-huh. Shall we inspect what Luke left behind?" She inserted one of the flash drives into the waiting slot on the computer.

But, as expected, Luke Wyndom had ensured that his father would be unable to access the material. It asked for a password.

****

Dinner was a drawn-out affair. The three at the table who were scheduled to take the stage to sing or play were definitely relaxing, letting the evening roll at a slower pace. It hadn't taken long for fake family conversation to take the turn to music. Cliff was the only one lacking a background in it, but he covered well, Gaelen felt. To those dining around them, she and Rika probably looked like the token girlfriends, along because they may or may not become part of that family. Pel's shoulder brushed hers frequently and Cliff's chair was cozied up next to Rika's. Considering the surprising greeting her two friends had given each other, Gaelen wondered why she'd never seen the attraction between them before. Rika would occasionally ask how Cliff was doing in California, but as Cliff had headed to LA with a wife in tow, it had never occurred to her to notice whether his eyes sought out the gorgeous Latina in the past. Then again, Cliff did fit the physical profile of the men who floated briefly through Rika's life.

She was sandwiched between Pel and Cliff at the table, so while Pel interrogated—for it definitely sounded like an interrogation—his father about changes to his playing style on the trombone, Gaelen leaned toward Cliff. "You have any ideas on what that password might be?"

"I was about to ask you the same thing. We need to throw every quirk Luke had that his father might not know about at it. The two things most likely are that it's going to be numerical and rival π in length," Cliff said. "The guy loved to irritate people with messages written in numbers."

"Which means the numbers translate to letters? That would be too easy for Hank to convert."

"Ah, but Luke wouldn't have used the normal substitution list. He'd use his own version."

She blinked. "Luke had a substitution version of his own?"

"Huh," Cliff murmured, looking surprised himself. "I thought he was the kind of guy who would leave love notes for you in it."

"Nope. Not a one."

"I'm not even giving you odds on whether that's what it will turn out to be," he said. "Unless he put a limit on how many tries there can be to feed the combination in, it will be a very frustrating evening ahead for me," the detective admitted.

Gaelen drummed her fingers lightly against the table. "Ah, um, I won't be here to help you. I'll be out at—"

Cliff cut her off. "I know. Security detail."

She gave him an irritated smile. "Luke wasn't the only one who liked to talk in code, was he? Yes, I'll have my client under intense scrutiny."

Cliff laughed. A nanosecond later he was serious. "I'm glad you decided to start living again, honey. Luke wouldn't have wanted you to give up on love."

"Lust," she corrected.

"A shared one, considering the way he looks at you."

"Not a topic for discussion, Cliffy. Password solution. That's what we need tonight. Starting tomorrow morning there will be little time to work on it. It's when more company arrives. You have any idea what number to begin with?"

"Pure guesswork, but I'm starting with 28."

"That's not even close to what he always said was his lucky number—six," Gaelen reminded.

Cliff took a moment to tilt back his no longer frosted bottle of beer, the same thing Pel was drinking. She'd gone with iced tea. To keep a cool head, not that that was possible when alone with Pel, but still…

"Why 28? If he's re-numbering the order of the alphabet, that's higher than the ABCs add up to."

"Not with Luke's system," Cliff assured, then leaned closer to whisper the secret in her ear. "He didn't use X, Y or Z, yet had 34 letters, so there could be duplications on some. The first letter in the code alphabet is L. Then it goes to W and reverses all the way to A."

"His initials? Then that makes the 28th what?"

"I thought that would be obvious. It's a *G*. For Gaelen."

****

"How are we going to work things tonight, boss?" Rika asked as the trio she usually worked with drifted in a little after nine. "We've got two singers and Jay's trombone to work in." They were all gathered in the hallway outside his office because Gaelen and Cliff had taken it over temporarily, hoping to stumble onto what Luke Wyndom had chosen as the password on at least one of the thumb drives.

Unscrambling the legacy Gaelen's husband had left her wasn't in his province, Pel conceded to himself. His job was to breathe life back into the ghost of Jace Hastings. Which, to his mind, leaned on an expertise he'd left collecting dust as his own answer to survival.

"Trust me. Dad has taken the measure of you all," Pel assured. Plus, if they hadn't measured up to his own standards, he wouldn't have hired them in the first place. Not that he could tell them that quite yet. "Dad was not only part of the audience Friday night, he soaked up your capabilities at the jam session afterwards. No one can toss a set together like he can on the spur of the moment, so ask him to help you. It isn't like I was running the music department side of things before anyway."

When Rika and her usual backup did a silent communication that involved rolling eyes, at least on her part, he realized he probably had been a real buttinski with his suggestions. All of which they'd taken to heart.

Apparently Jace Hastings didn't know when to shut his damn trap and leave Pel Flannery to do whatever it was Pel Flannery did around C.C.'s Place.

"Have a quick sit-down with him," Pel ordered. "Jay Flannery has been working that slide in full orchestras to small combos since he was eighteen. And, actually, he likes smaller groups like yours letting him sit in."

"Sit in?" the sax man echoed. "He isn't joining us on a regular basis?"

"Only if you ask him to, and that's up to the four of you. Right now, we're gearing up for the arrival of someone else who might want to sit in while he's in town. My godfather. You might have heard of him." Pel paused, winding them up for the pitch. Then he dropped the name.

"Oh, God. *The*—?"

"The," Pel assured. "But Montgomery doesn't arrive until tomorrow. Since I didn't know he was dropping by until earlier today..." A slight lie that bordered on the truth. "...I have things to do at home to prepare for company, so I can't serve as C.C.'s accompanist tonight. Rika, you and Cec can decide who does what. Maybe do a duet, or just switch off being background singers for each other. You know, harmony-type stuff. She's a trooper *and* she likes the way you sing. Play to each other's strengths. And enjoy yourselves, for God's sake! That's when you sound the best.

"And I'm talking far too much for a guy who just said Jay Flannery, not Pel Flannery, was the one you need to talk to. Get out of the hall. You're blocking traffic."

Rika laughed softly at the very idea as the four of them headed back to where Jay and C.C. had their heads together at the otherwise vacated dining table. The guitar player was breathing Montgomery's name in shock. Or so it seemed. Okay, one starstruck performer to warn Paul about. He knew his mentor well, though. His godfather was one superstar who preferred offering encouragement over being worshipped for his hard-won success.

The type of success Jace Hastings had been pursuing once upon a time. Would the old feeling return, Pel wondered? Or would the entry of Gaelen Shaw into his life temper it? Montgomery was the first to warn of the dangers of putting career before personal happiness. "Don't follow in *all* my footsteps," he'd counseled when Pel had washed up in LA fresh from high school. "You fall in love, you follow the girl as much as you do the music."

Except he hadn't fallen in love. Not until yesterday. Or had it been the week before, when he'd handed a damp woman his spare shirt in this same hallway, at nearly the same spot he now stood?

The trouble was, he'd been without both music and female companionship for so long, to have both fall into his lap now pulled him in two different directions.

Gaelen wasn't suffering from the same difficulties. Her responses showed she was as eager for the physical relationship they'd rushed into, but she was doing a damn good job of compartmentalizing, while he…

Was left clicking his heels rather than being more involved in her life. Something he wanted to be part of very much.

Odd that he felt that way after only a few hours in her company. He hadn't, after all, had a reason to follow all of Montgomery's advice. Music had come first because once that first taste of success arrived, he was suspicious of the reasons any woman who pursued him might have. Jace Hastings wasn't the guy who wanted a serious relationship with a woman. It was Pel Flannery who had, and he'd shoved that pathetic sap in the closet the moment he left DC for the bright lights.

Had there even been a woman to tempt him with a shared future, though? Or was it that at thirty-five he was ready to have one and Gaelen had turned up? Was he infatuated with her or the idea of her? Or was he following in his parents' footsteps? They'd always claimed it had been love at first sight when they met. C.C. had been auditioning as vocalist at the club where Jay's quartet was booked. He'd asked her out the minute the audition was over. They'd married within the month, spent six glorious (as his dad phrased it) months together before their careers went in different directions. But every day, before either headed for a gig, they talked on the phone for an hour. There had never been another girl for Jay but C.C., nor another man in his mother's life, either.

He'd always wanted that type of connection. Hell, he'd grown up with grandparents who were inseparable. Well, except when one was arrested during a protest, or they both were and lodged in separate cell areas. Not exactly your run-of-the-mill family in many ways, but fairly perfect in all others.

You're overthinking things, Flannery, Pel silently berated himself. He was simply suffering from an overdose of the two things he'd done without for so many years. *Prioritize. That's the way to go, pal. So, what's the* numero uno *priority?*

It was an easy answer. One that had nothing to do with becoming Jace Hastings again or surviving whatever Rowan McTavish was planning. A total world summed up in two syllables.

Gaelen.

Pel knocked lightly on his office door to alert her and Cliff of his invasion, then turned the knob.

****

Gaelen couldn't say her perch on a corner of Pel's desk was comfy. It put her back to the door and offered no place other than her lap to rest the spiral notebook Cliff had passed her. She'd found a box of #2 wooden pencils on the shelf behind the desk chair Cliff had commandeered and had already contributed worry marks to one of the bright yellow objects of said box, as her teeth settled on the length of it. It felt a bit like invading Pel's sanctum to acquire one, but he *had* told them both to help themselves to whatever they needed. The notes she'd made with the borrowed pencil included any asinine word or phrase she could remember Luke having said or called something, then added in things she'd called him. Cliff had chuckled when he looked at what she'd written down.

"Dip? Doesn't sound too lover-like, Gaeley."

"He did dippy things sometimes. A lot of the time. It was well deserved, and he seemed to like it."

"You said it in retaliation when he called you

201

'Done Deal,' didn't you? Did Hank know he called you that?"

She sighed. "Of course, he did. It was how Luke announced that we were married. Said I was his *done deal* wife and his trainee at Desert Wynd because I was now family."

"But did Hank know Luke called you that in private as well?"

Gaelen shrugged, which meant the suit jacket Pel had stripped off and draped around her shoulders tried to fall off. She made a grab for it, holding it in place, glad of the warmth it offered. She was never ever again going to let Rika pick out something for her to wear. If she needed to borrow another dress in the future, she was cruising her friend's closet personally. A backless dress when Paprika knew they'd be in a restaurant where the AC ran full out at this time of year! What *had* the woman been thinking?

"Probably not," she said. "If Hank borrowed anything Luke called me, it was *Gaeley*, and he did it because he knew it irritated the you-know-what out of me."

"Think phrases, then, Gaeley," Cliff said, putting a slight emphasis on the pet form of her name.

She swatted at him with the notepad. Cliff ducked it.

When she heard the light tap on the door, she knew it was time to leave everything in Cliff's hands for the evening. "I believe my ride is here," she said, sliding off the desk as Pel entered.

"Depends on your connotation of the word *ride*," he contributed, "though I could meet all the criteria for it if you want."

"Careful," Cliff warned him. "She's irked enough to hit you with this lethal notebook. The papercuts alone could do serious damage to a man."

"Hey, she's already knocked me down with one of those flying kicks, so I know it doesn't take the larger weapon or that little gun she's got strapped on tonight—"

"You're carrying while wearing *that dress?*" Cliff demanded. "Where?"

"Where you aren't going to see it, that's where," she said then pointed to the things she'd already written down. "This is all I can remember right now. See if any of them would help. Of course, knowing how long this password needs to be would help. Don't you have someone at that hot-shot firm you work for in LA who has a gizmo that would make this easier on us?"

"On *me*," he countered. "You are on security duty for your client until two tonight, then tomorrow afternoon again. In the morning you have more things to do to get Firebird Investigations up and running, don't you?"

She frowned. Looked from one man to the next. "Why do I get the feeling you two cooked something up before I got here this evening?"

"It's your cover," Pel said. "Rory Montgomery will need a bodyguard while she's here, and that's your excuse for being at the house during their stay."

"I've been demoted to security for the visiting celeb's wife?" Gaelen knew she sounded flabbergasted at the very idea. "I took this job on to protect *you*, Mr. Flannery. Not play nursemaid to—"

"Rory is a big deal in the fashion industry, even though she sold her company a long time ago," Pel explained.

"As you can tell from the way I usually dress and how I'm dressed tonight, fashion is not high on my list of interests," Gaelen countered.

"She's a billionaire in her own right, slick, and billionaires require a bodyguard when they go out on their own."

"To do what?"

Pel had the nerve to grin at her. Damn the man. He knew exactly how to fluster her, make her lose track of a conversation.

"Shopping was mentioned," he said.

"She lives in LA, and she wants to go shopping in Phoenix?"

Pel gave a theatrical shrug, which she thought was overplaying things. "It's the last thing she told me she wanted to do when I talked to her," he insisted. "You ready to leave for a bit?"

"Back around two then?" Cliff asked him.

"Yup."

"Yup," Gaelen parroted dryly as she studied him. "I have a feeling your vocabulary has suffered a few setbacks over the years."

"Yup," Pel agreed, but as he offered her his hand, she took it.

Before they left the room, though, she turned a steely eye on her old friend. "I expect some progress made during my absence, Quinnlan."

Cliff grabbed up the discarded notebook and hastily flipped through pages. "Now where was one of those pet names Luke used to call you that you hated? Damn, just when I could use one."

Gaelen pointed a forefinger at him. "You're on

report, buddy," she said. "Oh, damn! Luke used to say that. Did we—"

"I'll add it," Cliff assured. "Now get out."

****

"I have a confession to make," Pel said as he backed the SUV out of its usual spot in the back lot.

Gaelen twisted in her seat as much as the seatbelt allowed. The movement caused her skirt to slither up her thigh, putting the bottom edge of the black lace holster on display, though not the weapon secured within it. "Is it something I'm not going to like?"

"On that, I'm not sure, but I'm feeling a bit in left field here."

"In what way, Pel?"

"Luke Wyndom," he said.

"If you think I compare you to him in any way—"

He tossed her what passed, barely, for a reassuring glance. "I don't think that at all, but I need to know more about him. About..." Pel paused. "About your life with him, Gael."

She shouldn't be surprised. If the situation were reversed, she'd have already done a background check on the woman he'd loved. In a way, she had, in looking into Ashley Hopper's life at the start of the case.

If she believed Pel, Ashley had never been anything other than a part of the act, though. A part he had disliked catering to.

"All right," she murmured. "You're curious because of what we might find on the thumb drives."

"I'm curious because he's the man you married," Pel corrected. "The man Cliff claims you were so close to that you finished each other's sentences."

"Cliff exaggerates." And yet, she did remember

how easy it was to read Luke most of the time. It was that *most of the time* bothering her now. She had had no idea that he hated his father enough to begin digging into Hank Wyndom's business practices. Or had it been more than that? When had he begun collecting whatever was on the once-hidden portable data sticks? She needed to tune into the space where she and Luke Wyndom thought alike.

Needed to go back over their entire life together.

"He was different," she found herself saying in fond memory. "He was on a case when we met. Following some lowlife husband at an irritated wife's request. The trail led to the small club where I was singing."

And with that, she was back in time.

****

Six years, four months and five days earlier

She shouldn't have been able to see the man who sat alone at the table against the wall in the dim, late night lighting at The Horned Serpent Lounge, particularly with a spotlight nearly blinding her. She'd stepped aside from the mic to give her boss and his trumpet the solo spot, and perhaps being out of the glare allowed her eye to catch the man's movement as he lifted a tumbler to his lips. There was something about him that distracted her from the cry of the horn as the trumpeter worked the mute, making the sound weep on "The More I See You." Since they'd slowed it down, dragging out the bars rather than rushing through them as other versions of the song tended to do, it had become one of her favorite tunes to croon. Possibly because it now resembled something Jace Hastings might have scored, and she'd never gotten over her fascination with the man's ability to rework a Great American Songbook standard. Occasionally she wondered what Hastings would have done with the song himself if his life hadn't been cut short.

But not that night. That night it was the appreciative calm of the man who drank alone in a shadowed corner who caught her eye. When it was her turn to reclaim the mic, it was difficult not to appear to be singing directly to the stranger. She'd had to force herself to move her eyes over the room, as though seeking to make eye contact with each customer in turn, rather than peer toward where she knew he sat.

When the set ended, one of the waitstaff stopped her, told her the man in question had asked if he could buy her a drink during the break. Out of curiosity, she accepted.

He got to his feet when she was still a table and a half away. A tall man, she saw, but she had a preference for them, particularly if their legs were long, their shoulders were broad, and their build was lean. Even with the spare action of rising, the way he moved promised the treat of honed muscle beneath the suit of a businessman. Middle management rather than penthouse office, though, since the way his suit fit indicated it was off the rack rather than tailored specifically for him. His hair was a nondescript shade, not blond but not brown, caught somewhere between the two, and it had grown slightly past the stage where it needed a trim. He was clean shaven, too. Not something many men in her generation chose once the look of a scruff of beard had become the fashion. It was a pleasant face. Not overly handsome nor leaning toward plain. A face likely easy to overlook or forget.

When he smiled though…oh, there was a touch of the rogue in the curve of his lips, an implication that a girl might become quite addicted to any kisses offered.

"Is this your first visit to The Serpent?" she asked him. "I don't remember ever seeing you here before."

"My first visit," he confessed as he drew the chair next to his out for her to join him. "It won't be my last. What would you like to drink?"

"While I'm singing, just water."

"And after you've finished for the night?"

She grinned at the disguised suggestion that, should she be interested, their brief encounter would be stretched further. "Considering the bar will have closed by then, it will be just water once more."

He knew her name. It was on display just inside the front door in smaller print than the quartet's name. A name no one ever used. They'd had to accept being known as "The Serpent's band." She was simply the girl singer of the moment. But then, she didn't have what it took to draw a crowd. She'd been hired more as decoration than for her song stylings. How else could a woman trained just to sing cope with living expenses, though? Wait tables? Although there were no tips, the singing gig paid slightly better, but not by much. She was twenty-four and had been trying to make it on her pipes for over two years already, heading nowhere at a snail's pace.

He supplied his name. Luke Wyndom. Wyndom with a *Y* to distinguish them from those lacking bloated egos, he'd said. She laughed. Sipped at the water the waitstaff delivered, then returned to the slight rise of the bandstand and a fresh collection of songs. Well, fresh to those who didn't visit often. Luke waited her out.

Walked her to her car. Thanked her for sharing her beautiful voice and a small measure of her time with him that evening. Then they went their separate ways.

He wasn't there the next night, but he returned the one following that, and the one following that. She began naturally gravitating to his table during her breaks. He would sip scotch neat while she stuck with water. They learned they were both natives of Phoenix. He asked about her choice of career, and Gaelen found herself confessing that it wasn't as satisfying as she'd expected. He talked about anything and everything except what he did for a living, other than admitting he worked in his father's firm. What his father's firm did, she didn't learn, but hadn't asked, either.

"You never eat here, do you?" she asked one night. "Is that because your wife makes you supper, and when she's asleep you steal off to listen to the music here?" He had, after all, never asked to see her on her nights off. Had never asked if she would like to join him for an early dinner before it was time to go on stage.

"Nope. Never acquired a wife to duck out on."

"Girlfriend who works nights? I'll bet she's a cop. There is something about you that says you'd be interested in a woman you found dangerous."

Luke laughed. "You're the only dangerous woman in my life."

"I'm hardly dangerous."

"Very dangerous," he countered, then surprised her. "Do you ever get a weekend off?"

"No, but I will soon. My contract with the band is nearly at an end. The trumpet's the man in charge. He tends to keep the drummer, the bass player, and the keyboardist, but he changes girl singers three or four times a year. I knew that when I took the job, though. He thinks it keeps the clientele returning, wondering who'll be at the mic a month or so down the road."

She expected Luke Wyndom to ask if she had the next gig lined up, which she didn't since there were few clubs in Phoenix that catered to her type of song styling. She had intended to lie, say she was going to try her luck in LA or New York or whatever other place didn't make her sound pathetic. Instead, he apologized for never having taken her out to dinner or to a movie or to critique her competition on the nights she didn't work.

"I never know what my schedule is going to be," he said. "Sometimes it means doing an all-nighter or traveling."

"I wasn't curious," she claimed, though she had been. "I enjoy our talks during the breaks."

He was silent for a moment. Traced his finger around the rim of his tumbler. "I'd like to do more than just talk with you, Gaelen. A lot more."

That night when he walked her to her car, he kissed her.

She hadn't slept that night. She replayed the kiss. How much she'd liked it. How she wouldn't mind enjoying a few more. Quite a few more.

And a few other things, too.

He had stopped being a stranger, had become a friend, someone she trusted because he hadn't made a move on her that first night, nor the second, nor…

Well, she'd begun to wonder if she not only had an uninspiring voice but a total lack of sex appeal, too. He didn't read as gay. He was simply…careful. The next evening, he asked when her contract ended. A week later they'd moved to spending the night at his apartment. When her things took up part of his closet and she'd been allotted drawers in the dresser, the contract at The Horned Serpent ended.

And that was when Luke invited her to go with him to Las Vegas.

****

It was on the five-hour drive up Route 93 to Sin City, a road that passed through nothing but desert nearly the entire three hundred miles, that he told her what he did for a living. She'd been so full of questions. A private detective! It was nearly the equivalent of saying his name was Bond. Detectives were the stuff of television, movies, books! Luke had laughed. Said, considering the interrogation she put him through, she'd make a damn fine investigator herself. He even asked if she'd be interested in apprenticing for the job, and promised he'd teach her everything she needed to know. Her gig at The Serpent was behind her, so she nearly said yes without thinking beyond to what being a professional investigator might entail.

But she was also disappointed. "Oh, so this isn't going to be the sort of weekend I thought it was going to be, then. It was always a job interview and then shadowing you on a job."

In answer, Luke pulled over to the side of the road. "No, Gaelen, it's a thirty-year-old man making a fool of himself over a girl he does not deserve but can't stop thinking about."

She unfastened her seat belt. Slid as close to him as the stick shift on the floor between them allowed, and draped her arms around his neck. "I'll think about the job possibility, but right now, I'd like a demonstration of what else we can do besides talk this weekend, Mr. Wyndom."

Which is when she discovered that, although she'd been nearly living with him for a couple weeks, Luke Wyndom had been really holding out on her.

By Sunday afternoon she had no doubts about the future. She was in love, and he was in love with her. They would be working together. No more doing the rounds of auditions for jobs where there were more applicants than spots for performers. She was excited about what lay ahead. Then, as they did a final round at the tables, breaking even, Luke said the words she was enthralled to hear.

"This is really spur of the moment," he warned. "Not thought out in the least but, before we return to Phoenix, what do you think about marrying me?"

"Marry you!" she gasped.

"From the brightness in your eyes and the breathless way you said that, should I take that for a yes?"

"But—"

"There's a wedding chapel here at the hotel. There's a jeweler with a case full of wedding bands. And you'd not only make me the happiest man on the planet, Gaelen Ellen Shaw, I swear never to give you reason to regret becoming my wife."

She had no qualms when, a short time later, he placed a simple wedding band on her finger. But when the justice of the peace gave the official sanction that Luke could now kiss his bride, her new husband had first kissed the hand where he'd placed the ring and whispered, "I will love you forever."

Chapter Ten

Present

"You could say that in just two days, Luke Wyndom turned my life around. I went from unemployed singer to being both a wife and new hire at Desert Wynd Investigations," Gaelen admitted as Pel worked their way through the light traffic as they headed to the house. "The idea of being a P.I. was thrilling, though Luke assured me that I had what it took to get the job done. He laughed and said considering I'd spent many evenings attempting to pry information from him, I'd already proved my worth. But I was also newly in love. Or thought I was. It was closer to being intoxicated with the attention, his belief in me, and simply the idea of being married. That's not what you asked about, though, is it?"

"It's not *not* what I was curious about," Pel admitted. "You fell hard and fast, I take it?"

"I thought so at the time. It's only hindsight that makes things clearer. Still, it's difficult to admit we didn't have what I'd thought we had."

"Go on."

She considered for a moment, mentally skipping about, revisiting memories, emotions she'd thought shelved long ago. "He did silly, old-fashioned things that, while I insisted they weren't needed, he did anyway."

"Such as?" Pel prompted.

"Opening doors for me. Holding chairs until I was seated and only then taking a seat himself. Always getting to his feet when I came into a room. And flowers. Bouquet after bouquet of flowers. When we first met, they were delivered to the club with an apology note for missing the show, but later he'd come home with them just, as he phrased it, for the sight of me looking disgusted with him for doing so before burying my nose in the blossoms. He was always so attentive, so patient, and able to draw out what I thought of as my secrets. I had, after all, told him within a short time what I hadn't confessed to my parents or to Rika. That being a vocalist wasn't as satisfying as I'd thought it would be. It isn't the best paying or most secure job, as I'm sure you know."

"Piano player for weddings, one-shot backup singer, occasional arranger for songs," he murmured. "Different gigs, similar situation. Been there—"

"And oozed talent wherever you landed," Gaelen countered. "Jace Hastings achieved what every small-time musician I've ever met has dreamed of, Pel."

"But I've been there, Gael, even if it was for a shorter length of time. I changed my name to distance myself from Cec and Dad's successes, and although my godfather tried to throw jobs my way, it doesn't mean I took any of them on unless I was really hungry and short on the rent."

"What you can do with a song—"

"*Did* with a song. There's no guarantee that—"

"*Do* with a song," she reiterated. "It wasn't Jace Hastings that was a success. It was Pelham Flannery all along."

"Debatable," he countered, taking the turn that would eventually lead to the hermit's retreat the house in the desert had become. "We'll find out in the coming days, particularly the night of the show. We aren't talking about me, though, Gael. The topic is Luke Wyndom. Sounds like he rode in on a white horse and saved you from scrambling for gigs."

"Close, but it still took him a couple weeks to wear me down. We didn't have dates like other people. No dinners with wine and candles. No movies or nights before the television where whatever was on was ignored. He was just always there on the nights I sang, and he followed me home. Rika and I were roommates, and she used to call him my stray dog, though I stayed at his apartment more often because...well, I had a roommate. Then he asked if I'd like to accompany him on a trip to Vegas. It wasn't until we were enroute that he told me what he did for a living."

What a sap she had been back then. During the drive to Nevada, she'd practically grilled him for details.

"I'm good at this job, Pel, but Luke...Luke was amazingly insightful. Cliff is good in a different way, but together, well, with them teaching me everything I needed to know, the whole situation seemed idyllic. Then Cliff got headhunted by the firm in LA and left. Luke upped the time we spent on martial arts, forcing me toward the next belt level, and practice on the shooting range became a daily thing rather than a weekly one. I never caught him looking over his shoulder but got the feeling he was forcing himself not to do so, partly because it was a tell and partly because he didn't want me to worry. He'd send me out of the office to dig through news archives or sign me up for classes that upgraded my computer skills. I came back to the office early once and found the receptionist in the hallway rather than at her desk. She advised me not to go in until the shouting match between Luke and his father ended. When Luke stormed out, he wouldn't tell me what the argument had been about. A week later, the police called to tell me he'd been shot and which hospital he'd been taken to."

Outside the SUV, the desert stretched away, the light of a nearly full moon keeping it from becoming endless dark. Only the occasional security light on a tall pole broke up the vista. Overhead, stars glimmered, free from the blanketing glow of city lights. Gaelen was barely aware of the beauty of the landscape, the sky, as she stared ahead at the ribbon of narrow road.

"He was still conscious when I got there, but the doctor didn't offer me the chance of hope. Whoever fired the shots, they were a professional. Luke had been hit three times. Any one of those wounds should have killed him, yet he hung on."

She heard her voice tighten, threatening to break. Felt the first dampness as tears gathered at the corners of her eyes. Blinked them back into submission. Wished it was possible to control both the waterworks and the wavering catch in her voice. To be professional. Distant from emotion. And yet...

Apparently, she hadn't cried enough yet over the loss of Luke Wyndom.

"His eyes were closed, but apparently he sensed I was there. I took his hand—" She gulped at the air blasting from the car's vent, hard pressed to get her voice under control. "—it was cold, and not in the way a cooling system chills you. He whispered my name, but I had to bend closer to hear what he said."

Gaelen wiped at a tear as it rilled down her cheek. When others followed, the battle to hold them back was clearly lost. Her voice had grown so tight with emotion that the sound she made was the barest whisper. Which is when Pel silently pulled to the side of the road, released his seatbelt, and wrapped his arms around her. She felt his lips brush her hair as she buried her face against his chest and wept.

"We need to call Cliff," Gaelen said once the uncontrolled sobbing eased.

Pel didn't ask why, simply fished his cell from where he'd tucked it in his shirt pocket before giving her his jacket to wear. When the call went through, he handed it to her.

"Did I ever tell you what Luke's last words to me were?" she asked her late husband's former partner.

"Not that I remember," Cliff said.

She took a wavery breath. Pushed slightly back from Pel, though she kept her eyes focused on the concern in his handsome face. "He said to *always* remember what he told me in Vegas. Luke knew he only had minutes to live, but he very specifically accented that *always*."

Both men waited in silence for her to repeat those words.

"*I will love you forever.* Try that with Luke's code, Cliff."

She could hear the click of the computer keys as Cliff fed the numeric translation to the program. There was a pregnant pause. Then he breathed two words.

"We're in."

****

An hour had passed since she'd stumbled upon the password. An hour in which not a word had passed her lips, though they had been quite demanding of what she wanted of him.

Passion.

So Pel had followed his instincts. Gathered her up in his arms, letting his suit coat drop from her shoulders to the floor in the garage, and carried her to the bedroom. Had cupped her face between his hands as they stood next to the mattress and kissed her softly, then more urgently when her own response turned hungry. The borrowed dress slithered to the floor as though gravity alone urged its descent. He let her remove the small pistol from the thigh holster, but she handed it to him to tuck somewhere safe. Lacking a bedside table, he bent a knee to the carpet and tucked it under the bed, then stayed where he was to place kisses in a path that flowed from the midnight of the remaining holster up the line of the securing garter. Along the flat plain of her stomach left exposed by the miniscule scrap of a silk thong. His hand slid up the back of her thighs, over the firm round curves of her buttocks, caressing, savoring the satin of her warm skin.

Her hands gripped his shoulders. Her head tipped back as her breathing quickened, but she did nothing else but stand there, his to do with as he willed.

As promised earlier, he took his time over the garter belt that held the lace holster in place on her thigh. The black peekaboo weave let skin pale as parchment gleam through in the dim moonlight that found narrow gaps in the closed shutters. They created bars of washed-out cream across the rug, across her body and the bed. Slowly he removed what little she had worn beneath the backless blue silvered dress. When she started to step out of her shoes, he stopped her and removed each separately, as though reversing the actions of a fairytale prince intent on discovering a runaway love.

He swept her up again then, one arm around her back, the other acting as a crook for her legs, holding her naked form close to his chest. With her arms around his neck, she instigated the kiss that demanded more.

Rather than strip back the sheets, he placed her atop the simple white comforter. Bent, supporting his weight on his arms as their breaths blended. For him, it was a sweet inhaling of her essence. For her...

She gasped, a catch in the night that said he had awakened the music in her soul.

Shifting to kneel at the bedside, Pel traced the arch of her throat, the hollow at its base, moving lower to her collarbone. First, lightly, with the tips of his left-hand fingers, he played the chords of her desire as though caressing a keyboard, finessing the sounds she made into a new version of a song she'd sung before.

With Luke Wyndom.

With him.

When his lips took over the instrumentation, his hands slid lower, sketching out the measures he sought to tread. She breathed notes, notes that danced around him, demanded a physical *ostinato*, repeating the motif he played on her body as often as he wished.

Pel claimed her mouth once more, first stripping his already loosened tie over his head and discarding his shirt in haste. Toeing his shoes off, he climbed onto the bed still clad in trousers and socks.

She gasped when his tongue brushed the tip of her breast. Clutched at him. He licked a circle around the budded rose, then sucked it gently. Gaelen lifted herself closer, eager to quicken the pace of this *ossia*, this secondary notation following where the original had once sufficed but no longer did.

The song was of his arranging. Slow but ever building. The way he played every musical lyric another composer had originally written. He'd never asked how many men she'd known because it didn't matter. He rewrote what they had done in a way that was right for him. Right for her, if he judged by her reactions.

When he moved to her other breast to worship it, repeating the stanza, his fingers trailed down, skimming her ribcage, dipping ever lower to the waiting bower at the joining crest of her thighs.

Air sucked sharply through her parted lips when he brushed the pad of his thumb over a far more intimate bud. He thought a name was primed to fall from her lips. Would it be his or the man who had sworn to love her forever?

Rather than discover which she might whisper, he kissed her deeply once more while continuing to court music from her.

She inhaled him, her mouth unquenchable in its quest. Her nails clawed at his back, the sharp pain glorious because it signaled the first of many *subito fortissimo*s he intended to coax from her. When she shattered, Pel pressed further.

Then Gaelen tampered with his score, her hands plucking urgently at his belt, tugging at the zipper that held him captive. When her fingers closed around him,

Pel feared a *stretto* would approach far too quickly, his being the second voice to sing this particular song before her rendition had subsided.

"Not yet, love," he whispered, his voice gruff with the effort to hold back as he caught her hand. Drew the other next to it to hold them captive, stretched above her head. She stared into his eyes, his mock brown ones that tinted things around them in deeper shadow. He wished briefly that he'd taken the contacts out and thus be able to let his green eyes meet her beautiful blue ones. But only briefly. Since holding her sobbing form at the side of the road, there had never been a moment when he wished to be parted from her for even a brief minute in time.

Wedging his knee between her thighs, he nudged them wider. Transferred her wrists into the keeping of his right hand, allowing the left to tempt her body into another glorious *fortissimo*.

She was primed for an aria. He wrung it from her with one touch, then slid two fingers inside her.

Gaelen bucked slightly, her body quivering as though in the grip of a *glissando*, sweeping her from one pitch to another.

The notes were his undoing. Not bothering to rid himself of trousers, Pel pushed the cloth aside and slid within her. The gasp of pleasure that escaped her lips was a plea for more as well. So he obliged the command, driving deeper, but keeping the tempo still slow and steady, just as the most celebrated of Jace Hastings' reconfigured arrangements were created.

Gaelen was impatient of a *lentando* styling, though. She wanted no deceleration but a *prestissimo*. Pel let her demands lead to an acceleration—a very, *very* fast acceleration that soon had their voices blending in a *stentato* that resembled a shouted cry of exultation.

He collapsed on her, not wishing to withdraw, lacking the strength to move. Sometime during the crescendo, he had released her wrists. Her legs wrapped tightly around him, drawing him to her yet. He buried his hands in her hair. Gaelen's rested lightly on his bare back. When their lips met this time, they did so softly, the merest brush of mouth against mouth. Sweet now rather than hungry.

The air conditioning was cool against the sweat of his back, but he didn't roll away from her until his body made the decision for him. He left her only to strip off his gaping trousers and socks, then rejoined her, his arms tucking her firmly against him. Her cheek rested on his chest, her left hand covering a spot over his heart. She curled so that one long lusciously curved leg was hitched over his hip, her knee resting near his groin.

"Pel," she whispered against his skin. "I think I made a mistake five years ago."

****

He was silent as he considered her words, the brief moment of time seeming to stretch far more than the seconds that actually ticked by. She shouldn't be surprised, Gaelen decided. They were rather cryptic.

"In what way?" Pel asked quietly, his breath stirring her hair. "It doesn't sound like he ever changed his mind about how he felt about you, Gael."

"No," she murmured. "What I felt for him was never what he apparently felt for me. It's hindsight to realize this, but I loved him more as a friend, as a colleague. As the man who had given me a future I was more suited to. It wasn't a marriage like that of my own parents, or even C.C. and Jay's, considering they have spent most of their lives together living in separate, distant, temporary locations. Luke and I were partners with benefits, not really husband and wife."

"He did what he said he would do: *love you forever*."

Gaelen tilted her head to meet his eyes. Eyes that were green in her memory though hidden both by the shadows and the tinted contacts as he retained his disguise. She had failed to give Luke Wyndom what he wanted most—though she wasn't sure what that had been any longer—but she would not fail when it came to giving Pel back the life he should never have lost.

"Perhaps only because it was a short *forever*," she said. "Luke's own parents' marriage was certainly not one for him to copy. Hank ignored his wife. When she was dying, he visited the hospital only because Luke railed at him, using the only thing he knew would get through to his father. He insisted it looked bad to the clients to show them Hank really was an unfeeling bastard, which ignoring his wife made him appear. It is what Hank Wyndom is, though. Semblances mean everything to him. The post-funeral reception in her memory was just a way for him to schmooze with the men and women he courted for business, sop up the sympathies they murmured, wallow in the attention."

Pel shifted, turning slightly. "You really despise him, don't you?"

"*Despise* might be too tame a word," Gaelen admitted. Considering what Luke's secret horde of data might hold, perhaps she should consider *fearing* Hank Wyndom.

"No, where I made a mistake was in not following through on the circumstances surrounding Luke's death. In not talking to the detective in charge of the investigation. I don't think there was ever a satisfying conclusion. I don't know whether the man arrested was even charged with causing Luke's death. It's become a cold case, and that's my fault. At first, I was grieving for a dear friend, and then…"

She paused. Soaked up the strength Pel radiated, not just with the warmth of his arms around her, or the solidness of his broad chest but with his concern for her. The scent of their lovemaking mixing with the tang of his aftershave added to it. The memory of him buried deep within her and how perfect, how right it was to have him be so much a part of her so quickly. Had she tripped into loving him because her subconscious recognized who he was before she consciously did? Once she had had such a crush on Jace Hastings. Had that souvenir of her youth colored things, lent her lonely heart false wings?

Did she really know how real love felt? Love was what she'd once called what she felt for Luke Wyndom.

Pel's fingers brushed up her arm tenderly, stirring the embers of the conflagration their lovemaking had resembled.

No, she'd been right in terming what she felt for Pel Flannery as lust. Lust they possessed in bushel baskets.

"I want you," she told him.

She knew without seeing it that his mouth curved in that special, heart-stopping grin when he drawled, "I need a bit more recovery time, darlin'. And I'm still curious when it comes to your life. Whether you loved

Luke Wyndom the same way he loved you is no longer the point. It's what kept you from looking into the circumstances surrounding his death that is. Was it grief or something else at the time?"

Although she couldn't see the scars on Pel's torso in the near darkness of the room, she could feel the slight indentation of the ones a scalpel had created to save his life a decade ago. She traced one now, following the downward descent.

He grabbed her hand, brought it to his lips. "Luke Wyndom, Gael," he said, her late husband's name warm against her fingers.

"Not Luke," she corrected in a whisper. "*Hank* Wyndom. He is what kept me from following up on things."

Pel didn't press, merely waited for her to gather her thoughts. They were so tangled, though. She had expected Hank to tell her she was no longer a Desert Wynd asset, with Luke gone. Instead, he surprised her by taking over her training, intensifying it so that there was never an opportunity to question the police investigation. If she had even thought to do so at the time. With only a year of training, would she even have asked the right questions? With Cliff's resignation and move to LA coming barely two months before Luke's death, she had become the only operative left under Hank's thumb at Desert Wynd. He'd kept her close and swamped with work. The more days, weeks, months, *years* that went by, the less she thought about the crime scene report on Luke's death.

"I think Hank deliberately kept me unable to pursue inquiries into the case Luke was on when he was killed. Though Hank's idea of training differed from what Luke and Cliff taught me, if I wanted to be fully accredited, I needed to kowtow to his demands. And I did want that license. Investigative work spoke more strongly to me than singing ever had. But I let Luke down by not looking into things once the training was over. I think the time has come to rectify that error."

Pel shifted his position on the bed. His fingers glided along her ribs, seeming to cue them, play them as he would the keys on a piano, creating music he heard only in his mind. Or perhaps he pictured them as a musical staff and the spots he touched as placing notes in an arrangement, directions on how different instruments should blend, or to a vocalist on when they should be sung? "You don't trust the police investigation that was done at the time?" he asked.

"Honestly, I don't know if they even finalized things," she admitted. "Luke was killed rescuing an abducted child. Other than his dying as a result of saving the youngster, it was considered a case satisfactorily closed, in Hank's books. As he saw it, Luke getting shot was simply something that was likely to happen to anyone who carried a weapon, but it sounded like he expected it to be a credible outcome in any investigation. Even those that were free of confrontation."

"He thinks it's justifiable even when all you're doing is delivering a court summons?"

"Probably, and he had me deliver quite a few of those, terming them the bread-and-butter income, while he looked for fully accredited agents to fill both Cliff's and Luke's shoes. Only the fellows he hired weren't worthy to even buff their shoes, much less fill them. I always suspected they worked more cheaply than either

Cliff or Luke had."

"Then you know what needs to be added to your tally of things to work on tomorrow."

She sighed ruefully. "That list keeps getting longer and longer. Who knew being unemployed would be so time consuming?"

He chuckled. "It's called being in business for yourself, slick, not being jobless. It eases up a bit once you have employees or connections to people who can take on some of the work, but I'm sorry to say, the heavy lifting still falls in your corner."

"Is that advice being given by Pel Flannery, manager of C.C.'s Place, the C.F.O. of Cristofori Investments, or the semi-retired Jace Hastings?"

"*All* of them, though Jace Hastings didn't get a full night's sleep until he was unconscious in the hospital. Pel Flannery doesn't because a very demanding woman has moved into his bed."

"And does Mr. Flannery plan to do something about that demanding woman?" Gaelen asked, her face turned up to his.

"Other than upping the vitamin supplements to be able to accommodate her, he is pretty content with accommodating her whenever she wants," he said.

Gaelen snuggled closer in his embrace. "How much time do we have before heading back to C.C.'s?"

"Not nearly enough, as far as I'm concerned."

"Then—"

He cut off whatever she had intended to say through the simple expedient of kissing her.

Quite thoroughly.

****

Cliff would only admit that the information on the

flash drives was a trail Luke had been following regarding his father's activities—those outside of daily business at Desert Wynd. "We sussed that right, Gaeley, but it looks like Luke was rushed for time and nothing is organized, just loaded in a blitz of scanned documents and notes he made. Lists of names, some that I recognized but others that I don't. We'll simply have to keep up the appearance that I'm related to the Flannerys and have come for a golf holiday."

"Which is never a hardship for you," she had told him. Judging it safer for neither of them to carry the drives, they handed them over to Pel to tuck in the safe at C.C.'s, then waited in the parking lot for him to set the alarm and lock the rear door.

But, as Rika headed for her car, Cliff grabbed her hand, executed a move that had the singer spinning into his arms, where the two exchanged a prolonged kiss that would have surprised her, Gaelen admitted, if she hadn't seen the earlier welcome when Cliff had swept Rika off her feet to swing her around. The good-night kiss they now shared was obviously as heated as the one Pel gave her before tucking her inside her friend's car for the drive back to Phoenix. All Rika said when she settled behind the wheel was, "Wow," in a rather stunned voice. She smiled the entire drive back to Gaelen's apartment, though.

Although she'd had little sleep, Gaelen was up early the next morning and dressed in one of her usual concrete-gray suits, a simple white cotton camisole beneath it, and her favorite hammered copper torc at her neck. Her regular handgun was in its hidden holster at her waist, and Luke's pistol was tucked behind her back. The first stop of the day was the garage her father's friend ran. He gave her a list of things that would be done or checked on. While an oil change, tire rotation, brake check, and other normal items appeared on it, including a new paint job and interior detailing—she wanted more than sufficient things being done to make it reasonable to use a rental car the coming week—what was really being done was ordered verbally. A complete teardown, if necessary, to locate any hidden transmitters.

The rental agency was happy to deliver a new vehicle to the garage for her use. Rather than go with a clone of what she owned, Gael requested a luxury sedan that would catch the eye. The blue metallic luxury four-door sedan that pulled into the garage's lot definitely suited her purpose. Should Hank have put a tail on her, all they could report back to him was that she was performing security duties for a visiting fashionista billionaire. The car guaranteed there would be no missing them as they hit various shopping destinations.

Her dad's pal waved her off, after admiring the replacement wheels, but Pel's desert escape would not be her first stop in the coupe. That was the precinct office of the detective assigned to investigate the details surrounding Luke Wyndom's death five years earlier.

The type of cases she handled at Desert Wynd hadn't been ones that involved police intervention. Hank saved those for himself. Hers had been linked to lawyers, even though she'd put her foot down about following cheating spouses. Cliff, she knew, fielded many of those types of cases, but he also handled white collar crime. *And* he'd been a cop before joining Desert Wynd. At Luke's funeral, she'd seen him talking to a man whose very demeanor shouted civil servant, a man he mentioned having worked with while on the force. The man who had caught Luke's case.

It was only in calling to make an appointment to see Douglas Valente that she discovered he was a homicide detective. Had he been one when Luke was shot during the rescue of the kidnapped child? And if Valente had been, did that mean Luke's death had been treated as a homicide? She'd been under the impression that it was the kidnapper who had fired on Luke, but dipping into newspaper copies in the online archives she found he had gone to prison for abduction, nothing more.

Little in the articles mentioned anything other than that Luke Wyndom died of wounds related to the take-down. As far as public data sources went, her husband's death was just smoke pushed aside by a breeze created when the kidnapping case went to trial.

Since she'd called ahead, requesting access to the files dealing with the case, and Luke's death, when she gave her name and reason for visiting to the officer at the precinct's front desk, it wasn't long until a sturdy, sun-bronzed man with dark but silver-streaked hair came to claim her. If he'd worn a suit to work that day, the jacket had long since been discarded. His white dress shirt clung in a sweat-dampened patch on his back, and his yellow-and-blue-striped tie had been pulled loose. His shirt sleeves were turned back at the cuffs.

Valente had his hand out when he walked up to her. "Mrs. Wyndom? Doug Valente. Your late husband and I worked together briefly during the year before his tragic loss. He spoke often of you and the progress being made on your training. With both Luke and Cliff

Quinnlan as your handlers, I'm not surprised."

Gaelen shook his hand, her grip as firm as his, which meant he wasn't putting force behind his, but she was with hers. One of Luke's first lessons: *a firm handshake indicates you not only mean business but know your business.* "He compared me to a sponge, didn't he?" she said, her lips curving slightly in memory.

Valente chuckled. "He did. Come on back to the offices. I've already pulled the box of evidence and files for you to look over. Should I infer that something you've been working on at Desert Wynd has ties to that case?"

The detective held the door for her to proceed him into a network of offices. They walked through a room filled with desks holding computer screens and keyboards. "Nuts and bolts corral," he said when he caught her studying the layout as they moved past. A few of the desks were occupied, and a couple of chairs were, as well, as officers took statements from people who looked frightened, leery, angry, or merely pissed over being questioned. "Paperwork hell."

"I dislike it myself," Gaelen said. "Actually, as of this past Monday afternoon, I'm no longer a part of Desert Wynd. Hank and I didn't see eye to eye on an assignment. While I'm currently case free as I put together an agency of my own, I finally have the time to learn more about the one my husband was on when he was killed."

"Murdered," Valente corrected. When she stumbled in surprise, he paused. "You weren't aware of that?"

She took a deep breath, steadying herself. "I was

very much unaware of that. Hank knew?"

"Yes. I suppose he didn't want to upset you further, and thus kept the information to himself."

"Most likely," Gaelen agreed, though she knew Hank Wyndom too well to think that had been his reasoning. The case was closed as far as he was concerned. Yes, he'd lost his son, his only child, but the parents of the kidnapped kid had paid what he charged them, so all was right in Hank's world.

Valente stopped at the closed door of what she could see through the glass partitions was an unoccupied office. "For your convenience, I've had everything brought here. The detective it belongs to is currently on vacation, so you won't be disturbed. If you have any questions, or when you're ready to leave, just call my extension."

Gaelen took the business card he handed her and thanked him for his time and the trouble he'd gone to.

"Do you mind my asking what you hope to find?"

"Honestly, I don't really know. Perhaps simply closure," she said. "Was I wrong to assume the case is considered cold rather than solved? It was my understanding that the kidnapper was caught and sentenced."

"He was given a very long time to serve, too, although he claimed to be innocent throughout the proceedings. The missing boy was confined in his basement and drugged with prescription pills prescribed by the man's doctor. Everything pointed to his being the kidnapper. That's what he went to prison for, not for your husband's murder."

She had already stepped into the room, had put her briefcase-sized purse on an open space on a desk otherwise filled with photos of the resident detective's family. They had been slightly pushed aside to accommodate a bound collection of paperwork—a murder book, she realized, the step-by-step investigation of a homicide—and a typical storage box the size of a file-cabinet drawer. At Valente's words, she turned back to him, stunned by the revelation. Even though no mention was made of it in the newspaper articles she read, she'd simply thought she missed a follow-up piece at a later date. "He wasn't tried for Luke's death?"

"No, ma'am, and the reason why is that the man didn't own a gun, had no residue on his hands to indicate he'd fired a weapon, and—"

Gaelen found she was holding her breath.

"—no weapon other than the one holstered beneath Luke Wyndom's left arm was found at the scene. We couldn't produce the pistol that killed your husband, Mrs. Wyndom, and it still irks the hell out of me that we couldn't find it."

Chapter Eleven

"Well, what do you think? Is this what you had in mind?" Tina Kavanaugh asked as she surveyed the final arrangement of furniture in the front room—the great room, though "massive" had always seemed a more apt word to him. The wide open space of it looked winnowed down considerably with the addition of furniture and went beyond "great" now, verging on "incredible."

"I'm practically speechless," Pel admitted as he pushed a pair of thin black-framed designer aviators back to the bridge of his nose. Two long, extremely comfortable cognac-toned leather sofas were set like parallel lines leading from the once-empty adobe-faced fireplace. A couple of casual chairs in a slightly darker shade of brown leather closed the area off at the opposite end of the parallel. A huge Navaho rug covered the floor in colors that matched those in the sofa and chair but added rust, gray, and the alkaline white of the desert floor. Mesquite logs were piled in the wide, flat-fronted adobe fireplace and in a huge Pima Papago basket off to the side, as though ready for use. A large, colorful oil painting of a pale horse with feathers woven into its tossing mane and streaks of blue and red war paint markings on its face, neck, chest, and shoulders sat on the mantel, leaning against the adobe chimney piece.

"No footstools, or coffee table to set drinks on?" he asked.

"What, and hide the beauty of that rug? No way," Tina insisted. "Why do you think there are sofa height tables behind the couches and that antique chest between the chairs? That's where drinks go. There's plenty of room to stretch your legs out without a footstool involved. But I'd still like to move the piano to a spot in front of the window. That way the horse's head is turned to look directly at it."

He shook his head. "Nope. It's in the corner for the acoustics." Which was a bare-faced lie. It was there because anywhere else would turn him into a shadow to take potshots at.

"The dining table should accommodate nearly all the people you said would be arriving, particularly with benches rather than chairs. With the number of guests you'll have, is this a family get-together because your father is off the road now?"

"Sorta." It was the story they planned to trot out should anyone ask, though he hadn't volunteered it to the Kavanaughs. That meant it was a very logical invention, since Tina mentioned the same scenario.

"You're happy with what Brad and I put together then? We..."

She went into detail on how the former gym room now functioned as a bedroom for one of the women arriving, and the media room, which she really wanted to put the largest big screen available in, was set up for the larger number of men. His beyond-minimalistic home office was now a cozy guestroom for the Montgomerys. Considering they'd moved all the exercise equipment to the garage, it was convenient that he didn't have a collection of cars housed in the echoing space.

"Anything else you can think of that we might have forgotten?" she asked. "If so, just give us a call."

Pel smiled down at her. "Trust me, Tina. You and Brad did a hell of a job here. I'm definitely keeping everything but the rented single beds."

"Next stop, then, is decorating the patio outside," she announced. "While we don't do plants, we do have outdoor furnishings and the name of an excellent landscaper. It was a pleasure doing business with you again. Call anytime."

Brad gave him a wave when Pel escorted Tina out the front door. She hopped into their van, which then left the larger delivery truck to follow in the dust of their run back down to the road. On his own temporarily, Pel wandered through the house once more, feeling like he'd been sideswiped by an extremely efficient local small business. From echoing rooms to truly decent living quarters in under two hours. The lone bar stool in the kitchen had been relegated to the garage, replaced by four adjustable-height swivel bar stools with high backs that leaned toward industrial modern. Hell, there were even two dressers, bedside tables, and a further Navaho Yei-design rug in shades from desert white to obsidian draped over the foot of his bed in the master suite now.

Buddy, he told himself, *you've been on the road far too long.* This *is what settling down in one spot looks like.* Now if only he could stay put and not be constantly looking over his shoulder, it would feel like heaven.

Well, almost. As comfortable as the house was, he

was still the lone occupant. Since that occupant had to be the one the incoming horde would recognize, he returned to the house, got rid of the plain glass frames, and took the brown-tinted contacts out. The green-eyed Jace Hastings was back in residence. "You'd better know what the hell you're doing," Pel told the man who looked back at him in the mirror. Unfortunately, Jace Hastings didn't look like he was all that confident either.

Half an hour later, the parade arrived. Or so it seemed. Cliff's pickup truck led the way up the long dirt drive, kicking up a dust trail. Whoever was driving the first of a diverse fleet of SUV rentals and the lone do-it-yourself moving truck was smart enough to hang back as they followed him. Even when everyone had pulled to a stop in the wide oval of gravel before the house, the dust cloud following them took its time to settle. That didn't stop those in the vehicles from pouring out the doors, though. His mother tumbled from the back of Cliff's truck and gave him a quick kiss on the cheek as she breezed past, eager to see what the Kavanaughs had done to improve living conditions in what she called his Casa Grande. His father thumped a hand down on Pel's shoulder and followed close on her heels for his first look at what a large bank account could accomplish in the stroke of a key. As with every transaction he made, money would vanish from the BCI offshore account into the Kavanaughs' local one electronically.

His godfather was the next in line to greet. Not that there was a line. More a swarm of people standing around gawking. Montgomery gave him a crushing hug that mixed pleasure to have him back in circulation and concern about the past, in equal parts. They hadn't seen each other since before the metal-mangling crash a decade before. With Paul being a very visible icon, he had agreed to keep his distance, making it far more viable a conclusion that Jace Hastings hadn't survived, though he'd known Pel had. After that, it was kisses from both Rory Montgomery and Nan Rawlins, more back thumping from the men he knew from of old, and handshaking of those he hadn't met in the past.

Scott Rawlins handed over already signed nondisclosure agreements from everyone he'd pulled from the Visions Records studio. "God, it's great to see you again, Pel. Don't worry, everyone has pledged in blood to keep Jace Hastings' survival to themselves under pain of professional death."

"Your uncle Paul's favorite threat," Pel mused.

"One he has used with great success for far longer than either of us has been alive," Scott agreed. "So tell me what we're going to do here. Other than resuscitate the Hastings career."

Since everyone else was either on a tour of the house or dropping suitcases and duffle bags in the hastily constructed men's dormitory room, Pel waved Scott inside and out of the heat. "Hopefully, nothing more than resuscitate Jace Hastings," he said as Scott spun one of the new barstools around to straddle it, his arms folded on the tall back. Pel pulled two frosted bottles of beer from the refrigerator and passed the recording engineer one. In sync, they twisted the caps off, then clinked long necks before taking a swallow.

"You don't sound as sure that it's possible to pull off as Uncle Paul does," Scott noted before knocking a second gulp back.

"With good reason. I haven't sung since the close of the show in LA ten years ago. The piano's still working for me, and I've never stopped rescoring songs, but doing vocals?" Pel sucked air through his teeth. "Not all that confident on what those will sound like. Probably sadly out of pitch."

"You haven't sung at all?"

"Not even in the shower. I was constantly on the road and attempting to pass without anyone noticing me. As too many people in the past have noted, my song stylings are very recognizable, as is my voice because of that."

"But you were playing the piano."

"Nope. Not until C.C wanted to get off the road and still have a place to perform herself. Then I got back in the habit, but only as her accompanist."

"No music at all in your life for nearly a full decade? Pel! How'd you stay sane?"

Which was probably the heart of it. Trust Scott, a man who had grown up with music a constant in his life, either because his uncle was performing or his father was producing someone's latest recording, to realize what he'd missed the most.

"I did take up the harmonica," Pel confessed. "Got pretty good at it."

"A harmonica," Rawlins mused. "We could work that into something."

"I was thinking the same thing. Everyone knows what Jace Hastings was best known for in the wayback, yet if he hadn't vanished but returned to performing, there would be things about his style that changed over time. Now we just have to sort out what those might be."

"Like?"

"Faster-paced songs. Oh, not all of them, but fewer of the snailed-down standards."

"*Snailed-down?*" Scott choked.

"Drawn out, then, like with 'Misty.' "

"Actually, I like the *snailed-down* connotation," the recording producer said. "Is there an already chosen date for when this *Live at C.C.'s Place* session happens?"

Pel stalled by tipping back his brew. "I don't think that's up to me to decide. It's going to depend on how sad my pipes are. And, believe me, buddy, I gave 'em a try yesterday while I was here alone, and it was disaster city."

"In a playback—"

"Recorded to the laptop, played it back. Felt suicidal. Nearly."

"Ahh, but that's only because you didn't have me to play coach," Montgomery said as he joined them. "You got one of those frosted bottles to help me wash the dust cloud away, Pel?"

As he handed a bottle over and supplied Scott with a fresh one, Pel studied his godfather. "That sounds suspiciously like you've already decided on a date for this gig."

"I was talking to your fake cousin Cliff," Paul admitted, "and we both think this needs to go down next week."

"Next week!" Pel sputtered. "It's already Wednesday."

"Which means we do it no later than Tuesday. Monday would be even better. C.C. tells me either of those nights are lightweight ones for clientele, and while Scott may not be in a hurry to get back to LA, Visions executives won't want their number one recording team playing golf in Arizona while still on the payroll."

"Golf!" Pel coughed.

"I told those that played to bring their clubs because there will be downtime," Scott admitted. "Plus, it had everyone really eager to sign those nondisclosure forms."

"And, to make it look like nothing much was going on, I asked Jay to throw together a tournament for them," Paul admitted. "We're calling it the Flannery Family Reunion Playoff."

"But *you* don't play golf," Pel said.

"*I* don't have to play. *I'm* not a Flannery. My lovely wife Red is pretending to be one through her mother's side of the family, and she does know her way around a golf course, as do Nan and Scott here."

"So, while they are all off on the greens, that means..." Pel left the opening wide for his godfather to supply what would be going on.

Montgomery smirked at him. "You and I, buddy, will be working on those vocals. Now, have you got suggestions on things worth singing?"

Pel reached into his jeans pocket. "Funny you should ask," he said and handed over the playlist.

****

Detective Valente had warned her that the murder book featured photographs of Luke's body in the morgue, but Gaelen steeled herself to look at them dispassionately.

It didn't worked.

Her last glimpse of him had been at his funeral,

dressed, primped by the undertaker to look natural and at peace as he lay in the coffin. The case details showed her a man with three bullet holes in his chest. She went through an entire fresh packet of tissues before tears no longer blinded her.

It wasn't Luke, she told herself. Not really. Merely his body. A body that had held her close. Had made love to her. Warmed her when he encircled her with his arms because she had forgotten to bring a heavier jacket when they went to hear Rika sing on the first night of a new gig their first January together. Comforted her when she was down over failing to master a move that would inch her into collecting a new color on her martial arts belts. Hugged back and kissed her passionately when she squealed in excitement and had thrown herself at him after opening the birthday gift he'd gotten her—the handgun she'd been lusting after and still carried.

She averted her eyes while crying. Closed them against the pain, the sight of a Luke she didn't know. The pale, shattered shadow of the man who'd given her everything she ever wanted, even when she hadn't known she wanted it.

The man who, despite it all, had not been able to win from her what she already felt for Pel Flannery. Had Luke known there was a spark he hadn't kindled in her? Had he mourned his inability to raise that flame, or had he told himself that the time she spent with him would suffice?

That, in the end, she was destined to leave him?

I will always love you. His last words, though he hadn't whispered them but just the reminder that he'd said them.

"I'm sorry, Luke," she whispered. "So sorry."

But he wasn't there. If spirits lingered around those they loved, Luke had moved on long ago, knowing she wouldn't know whether he was there or not. There was no disturbance of her hair by the air-conditioned breeze that blasted from a vent in the ceiling that she could match to the way he had once brushed a stray lock of hair back from her face, tucking it behind her ear. No imagined echo of his voice.

The chair in the vacationing detective's office swiveled. All she needed to do was swing away from the desk and the case file photographs. Stare out the window that was currently at her back. But it wouldn't erase the picture of Luke that now held precedence in her mind's eye. Nor make it any easier to do what she'd come to do, and that was to find facts to work with. If Valente and his team hadn't found the murder weapon at the scene, that meant whoever had killed Luke Wyndom was just as free and enjoying that they'd gotten away with murder as Rowan McTavish was, getting away with the same thing in regard to Ashley Hopper.

In the now six years that she'd been learning and working in her new profession, murder had not been a crime she'd been called upon to deal with. That didn't mean she lacked the knowledge, the investigative skill to follow the trail of evidence to discover the identity of Luke's killer. Her husband had believed in her abilities. Time to prove them to herself by…

She took a deep, spine-stiffening breath, gathering her courage.

By looking at the evidence. *All* the evidence.

Gaelen took several more bracing gulps of

refrigerated air. Gritted her teeth. Opened her eyes and attempted to look at the photo of Luke Wyndom's desecrated torso dispassionately. To help, she ripped a blank sheet of paper from the notebook she'd brought along, folded it, and laid it across Luke's face, turning him from a man she'd known intimately into the corpse she needed to concentrate on.

She knew little about anatomy, but the shots had been grouped. According to the attached coroner's report, one had just missed his heart and a major artery, though it had nicked a minor one. Another shot had ripped through a lung. The third had plowed into muscle. If it had been the only bullet to reach him, he would have recovered. It was the other two that killed him. Too much damage too close to his heart, and a lung filling...

Gaelen set the report aside, not able to read more. Concentrate on the visual, not the interior damage she told herself.

Grouped shots.

Was that possible to do when a target wasn't stationary? Her experience was entirely tied to practice on a shooting range. Grouping shots on a paper target. An unmoving target.

But a man who had been moving, as witnesses had claimed Luke was doing, running toward the kidnapper when he was shot, would not have been stationary. Even if the first shot had been a killing one, he would have jerked with the impact, which would have moved him in a different direction than his run. Would it have been to the left, to the right? Backwards?

Yet the shots were grouped.

Gaelen leaned back in the chair. Stared at the

ceiling. What had Valente told her? Something beyond that they hadn't found the murder weapon at the scene.

The kidnapper Luke had uncovered had drugged the boy with his own prescription medication.

The accused insisted throughout questioning and the trial that he was innocent, that he hadn't taken nor doped the boy.

That the man hadn't owned a gun.

That...

Gaelen sat upright, stunned at what she'd just realized.

Luke's had been the only weapon at the scene, and it was still in his shoulder holster when he was shot. That meant he'd known the kidnapper was unarmed. Had planned to tackle him or grab and restrain him.

She knew Luke Wyndom. He would have been running at the man, his suit jacket open and flying as he darted forward. She could even picture his tie flipped back over his shoulder, his hair moving with the wind of his passing.

You've watched too many shows that slowed the action sequence down for dramatic effect, she told herself. Yet that was Luke. Her Luke. The Luke she remembered. The guy who had a hero complex that wouldn't quit, whether he was saving a pathetic girl singer from a life of few gigs or running toward danger if it meant there was a chance to save someone.

Luke Wyndom, who had been killed by someone targeting him *specifically*. An assassin with the ability to not only closely group shots, but to do so in such quick succession that they left a signature on a man in motion. Five years ago, someone had contracted a professional hit on her husband!

****

When Gaelen left the police station, it was without mentioning her revelation to Detective Valente. No doubt the police had come to the same conclusion. They dealt with murders on a regular basis. But the realization that Luke's name had been given as a target to a professional killer made her wish she hadn't let her temper get the best of her on Monday. If she were still at Desert Wynd, she could be digging through the cases Luke had worked prior to that final one.

Then again, the answer itself might be among the data on the flash drives he'd left for her to find. That seemed just as logical, considering the timing. Someone mentioned in one of those documents hadn't wanted him investigating them any further. Yeah, she and Cliff suspected that everything on those data sticks related to underhanded deals Hank was involved in, but that didn't mean other people mentioned in those documents wanted their involvement known. Hank was probably hired muscle. Beating a man was his preferred way of getting answers. She'd never seen him do so, but Luke had come home fit to spit after having pulled his father off a suspect.

"God, but I hope Mom had an affair with someone and I'm the result of it. Anybody's DNA would be better than having Dad's," Luke said that night, despair fairly dripping from the words.

And yet Hank had been right about the best way to find Jace Hastings. That really irked her. She had stumbled upon Pel not by following the money, but via a music angle. She'd been off the clock, just accompanying Rika to the audition in Surprise, and met a man who lent her his spare shirt. Still, if Hank himself had taken on the case, she doubted he would have found his way to C.C.'s Place. McTavish had told him Jace Hastings was in the Phoenix area. Hank wouldn't consider a community best known as being a retirement one having a strong enough musical connection to be worth investigating. Particularly when the man they'd been hired to find was only in his mid-thirties.

At least she didn't think he would.

She hoped the appearance of having been hired to be Rory Montgomery's security and shopping tour guide was enough to keep Hank from suspecting her of doing anything other than catching any type of case that surfaced. She was still putting the fledging Firebird Investigations together. Which reminded her that a visit to Luke's IT friend was also on her To Do List.

Before she had put everything back in the evidence box, the last thing Gaelen studied for a length of time was the plastic bag that housed three bullet casings. The ones retrieved from Luke Wyndom's chest.

The marks inscribed along the sides by the rifling in whatever pistol had fired the shots was different from those her gun made on the spent bullets she collected after time at the firing range. That simply meant the gun in question hadn't been created by her manufacturer of choice. She wondered whether Luke had any from his gun. If they were a close match, it meant the assassin had used what he carried. But considering how many makers of pistols there were, that left a lot of possibilities open. It was also something the police would have noted. All she needed to keep in mind was Valente's mention before she left that shells with similar markings were connected to other unsolved crime cases. That probably indicated the shooter was a local, but nothing else.

As she got back into the rental car, she touched bases with Cliff to see if the visitors from California had arrived and whether she was needed yet.

"Everyone's here, and they arrived with already-signed nondisclosure docs. Pel's godfather is one very thorough man. He's already pushing for a show date for early next week," Cliff related. "What have you been up to this morning?"

"Investigating," she said. "I met your friend Detective Valente—"

"No better man on the force than Doug Valente," Cliff interrupted, possibly to reassure her.

"—and went through the evidence box they have on Luke's murder. Did you realize he *was* murdered and just kept it from me?"

He was slow to answer, which was answer enough.

"I was still new to the job in LA, Gaeley. There was no way I could look into it, and I trusted Valente to do everything possible."

"You didn't think I was ready to handle the truth, Cliff?"

"Far from ready," he admitted. "Since the police hit a brick wall on it, there was nothing either of us could have—or should have—done differently."

"Would you have asked to sit in on the interrogations of the kidnapper if you'd been here?"

"It only works that way in a television show, honey. The guy had nothing to do with Luke's death."

"But he might have seen someone who did."

"Doubtful."

She fumed silently, then made her decision. "I'm going to ask to talk to him in prison, see if he remembers anything that he didn't realize might tie into the shooting."

"Gaeley." The way he said her name was warning enough. "Sweetheart. That's not going to happen."

"Because I'm the victim's wife, or because I wasn't involved with the case five years ago?"

"Because," Cliff said softly, "he's dead. Less than six months after he was sentenced, another inmate—an inmate never identified—stabbed him with a shiv. The case is closed, Gaelen. There's nothing more anyone can find."

****

"What I was thinking," Pel told his godfather, "was giving myself breaks where I wouldn't be singing, just being the guy at the keyboard."

Montgomery had pulled one of the chairs from the living room over next to the piano where a spill of sheet music spread across the closed cover of the full-sized grand. "Go on," he urged.

Pel shuffled through the sheets. "When you told me Nan was being dragged into this—"

"You try stopping her from doing something once she gets wind of a performance by one of her pets," Paul interrupted.

"I am not one of her pets."

"Sure you are," Montgomery said. "When you turned up in LA, she was feeling her oats. She'd been a chart topper on her own for over a decade and eager to spread her mentor wings. Sorry, pal, but you got the designation of *pet* stamped on you from that day on."

"Our style is nothing alike," Pel argued.

"Neither is yours and mine, but here we sit. But you were about to say something about Nan?"

Pel frowned. "You're a real pain sometimes, Paul."

His godfather grinned at him. "It's part of my charm."

"Is that what it's called? Okay, to business. If there are built-in rests for my voice, I might be able to pull this off. Scott had me sing something for him and says I'm not as bad as I think I am currently."

"You were singing? I didn't hear you!"

"We hid out on the far side of the garage with the buffer of three parked SUVs and the doors closed to keep the rest of you at bay. But in regard to those rests—if everyone is agreeable, we've got you, Nan, and C.C. to break things up. I'd also like to include a local singer—Paprika Mendez. C.C. hired her for Friday and Saturday nights. I found backup in the form of a sax, guitar, and drums for her, and they've melded into a heck of a team in a very short time. Rika's a powerhouse whose talent is wasted on Phoenix audiences."

Montgomery was smiling when Pel finished. "Even with a decade away from the biz, you've shrugged on the mentor cloak."

"Oh, I'm sure you'll agree with me. And we'll be using this team for the show, augmenting the sax with Dad's trombone. I saw a guitar case come in the door with you, Paul, which means you intended to be part of this dog-and-pony show the moment you heard about it. Our local guy switches from playing lead to doing just bass guitar, so we can talk to him about sticking to the bass. We even have backup singers in C.C., Nan, and Rika, unless you'd like to lend to the mix as well," Pel suggested. As if his mentor could resist any of what he'd laid out. The man might claim to be retired except for the occasional television special, but he had the stage in his blood. It had one hell of a Lorelei call, too. One that had been whispering seductively to him for a long time now, Pel admitted to himself.

"Although the brass section is miniscule, it still needs to be rounded out with a trumpet," Montgomery murmured thoughtfully. "Otherwise, you're suggesting that, with me, we've got four singers to spell you as well as do backup duties. I think I'd like to hear your local team first."

"That's on the schedule for later tonight. Since they're filling in for Cec while we have company, they go on at ten p.m. I'll warn you, when I mentioned you'd probably stop by C.C.'s Place tonight, the guitar guy got a stunned look on his face and was heard to whisper your name in a worshipful manner."

Paul laughed. "Hell, I like him already! Now, about that trumpet…"

Which is when Cliff strolled back into the front room, his cell phone to his ear. "Gael's on her way. She wants to know if she needs to stop and pick anything up."

Pel glanced at the superstar seated next to the piano bench where he'd parked. Raised an eyebrow in query. "Pizza?"

In answer, Montgomery blessed him.

****

It both looked and sounded as though a party was in process when Gaelen pulled the luxury rental car onto the gravel lot before the desert house. Cliff had been on the lookout for her, but when he left the house, he was trailed by strangers, all men, their ages spanning from late forties to mid-twenties. All eager to carry the multitude of pizza and salad boxes through the front door. While she fielded a few appreciative glances, Gaelen figured they were meant more for the food delivery than for herself.

"I'd introduce you," Cliff said as the men trouped away, "but I can't remember half their names yet. You didn't tell me Pel's pad was palatial. Way to go, partner."

"It has next to no furniture," she said.

"Make that *had* next to no furniture, then," he corrected. "It was decked out when I got here after leading everyone from the airport. I'd say take a quick tour of the joint, but if you do that first, there's a good chance there will be no food left when you return to the kitchen."

"So what's been going on since they arrived?"

"Work," Cliff murmured. "Nearly every room in the place has some sort of music-related thing going on. Jay, C.C., and Nan Rawlins have had their heads together in the master suite, Mrs. Montgomery has been on the phone making calls and checking off names on lists in the guest room. Scott Rawlins and his engineers have been back in the media room looking over the blueprints Pel had of C.C.'s Place, to plan the placement of their equipment—"

"There's a media room?" Gaelen demanded. "I never saw it when I was here before."

"As there's no media equipment in it but enough single beds to look like a barracks, I'm not surprised. Pel and Montgomery have been sequestered at the piano. I've been twiddling my thumbs and keeping an eye on the vista outside. It's quite a view," Cliff noted.

"Tell me about it," she said. "Night and day from

reality. It's hard to picture Pel having lived any differently, though I know from what he's told me that he's been living far below this pay grade for nine years, never staying anywhere for longer than a few weeks, if that long, before moving on to yet another cheap motel in another small town."

Cliff nodded. "When you're trying to stay under the radar, it's amazing what you can put up with. You and I've only had to do undercover surveillance a few times—"

"And mine was usually as a file clerk in an office where the crime was petty cash and office equipment disappearances," she admitted. "Nothing much downscale from what I did between gigs as a singer."

"Lucky you," he said. "I did a hitch as a hod carrier."

"You carried pigs?"

"*Hod*, not hog, Gaeley. Heavy lifting, mixing and toting the stuff brick layers stick the bricks in place with."

"Geez! I'm glad I just did filing, now. Sounds like there's nothing for us to do but keep our eyes peeled here, though."

Cliff swung an arm around her shoulders. "At least for today we're superfluous to the proceedings. Tonight, everyone is headed to C.C.'s for dinner and to hear Rika and the boys. From what I overheard, when moseying through the front room, Pel wants to put them front and center in the show. Well, as much as can be when they share a stage with the likes of Montgomery, Nan Rawlins, C.C., and Jay, plus Jace Hastings."

Gaelen chuckled. "Yeah, like anyone will notice the rest of us in such company. Which is good for you and me, but for Rika and the others, well, it will look good on their performance resumes to have played with such stars."

"You're the expert on that," he allowed. "Now, we'd better get inside before lunch is nothing but crumbs in those pizza boxes."

The first thing she saw when she entered, though, was Pel seated at the piano, his hands on the keyboard, working through a song. A very recognizable Nan Rawlins was standing next to him. "Here," Gaelen heard the woman say, offering a wedge of pizza to him. "Eat. You're going to need your strength."

"Not near the gra—" he started to say and was stopped when she shoved the piece in his mouth.

Gaelen recognized the exasperated look he gave her as he chewed.

"I like the song, really, I do, Pel," Nan insisted, "but other than the desert theme, it doesn't tie into everything else. I want to sing this one. I've wanted to do this song for a long time, but Scott has shot it down for every recording session. This time I think we can sell him on it. And since—"

She broke off when he stood up, rounded the magnificent grand piano, and swept Gaelen into his arms for a quick kiss. He tasted of tomato sauce, melted cheese, and pepperoni, but the embrace felt like home.

"Thank God," he murmured. "The cavalry arrives. I need saving from these vultures."

Gaelen grinned up at him. "Didn't you invite them?"

"Throwing it back in my face, huh? Yeah, I did. Kick me next time I suggest such a thing."

But she wasn't paying attention to what he said.

She was staring at his eyes. "You took the contacts out! Your eyes are green again!"

Pel shrugged. "Solidifying with this group that I really am Jace Hastings, though the hair color is still off."

He was dressed casually, something she hadn't seen him do often in their short time together. Rather than the well-worn jeans he'd pulled on when she'd prevented him from going back on the run, the current pair simply showed that they were no longer new, but not to the point of being very faded. A pale blue T-shirt clung to his shoulders, pulled attractively over his chest, hinting at the firmly muscled body beneath the cloth. The rises and dips she loved to run her hands over as she traced his scars. The varied shades of azure ended with a pair of navy running shoes that looked comfortably broken in. Since everyone else in the room had chosen denim as the cloth of choice when dressing, she felt terribly overdressed in her gray business suit.

She was too used to blending into the surroundings, Gaelen decided. That was what made her feel disconnected from the other people in the room. Not just because they were all talking music, even around the pizza in nearly everyone's mouth. Part of her remembered being one with this world once upon a time. A long time ago.

C.C. and Jay came over to greet her. C.C. kissed her cheek, squeezed her shoulders. "Take your jacket off and relax, Gaelen," the older woman said. "We're just a group of old friends hanging out together here."

Apparently Pel's mother had noted the quick glances she'd given the famous people in the room—Montgomery and Nan.

Jay went with a more forward kiss on her lips and his arms around her torso for a hug. "She can't take the jacket off, Cec," he told his wife. "She's carryin'."

C.C. blinked and gave him a frown. "Carrying what?"

"She's armed," Pel explained, then gave her a studying look. "The usual pistol in the holster, but what's the one behind your back?"

Gaelen shook her head. "All the Flannery men are gropers, are they?"

"At least the two who *are* Flannery men," Jay said then jerked his chin toward the other men in the room. "I'll bet some of the fake ones are, too, though."

"I'll watch out for them, then," she replied and turned to Pel. "It's Luke's gun, same make as mine. What you carry said FBI and state police to him."

He groaned. "I think I've just been insulted."

"Well," she said, drawing the word out, "I did note that beneath the tail of that shirt that you, too, are still armed, Mr. Hastings. Anyone else realize you are?"

As C.C. looked shocked and Jay amused, she figured that some had and some hadn't.

"I believe there is a salad with my name on it somewhere, so if you'll excus—"

But lunch was put off yet again as the two superstars in the room pushed through the crowd of people standing around a dining room table rather than sitting at it. Open pizza boxes filled the surface. A surface that was extremely long and wide and yet totally hidden from view.

"I believe it's time to introduce me to this very special lady," Montgomery's sandpaper voice declared. Gaelen looked up into the face of a sun-weathered man in his late seventies. His white hair was still as thick as it had been in his youth when the color had been dark, and seemed just as disinclined to behave itself as it had on any photograph she'd ever seen of him. The creases at his eyes and around his mouth were quite obviously more the result of smiles than years.

Pel put his arm around her shoulders. Placed a quick kiss against her brow. "My disreputable godfather, Paul Montgomery," he said, but he looked beyond him to the mid-forties woman at Montgomery's shoulder. "And the irritating Nan Rawlins. Paul, Nan, Gaelen Shaw, the one whose idea all of this was."

"Then let loose of her, scamp, because that deserves a hug of appreciation," his godfather said.

"I know you," Pel warned. "You're never satisfied with just a hug."

Montgomery winked at her. "I didn't make a living writing love songs for nuthin'," he told her, then did indeed not only hug but kiss her, but on the top of her head.

"And I'm not chopped liver, either," Nan Rawlins insisted, shoving her uncle aside. "I'm so glad you convinced Pel to come back to us." A further hug accompanied by a brushing of cheeks happened.

"It's nice to meet you all."

"We're family," Paul said. "I understand you soon will be, too."

Gaelen frowned at Pel. "A pretend engagement."

Nan looked from her to Pel and back. "Sure, it is," she murmured. "Excuse me. Pizza is calling."

Montgomery cocked a brow in Pel's direction, then turned to C.C. and Jay. "Either of you two come up with a trumpet for us, or do we go with Lance?"

"Nan's husband's another brass man," Pel whispered near Gaelen's ear. Of course he was. She was definitely out of her depth with this crowd, musically speaking. *Remember what you* are *good at,* she lectured herself. It might not be singing, and she'd never played an instrument of any kind, but the twin Sigs she carried were good reminders of what she could do that these people couldn't do.

Keep Pel Flannery safe.

"Lance is good, though I think we could entice someone even better by dropping Pel's stage name," Jay said. "But with the limited time we have to pull things together, it makes sense to have Nan make the call."

"That's a terrible thing to say about Lance," C.C. insisted. "Personally, I think he's a better performer than you were at the same age, dear."

As they moved off toward the table, Gaelen heard Jay protesting, but it sounded to her as if he did it simply to get C.C. wound up for a brass-related argument. Montgomery trailed behind them looking amused.

Next to her, Pel sighed. "Welcome to life in the eat-'em-alive realm of the music world."

"You've missed it," Gaelen said. "I can tell. Grouch though you may, you're more relaxed despite the fact that, as I understand it, the plan is to do the show next week already."

"Monday," he affirmed, though he did so with a groan. "It will be a miracle production."

"You can do it, Pel."

He wrapped his arms around her more securely. "I need to kiss you much more thoroughly and quite often to make it through this, Ms. Shaw."

"Publicly?" Gaelen knew she sounded aghast at the idea.

"I do my best work *privately*. Why don't I give you a tour of the changes around here? One that will end in the master suite with the door closed."

"Pel," she warned.

"Just kissing," he promised. "One of these people will hunt us down—"

"Hunt *you* down," she countered.

"—and drag us apart with some question that could wait an hour or so for the answer, in normal circumstances."

"Which these aren't. I can see the changes here in the main room. No more sex on a hard floor before an empty fireplace." She sighed. "I might miss that."

"Personally, I've been thinking about all the furniture that needs to be christened by just that sort of fine detail."

She put her own arms around him. Settled into what she felt was the most perfect place to be— snugged torso to torso with him. His was brewing currently impossible scenarios, she noted.

"Will everyone be leaving the day after the show?" she asked.

"Yup."

"Then just six nights on your own to get through."

"Not that I'll be sleeping much," he said. "I'll be missing you."

"Liar," she countered. "You'll be fretting about the show, reviewing all those excuses you've made about it being a bad idea, either because it brings Jace Hastings back to life or that you think you've forgotten how to be him after all these years."

"Far more missing you will be in the mix, but you're right about the fretting. I suppose you'll be enjoying the sleep of the just?"

"I wish, though that's doubtful. My plate is pretty full right now. Mostly it will be…"

When she paused, he waited her out.

"I'll be missing you," she said.

Pel rested his forehead against hers. "You know, Ms. Shaw, I think you deserve the biggest, flashiest engagement ring Phoenix has to offer."

"For a fake engagement?"

He gave her the grin she loved. That patented Jace Hastings one. Or so she thought it, and only because the first time she'd fallen under its spell was in watching a video of Jace Hastings flashing it. There had been no beloved Pelham Flannery back then.

The grin widened. "Darlin'," he drawled. "Do you think there is a single person in this house right now who believes that we're only *fake* engaged?"

Over his shoulder she caught the quick glances and the wider smiles as the strangers in the room responded to the sight of his arms around her. Of hers around him.

"Come on," Pel urged. "Let's take that tour and hide out for a while to really sell the story."

"Someone will have eaten my salad."

"I've had my fill of pizza, and I've only had the bite Nan forced on me. I want something better for lunch."

Gaelen stared up into his face. "Would you give me a tour of the newly decorated house, Mr. Flannery? I need to check it over for security purposes, you see."

"Absolutely, Ms. Shaw. It's what I hired your firm

to see to."

As he led her out of the room, Gaelen glanced back and caught at least four people checking the time on their watches.

Chapter Twelve

The days went by as though driven by Santa Ana winds, something Phoenix didn't have, but Pel could think of no other comparison that fit as well. He'd probably lived in LA just long enough for the similarity to strike. The Virginia-DC area where he'd grown up didn't have anything quite the same for comparison with the speed at which everything came together.

Wednesday evening, the LA team had taken over several tables at C.C.'s for dinner, soaked up Rika and the trio's performance, then stayed on beyond closing. C.C. had introduced Montgomery and Nan, and Paul explained they'd like to add the locals to the recording session Monday night. The nondisclosure contract was laid out, and then the grand reveal—or so Pel thought it had felt like, since his godfather had beat a drumroll on the tabletop—of Jace Hastings, complete with contacts removed before their very eyes. Only one of the trio, the youngest, the drummer, had said, "Who?" The sax and guitarist stared at him in awe. But it was Rika who didn't look at him. She jumped to her feet and wrapped Gaelen in a hug that might have cracked ribs in its enthusiasm as she breathed, "You found him!" After that, it was all work.

Mornings he spent with his godfather, honing his performance skills once more. They settled on the final queue the songs would be played in, a plan that put him front and center for three fairly fast songs at the start. After that every few tunes one of the others took the mic for a single song before passing the buck back to him. By mid-show, things went into the most snailed-down score. After that it felt like a free-for-all.

With Nan's trumpet-playing husband's arrival the day after Nan called him, there had been a shift, with the couple taking C.C.'s spare room and Cliff moving into the room previously prepared for Nan at the house. The P.I. augmented the furnishings by hitting local businesses for three card tables, two folding metal chairs, a printer, and accompanying supplies. Printouts of Luke Wyndom's hidden cache proved to be the fastest system for sorting things, the detective had found.

For his own part, whenever he was allowed some downtime, Pel headed for the master bedroom, where his own laptop waited, and checked the status of his stocks. In those brief minutes of financial juggling, he realized that, given a choice, he'd rather be dealing with the thing that had made him far more money than Jace Hastings could ever bring in with recordings and tours. The stock portfolio had already acted as the launch pad for over a hundred projects financed by his one-man non-profit, Blue Marble Aid. Had he missed music enough to want to truly resuscitate Jace Hastings' career? Or was it that until the attempt was made, he'd never be able to shake the feeling that Rowan McTavish still waited like a spider to pounce and kill him?

If he could travel without that threat—*live* without that threat, there were so many more people he could help better their lives. More kids with instruments to use, whether it was with a career in music they craved or just a place in the school band. More wind farms, solar power facilities for small communities, more…

More of everything that made him feel like a man worth a fig. A man who still, occasionally, played music.

Until McTavish was no longer a threat, everything was nothing but a dream, a possibility. A lure.

Just as a life shared with Gaelen Shaw Wyndom had become, despite meeting her just ten days ago. Making love with her for the first time four days ago.

Being without her next to him in the suddenly far-too-large bed the past two nights had made them endless and restless ones.

A pattern to their days emerged quickly. An exodus of mock Flannery clan began early in the morning as nearly everyone headed for the golf course. At ten, Gaelen would arrive to pick Rory Montgomery up for shopping trips. Rory's forte was costuming, and not merely for C.C., Nan, and Rika. She'd included Gaelen in the list of women to deck out. "She's the most challenging to find something for," Rory told him. "I've never had to find an outfit that would keep an automatic pistol hidden before." When he'd called her in LA, the fashionista had been in total agreement that to sell the engagement, whether it be mock or not, Gaelen needed to be sporting a ring that combined conservative flash with elegance. Pel hadn't envied Rory the argument that would ensue at the jewelers, though. Although what was purchased suited the mission to sell their engagement, Gaelen had refused to put the ring on until absolutely necessary—which to her meant just before they opened the doors to the arriving journalists the night of the show.

A day and time that scared the living hell out of him. That fear needed locking down. The days were long, but they were filled with everything he'd missed for ten long years—family, friends, and music.

From the women's clothing needs, Rory had moved on to outfitting the C.C.'s trio in tuxes. The guitarist surprised everyone by lugging a huge double bass into the house rather than the expected bass guitar. He confessed to owning a tux because he occasionally picked up chamber music gigs with the fiddle. Paul, Lance, Jay, and himself had the required formalwear from awards show appearances. Just in case, Rory had made him try his on, since it had been hanging in C.C.'s closet during the years he'd been in hiding. If anything, she'd thought he looked better in it now, since he had a few more years of wear and tear on him.

Around the time the golfers drifted back, the local trio and Rika turned up for rehearsal, intense hours that left the C.C.'s group with three hours in which to have dinner and prepare to take the stage each evening at the restaurant.

A sign on the door at C.C.'s Place already announced that the club would be closed the following Monday for a private party but open for business as usual on Tuesday.

It just wouldn't be open for business as usual with him, Pel admitted. Monday night was going to change everything. Either he'd be back in demand as Jace Hastings, or Rowan McTavish would make a beeline for him and kill him successfully despite whatever Gaelen and Cliff did to protect him.

The first sign they were rushing things came Friday

when neither C.C. nor Nan could remember the Spanish words they were supposed to be singing as Rika's backup. Gael and Rory had just returned from another shopping trip when Montgomery called a halt.

"Paprika, *mi querida, cariño, chica*," he growled in fond exasperation as he put an arm around her shoulders. "Do you know anyone we can trust to not flub up your beautiful family tongue as these two *gringas* do so painfully?"

"*Si profesor*," Rika cooed. "*Mi amiga Senorita Gaelen. Ella habla bien el español.*"

"She lies," Gaelen said as she dropped her purse on the broad surface of one of the sofa tables.

"Do not," Rika countered.

"Children," Montgomery chided as he strode past the patiently dormant drummer with his bongos and snagged the lyric sheet from Nan. "Give it a try, Gael. At least show C.C. and Nan that it is possible to master."

"Go on, Gaelen," Rory urged. She tossed her own purse aside and dropped into the comfort of the sofa that faced the piano where Pel sat with C.C. and Nan bracketing him on either side.

"Come on, slick," he urged. "Prove to me that you have pipes."

"My pipes are rusted from disuse," she insisted.

"Not as bad as mine," Pel countered.

"Yours were always better, Mr. Hastings."

He snorted. Montgomery chuckled. "Gaelen, come on. Be a sport. It's not like we're asking you to step on stage, just act as a crutch until Cec and Nan get their tongues around things."

Which was a lie. They needed a third backup

singer for the song, and every word Paul and Rika said had been planned beforehand. Even Rory knew they planned to lure Gaelen on stage. She'd made sure that what Gaelen would be wearing Monday night was jet black and featured sequins like the things chosen for the other three females to wear. To make the lovely P.I. think it was simply a theme that everyone would be wearing, Rory had a similar outfit. They were even sticking Cliff in a tux.

Besides, C.C. and Nan weren't mispronouncing the words in a mock backup disaster. Neither was used to singing in a foreign tongue and clearly showing why that had always been a wise decision on their parts in the past.

When Gaelen relented and took the page of lyrics from Paul, Pel felt his mother rub her hand against his back, giving a light massage of approval for the tactic.

"Give me a minute," Gaelen said. He could almost hear her caressing the words although she made not a sound as she perused them.

"I'll give you five," Paul said and turned back to Rika. "Now, *chica*. What happened to those sexy moves we've all watched you make on stage the past two evenings? Pel arranged this with a Latin beat, probably just for you, if I know my godson."

Rika's dark eyes widened as she looked across the top of the grand. "You did? Pel!"

"So do it proud," he told her.

She flashed him a wide thank-you smile, then turned back to the team mentor. "You want me to dance as I sing, Professor?"

"In the parlance of my era, I want you to shake your booty, *chica*. Performance is what that Ph.D. says

I drum into heads best. Taught the two youngsters over there all they know."

"Did not," Pel and Nan said in unison.

"Pay them no attention," Montgomery insisted. "Ingrates, both of them. You want the audience's eyes on you, not them. Give the crowd a reason for their eyes to stick on you when you're front and center."

"This is a great choice for a song," Gaelen noted, glancing up from the lyrics.

"Pel's idea. I give credit where credit is due, but he isn't very original. India did a Latin version of this song back in the Nineties."

"When I was in elementary school!" Pel complained in exasperation. "I lived with people who listened to folk music at the time, too."

Paul looked at his niece. Then, in sync, they played invisible violins.

Even from across the room, Pel could see Gaelen was fighting not to laugh.

"I'm waiting for a performance here," Rory Montgomery reminded them. "I could be taking a nap—"

She was booed by the performers in the room, all of whom had been hard at work for hours without a break. A break they couldn't afford to take. Well, *he* couldn't afford to take, Pel admitted. Monday was galloping at them. There were two days left to practice, then Monday afternoon would be a full run-through, followed by a dress rehearsal. He'd be hoarse by then. Despite palming off some songs on the others, he'd still be the main performer for fourteen songs and, if pushed to it, a fifteenth as an encore.

"Do I stand behind Pel, then?" Gaelen asked.

"Nope, when singing, we've had our backup team stand against the wall next to the piano," Montgomery said.

"In line for the firing squad," Nan added.

"You stand between the two of us," C.C. said. "That way we can both hear the correct pronunciation when you sing it, Gaelen."

"We've got the English bits down pat," Nan explained. "It's the Spanish tail, after that, we aren't wagging to Uncle Paul's—"

"Or Pel's—" C.C. griped.

"—satisfaction yet."

"People?" Paul picked up the conductor's baton he'd brought along.

Pel flexed his fingers. Kept his eyes on his godfather as Montgomery raised the stick, gave them a count of four, then cued the bongos and the piano. Six bars in, Rika burst into song.

And when the backup singers joined in, he discovered that Gaelen Shaw Wyndom had lied to him.

Her voice was strong, lyrical. Equal in every way to the other talent taking the stage Monday night. She simply didn't believe it was.

****

Montgomery gave the backup singers a break, shooing them off to practice their Spanish, with Rika the stand-in teacher. Gaelen bowed out with the excuse that she needed to see how Cliff was doing in unraveling Luke's secret gift.

She found him leafing through a batch of print-offs as though looking for something specific. He also had high quality headphones on. To block the sound of voices and instruments? In the main room, the three men making up the brass section were running through an old Sixties song, melding the blaring voices of their horns with the piano. It sounded like Paul Montgomery was lending vocals and that any backup voices were those of the guitarist, the drummer, and probably Pel. From the other end of the house, men's voices swore at recording equipment that wasn't cooperating with them. She could barely hear the Spanish lyrics being warbled, which meant when C.C. led Nan and Rika to the master bedroom, she'd probably closed the door to cut down on interference from the racket around them.

But as she moved farther into the guest bedroom Cliff had requisitioned, Gaelen realized he was listening to audio from a recording that was playing on his laptop.

And that on the screen was a very intense Luke Wyndom.

Cliff glanced up, saw her fixated, and hastily stopped the playback. Took the headphones off. Pulled the spare metal chair up and forced her to sit down. Then he closed the door she'd left open behind her and returned to his chair.

"I found this maybe ten minutes ago," he said. "It isn't long. I've watched it twice already and am trying to find the documents Luke's talking about in the recording. If you're up to listening to it—"

"I need to," she interrupted.

"You need to," he agreed. "Mostly because he's talking to you on it, Gaeley. You listen while I keep searching for the documents in question." Then he handed over the headphones, backed the recording up, and set it in motion once more.

On the screen, Luke leaned forward, apparently

adjusting something. As she watched, he settled back in his chair. From the background, she knew he'd made the video in their apartment. The apartment where she still lived. She could see the kitchen cabinets behind him. See the patterns the late afternoon sun made on them as it streamed through the western-facing window.

He was still dressed for the office, his favorite blue dress shirt on, the one he said was his favorite because the color matched her eyes. He'd stripped off the tie and unbuttoned the shirt halfway down his sun-bronzed chest. He'd been wearing what she always told him was *her* favorite among his shirts the day he'd been killed, the lovely aqua-checked one. She remembered briefly straightening the collar as he slid the double Windsor knot of his tie into place at the base of his throat that morning.

Two days after his death, she'd emptied the laundry hamper and found the blue shirt. It was the only item of his clothing that she'd kept. She'd washed it only after the scent of him on it was as gone as Luke was. The bared chest visible on the video was still alive and not sporting gunshot wounds. She was glad she had this version of Luke to block out the one of him in the morgue. While his appearance shouted that he was a man ready to relax at home after a long day at the office, his expression was tense. He looked tired. Frustrated.

Worried. Perhaps even a bit frightened.

"Gaeley," he said, his voice nearly harsh with emotion. "I'm leaving this for you as an insurance policy. One that I hope to God you never have to see, but that's beginning to look like the only option we'll be given.

"You know I haven't trusted Dad in a long time, but I just thought it was because of the way he ran the agency. The way he treated Mom. You know how cold he was when she died. Told us to take what furniture and keepsakes we wanted because he'd listed the house with a realtor and scheduled a charity shop to come take the rest of the things away at the end of the week. Mom hadn't been dead two days yet."

She remembered all too well. While Hank had offered the things to them, he hadn't wanted to give them any time off from the cases in progress to actually have time to pack things up. If Cliff and his wife hadn't helped toss things into a rental truck, the apartment would have continued to be very empty. When they'd married, she'd been Rika's roommate, but just as they did, Luke had lived in a furnished place. Her apartment still looked like someone else's home because, other than the bed, she and Luke hadn't chosen a single piece of furniture as theirs alone. Even now, for the few times she fixed something to eat at home, it was served on the china his parents had gotten as wedding presents. Hank himself had moved into an extended-stay hotel, his reasoning being that not only was the place cleaned regularly by staff, but the service included everything a man needed—cable television, wi-fi, a landline, and a free breakfast.

"I started looking into a few things that rang warning bells to me about Dad's business practices," Luke explained on the recording. "Today I talked to an FBI agent that a cop named Valente set me up with. The Feds were already keeping an eye on Desert Wynd. I'm just glad I convinced them that you and I had nothing to do with Dad's cases. His *secret* cases, honey.

There's not enough time to explain it all to you. The stuff I've loaded to the flash drives should speak for itself. I probably should have just turned it over to the Feds, but I didn't. We—you and me—need the leverage in the event things heat up more with Dad. I know you don't trust him because I don't trust him, but you've never really known why I don't trust him. It has nothing to do with the way he treated Mom, though that was bad enough. She never let on, and since he wasn't physically abusive, I'd no idea what was going on. When she was dying, she told me to never let him treat you the same way."

Luke paused. Grinned. "As if you'd ever put up with it. You're strong, Done Deal. You're feisty. But get the hell out of Desert Wynd. Call Cliff. He'll find you someone to complete your training. Then turn everything on these thumb drives over to Valente. The FBI is only interested in some of this stuff. Valente will slaver over all of it. It should clear up a lot of local cases that have gone cold."

He took a deep breath. "Sorry I couldn't be the right man for you, honey. You were always the right gal for me, though. I will indeed love you forever. But if you're watching this, it was a very short forever."

Through tear-drenched eyes, she watched as he kissed his fingertips, tossing the kiss across the table at the screen just as he'd often tossed a kiss across that same table to her at the end of a meal. Then Luke Wyndom leaned forward, reached toward something she couldn't see, and the screen went blank.

Silently, Cliff handed her a handkerchief. "I'm looking for the things Valente will be most interested in," he said as he continued to rummage through the pile of papers scattered around on the card tables. "Nearly everything is a homicide, but there's also drug running, money laundering, and a few other things that are probably what the Feds are interested in, as they seem to cross state lines. I remember some of this from news reports even back when I was a cop here in Phoenix."

Gaelen reached over and squeezed his hand. "Without you knowing Luke's numerical code, we'd never have found any of this, Cliff. I've been thinking about the things I packed and those I tossed after Luke died. There were pages with lists of numbers on them, but they also had his usual doodles, you know, the ones he'd make while on the phone. I can't help wondering whether he'd added those silly pictures so it didn't look like he was leaving me a code. Not even to me, because I threw them out. If I'd opened that paperback book back then—"

Cliff squeezed her hand in return. "You would have called me, Gaeley, and asked if I had any idea of what the password might be. We'd have found this sooner, but Luke was just as lost then as he is now." He'd stopped going through the papers as she watched Luke's last message to her but now released their shared grip to continue sorting documents. "If it's all right with you, I'll be the one to connect with Valente. Your priority is keeping Pel alive. And yourself."

"Myself?"

Cliff stopped rifling. Looked her in the eye. "Honey. Rowan McTavish isn't just going to want to finish what he attempted to do a decade ago in getting rid of the man he saw as his rival for Ashley Hopper. He wants to get back at Jace Hastings for losing him

Ashley Hopper simply by letting her drive his car. The car everyone knew he never let anyone else *ever* drive. The best way to do that is not just to kill the man then known as Jace Hastings, but to even things by…"

"By killing the one thing he will think Jace Hastings needs stolen. A woman."

"A woman who, as of Monday night, will be touted as the fiancée of Jace Hastings."

Her eyes were dry now. "Nice of Pel to suggest it, then, wasn't it?"

"You didn't fight too hard against the idea."

"As long as it wasn't a real engagement."

"It will be as far as Rowan McTavish is concerned. And I agreed with Pel on the idea, if you remember. Why did you agree?"

She bit the corner of her lip before answering. "Because it gave me the best reason to stay close enough to protect him. Did you have a different reason in mind when you agreed with the idea?"

"I did, indeed. It splits McTavish's goal, makes him less intent on Pel because he'll see you as a way to hurt Jace Hastings more."

"Before he kills Pel, as well."

"Gaeley. The only one likely to die is Rowan McTavish, and that's only if he isn't as insane as he might be. The man has illustrated that he does have a logical mind. He figured out a way to beat the system. Gave himself a profession where it wouldn't matter that he was an ex-con but possibly enhance his worth to the group that invited him to join them. Remember, both Pel and you will be safe until the news hits the Internet that Jace Hastings is alive, about to return to the stage again on a regular basis, *and* is in love. Not only do I intend to shadow the two of you, but I also know that neither of you are ever without a weapon of your own. There is little chance that McTavish knows that."

She sighed, knowing Cliff was right. She'd made Pel bait to draw McTavish out by getting Jace Hastings performing once more. Being bait herself was the right thing to do.

"Then I think it's time to take potshots at targets at the range," Gaelen said. "Don't want to be rusty."

"I'll go with you. We should take Pel with us. We set up some targets on the property yesterday during a break, and he's pretty good, but pretty good might not be good enough. While the others hang out at C.C.'s, the three of us will hit the range later tonight and possibly the next two nights as well, if that's possible. Montgomery runs a tight ship, but it's amazing how quickly he's got things running smoothly."

"He just suckered me into singing backup behind Rika a little bit ago. I'm hoping it was just to help C.C. and Nan master the Spanish, and not something more."

Cliff grinned. "No telling with this crew. You okay with me taking over the stuff Luke left for you?"

"In a roundabout way, he sorta told me to involve you just a bit ago," Gaelen said, gesturing toward the now sleeping laptop. "I've still got my cover of being Rory's muscle to live through. I don't think I've ever done so much shopping in my entire life. That muscle I mentioned? It's all tied up in hefting packages. She's moved on from choosing costumes to cruising the various shops for squash blossom necklaces, Navaho rugs, Papago basketwork, and whatever else catches her eye. I will admit that her taste is impeccable. It shows me how lacking in it I am."

"You're getting an entire new wardrobe out of it, aren't you?"

"How did—" she began, then ground to a halt. "Rika told you, didn't she? You two have been acting very cozy."

Cliff shrugged. "So maybe your problem wasn't the only thing luring me back to Arizona. It wasn't exactly my idea to move away. Eve claimed she missed the ocean."

"It's what happens when you marry a coast girl," Gaelen said. "She could go on *ad infinitum* about sailing, surfing, beach parties her senior year, and doing nothing but lying on the sand while waves rolled in over her. Gotta admit, I tuned her out pretty fast. It all sounded boring to me. I'd rather be working on something. Once it was on song stylings, but investigative work is even better. You never mentioned why the two of you divorced, so what caused the breakup?"

"A guy thirty years older, with a yacht, looking for a decorative item to have on his arm. Actually, I was ready to shake his hand for taking her off my hands by then."

"So you've taken up with Paprika Mendez, the ultimate glittery item to have on a fella's arm. I think Pel and Montgomery have plans to make her a star, Cliffy. What will you do when she heads to California herself?"

He leaned back in the uncomfortable metal chair, a grin on his face. "Follow wherever she wants to go. And you know why?"

"Why?"

"Because, Gaeley, Paprika Mendez doesn't see

herself as a glittery item to grace any guy's arm. She's a force of nature unto herself, and I have always found her the most exciting woman in the universe."

Gaelen leaned forward. Poked her forefinger into his chest. "If you ever stop feeling that way, you've got me to answer to, buddy," she warned.

If anything, his smile was wider. "Wouldn't have it any other way, honey. Swear ta God."

****

The first leak about the show had only one thing going for it, in Pel's estimation. It didn't mention Jace Hastings.

But it did mention Paul Montgomery.

Spotted enjoying the entertainment at C.C.'s Place in Surprise, the man who could be said to have put the 'M' in music, Paul Montgomery, a reporter at the *Phoenix Herald* gushed in the Saturday online edition.

"Where did he get a sappy line like that?" Paul demanded, handing back the tablet Pel had passed him. Then Montgomery picked up his cell and logged onto the Net. Since Pel was standing behind the sofa his godfather had stretched out on, he had no problem reading what the man Tweeted.

#paulmontgomery baking in the arizona desert with friends and hosting a show monday night

"Are you insane?" he demanded. "This is supposed to be top secret until after the show, when you go back to LA and I most likely get killed."

"You won't get killed," Paul said. "You've got the crack team of Gaelen and Cliff to take a bullet for you."

"Not what I want them to do."

"Not what they particularly want to do, either. It's not like you're the president, or me."

"You don't travel with a security team."

"I don't go around armed, either," Montgomery reminded. "Considering I haven't managed to go anywhere for decades without being recognized, it's fate that someone saw Red and me at C.C.'s one of the past nights. Add Nan to that equation, and there was no keeping a hat on things. All they know is that something's happening, but not with whom or even where."

Pel leaned a hip against the long narrow sofa table that separated them. "They can guess the *where* easily enough. There's a huge sign on the door at C.C.'s that the joint is closed for a private party on Monday."

"It's an eleven-by-eight-and-a-half sheet of paper you printed off in your office, kid." But as Paul then swung his legs off the sofa and stood up, phone in hand as he crossed to the patio doors, Pel knew his godfather was totally enjoying making him jumpy. When Paul slid the door open, went out on the paved expanse, walked to the far end, lifted his phone and clicked the camera feature on it, immortalizing the natural desert landscape around them, Pel ground his teeth. "This'll look good on my social media pages, and you don't have to worry. There is nothing in the picture that pinpoints our location here."

Not to him, but to a local? Pel doubted the landscape was that blasé.

"I'm telling your wife on you," he declared, the ultimate weapon to use against this particular superstar.

"I am quaking in my boots," Montgomery assured him. "But she'll agree with me. Red's gotten to be extremely savvy when it comes to media promotion. She's the one who knew which people to invite to this shindig. She's the one who lured them in without telling them a damn thing."

"And here I thought she liked me," Pel moaned.

"You're the son we never had and are just glad C.C. and Jay don't mind sharing you."

"I'm all choked up," Pel said, not sounding like it in the least. "About the show…"

Montgomery moved back inside the house. Slid the door closed, blocking out the heat once more, and sighed quietly in relief as the air conditioning wrapped around him again. It was August, which meant the desert roasted under a blanket of at least 105 degrees. Indoors, the cooling kept it at a steady 68. "What about the show?"

"C.C. and Dad want to add a song. It would just be the three of us doing it and cancels out what we originally planned for her to sing. It's my own fault. A while back I scored 'Desperado' for her, and she claims it suits the show, which since more than one of the songs make a guarded reference to my hiding out for years and that I'm now in love—"

"Which you have all the indications of actually being, this time out," Paul added.

"That transparent, am I?"

"To those who know you best. To those who watched you fake the feeling for the cameras with Ash, yes, we can tell this is real for you. However, it's Gael you have to convince."

"Not an easy task," Pel admitted. "On Monday, it will be two weeks since we met. That doesn't sound like enough time to know this is it, does it?"

Montgomery grinned and dropped back down on the sofa again. "No law that sets a time on how long it takes to fall in love. Sometimes you know right away. Sometimes you fight it. Sometimes you welcome it. It all depends on where you are when you meet the right person."

"I think I'll agree with Rory. All those love songs you've written have warped your brain."

Paul snorted at the very idea. "I wrote every one of them with her in mind."

"Good thing I don't write love songs," Pel said.

"You just sing them, and, pal, the way you're singing the ones on that list you gave me, you got it bad. So where would you like to slip 'Desperado' into the lineup?"

"It doesn't fit as well where we had Cec's original song, so preferably another spot where my voice needs a rest. All I'm required to do on it is play the piano a bit as Dad's soloing on the trombone."

"Then how about dropping the Debarge number, which is rather long, so we can save some time with the switch. Move 'What You Won't Do for Love' into that spot, and stick 'Desperado' between 'Quiet Fire' and the instrumental take on 'That's the Way of the World'?"

Damn, but it was great to work with Montgomery again. He might be edging on eighty, but his mind when it came to music was as sharp as ever.

"Work for you?" his godfather asked.

"Yep. Particularly since, after that, it's all on me to bring this thing home," Pel said.

"Drop in the bucket, kid. And, while we're talking music, I want to add you to my line-up for the holiday special at the network. It won't run until after Thanksgiving, but we're filming it in early October.

Interested?"

Pel stared at the ceiling a moment or two, as though evaluating. "What's it pay?" he asked at length.

Montgomery chuckled. "Yeah, you're doing it," he said.

As if there had ever been a doubt. The only reason he wouldn't do the guest appearance was if Rowan McTavish made good on the threat issued a decade ago. *Catch ya later.*

****

For a man she actually liked as a person and admired as a performer, Paul Montgomery really knew how to get under her skin, Gaelen admitted when yet another social media note popped up dropping hints about the Monday night performance. Fortunately, while he mentioned his long-time friends C.C. Pelham and Jay Flannery, his niece Nan Rawlins and her husband Lance, called Paprika Mendez a powerhouse that Phoenix had been keeping under wraps, and named the three guys in the trio that backed her up at C.C.'s, he made no mention of a secret performer. To all intents and purposes, this was simply a by-invitation-only for entertainment critics that featured performers whose careers ranged from legendary (Montgomery's) to budding (Rika and the trio).

Between them, she and Cliff had kept Pel away from the group the past two nights. He was fine with drive-thru take-out for dinner and a destination of the firing range as entertainment. She found that Cliff had downplayed Pel's skill with his gun. The man was her equal when it came to ripping the hell out of the center circle on the paper targets.

But it also gave her a chance to look at the

markings of the spent bullet casings from his gun and mentally compare them to those she remembered studying in the evidence box at the precinct. All she learned was that whoever had killed Luke Wyndom hadn't used something from the same manufacturer. They hadn't used one from the maker of Cliff's preferred weapon either.

"As I see it," Cliff told them both as they climbed into his truck Saturday night after the practice session, "the only problem we have is that neither of you two has ever done anything other than fire at a stationary target on the range. Unless you're holding out on us, Pel, and actually have needed to take potshots at another shooter."

"Only served as a target for someone else," Pel admitted, taking the shotgun position when Gaelen waved him toward the forward door.

"And I've seen the scar to prove it," she verified as she climbed up to the banquette seat in the rear of the cab and swung the door closed. "Right along his ribs."

"Too close for my comfort," Cliff said. "This means that from the moment the people we allow in the door begin posting to their media accounts after the show, I'm shadowing you both. As a former police officer, I *have* sighted down on an armed person and had to take them down."

"Have you needed to do it as a P.I. in LA or while you were one in Phoenix?" Pel asked.

Gaelen thought it a fair question. She was a P.I. in Phoenix and had never needed to draw her weapon on a case, though that was probably because Hank had never given her a case that might require that sort of action. Either he or one of the male idiots he'd hired took on those assignments, and they were few and far between as it was.

Cliff turned the engine over. It purred contentedly. She'd been surprised that he hadn't switched to a sedan once he'd moved to LA, but apparently you could take the man out of the desert, but you couldn't take the desert out of a man who'd grown up as he had in Apache Junction, a small community *in* the desert.

"More than once," he admitted, "and it's never a nice thing to need to do. But when it's a them-or-me situation, I'd prefer them to be the ones going down."

"Don't we all," she said. "You're worried that we'd freeze, aren't you."

Cliff tapped the end of his nose as he pulled back into traffic. "I sure the hell did as a rookie cop, and you've never been a cop. Now, am I right in thinking this is our last evening of fun without the rest of the group?"

Pel sighed. "Far too right. Tomorrow's the last chance to hit all the notes and all the words right."

"You're worried C.C. and Nan are still struggling with the Spanish?"

"Naw, they've made great strides," he admitted. "I've flubbed up the words in a couple songs. Didn't hit the note dead-on in others. I'm afraid tomorrow it's like studying for a final exam. But I'll admit that back when Jace Hastings was drawing in the crowds, up until the day of a performance things went wrong. Paul admits the same thing. There is something about being on stage that cures it. At least it did for him, and it used to do it for me, too." Pel twisted in his seat, glancing to where she sat in the center of the rear seat. "You have that problem when you were singing for your supper,

Gael?"

She shook her head. "But I didn't have a specialized type of performance as you and your godfather have always had. Even when Pel Flannery accompanies C.C. Pelham and doesn't sing himself, there is still something about what you do that isn't like what we run-of-the-mill performers achieve. It's why Rika has star power and I lack it. I was a hack singer, and hack singers don't attempt things that others do."

"It wouldn't take much, slick," Pel said. "I could turn that around with a bit of coaching."

She grinned at him. Outside the window, Phoenix whipped by as Cliff got on I-10 west, headed for the Route 60 link northwest into Surprise. "Thanks for the offer, but I found what I do best and what I am not a hack at, and that's investigative work."

"Then how goes the investigation into the things Luke left for you on those thumb drives?"

"Cliff took them out of my hands. He told me I already had a case, and that was keeping you safe."

"And I passed them along to a local detective on the police force that both Luke and I knew. He's handling things in that regard, so I too am on Pel Flannery preservation duty," the LA P.I. said.

"Rather anticlimactic, isn't it?" Pel queried. "Like reading a mystery story and finding someone ripped the final pages out."

"At least when that happens you can always get another copy of the book. Valente promised to keep me in the loop, so when I learn something, I'll fill in those final pages for you both."

Which was good to know, Gaelen admitted to herself, but it also meant that Sunday was going to be a very boring day for both herself and Cliff. All the musicians and recording techs would be harried, but they wouldn't be leaving the house, either. Even with Montgomery's—and Nan's—social media posts tantalizing their fans, there were no hints that Jace Hastings was alive and would be the main attraction on Monday night. Even if they tricked her into singing backup for Rika, she'd just be in the way. It felt strange to get pulled back into the music business and yet not be a part of it. This time she was truly on the outside looking in, and the view was nothing like she'd ever experienced during her short career before a mic.

"I take it there will be no visits to the golf course tomorrow morning, then?"

"As I understand it, trophies are going to be exchanged over dinner at C.C.'s tonight, so the Flannery Family Reunion ruse has ended," Pel said. "Why?"

Gaelen shrugged, attempting to look casual, though the closer they got to the day of the show, the stiffer her neck felt. "Just wondering if I should bring donuts when I show up tomorrow morning."

When he chuckled, she envied his ability to act relaxed when he was anything but that. "I've seen the way this horde inhales any type of food. Better make it four dozen, at least, and heavy on the icing and cream filling."

"You got it," she promised and settled farther into her seat for the rest of the drive back to the desert house.

****

Monday came too soon. And not soon enough for Pel's peace of mind. The evening before, after extremely tense run-throughs, Rika and the local trio were given the evening off to recover in preparation for yet another extremely long show day. In their place, his godfather, C.C., and his father had volunteered to perform Sunday night at the restaurant. Paul was taking over the piano, Cec planned to hoard the mic, and Jay claimed he was just going to enjoy himself by winging things. It was to be an unplanned show, and thus they were simply going to ask for requests and patch something together on the spot. "Which is always the most fun you can have on stage," Montgomery claimed. C.C. and Jay agreed with him.

Cliff invited Rika out for dinner. Nan and Lance planned a computer chat visit with their kids. The Visions Records crew had opted for a night of bowling as a way of relaxing. That left the desert house empty but for himself and Gaelen. Pel intended to make the most of the few hours they had alone. The only downside to it was that other than a few cold cuts left over from lunch and the five glazed donuts that remained from breakfast, there was nothing to eat in the place.

Fortunately, Gaelen appeared to be hungry for the same thing he was—sex. Although the clock was ticking on the limited time they'd have alone, he'd taken his time, enjoying the feel of her, the taste of her. She hadn't felt the need to talk either but had an intent need to trace each of the scars he carried. It had been as erotic as hell.

And had merely whetted his appetite for more in, hopefully, a shared future with her. A future alone was no longer thinkable. He only hoped she would not have to see him as she had Luke Wyndom in the police file, a bullet-riddled shell on a morgue table.

"When this is over, I don't want *this* to be over," he whispered when she was tucked against his side, his arm around her shoulders, her leg hitched across his body.

"I don't either," she murmured, running a finger along the Jace Hastings scruff he'd been cultivating for two days. "But things will have changed. Jace Hastings will belong to the world of music. You'll need to be on the road again, only this time traveling as you did as a performer, not a man in hiding."

"I don't *have* to go anywhere. I can live Pel Flannery's life instead. I like his latest life." He let the fingers of his free hand brush across her collarbone, drop lower to tease the rosy tip of her breast. "It has benefits that were lacking in Jace Hastings'."

"Pel Flannery doesn't belong to the world. Jace Hastings does," she insisted. "I know you've already said yes to being part of Paul's holiday special, but Nan asked you to be part of her tour early next year, too. The recording of tomorrow night's show will be released prior to that, won't it?"

"Paul's throwing his influence around, urging it be available for download and in stores in December. Ride the wave of the televised appearance into gifts under the tree, he says. I put Nan off because, despite how you feel about it, Jace Hastings doesn't belong to the world."

"Pel," she chided, placing her hand over his roving one. Since that merely stilled it, pressing it lightly against her soft, warm skin, he soaked up the intimacy. "There are a lot of people out there who haven't forgotten what Jace Hastings did with a song."

"Fans who found someone else to follow when they thought Hastings dead, Gael. They can live without me."

"This fan can't," she said.

"*This* fan doesn't have to. I'll sing for you, play for you, anytime, slick. An audience of one suits me just fine."

She sighed. "You say that now. But wait until you hear the applause, have the wave of adulation wash over you again. That's heady stuff, Pel. I know it is, and I never had more than the appreciation of a small audience. After the last note has been played, the final lyric sung tomorrow night—"

"I won't have changed my mind," he said. "That's not what I want any longer. It's not what I need. Yes, I missed music when I put it aside as a precautionary measure. But music is not necessary to keep my sanity any longer. This is."

She pushed upright, leaning on one arm as she brushed back the swing of chestnut hair that fell forward over her bare shoulder. "*This* isn't a guaranteed thing, Pel."

He played with a strand of her hair. "Do you think Luke Wyndom was the only man who has wished to love you forever, Gael?"

"No," she whispered. "I'm afraid it isn't how you think you feel, or how Luke claimed he did. The problem, Pel, is that *I've* never loved anyone that way. I'm not sure I'm capable of doing it. I can only ever promise to love you the same way I did Luke. Just until I'm ready to move on."

"Then that, Gaelen Shaw, is what I'll take," he said and drew her down to seal the promise with a kiss.

Chapter Thirteen

Monday morning, Gaelen found her role in things had changed once again. Rory Montgomery slipped into the role of coordinator, and Gaelen became her nearly overworked assistant. It was like doing undercover work in an understaffed office or taking on a between-gigs clerical position where she felt clueless about the assignments given.

Scott and his recording crew took off in the moving van they'd rented for the equipment. Tom, the chef at C.C.'s, was scheduled to meet them to open the door and turn off the alarm system. The day before, C.C.'s staff had been let in on who they'd been working for, complete with those nondisclosure forms. Gaelen felt an entire forest had been felled to accommodate the legalities. By the time she and Rory arrived, Tom and his staff were elbow deep on preliminaries for the hors d'oeuvres to be served at the post-show cocktail party. By noon, the van had returned to the desert house to load the rolling racks with the costumes hanging on them. Rory refused to let anyone don what they'd wear on stage prior to suiting up for the dress rehearsal. "We'll have no wrinkles," she ordered. A few saluted her. Those with far more sense had just followed instructions.

Not counting time for applause, the combined length of the songs being performed was clocking in under ninety minutes. A decent length for a CD, those who had CDs for sale agreed. There would be two run-throughs, one dressed in what everyone had thrown on that morning, and the second in full show regalia. The first guests were due to arrive at eight. The performers were left wondering at what time they'd take the stage, though, because Rory insisted it wouldn't be until every guest was in the door. She already had plastic bags with guest names on them where each arrival would be forced to deposit cell phones and any other electronic device before being allowed inside. Cliff had applied to Valente for four off-duty police officers in dark suits to be on hand, two to be stationed at the front door to frisk people for electronics or weapons, though electronics were what they expected. One would have the rear door as his station, and the fourth was stuck with the doors leading to the outdoor patio. The only reason anyone inside would be allowed out was if the place was on fire.

Gaelen met the cops quickly in passing, letting Cliff handle security. Rory had her stationed at Pel's computer to take dictation. An electronic document would be sent to the email boxes of all the invited music columnists once the last one had left C.C.'s Place that night. The documents would list all performers and songs plus give information about Jace Hastings' Blue Marble Aid nonprofit, which would be reaping all royalties from the sale of *Jace Hastings Alive and Kickin'* when it released. Once all the performers were suited up, Rory insisted they needed a group picture to include and enlisted Cliff to take one. It wouldn't stop some of the guests from hanging around the parking lot to take their own candid shots for immediate posting once their electronics were returned, they all knew.

"How long ago was it that you gave up your fashion business?" Gaelen asked between the assignments Rory gave her.

"Sold it the summer of 1994," Montgomery's wife said. "Paul was insisting he was giving up performing, but I knew he was kidding himself. Plus, he belonged on a stage. It's where he's most alive. So I transferred what I knew over to promoting a show. Not just for Paul but for anyone he took under his wing."

When the woman paused, Gaelen found herself being studied. "What will you do when Pel is back on the stage regularly? Stay in Phoenix and run the investigation agency? Or will you go on the road with him?"

"I doubt the situation will come up," Gaelen admitted. "This is just a fake engagement, you know."

Rory smiled in a way that said she didn't believe it in the least.

"It's the only reason I agreed to it." Yet, at the same time, there was a part of her that wanted it *not* to be an act. Was it the part of her that had been a diehard fan of Jace Hastings in college, though, or was it the woman she was now? The one Pel said he'd be content with for as long a time as she wanted to give him. She hadn't even been in love with Luke Wyndom a year before realizing she wasn't any longer. What if that was all the time she'd believe herself in love with Pelham Flannery?

"Subject closed, then," Rory said. "Now, proof-reading time. This has got to be perfect before it gets sent out electronically later tonight. This has been a really intense stay, but tomorrow morning the exodus to the airport and LA begins. I think I'd like to come back and visit Phoenix during one of our downtimes. Can Paul and I count on you to be our local guide when we do?"

"Without a doubt," Gaelen promised, then gestured to the computer screen. "Now, I just have two questions. When did my name get added to this tally, and why is it there?"

"Oh, didn't anyone tell you, darling?" Rory queried totally failing to look surprised. "I added it because you're one of the backup singers—at least when Rika needs an extra one."

****

It took longer than expected to get the guests in the door and settled with free drinks to keep them happy, mostly because very few were willing to give up their electronics without an argument. Gaelen and Rory were the greeters needing to deal with the resistant, though it was Rory Montgomery who stared them all down to compliance. Gaelen wondered if it was a trait the woman had honed in her fashion career or afterwards.

Once everyone was inside C.C.'s Place, the extra security closed the blinds on the entrance door, the side windows, and the patio doors, cutting the sunlight out and throwing the dining room into cozy obscurity.

There were fewer tables and chairs than during normal business hours, since they'd needed to clear room for the recording equipment, but they'd also wanted a wide enough margin between the stage and the reporters.

Once he'd been miked, Montgomery took the stage to welcome everyone.

She and Rory stood at the back of the room, their

dresses glinting. Montgomery's wife had chosen a different style for each of the women, though all were black and featured sequins. Rika's was the most eye-catching—a strapless, tight-fitting gown drenched in the glittery bits of light. Gaelen was simply glad the jacket that covered her black dress was the only item that glittered, though the simple styling of it seemed cut from sequin-enhanced cloth. She couldn't do without the jacket, though, for Rory had stuck her with a halter top that left her back bare and tumbled in a waterfall of ebony silk that barely hid the fact that nothing held the bodice together but perfect posture. It did, however, hide the holster just within the waistband, with her handgun snugged inside it.

When Pel had seen her in the costume, a special glint had appeared in his gorgeous green eyes. Perhaps there had been a similar glint in hers when she saw him in the conservative black tuxedo, white shirt, and black bow tie. He was a very recognizable Jace Hastings, since his hair had been dyed dark again. The couple days' growth of groomed dark scruff along his jawline solidified the Jace Hastings mien. Amazingly, he looked cool, calm, collected. If she slipped her hand inside his jacket and rested it over his heart, would she find it was anything but calm? Her own nerves seemed stretched to the limit. This was worse than getting on a stage by herself. Perhaps it was because she hadn't been surrounded by music icons before? Or was it that there was more at stake than just a musical performance that night?

"Ms. Shaw," he purred, slipping an arm around her. Beneath her jacket, she noted. "Only one weapon tonight?"

"I'm trying to cut back, Mr. Hastings," she murmured as his fingers brushed up her bare spine.

"You look extremely delectable, slick."

"I doubt Rory ever chooses wrong when it comes to wardrobe."

"Indeed not," Pel said, "although there is one thing missing to make this outfit absolutely perfect."

His free hand dipped into his trouser pocket and produced the diamond ring. When he placed it on her left hand, her costume was complete. She was now playing the part of Jace Hastings' fiancée, and thus had become as tempting a target for Rowan McTavish as Pel himself was.

"Looks good on you," Pel commented, "and yet it isn't quite you either, is it?"

She was glad he realized that. It wasn't an overly large stone. Merely one carat, the jeweler claimed, but it was an emerald cut and featured two tapered baguette stones on either side. The setting itself was platinum. It was right for a performance as Jace Hastings' intended but would never have been a choice she made, had she been asked. Briefly, she wondered what Pel would have chosen on his own. "Too flashy for me," Gaelen said, then added, "I'd tell you to break a leg, but I think you already had help with that in the past."

"Plus having one seriously limits bedroom agility. Warning, though—I have no intention of letting loose of you throughout the cocktail party to follow."

"Suits me just fine, Mr. Hastings," she agreed, then drifted away as Paul Montgomery's voice floated back to them from the stage.

****

His godfather was in his element, Pel mused. In

total control of their audience, Paul whetted their appetite for what was to come.

"We're recording this live, folks," Montgomery said, "so while we appreciate applause, we'd also appreciate it if you'd keep it short. Saves the crew from cutting long bits out. There's only so much room on a CD, although the downloadable version will likely get a couple extra songs added. At least if I can wring 'em out of our performers tonight.

"This isn't just any CD, though. It's one to benefit a charity that I've been shoveling money into for years, as has my wife, Red, who some days is worth more than I am."

The audience chuckled as though cued.

"The charity in question is one founded by my godson. Now, you all know how difficult it is to pry personal information out of me."

"Tell us about it," someone in the crowd yelled.

"Yeah, I'm one secretive bastard, aren't I? Well, tonight I'm going to tell you whose parents were foolish enough to name me their kid's godfather. You might remember him. The guy was breaking hearts a decade ago: Jace Hastings."

From where he was stationed in the shadows at the back of the stage, Pel saw a few startled glances exchanged.

"Yeah, everyone thinks of him as the late Jace Hastings, but the only reason he's *late* is that the man apparently can't tell time. Years went by before he remembered he had family, friends, and possibly fans who'd like to have him back among them. What he's been doing is something that was always dear to his heart, though—helping those in need and doing what he could to save the planet. He's been totally on board with Blue Marmalade."

"Uncle Paul. That's Blue Marble Aid," Nan said into her own mic from just offstage.

Montgomery turned to look back to where he knew she stood. "That's what I said. Blue Marmalade."

Which was Pel's cue. "Blue. Marble. Aid," he said, his disembodied voice firmly separating the words.

On stage, Paul frowned. "Blue. Marble. Aid," he repeated. "You mean I've been writing checks to the wrong place all these years?" Then he faced the chuckling audience again. "Okay, now that that's clear, you'll be getting all the particulars sent magically to your email boxes at the close of the show. We even took a cast picture for you earlier today. But I know that's not what you came here for tonight—and we really appreciate that some of you actually flew in from the East Coast—however, the lure was the free drinks and horses' doovers we'll be serving after the show, wasn't it? You'll also be able to schmooze with those of us who have actually sung our hearts out tonight, cliché though it is."

He looked down at the technicians, most of them hunkered down over equipment placed on the floor. "Ready to kick things off, gents?"

"Roger wilco," one of them said.

"Nobody by that name here," Paul announced. "However, we do have the awesome Nan Rawlins, the amazing C.C. Pelham, the legendary Jay Flannery…"

As each took their place on the miniscule stage, Pel edged his way behind the screens they'd set up so that his entrance spit him next to the piano bench without needing to cross the stage.

"…and the long-lost Jace Hastings!" Montgomery ended.

Pel slid onto the piano bench as Nan, C.C., and Rika leaned together and crooned, "Comin' home to you." The spotlight hit him a second before he followed with a partially growled, "I'm comin' home, baby." An instant burst of welcoming applause flowed toward him from the gathered critics. The drums rattled a staccato beat. Then Pel hit the ivories, adding the base rhythm, and the show took flight.

****

Phoenix Herald online:

JACE HASTINGS LIVES! A decade after the traffic accident that we all thought took musical wonder boy Jace Hastings' life, it turns out that he didn't die, just spent the next year getting back on his feet and then wandered the world under the musical radar. Last night at C.C.'s Place, a jazz club and restaurant new to Surprise, Paul Montgomery reintroduced Hastings to the world he belongs in.

The venue was limited to an audience of music critics from across the country, but as the show was being recorded for distribution this autumn, shortly the world will indeed be Hastings' playground once more.

In the ten years he's been away from performing, Hastings' style has mellowed and become more diversified than it was when he was in his twenties. But the magic is still there. A decade ago, he could bring tears to even the toughest guy's eyes, and he did it again in Surprise last night. Not just with the iconic "Misty," which closed the show, but with "In the Wee Small Hours of the Morning" where the lyrics switched in mid phrase from Hastings to C.C. Pelham, then on to

Montgomery, and back to Hastings more than once. The weeping solo by jazz trombone great Jay Flannery nudged this rendition of the tune into the history books.

This is the same Jace Hastings, and yet it's a new version of him. This one is playful. On some tunes the music seemed to actually strut. When Nan Rawlins sang a flirty version of "He's A Tramp," she trailed her fingers through his hair and across his tuxedoed shoulders and ended the song by planting a smacker on his cheek. Hastings made no effort to wipe the bright red lipstick away until after the show.

Montgomery himself sang a peppy "You've Got a Friend In Me," to which he, Hastings, and their lovely backup singers all waved jazz hands above their heads as the downsized numerically but not sound-wise brass section nearly stole the show. Hastings now plays the harmonica as well as the piano—a baby grand on this smaller stage but still the iconic Hastings stage dressing—and his rendition of "Hi-De-Ho" benefitted from the addition. But then, every song performed was clearly marked as a Hastings arrangement.

From the applause and standing ovation, Jace Hastings was most definitely welcomed back to the world of popular music.

****

Billboard, online edition:

Superstar Paul Montgomery is known for surprising audiences, but he's also known for keeping secrets. In the small Phoenix suburb of Surprise Monday night, Montgomery not only let one of his secrets out—that he is the godfather of another great musical talent, but then surprised us in Surprise by reintroducing that godson to the stage. His name? Jace

Hastings.

Hastings hasn't set foot on a stage in the decade since the traffic accident that killed singer Ashley Hopper and landed Hastings in intensive care. In fact, everyone thought he'd succumbed to injuries and died himself.

His reintroduction came with a string of talented friends. Not just Montgomery but...

****

@Nuts4JaceH Knew you couldn't be dead! Dying for the new release!

#jacehastings #bluemarbleaid is awesome. Gave— just GAVE—me my first guitar. A Fender!

NanRawlinsSings on Facebook. Join me for my weekly podcast and meet my new best friend Paprika Mendez who I met on stage with Jace Hastings. We'll be talking music, and all things Jace Hastings!

@Fan4Life4JaceH Remember me? I gave you a single red rose when you autographed my arm in Denver 12 yrs ago. Still planning to marry you. Call me. # the same.

@JaceHastingsSings Sorry @Fan4Life4JaceH I'm engaged.

@Fan4Life4JaceH NOOOO!!!!!

****

"What the hell? I don't have any social media accounts!" Pel snarled as he stared at the screen of the cellphone his godfather handed to him in exchange for a cup of coffee.

"You do now," Rory Montgomery said as she dunked a tea bag in and out of a cup of hot water. "Don't worry. I answered that message for you. In fact—" She paused long enough to push a sheet of paper across the table to him. "—here are your account log-ins and passwords. If you can't stay on top of them, Pel, hire a media go-fer to do them for you. It'll likely be a full-time job."

****

Gaelen had said her farewells to the visitors from California when the last of the media guests finally drove away from C.C.'s Place. Scott Rawlins and his team of technicians weren't trusting an electronic alarm with their equipment or the now priceless—at least nearly priceless, the way they were treating them— sound recordings and reloaded the truck with everything while there were still rented cops to keep the curious critics away. She'd lost count of the number of times her picture had been taken once electronics were returned after the food ran out, usually with Pel's arm around her waist, and once someone had caught them kissing.

"Should have locked the office door, I guess," he'd said and then returned to kissing her.

The scenario was well and truly sold. He'd kept her by his side throughout the cocktail party, always staying on her left to leave the pistol available should things go to hell sooner than they expected. The Phoenix cops had been warned that a stalker from ten years ago might surface, but that was all they were told. The only people stalking him at the party were those who wanted details on where he'd been and what he'd been doing for the past decade. Pel admitted to traveling in disguise but said he was doing it to be at the people level, the people who could best use aid from Blue Marble.

"If any of you remember the old me, I was just as

determined to promote renewable energy sources and saving this big blue marble—you know, Earth—though one guy with a small nonprofit foundation can't change the world alone. He can help others do things that will begin to make a difference, though," he said over and over again, just using different words. The message didn't change. It wasn't the past he wanted to concentrate on, as far as the reporters were told, but the future.

"Speaking of the future, that's some ring Ms. Shaw is flashing," one of the columnists noted.

"Yeah, it is," Pel—or rather, Jace Hastings—told them, "but Gaelen says it isn't to her taste. Wants something smaller, more in keeping with the woman she is, so it'll be going back to the jewelers this week as we look together for something she does like. Right, darlin'?" To which she always smiled and agreed, though she intended to refuse a replacement ring. "The only thing I don't want her considering replacing is me," he added, tossing in a fond look and the grin that still took her breath away. Perhaps it always would.

"Welcome to Phase Two of the plan," Cliff said after seeing Rika off in her car. "While some of the social media posts and reviews are already showing up, it's three in the morning. I doubt McTavish will know Jace Hastings is back in circulation for another few hours. Depends on how addicted he is to the Web. I'll still be on duty at the house with Pel after everyone leaves tomorrow. Gaeley, you return to seeing to the set-up of Firebird Investigations. Should we three rendezvous at C.C.'s for dinner, or will it now be a mecca for Hastings fans?"

"It'll definitely be a shrine for the next few weeks,"

she said, then turned to Pel. "Name your takeout, but be warned. When this is all over, you're getting a humongous list of reimbursable expenses from Firebird Investigations despite having financed the start-up for it."

He gave an extremely fake world-weary sigh. "It's to be expected when the owner only requires a buck to take on a case."

"You better believe it," Cliff commented. "You're just lucky she hasn't made up a price sheet yet."

"True," Pel agreed. "Considering I know you a bit better than when I handed that sawbuck over last week, what will you be doing *instead* of creating a price sheet in the morning, slick?"

"And it better be staying the hell away from any place Dr. Rowan McTavish might be," Cliff warned.

"Lots of boring things, boys. Rented car to return, refurbished car to pick up, and an IT guy to talk to."

"About what?" Cliff demanded.

Obviously, he didn't trust her not to attempt something. If she could think of something that could be done and not risk Pel's or her own safety, she'd have it on her mental To Do List. As it was, she was too tired to think. Post-show miasma, that was what one of her professors at the college called the day after a performance where prep time had been short and the cast frantic as they learned their parts.

"Computers for Firebird, of course. However, first I think I'll sleep until noon."

"Wish I could," Pel admitted, then gave her a quick goodnight kiss. Cliff followed through with one of his own on her cheek.

Before she got in the rental, though, she took the

engagement ring off and handed it to Pel. "You should keep it a while longer," he said. "We're still on stage as an engaged couple."

"It's safer in the safe at the house until it's returned," she insisted. "After all, I know what it cost—nearly as much as a new vehicle with all the bells and whistles added. With a car, at least you get more weight for the buck than with this."

Reluctantly, he'd held his hand out. She dropped it in his palm while wondering whether it would be returned to the jeweler or stay hidden in the safe behind the towels.

When she'd glanced in her rearview mirror before pulling out onto the street, it was to see both men standing in the shadows, just watching her leave.

****

Since the LA crowd had rented a private plane, departure time was when they finally got around to going to the airport, which ended up being after noon, since the celebrities were slow to revive. Whether any of them had slept much, Pel knew he'd simply spent the night tossing and turning.

C.C. and his father had arranged to meet with Rika and the trio to rearrange the C.C.'s performance schedule. Jay mentioned in passing that if it was all right with Cec and Pel, he'd like to stay and learn how to run a jazz club. He didn't mind seating customers, but Tom ran a tight ship in the kitchen, and the bar manager handled beverage inventory like he'd been born with an order form in his hand. They didn't need supervising. "If either of them have a problem, they can call you while you're off touring," his father claimed.

Jay was interested in getting more jazz enthusiasts

in the door and had some ideas to put in motion. Otherwise, he'd be joining the trio. "We'll just need a piano man to replace you, Pel," he said. "If Jace Hastings is on hand every night, we'd need riot control."

He'd laughed along with his father but had also felt booted to the curb.

"Just wanted you to know that when you go back on the road, things here will keep running smoothly," his dad assured.

Odd how in all the years of hiding, the one thing he'd missed was being on stage in one city after another, and now...now it felt like something he was required to do, not something he wanted to do.

It was even harder to settle to anything. The stocks were doing fine and didn't need his finessing—or if they did, he hadn't spotted where. While he'd been talking up Blue Marble, there were already aid projects in process in various places around the world. But when a man expected a mad man to turn up and kill him, it was even harder to think about the future, although he'd talked enough about it in a vague sort of way the previous night.

So while Cliff sat at his computer doing distance monitoring of things on his desk in LA, Pel scanned the Web for anything related to Jace Hastings and wondered which story or post would be the one to get Rowan McTavish's attention.

And whether he actually should show up at C.C.'s to wave a red flag before this particular bull's face.

Or perhaps...

Pel pulled up listings for upscale restaurants in Phoenix and choose one. Once reservations for three were made, he ambled down to where Cliff was still holed up in a guestroom and told him that for the night he needed to be disguised as a rabid journalist who'd cornered Jace Hastings while the newly visible celebrity was out for dinner with his fiancée. Then he called Gaelen and told her to forget ordering to-go meals, that he was taking her and Cliff out for dinner.

She balked at first, then was quiet long enough for him to think they'd lost the connection. "You want this all over with, don't you?"

"The sooner the better, slick. And to make sure we're seen, when I pick you up, could you be wearing that sexy red dress?"

****

She could have shown up in a gunny sack, Gaelen decided when they reached the restaurant. He'd made the reservation for Hastings, and it had most definitely been Jace Hastings who followed Cliff's truck to her place, since Pel had never been there before. He pulled into the lot behind the apartment in a bright red sportscar. The same make as the one creamed by the semi a decade ago. She half expected to see him in the tuxedo again, but it was one of his many Pel Flannery business suits. The shine on his shoes could pass for a mirror finish, though.

His once-again dark hair was tousled as though a woman had run her fingers through it. His jaw still bristled with scruff, and his eyes were the intensely bright green she remembered so well from photographs and videos. She found she missed the lighter shade of hair and the brown of the contacts he had used as Pel.

But this was the man he was. Confident, assertive, contemptuously defiant. He'd overcome the fear that had nearly sent him back to a vagabond's life a week ago. The impulse to flee had been crushed under a need to turn and fight. He'd found a reason to take back what Rowan McTavish had stolen from him—the right to live his life.

"You look fantastic, Gael, and smell even better than whatever this restaurant serves," he said.

"You don't know what they specialize in?"

"Picked a place blindly, based on the décor featured on their website. Does it matter what's on the menu? Chances are that if Jace Hastings fancies it, they'll send someone out to a competitor to pick it up rather than disappoint him."

"Disappoint *you*," she countered. "You're Jace Hastings again. Isn't that the man you missed being?"

"I thought so once, maybe even just a few days ago, but not now. He's a construct. He's what he needs to be. Hell, overnight he's ended up with more social media accounts than he cares to count."

She smiled softly. Reached up to smooth an out-of-place lock of his hair. "Rory's doing, no doubt."

His left arm slipped around her waist. Drew her in tight against him. He dipped his head to brush a light kiss against her lips. "On the nose, but I don't need to deal with most of it. I believe there are people who do that for a living."

Gaelen laughed. "There are. I just don't know any. Let me get my wrap, and we can be on our way."

When she attempted to slip away, he stopped her. "You aren't entirely dressed yet," he murmured and unearthed the diamond ring from his pocket, just as he had the evening before. "Show time, Ms. Shaw, remember?"

"You're a stickler for appearances, aren't you?"

"In this case, yes," he agreed and slipped the ring on her finger once more, "even if you don't like it. But before we go, I want a tour of your home. You've seen mine. Time for me to see yours."

With nearly everything being a hand-me-down from Luke's mother's house, the apartment wasn't a reflection of her tastes, of the woman she was. She had made do rather than made her surroundings say who she was. Even though she knew Pel hadn't chosen any of the furnishings in his home, the firm that had decorated the desert house had taken his measure, had recognized what suited not only the man he was on the surface, but the man beneath that surface.

"It's...sad, I suppose," Gaelen admitted. "It looks just the way it did when Luke lived here. Not because I was being sentimental, because this was never our stuff but someone else's. I simply stopped seeing it. It's pitiful rather than anything else."

"Slick, I'm not here to judge it. I'm merely curious."

"Then wait until the Firebird office opens for business. What I chose there reflects who I am, not this place. This was always...temporary. A temporary that I stopped seeing because I wasn't looking at it."

"It's Luke Wyndom's place," Pel said quietly. "The cocoon where you still feel safe, cared for. Loved."

He was going to make her cry if this conversation continued. "Cliff's waiting. The restaurant expects us," she reminded him. "Luke doesn't live here anymore. I haven't lived, period, in a very long time. Let's get this fiasco over with so that both of us can find new lives to live, Pel."

In answer, he offered her his arm.

****

Cliff's shrugged-on identity as a reporter included a small recording device to place on the table and a list of questions in the notepad feature on his phone. He waited five minutes before following them into the restaurant and arrived in sync with a waiter with a bottle of wine. Pel had left the vintage choice up to the sommelier. Around them he saw heads turn, people lean closer together while they continued to stare across the room to the table where he and Gaelen sat across from each other. "Isn't that Jace Hastings?" he fancied they murmured. Or perhaps it was, "What did that guy do to win a woman like her?" The idea sent his lips curving with pleasure. What had he done to win her? If indeed he had won her, that is. He fancied it was not that he was the elusive Jace Hastings but that he'd been the man to offer a shirt to a woman drenched by a tray of cold drinks.

When Cliff arrived on the maître d's heels, Pel got to his feet to shake the P.I.'s hand, both acting as though they'd never met.

"Mr. Quinnlan? I hope you had no difficulty finding this place," Pel said as he regained his chair.

"None at all. Thank you for agreeing to the interview, Mr. Hastings."

Pel waved the intrusion off. "Nonsense. It was perfect timing since my fiancée and I had planned to come into the city tonight."

"I hate to intrude," Cliff murmured insincerely.

"Please," Gaelen said. "Intrude away. Jace needs to get used to being back in the media, and this will wet his feet for the job."

After that, his only thought was whether, between the three of them, they had sight lines to everyone who came in or out of the dining room. Whether Rowan McTavish had picked up Jace Hastings' trail yet or not, they were ready for him. Gaelen had her smallest pistol strapped beneath her flowing skirt once more. Cliff's suit was modified to disguise the shoulder holster where his weapon rested, and every time he leaned back in his chair, Pel was very aware of the handgun tucked in his back waistband.

Although he understood the food gained rave reviews from gourmands, it was tasteless that evening. He couldn't remember what he'd ordered, only that he remembered to eat as he answered Cliff's mock interview questions.

The waiter was patiently waiting for them to decide on dessert when both Gaelen's and Cliff's phones rang like a well-rehearsed duo. "Anything chocolate," she said, then glanced at Pel. "This can't be good."

Cliff fished his phone from his suitcoat. "You're right," he agreed with her, then snapped his name in answering the call.

Gaelen was a few seconds behind him in digging her cell from the small purse she carried. It sounded like she was holding her breath when she said, "Hello?"

"Where?" Cliff demanded. "When? We'll be there shortly, Valente. Thanks for the heads up."

"What!" Gaelen gasped. "Yes, yes. Of course. I'll leave now, though I'm on the other side of town, so perhaps thirty minutes?" As she disconnected, she looked across the table at Pel. "Cancel dessert. I'm needed at the Desert Wynd office."

"We both are," Cliff said as he tucked his phone away. "But there is no way in hell we're leaving you alone, Flan—Hastings. From what Detective Valente said, things are heating up."

"And fast," Gaelen added, then dropped her voice to an emotion-filled whisper he barely managed to catch over the noise in the restaurant. "Oh, Pel. Hank Wyndom has just been found in his office—beaten to death!"

****

The parking lot of the building wherein Desert Wynd Investigations leased an office was attracting more attention than any of them would like, Pel thought upon arrival. Considering it hosted an ambulance and two patrol cars, it was impossible not to be of interest to curiosity seekers.

The lightbars on the vehicle roofs flashed blindingly although it was still daylight out, the sun merely ambling its way to the west, though hanging low in the sky. The vibrant shades of sunset in the sky seemed mocked by the strobe effect on the vehicles. Although it was long after normal work hours, Gaelen pointed out her father-in-law's late model truck and an agent named Nagel's battered pickup. Where other tenants and visiting clients parked, a variety of sedans sat with single magnetic beacons affixed to the roof just over the driver's seat, their blasts of light just as blinding as the grill and wigwag flashers on the patrol cars.

The splashy red electric sportscar slipped silently into an empty place away from the official vehicles. Cliff's truck pulled in just behind him. As though rehearsed, the three of them pulled the doors open and got out.

A uniformed officer stepped in front of them as they headed for the building's rear door. "I'm sorry, folks, but the building is currently off limits as a crime scene," he said.

Cliff already had his I.D. out. "Detective Valente called me to meet him here. And I believe a federal agent requested Mrs. Wyndom's presence. As we are currently Mr. Flannery's security team, we need to bring him in with us."

Considering the ID he carried wasn't issued to Jace Hastings, Pel was glad the LA investigator had reverted to his real name, though wondered if Cliff had realized the driver's license had been issued to Pelham Flannery or whether he'd forgotten they were still playing parts and the name was a slip of his tongue.

"Let me check if it's all right before I let you through," the man cautioned as he freed the portable radio on his belt.

"What was the name of the Fed who called you, Gael?" Cliff asked.

"Special Agent Spenser Nelson. I've never met him, but something about his voice was familiar, I just don't know why. Do you know him?"

Cliff shook his head. "Since I handed Luke's doc files over to Valente, could be he's here because of something in one of them."

When she nodded, Pel realized that he stood with two people who had become strangers to him in under thirty seconds. Neither wore a uniform nor carried a badge, but they were professionals in law enforcement, nonetheless. He felt totally out of place and wondered whether Cliff had felt that way around the music crowd the past week. With Gaelen it was harder to tell. At times he'd caught her looking wistful as they'd rattled off jargon that she had probably been very familiar with in the past. But this Gaelen...

This Gaelen was the woman she wanted to be. The woman Luke Wyndom had recognized lay beneath a singer's surface and lured forth.

"They aren't going to like that you're armed, Pel," Cliff said.

"Gael said the same thing. My gun is in the glove compartment, and the car's security system is on duty," he told the P.I.

"Since I no longer have a Desert Wynd license, but a Firebird one, I also left the weapon I brought along in the same place," she assured. "You think the fact that your license is a California one will give them pause?"

He shook his head slightly. "Not with Valente to vouch for me with this Fed. They did call us," he reminded.

The uniform reattached the radio to his belt. "All three of you are okay to go in. Forensics hasn't been over the place yet. We're still waiting on the coroner. They have the stairwell doors propped open, though, so don't use the elevator or touch the railing."

When Cliff and Gaelen nodded, Pel followed suit. Another officer held the rear door open for them.

"Is it possible they called you to identify the body?" Pel asked as they began the climb.

"Since Agent Nelson specifically named Hank, I doubt it. I certainly hope that's not why they called," Gaelen admitted.

"Probably whoever found him was able to do the identification," Cliff said. "At this time of night, another of the Desert Wynd staff or someone in one of the adjacent offices returning for some reason? If anyone was in the building during the beating, though, they either kept quiet and hid, or they're dead, too."

The answer came when they reached the third floor. A man in a cheap dark suit with a lanyard slung around his neck sporting official federal ID was waiting for them. Pel nearly bumped into Gaelen when she froze on the stairs. "Nagel. Why are you here, exactly?" she snapped.

Pel glanced at Cliff, hoping for clarification on who the man was, but Cliff lifted one shoulder in a slight shrug, clearly as clueless about the man's identity and how Gaelen knew him.

"Hoping to get a few answers, Mrs. Wyndom. My name, by the way, isn't Zeke Nagel. It's Nelson. Spenser Nelson. I'm with the FBI. Your husband Luke contacted me shortly before his death. From what he gave us at the time, the Bureau decided someone on the scene was needed. I'm sorry I had to deceive you, but secrets are rather our specialty." Then he looked past her to where Pel stood. "Jace Hastings, I presume? Or is it Pelham Flannery?"

It was unnerving to hear both his names uttered by someone his Pelham grandparents wouldn't have trusted to rescue a kitten up a tree because he was a Fed. "Flannery. The Hastings is my version of your Nagel apparently," Pel said, leaning past Gaelen to offer his hand.

Nelson's clasp was strong but not threatening. Then the government man offered Cliff his hand as well. Since Gaelen had bristled the moment she saw him in the doorway above her, Pel wasn't surprised that the agent didn't offer his hand to her.

"You said Hank was dead." Her voice was as cold as Minnesota at midwinter. "When was he found?"

"And by whom?" Cliff added.

"Cleaning staff. They called 9-1-1."

"Yet you turned up?"

"I was in Valente's office at the time," Nelson explained.

"Was he the one who gave you my number? I've changed phones since I left Desert Wynd."

Nelson tempted fate, Pel felt. He smiled wryly at her. "We have our ways, Mrs. Wyndom."

She arched a single eyebrow. Stared him down. "Are we expected to stay in the stairwell, Agent? If you're here to block us from the crime scene, I'd just as soon wait in the lobby where there are benches to sit on."

He bowed his head in what Pel identified as concession rather than anything else. "If you don't mind, Valente has a few questions for you. I'll be sitting in, but we need you to use the bullpen rather than your previous office."

"That sounds suspiciously like it became your office," Gaelen snapped.

"Not mine," he said. "But Akane Fujihara's."

She looked stunned at the news, which merely heightened the taunt apparent in Nelson's voice.

"I see you didn't realize how *closely* Ms. Fujihara was working with Wyndom, Gael," the agent remarked.

Because he stood nearly brushing her shoulder, Pel felt her quiver in irritation over Nelson's use of her name, but the rein on her temper was held tightly. "What I *see* is that when an FBI agent goes undercover, they don't necessarily disguise their true self, Zeke," she snarled, then pushed past him, leading the way toward what Pel supposed was the bullpen.

"Well done, Gaeley," Cliff murmured quietly as he trailed behind her. Hot on his heels, Pel found himself smiling. *And that willingness to take the fight to the combatant, buddy, is why you fell in love with this woman over all others.*

****

Gaelen waited in silence for Valente to join them. Since the Desert Wynd bullpen was what served in other office suites as a meeting room, it was long and narrow. Three desks filled the space, one end pressed against the wall, the other leaving a narrow area that hosted more file cabinets and a few spare chairs. She specifically took a seat at the center desk, Nagel's desk. Pel settled in at the one that held no personal items. It had been Akane Fujihara's. Obviously following her lead, rather than just take a seat, he arrogantly swung his feet to rest on the desktop, his ankles crossed and his arms folded across his chest. Cliff pulled the rolling desk chair at the third desk out, the one belonging to the other idiot Hank had hired, and leaned back, his suit coat open to display the weapon holstered beneath his left arm.

She knew why the voice on the phone had sounded vaguely familiar now. Nagel—or rather Nelson—had dropped the western drawl he'd used as a Desert Wynd employee, though she noticed he was still dressed as Nagel. She doubted as a government agent his suits were as ill-fitting or that he wore dust-covered western-tooled boots to work. His personality was still the same, snide and greasy. He smelt of tobacco, though a cigarette had not been bobbing on his lip. Probably because he needed to appear law-abiding now that he was unmasked.

When the Fed and Valente joined them, they were stuck with what she knew were extremely uncomfortable, barely padded, and mismatched waiting room chairs. To apparently show that her requisitioning of his desk didn't bother him, Nagel/Nelson spun one around and straddled it. Valente chose to stand.

"Considering you already had an ID on the body, either from whoever found him or from Nelson here, why did you call us to the scene, Valente?" Cliff bristled. "To interrogate us? Find out if Mrs. Wyndom or I killed Hank?"

"Mrs. Wyndom had cause to want him out of the way, according to Agent Nelson," Valente said. "A week ago, she walked out over a disagreement involving a case she'd been assigned. Plus, she's the one who profits by his death. She is now the only surviving owner of Desert Wynd."

"I'm not," Gaelen insisted. "I sold the shares in the company I inherited from my late husband to Hank last Monday when I resigned."

"Do you have a document to that effect, ma'am?"

And to think she'd actually liked this man last week, Gaelen thought. "Considering I sold it to him for one dollar, I didn't consider a bill of sale necessary. Hank would have laughed at the idea, had I insisted. He knows…knew me well enough to consider my word sufficient. I wanted no further part in anything to do with Desert Wynd."

"So you say," Nelson quipped. "We only have your word for that."

She bristled. "Perhaps I should call a lawyer before we go any further with this, if Detective Valente agrees with you."

"If you wish, though this is just a preliminary, Mrs. Wyndom. Can you tell us where you were between seven and nine this evening?"

"We three were together," Cliff said. "Very visible, in a restaurant, having dinner. Not only the maître d' but the waiter and a room full of guests will vouch for us."

"An entire room of diners will remember you?"

"Jace Hastings and his fiancée were dining out for the night," Pel said. "After the show in Surprise last night, the fact that we were there drew attention, though there might have been a few tables where the guests paid us no heed. Mr. Quinnlan was with us moments after we'd been seated. I'm sure the valet parking attendant remembers the red vehicle Mrs. Wyndom and I arrived in, as well."

"That's the window for Hank's murder? Between seven and nine?" Cliff turned his attention to Valente. "Since the officer in the parking lot mentioned that you were waiting for the coroner, I suppose that means someone saw Wyndom alive at seven, but he was found bludgeoned at nine? If the cleaning crew discovered him, why invite Nelson to the party so quickly?"

Nelson offered an oily grin. "Because we were discussing the data that Luke Wyndom hadn't supplied five years ago, but that only surfaced last week through Mr. Quinnlan."

"Via Mrs. Wyndom," Cliff added. "She'd never gone through her husband's things after his death until I suggested she do so. She is the one who found the flash drives. She is the one who managed to find the password phrase to open them."

"Which I find suspicious," Nelson murmured.

"Only because you are a bastard. You were one the day Hank introduced you as a new hire nearly five years ago, and you apparently weren't faking that the way you did your accent, Agent Nelson," Gaelen snarled. "Considering Luke was combing Hank's files for what is on those data sticks, I would have thought you'd have done the same, in all this time."

When Nelson bared his teeth at her, she knew she'd hit a nerve. "I did, Mrs. Wyndom. The information on the drives was not in Wyndom's files any longer. I suspect your husband either destroyed them or hid them somewhere. This was his father, after all."

If he'd heard the venom in Luke's voice when mentioning Hank in the video he'd left her, he'd know Luke had no intention of letting his father escape justice. Which meant that Cliff hadn't left the personal message in place on the thumb drives before turning them over to Valente. He had erased Luke's message from them. Probably after saving it to a file on his own computer, though. Saving it in the event she wanted the connection to Luke even if she never opened the file to see his face or hear his voice again.

Before she could decide whether to comment on Nelson's innuendo, one of the uniformed cops leaned in the open door and cleared his throat. "Sir?" he said, looking at Valente. "We found this in the victim's desk. I thought you'd want to read what it says immediately."

What he handed across was a folded document consisting of quite a few legal-length pages. It also was stapled between cover sheets that were pale blue in covering. Gaelen knew what it was immediately. Luke had had a similar document.

Valente took what had to be a copy of Hank Wyndom's will and leafed through it. When he looked up, his gaze was firmly centered on her.

"It appears that you have an excellent reason to want Hank Wyndom dead, Mrs. Wyndom. You are now sole owner of Desert Wynd Investigations," he said. "Your father-in-law didn't bother to change his will after revising it after his son's death. He names you, and only you, as the person to inherit his entire estate."

Chapter Fourteen

"It was McTavish," Gaelen said.

"It was McTavish," Pel agreed. Once the police had let them leave, she hadn't wanted to return to her apartment. Now, her back against the padded leather as they lay on one of the two long sofas at the desert house, she nestled in his arms. He doubted she had any intention of leaving the comfort of the embrace that night.

"Without a doubt it was McTavish," Cliff agreed from his post on the opposite sofa. "He hired Hank to find Jace Hastings, and Hank assigned the one person he thought capable of finding Jace Hastings. Who subsequently quit after finding Jace Hastings."

"That wasn't the timetable," Gaelen corrected. "I didn't know Pel was Jace Hastings until hours *after* I resigned from Desert Wynd. I didn't find Jace Hastings. He found me."

"Let's say I simply stopped being cautious around you," Pel said. "And I wish you'd both stop saying 'Jace Hastings.' I'm getting tired of hearing the name."

"We need a game plan here," Cliff said. "It's convenient that we were all at the restaurant and our presence noted."

"If the police don't find that a bit too convenient, I'm sure Special Agent Nelson will," she grumbled. "However, it is much better than needing to say we were all here where no one else would be able to verify where we were."

Pel dropped a kiss on the top of her head. "Sometimes it is handy to be famous. Or is that infamous?"

"Famous," she said. "Always famous. But as soon as Hank's office is no longer an active crime scene, I'll need to be at Desert Wynd to close the place down. It left a bad taste in my mouth before, and it still does. When do you have to be back in LA, Cliff?"

"Not for another week, and I can extend it. I haven't taken vacation days in quite a while, plus there are sick days to use if necessary. I can stay glued to Pel while you do what's necessary."

"That's not going to work," Pel insisted. "Gael's marked as a target as much as I am in McTavish's sights."

She tilted her head back, staring up at him. "Are you implying the three of us need to be as close as Siamese twins…well, triplets, if such exist…from now on?"

"We all tote guns. We all have each other's backs. Three pair of eyes are better than two."

"I'm with Pel on that." Cliff leaned forward, his forearms resting on his thighs. "What needs to be done at Desert Wynd?"

"The same things that need to be done when any business closes shop. The last clients either taken care of or shifted to Firebird to close their files. The paperwork from every case Desert Wynd handled boxed up and stored someplace. I suppose that place can be the Firebird offices for now. I'll need to find out how long they need to be kept. I'm afraid the answer will be 'forever.' I'll need to call the remaining employees, though it's just the bookkeeper, the receptionist, and the two investigators left, and tell them the office is temporarily closed. At least until crime scene cleaners have dealt with Hank's office. Then tell them they're out of a job."

"Keeping any of them?"

"Only the office manager, who is also the bookkeeper, if she's interested in moving to Firebird. The rest—no. Akane is going to be very surprised when I withdraw the offer I made her to be one of my investigators."

"Maybe only surprised that you know she was in cahoots with Hank and stringing you along," Cliff suggested. "While she told you Hank had taken over the case you'd been assigned, I'll bet he either gave it to her or had her birddogging you."

"And if it's that latter, she'll be suspicious about all the times you turned up at C.C.'s. She might even have followed you out here to the house. What's she drive, slick?"

Gaelen sighed. "Something as nondescript and common as I do. I only knew Nagel—well, Nelson—had followed me because his truck was easy to spot, although in some areas it would blend in as well as my sedan does in the city."

"Then we don't know whether Hank just had her following you or whether she was hunting Jace Hastings, Gaeley. Since Hank gave her your office, I'm guessing she not only caught the case but, unlike you, may have been introduced to McTavish himself."

"She did know I was monitoring the comings and goings at the Hakathi offices," she admitted.

The LA P.I. flinched at the news. "When?"

"Day after I quit. The day I started paperwork for Firebird, I invited her to lunch, which we ate while parked in the lot of the building next door to McTavish's building. I even took her with me when I met the leasing agent who handled the office suite I took for Firebird. Obviously, I'd no idea she was in thick with Hank at the time."

"Could be she only became his favorite after that, when she squealed on you," Pel said.

"*Squealed*?"

He shrugged. "Remember, I watched a lot of really old movies while healing, in the wayback."

"I'm inclined to agree with Pel on that, honey. Akane sounds like a climber. Moving to Firebird would be starting from scratch since the new firm didn't have contracted cases yet. Desert Wynd, though…"

"Saw herself as the next Mrs. Wyndom if she played her cards right?" Pel suggested.

Gaelen snorted. "Like that was ever going to happen. As Luke told it, his father only got married because it looked good to be a married man, and when a son was added, that only helped the profile he wanted to project. He thought that, as a family man, clients would see him as solid, trustworthy. Neither things Hank was."

She pushed away from him. Pel recognized the move for what it was. Gaelen was ready to rejoin the battle. Though he missed the warmth of her pressed against his side, the feel of her resting against his chest, he knew he had to let her be herself. Knew she didn't need him for what lay ahead but wouldn't leave him behind as she pursued it.

"I'm not going back to my apartment until this thing with McTavish is over," she announced, sitting up once he swung his feet to the floor to give her room. "But I don't have any clothes except the ones I'm in right now. A red party dress and spike heels are not going to make me anonymous. I'm also down to one gun, and it's the smallest I own, but that can't be helped right now. It's better than nothing.

"Cliff, if I call Rika and ask to borrow some clothes, can you pick them up for me? We also need another vehicle. This one needs to be something Mr. Flannery is unlikely to choose for himself, based on the two vehicles in the garage currently."

She turned to him. "Is it possible to transfer funds into my parents' account so that it's there when the bank opens for business?"

"Or at least within minutes of it opening," he agreed. "Why and how much? All I really need is the account and routing numbers."

"Dad has a friend who runs a garage. I had him totally overhaul anything and everything on my car while I had the rental car. When I picked it up earlier today...well, I suppose that's yesterday now...I noticed that one of his mechanics had an extremely well-used pickup with a For Sale sign in the window. It's scratched, dented, and probably has 200,000 miles on it, but since he's a mechanic it runs great, or so the sign claimed. We need to buy it because no one will expect to see Jace Hastings in such a disreputable vehicle. You've already got the wardrobe to go with it—it's your 'runaway' stuff."

He nodded. "Which all came from secondhand stores to begin with. Tinted contacts back in?"

"Absolutely, and baseball cap to disguise your hair. Keep the beard, just don't trim it in the coming days, so it's ragged."

She turned to Cliff. "You need a similar wardrobe and scruffy appearance. The three of us need to look like we're migrants just passing through the city, and hole up at a down-and-out motel. Maybe even move to a different one every day."

"That system always worked for me," Pel said. "We pay cash, and I have more than enough of that in small well-used bills to keep us for a month if necessary."

"Doubt McTavish is patient enough to wait that long," Cliff contributed. "I say we push him. Have one of my team in LA call him posing as a true crime writer interested in interviewing him for a book about the accident that sent Jace Hastings on a different path for ten years. He can claim to have a publisher already interested in the story, since Hastings has resurfaced, and offer McTavish a share of the royalties. He can mention that McTavish is his first call because it takes getting him on board to make the deal really fly. Jace Hastings will be his next call. And McTavish knows that you'll tell an entirely different story from the one he spins. That should force him to make a move."

Pel glanced at his watch. "I like it, but it's still the middle of the night, so we can't get moving on any of this until morning, which is still a few hours away."

"We need at least a few hours of sleep," Cliff agreed. "Gaeley?"

She got to her feet. "Agreed." Then she headed down the hall. Toward the master bedroom, Pel was glad to note.

He exchanged a look with Cliff. "The bit's firmly between her teeth," he murmured.

"Damn right," the other man agreed.

****

Local news, both that broadcast on Valley of the Sun morning shows and on the Web, had the murder of Phoenix professional investigator Hank Wyndom as the lead story. Probably, Gaelen thought, because it was sensational for the gore alone. She was relieved Valente hadn't required her to see either Hank or the crime scene. He'd simply said they'd let her know when the police were finished there. Specialized cleaners would then be needed to erase the signs of violence in the room. With the investigation ongoing, that was likely to be days away.

Rika was not only willing to lend clothing, she offered to go shopping at a charity shop for things, though said she'd hit a lingerie specialty shop and then a shoe clearance store for footwear. "You can make do with cheap shoes but not discount underwear," Rika insisted. Gaelen made sure her friend would not purchase only sandals. "Running shoes," she emphasized. "I can't run in sandals, and I've got to be able to run." She didn't add "for my life."

Once Cliff saw how Pel dressed that morning, he decided to grab a few things himself when Rika went shopping for previously owned clothing. "Neither of you leave the house while I'm gone," he ordered.

Considering she was wearing one of Pel's shirts in place of the red dress and was barefoot, she gave him a dirty look as he headed for his truck.

Next was the call to her parents, explaining about the truck and getting their bank information for Pel to do the transfer of funds. "Do we finally get to meet this man we understand from newspaper stories that you're engaged to?" her mother inquired irately.

"When we pick the truck up at your house," Gaelen promised. "But it will be a quick trip. I'm sorry I didn't tell you about him before. It's all been rather sudden. You'll like him."

"We liked Luke," her mother reminded, "and still haven't gotten over how quickly you went from seeing him to marrying him. Is this a similar case?"

"No," Gaelen said firmly. "I promise."

"Then bring him here for dinner tonight, darling. I'll make sure your grandmother is visiting, as well."

"No dinner, Mom. It's too dangerous for us to stay long right now."

Her mother sighed. "And why is that?"

"Can't tell you," Gaelen admitted. "At least not until it's all over."

As she disconnected from the call, she sighed. "Prepare yourself, Mr. Flannery. It appears the price of having Dad buy the truck for us is that you have to meet the family, even if it's a glancing blow of a visit."

He grinned at her. "How could they not like me instantly? I'm rich."

If the decorators had supplied toss pillows, she would have hurled one at him. Instead, she moved on to calling Desert Wynd employees, telling them to stay away from the office and that Hank was dead. Only the receptionist hadn't discovered that ahead of time. She just said, "I'm out of a job, aren't I?"

"Yes, you are. But with a month's salary as severance pay. I don't know how soon funds can be released for transfer. However, I'll let you know when it's been made. I'm afraid I won't be writing any letters of recommendation, though."

"That's okay," the woman said, her voice chipper. "I've been considering quitting and going to beauty school to become a manicurist."

With the amount of time the receptionist spent on her nails during work hours in mind, Gaelen agreed that it was a smart move.

The bookkeeper declined the offer to work for Firebird. She saw Hank's death as a sign that she should bow to her son and daughter-in-law's wishes and make her home with them in Oregon. She did, however, agree to take care of all severance pay deposits to accounts and issuing final tax documents for Desert Wynd in the coming days. "There won't be much left in the account after that," she warned. "Hank took money out faster than he put it in. I suspect it went into his private account."

The idiot Hank had hired along with Nagel was tracked down to the drunk tank. His being there was an occurrence the officer Gaelen talked to said was so common the man might as well give the address of the jail as his home. Another letter she wouldn't need to write, though the word *recommendation* would not have applied anyway.

Akane Fujihara didn't answer her phone. Whether that was a bad sign or because Akane had the number of the disposable phone she was using and didn't wish to talk to her was a puzzle Gaelen didn't wish to solve.

Pel had vanished into the back of the house, mentioning his stock portfolio needed some work. After all the activity of the days leading into the show, the place was nearly tomblike in its silence. She'd done everything she could currently and was at a standstill. She couldn't leave without clothes, and her car was back at the apartment. Even if she could leave, there would still be nothing to do. She couldn't even eat, since Pel's refrigerator held a few remaining bottles of beer and a selection of condiments but nothing more.

"I'm getting very partial to outfits like the one you have on currently," Pel said when she arrived in the doorway of the room he'd reclaimed as a satellite office.

"It means your laundry bill will be going up, since more shirts are being shipped to the cleaners."

"Not a problem. What's up, slick?"

"Nothing, and that's the problem. I don't know what to do with myself. There's so much that needs to be done that can't be done yet."

He tilted his head to the side. "Cliff's calling when he's on the way back with the clothes Rika finds for you, right?"

"Uh-huh."

Pel clicked a few buttons, obviously signing out of his business account. "We could always do what we've done every time we've managed to be alone," he suggested.

"Yes," she said. "We could."

"Could or should?" he pressed, tossing in the grin she couldn't resist.

Gaelen leaned a shoulder against the doorjamb. "Should? Even if we get interrupted by Cliff's call?"

"As long as it gives me time to pull a pair of pants on, I think we're okay, darlin'."

She tilted her head. "Race you to the bed, then?" He caught her before she'd made it five paces.

****

Three days went by in which Rowan McTavish made no attempt to find them. Or, if he had, they'd outmaneuvered him by changing motels every day. The idea was to avoid being sitting ducks or as isolated as staying at the house would have made them. Gaelen was the only one totally affected. Pel watched as she paced the current small motel room like a caged lioness. He'd brought his laptop along and bounced between the stock market, requests made to Blue Marble, and answering a few of the less stalkerish social media posts that now came into the various Jace Hastings' accounts. The Montgomerys let him know they were off to Alaska for a few weeks, but he'd be hearing from the producer of the holiday show before they were back. Nan also touched bases, still attempting to lure him into being part of her own tour in the new year. Cliff was distance-monitoring cases still in play in LA. Although his room was next to theirs at the latest motel, there wasn't a connecting door as they'd managed at other locations, which stopped Gaelen from extending the distance she traveled back and forth into Cliff's quarters.

Pel sympathized with her. He'd felt the same restlessness whenever the weather stranded him temporarily in any now-forgotten small towns in the past. Particularly if the place he stayed lacked Wi-Fi or variety in cable television channels. This time they had both, but she hadn't found anything to hold her attention on daytime broadcasts and taking him up on offers of making love was out, as she was too aware that housekeeping or Cliff might knock on the door anytime during daylight hours. At least that last he understood as well. He might look calm on the surface, but it was a lie. He wanted this all over with as much as she did. Possibly more.

When Cliff did knock on the door, it was to ask if they felt safe enough for him to take Rika out for dinner. Although it was one of the nights she'd originally been hired to sing at C.C.'s, the schedule had undergone some shifting in the wake of the show Monday night. Since they'd left his truck with Gaelen's parents upon claiming the disreputable truck, Cliff suggested taking a cab to Rika's and leaving the truck for them in the event they needed to run.

"Better safe than sorry," he said, then added that he'd be back but probably late. Very late.

Obviously Gaelen wasn't the only one the waiting was making twitchy, Pel decided.

Left on their own, they ordered pizza delivered to the door and spent the evening switching channels, never able to find something to hold their interest. By midnight, they were in bed, his pistol and her smaller gun within easy reach on the bracketing side tables.

"Is this what it feels like to go insane, do you think?" she asked into the dark.

"This is what it feels like to be on the run," Pel countered.

She shifted, causing the mattress to groan. Lying on her side, she faced him. "How did you do it for so long?"

He put his hands behind his head, staring at the ceiling. "I kept moving," he said. "Every day a different place until I got tired and stayed longer in one. The longest I stayed anywhere was three months. When the invisible target on my back began itching, I was back on the road. Sometimes via bus, sometimes grabbing a ride with a trucker, other times buying a junker and then leaving it in the next place I stopped."

"And in the evenings?"

"I wrote arrangements for songs."

"Without something to play them on?"

"Without something to play them on," he echoed. "Well, other than the harmonica, once I mastered it. When the pile of sheet music got too bulky to carry, I mailed things back to my grandparents to hold for me. When Cec and I decided to head for Surprise, once there was an address available, they shipped them all to us."

"So you lost yourself in music to stay sane."

"I suppose so. That, the stocks, and Blue Marble, though the music was mostly a silent type. What did you do when Luke died?"

"Hank didn't give me an option, really. A short time off to deal with taking Luke's name off our bank account, off the lease, selling his car, changing the insurance…arranging his burial service. The last shovel of soil had hardly fallen on the coffin when Hank dumped a pile of cases on me. I wasn't even qualified to be a P.I. yet, but as they were mostly skip traces— which I hate doing, by the way—no one was asking about my license. But when I got home each night and Luke wasn't there, I felt guilty that I hadn't the energy to mourn him."

They were both quiet for a while, each lost in their own thoughts. "Listen, Gael, if something happens to me—"

Her lips stopped him from finishing. "Don't even think it," she breathed against his skin when they

333

parted. "If you do and then give it voice, I'll feel jinxed. On that recording Luke left for me, he was expecting the worst, and the worst found him. We. Are. Going. To. Survive."

He made his promise with a longer, more intense kiss. "Yes. Together we will. And, when this is over, I want you to do something for me."

"Anything," she said. "Except wear that ridiculously expensive ring."

Pel chuckled. "No, what I want you to do is introduce me to Luke Wyndom in greater detail. I'd like to get to know the man who discovered the woman you were meant to be."

"Done," she said.

"Oh, and just so you know. Hiding out this time, things are better, slick."

"Better? How?"

"You're with me."

****

Gaelen's phone buzzed to life at 1:30 a.m.

"Gael!" Rika breathed. "Thank God. Are you all right?"

Pel fumbled the light on as his cell began vibrating on the side table. "It's Cliff," he mouthed a moment later.

"Yes, I'm—we're fine," Gaelen told Rika. "Why?"

"The police called Cliff, somebody named Valente? Gunshots were heard at your apartment. The police are on their way there."

Gunshots in an empty apartment?

"We're on our way," Pel said into his cell while reaching for his jeans.

"Are you with Cliff?" Gaelen demanded of her

friend as she scrambled from the covers.

"Not right now. We were at the musicians' union with C.C. and Jay when Cliff got the call. Don't worry, he told us to all stay here. That it was the safest place for us to be right now. Then he took off in my car."

"He's right. It's the best place for you all to be. I'll call as soon as we know more. Pel's on the phone with Cliff. We'll be headed to the apartment." *My* apartment, she thought. McTavish had bitten on the engagement lure.

"Don't do anything stupid," Rika said.

"I'll try not to," Gaelen promised, though with mental fingers crossed. She disconnected the same moment Pel did.

They looked at each other across the expanse of rumpled bed. "McTavish is really ticking me off," he said.

"At least he's moving."

"Yeah, but it was against *you* this time," Pel grated. "It's past time to finish this."

With that she agreed wholeheartedly.

****

The parking lot behind her building was nearly a clone to the one at the Desert Wynd offices on Tuesday. It only lacked an ambulance.

Cliff was already there, which made entry into the apartment swift. They slipped past the officer stationed at the door and took the stairs to the second floor nearly at a run.

The door to her place was open wide, and down the way, the college-age couple in the end apartment were being interviewed by one of the uniforms.

"They called it in, then locked themselves in the

bathroom until they saw the cops arrive," Cliff explained. "Only saw a man and a woman leaving, but it was dark, and they were facing away when the kids peeked down at them, so no description."

Apparently hearing their arrival, Valente stepped into the hall. "Mrs. Wyndom, Flannery," he growled. "This is beginning to become a habit with you two."

"Price of success," Pel quipped.

"I understand there were gunshots?" Gaelen snapped. "That I don't understand. I haven't been home since Hank was murdered."

Valente gestured toward the open door. "Let me walk you through it. First, the lock was picked, and not with any finesse, as there are fresh scratch marks. Since your car is in the lot—"

At Gaelen's frown, he sighed. "We checked plate registration. That's how we know. Anyway, it seems likely that upon finding you weren't here, the intruder took out their frustration by turning the place over. Now, to the shots. Follow me."

This time he led them through to the bedroom. In the living room, sofa and chair cushions had been torn off, the couch overturned, books and framed photographs swept from wall shelves, and the landscape painting Luke's mother had bought was ripped from the wall and apparently kicked with enough force to shatter the glass and put a hole through the canvas itself. The frame was twisted enough to splinter it. In the kitchen every cupboard was open, the china and food stuffs stored inside now littering the linoleum, the dishes all broken, and boxes torn open to spill rice, cake mix, and other dry items over the damage. The table and chairs had simply been pushed askew.

Gaelen's stomach turned at the useless violence since it indicated unleashed hatred as well as frustration. In the bedroom, the door to the gun safe was open, and both Luke's and her handguns were missing. *The price of wearing a party dress that wouldn't hide either of them*, she sighed in remorse. If she looked closer, she was sure the same signs of impatient lock picking would be in evidence. Or perhaps McTavish was simply out of practice after his years in jail followed by the reinvention of himself as a psychologist.

The coverlet on her bed had been torn by several shots fired into it.

Even more disturbing was the blood staining it.

"I think this speaks for itself," Valente said. "Any ideas on who might have done this? Or whose blood this might be?"

"Ideas, yes. Evidence, no, unless you find something."

"Humor me, Mrs. Wyndom. Give me a name."

When she did, he frowned at her. "And why would a psychologist wish to kill you? Of course, I'm only guessing that's the message given by the shots fired into your bed."

"For the same reason that he probably killed Hank Wyndom," she said. "Because we didn't serve Jace Hastings up to him on a silver platter."

"He doesn't like me," Pel contributed. "Tried to kill me ten years ago."

"Those are serious charges," the detective said.

"And we can't prove it," Gaelen admitted, "though that doesn't make it any less true. Have you found the guns from the safe here?"

"Guns as in plural?"

"My late husband's and mine," she said, then described the specific models of the Sigs in more detail. "If they aren't here, then he took them with him."

Valente looked up when he'd finished noting the details in a small spiral notebook. "If indeed the intruder was Dr. McTavish, do you think the blood is his or that of his accomplice, and if you have any idea on who that accomplice might be, it would be well to supply a name."

"We can't be sure," Cliff began.

"Of course not," Valente interrupted. "But give it anyway."

"Akane Fujihara," Gaelen said, "one of the investigators at Desert Wynd. I haven't been able to get in touch with her, which is rather suspicious. But, believe me, Detective, it is pure speculation that she may be with McTavish."

Valente grunted but added Akane's name to his tally. "I can't see that you can do anything more here tonight, Mrs. Wyndom, but I'll need to see all three of you in my office tomorrow afternoon. With this, I'm looking at a really long shift tonight."

They were just turning away when Pel's cell burst to life with a peppy short and repeated generic bit of music. The same ringtone the discardable phone he'd given her used. "Flannery," he snapped in answering, then within seconds added, "I'm on my way."

Rather than leave the apartment immediately, though, he faced Valente. "You might want to touch bases with the police in Surprise. That was the company monitoring the security system at C.C.'s Place. Someone's just broken in."

****

"McTavish is making the rounds," Cliff noted when they reached the lot behind the apartment.

Pel glanced at his watch. "At least he didn't get there until everyone was long gone. With Cec and Dad with you and Rika at the union hall, who was minding the store?"

"Your bar manager, I understood. The trio were on their own tonight and out the door on the stroke of two. Your guy had the system turned on and the doors locked minutes after them. He called Jay as he was leaving."

"That means McTavish headed straight there after leaving here."

"Seems likely," Cliff agreed.

"But why?" Gaelen asked. "He can't have expected to find us there."

Cliff shrugged. "Making a statement? He trashed your place so he's trashing the one place he knows belongs to Jace Hastings? Probably to lure him to the location."

"Hell," Pel snarled. "Just when we started pulling people in for dinner and entertainment. Based on the destruction in Gael's apartment, my piano is going to be only good for kindling when we get there."

"Armed?"

"Gun's in the glovebox, but since we didn't return here after leaving Desert Wynd, Sundance is down to the peashooter she was wearing Tuesday night."

"Sundance?" Gaelen echoed. "Wasn't Butch the one with the plans?"

"We have actual plans?" Pel countered. "I thought we were just reacting to whatever happens. You know, riffing on what we're given."

"Just don't get yourselves killed like Cassidy and the Kid did," Cliff said. "Rika will never speak to me again if you do. I'll be right behind you, in any case. Remember, McTavish has Gael's two pistols, but there is nothing to indicate he carried in the past. He was a B&E specialist."

"Which doesn't mean he hasn't taken to firepower since then, Cliffy."

"Illegally," he agreed. "Giving a permit to ex-cons is seriously frowned upon. We don't know if he took extra ammunition when he took the guns, but we do know that three shots were fired at the apartment. The neighbors heard them, and the bedspread's wounds back them up."

"Bedspread's wounds? Next you'll be spouting sappy poetry," Gaelen grouched as she pulled the door of the beat-up pickup open. "What you're saying is he's still got plenty of bullets to shoot us with, although whoever he shot here obviously wasn't dead when they left. You think he'll still be at C.C.'s?"

Pel yanked the driver's door open. "Hell, no. By the time we arrive, Surprise's cops will have responded to the alarm. McTavish will have vanished. It's where he'll turn up next that bothers me more."

"Just stay alert," Cliff cautioned and headed for his borrowed vehicle.

****

As expected, the local police were on hand and expecting them. Or at least Pel. "Mr. Flannery?" a man in uniform with the insignia of a sergeant asked, looking first at Pel, then Cliff.

Gaelen watched as Pel dug his wallet out and

flipped it open to his driver's license. She reached for her private investigation license, as did Cliff as he climbed from Rika's VW.

It was easy to see McTavish's entry method from the front lot. The glass door was shattered, the glittering shards catching the light from the tall security beacons that kept the area nearly as bright as it was at midday. Gaelen suspected one of the stolen weapons was responsible for the destruction.

"How bad's the damage?" Pel asked.

"Mostly the door," the sergeant said. "We did a search upon arrival, though we're waiting for the lieutenant to arrive. However, the rest of the place seems to have been left alone, but it seems unlikely that whoever broke in intended to rob you. They left a present instead."

"Like a bomb?" Cliff barked in surprise.

"No, sir. A body."

Gaelen sucked in a gasp. "A female? Asian features?"

The officer's attention jerked to her, his brow raised. Clearly, he was stunned at the description. "Yes, ma'am. How did you know?"

Hastily she confessed to not having been able to get hold of Akane Fujihara, though she would have to see the body to verify that was the victim's name.

Although obviously reluctant to allow them closer until his superior arrived, the sergeant was also anxious to have the body identified. He led them toward the entrance. There was no need to enter the crime scene, though. Akane had been left in clear sight.

"Geez," Pel hissed. "He's a damn dramatic bastard."

Akane had been bound to the host's pedestal, her position that of a maître d' waiting behind it to greet visitors, though her chin was propped up on the thick casing of an open menu, using it as an easel.

Gaelen turned away quickly and found Pel's arms ready to enfold her. While she buried her face against his chest, she also raised the back of her hand to her lips and closed her eyes. "Yes," she said faintly, "that's Akane Fujihara."

"Can you tell how she died? Was she shot?" Cliff asked.

"Yes, and no," the officer admitted. "It's for the coroner to decide but, while she does seem to have been shot in the upper arm, strangulation is likely the cause of death. There appears to be a thin wire twisted around her throat."

Pel groaned at the news. "Then it's probably a piano wire. Have your techs check to see if the baby grand is missing one when they arrive."

A moment later, another dark blue sedan with the white door panel insignia of the Surprise police arrived. An ambulance was right behind it, its light flashing but the siren silent.

The man who climbed out of the car had dressed quickly, not bothering to don a suit, though he wore a dress shirt over a pair of dark jeans. The sergeant excused himself to meet his superior, and Gaelen wasn't surprised when the new arrival looked them over as his officer filled him in on what they knew. Moments later he came over, introduced himself, and said he'd be with them after observing the scene himself.

Before he could leave, Pel's phone rang again.

This time he didn't identify himself to the caller but snapped, "Don't tell me. The house. On my way."

"Lieutenant?" he called after the departing man. "We have to leave. Someone's just tripped the alarm on my house. Probably the same person who visited here."

"Address?" the man demanded. But when Pel supplied it, the lieutenant sighed. "That's out of Surprise's jurisdiction. I'll call the county sheriff to get someone on their way."

Cliff was already in Rika's metallic orange Jetta. His phone was to his ear, letting those sequestered at the musicians' union know where they were bound, Gaelen guessed. She hoped he included a warning that they should stay away from C.C.'s Place.

Pel's face was as expressionless as marble when he slid behind the wheel. "This has got to be the last stand. The man is more of a monster now than he was ten years ago, Gael. Hell, what he did to that woman…"

What McTavish would have done to her, Gaelen realized. That's what he really meant. It also showed that the bastard would go for her first because that was how he could hurt Jace Hastings the most before he also killed the man he'd hunted for ten years.

McTavish didn't know it wasn't Jace Hastings he'd be facing, though. It was Pelham Flannery, and Pel was no longer the man McTavish had tried to kill all those years ago. In the past two weeks he'd become a man ready to turn and face the enemy.

All because he'd fallen in love.

With her.

How long had it been since Hank Wyndom sat

across from her stabbing his finger at one newspaper article after another, listing the reasons why Jace Hastings wasn't dead but out there somewhere, and telling her their latest client wanted him found? Barely three weeks? How long since she'd tumbled to the idea that the mysterious client didn't want Hastings found to shake his hand or for some other asinine reason? Within three days of gathering data.

Part of her wanted to protect Pel. But part of her realized that Pel didn't want to be protected any longer. He wanted closure, and only one type of closure would suffice. McTavish could hire the best lawyers to get a case against him thrown out of court, which meant McTavish had to die.

Killing a man, even in self-defense, would destroy part of the man Pelham Flannery was, and that was something she couldn't bear.

She had to save Pel Flannery. From himself. For himself.

For her.

Could she do it? She'd never fired on any living thing. Would she do as Cliff feared? Freeze when the microseconds to make the decision to pull the trigger were upon her?

She wasn't a woman who believed in prayer, in miracles, but a miracle was what she needed.

Pel stared silently and grimly ahead as they rushed through the night, but Gaelen closed her eyes and cast a wish into the cosmos.

Luke. I need you with me. Need you to help me do what needs to be done to save this man. Save him from a mad man. Save him from making a mistake that will kill part of him. Be with me when the time comes. Either I succeed or I'll be with you shortly—and actually, I'd prefer to live through this, but not at Pel's expense.

Whether the request was just words tossed into the void or having thought them stiffened her backbone, she was ready. While Pel drove like a maniac, leaving Cliff to find a way through his cloud of dust, Gaelen calmly checked the rounds in her secondary and much smaller gun, slipped it back into her waistband, then took Pel's from the glovebox and checked the magazine on it as well.

While the house was battened down so that no light from inside crept outside, the exterior was flooded with light on all sides. No one could get close and not be seen by one or more of the motion-activated cameras attached at strategic points. She should have discovered whether they were monitored by the alarm company or were tied to Pel's computer in the house. For someone who claimed to be a security expert, she was damn lax when it came to checking her own client's system. In the glare of the lights sat a glistening azure blue convertible. McTavish was not only doing well for himself, he didn't mind attracting attention.

Pel's foot didn't let up on the gas pedal until he was nearly on the sports car. When he slammed on the brakes, he yanked the wheel to send the pickup swerving, ensuring that the battered truck's tires slewed gravel and dust to batter the side of the convertible. When he switched off the engine, he left the keys in the ignition and held his hand out to her, palm up. Gaelen slapped his weapon in it.

"Don't do anything I *would* do," she said.

"Well, that really limits things," he growled, but made no promise.

Yep, he was going to get himself killed, she thought. *Luke, what should I—*

When Pel's momentum sent him skidding on the uneven footing and nearly falling, she sent a thanks into the cosmos, and had reached his side before he regained his balance.

Together, they pressed against different sides of the house on either side of the main door. "Count of three?" he asked.

She nodded but went on two, barreling through the door.

The chandelier that dangled above the Navaho throw rug was lit but adjusted to a brightness that only warmed the room. Not bright enough to read by but shedding enough illumination to not miss a target by.

The glow highlighted the man who sat at his ease on the sofa to her right, a tumbler of Pel's bourbon in his hand. A man she recognized as McTavish from his picture on the Hakathi website. And he was wearing driving gloves. The doctor was taking no chances on leaving fingerprints. Gaelen wondered whether the wire he'd twisted around Akane's neck had left marks on them. She hoped so.

"Mrs. Wyndom, I presume?" he queried, looking up. "And trailed by the infamous Jace Hastings, too. I suggest you both put down your weapons."

"And I suggest you…Put. Down. My. Whiskey," Pel said sternly. "You're not fit to read the label."

"So unsociable, Jace," McTavish chided, though he did place the tumbler on the table behind the sofa. In his off hand, one of the stolen guns rested. He gestured with it, waving it to sweep them both with the threat of the muzzle. "And so difficult to get rid of. You were supposed to die ten years ago, not Ashley. I had such plans for her. A glowing future. But you ruined that."

"I had nothing to do with it."

"You stole her. Made her take out that restraining order against me."

"She did that on her own, McTavish. She didn't need you any more than she needed me, and frankly, we couldn't stand each other."

"Oh, I'm sure she was using you, Hastings, but no man could resist Ashley. It was why she needed me to keep her safe from your kind," the mad man said in a calm conversational tone.

"The police are on their way," Gaelen said. "They don't take kindly to breaking and entering, which is what the security cameras will have recorded you doing."

McTavish shook his carefully shaved head. "Oh, didn't I mention? The first thing I did upon entering is search out any computers and shoot them into microparticles. Then I did the same with the security system. If there was a returnable deposit, Jace, I don't think you'll be getting it back. Not that you'll be around to file a request for the return."

He gestured with the gun once more, but this time he pulled the trigger, putting a bullet through the head of the horse in the picture that rested on the mantelpiece. "Just a little demonstration to show I do know how to handle a gun and never miss what I aim for." Slowly, he got to his feet. "But, as Mrs. Wyndom so thoughtfully reminded us, the police are on their way."

"It's two against one," Pel said. "We have a better chance of bringing you down than the other way around."

"Yet you haven't tried," McTavish scoffed. "I've given you a fair chance, too."

"Like you did Hank or Akane?" Gaelen demanded.

"They failed me. In fact, your dear father-in-law attempted to blackmail me after he looked into my background and where it intersected with that of Jace Hastings. He felt he was safe from retaliation, but time in prison teaches a man things he might not have known before. Each visit the state forced on me supplied new and different information. It was a far better school than the one that gave me actual degrees."

Gaelen edged to the right, putting more space between herself and Pel. "Put my gun down, McTavish. It's over for you."

He laughed and fired a shot into the wall behind her. "So dramatic, Mrs. Wyndom." As though totally discounting her as a danger to himself, he swung the pistol in his hand to center on Pel. "I can see why you like her, Hastings. She's obviously feisty. In other circumstances, I might have taken her from you for my own entertainment, but I like women who are more compliant."

"Was Ash compliant?" Pel asked. "She didn't seem the type. She was a bitch in and out of the studio, and everyone knew it."

Gaelen attempted to throw a warning glance at him, but Pel had eyes only for Rowan McTavish.

"She laughed about how easily you were manipulated," Pel continued. "Said she was playing you until she got tired of you. And she was tired of you, McTavish. Really tired of you."

"I'm going to kill you," the man growled, his veil of calm pierced by the jibes.

"This isn't California, you pathetic ass. It isn't LA. This is Arizona. The last state that qualified as the Old West. Stick that gun in your belt, and I'll do the same. We can see who draws first, who dies last," Pel snarled.

In answer, McTavish seemed inclined to accept the challenge, then he raised the pistol and fired. Gaelen felt the punch of the bullet as it hit her, heard the small weapon in her hand drop to the floor, and then she was falling, falling...

"Gael!" Pel shouted.

But their enemy was back in control. "Put your pistol down, Hastings, or I'll put another hole in your girlfriend. Do it slowly."

Through a fog, she watched as Pel did as ordered, bending to place his gun on the Navaho rug.

"Kick it away," McTavish ordered, "and not in Mrs. Wyndom's direction."

"Gael? You still with me?" Pel asked though his eyes never left McTavish as he sent the weapon skidding across the wood flooring to the left.

"Nowhere close to dead," she said, though her voice faltered on some of the words.

"You'll get closer," McTavish promised. "Now, where is the most appropriate place to kill you, Hastings? I'd thought your flashy electric car fitting, ten years ago, but that proved to be an error on my part. Perhaps at something else linked to your image. The piano. Get your hands up where I can see them." The weapon jerked, indicating Pel should precede him to the grand.

Though he moved slowly, his hands held at shoulder level, the instrument was reached far too soon for her comfort.

Through a haze of pain, Gael noted that McTavish stayed where he was rather than follow Pel, but he had taken his eyes off her, turning so that he faced the piano in the corner of the room.

"The bench," McTavish said. "Sit down."

Where was her gun? She'd dropped it, but with McTavish's attention turned away from her, what ran through her mind was *eleven plus one rounds*. Even wounded she could bring the mad man down. Hopefully before he shot Pel.

Her left shoulder was damp. Her fingers felt numb. But the small pistol lay only four feet away, just under the edge of the nearest sofa. If she could reach it, would she be able to fire? Be able to come even close to hitting the mad man?

"Oh, look," McTavish purred. "The stupid woman is trying to get up. If you're looking for your gun, sweetheart, it's way out of your reach." To get his point across, he placed a foot on her reaching wrist and put weight on it.

She gasped in pain, which seemed to irritate him.

"What, not a screamer? Bad luck for you, Hastings."

"Stay where you are, Gael," Pel said.

She was surprised that he sounded calm. His voice controlled. For a man who had taunted

McTavish only minutes ago, he now seemed to have accepted the idea that a bullet would soon find him.

Then she remembered. The county sheriff's men were coming. They were just taking their good old time about it.

But Cliff had been behind the battered pickup Pel had driven. And Cliff hadn't come through the door with them.

She didn't dare look toward the entrance for fear McTavish would follow her gaze. Pel must have seen something. His voice wasn't broadcasting it, but he was probably coiled to move the moment Cliff entered the house. He no longer had his hands raised. Were they resting on the piano keys from habit?

McTavish apparently remembered once more that local law enforcement was on their way. No doubt he discounted them as country bumpkins simply because they lived away from the city. As he ground his foot into her wrist, McTavish wrapped both hands around her gun, the one taken from the apartment.

No. It was Luke's gun, she realized. They were similar but different models, his model was bigger and capable of holding seventeen rounds to the ten in hers. And when she'd cleaned and loaded Luke's weapon, there hadn't been enough ammunition to fill the magazine. The clip she'd shoved into place carried only six bullets. If McTavish had been using it because he liked the heft of a larger weapon, he'd put three in the mattress, one of them obviously grazing Akane, one in the painting on the fireplace, one in the wall behind her and one in her shoulder. The next time he pulled the trigger it would be on an empty chamber.

If, that is, he'd used the same weapon at her apartment.

Then she remembered he'd just told them he'd shot up the computer and security system. There was no telling how many rounds the gun in his hands held.

"You know, Hastings, I can almost hear your girlfriend here thinking. What do you think is running through her mind? All the things she meant to do but put off? The happily ever after she was imagining at your side?"

"You're using her weapons, McTavish. She's probably wondering if the taint of your mitts around them can be scrubbed off after you're dead," Pel said, careful to keep his eyes on the man whose goal in life had narrowed to killing him a decade ago.

"Quips off the stage as well as on it? I'm impressed with the bravado, Jace. Really, I am. In different circumstances I might even applaud. Have you any idea the number of hours I spent planning how to kill you?"

"I'd probably fall asleep due to the tedium of even trying to count them. Are you just going to fondle that gun or actually use it? Personally, I think those were lucky shots you fired. Did they make you feel like a man, Doc? Did shaving your head, getting that tat, buying the splashy convertible? Did beating Hank Wyndom or strangling Akane Fujihara make you all fluttery with excitement inside?"

The gun in McTavish's hands wavered as he gritted his teeth in fury.

"Tell me, Row, were you the bitch they passed around when you were in prison?" Pel taunted.

"I'm going to give you a treat for that one,

Hastings," the man snarled and moved his foot off Gaelen's wrist. Keeping the gun in his right hand, he reached down and dug his left in her hair, dragging her up. This time, she did scream as she clutched at McTavish's arm while trying to scramble to her feet.

Their adversary smiled when he got the desired effect from her. But as he did so, McTavish's attention shifted briefly away from Pel.

Moving slowly, Pel reached beneath the bottom lip of the piano bench and slid a small pistol from the hidden holster attached there. With his hand atop where it rested on the bench on his left, it blended with the black finish and was shadowed by his body.

"Over next to wonder boy at the ivories," McTavish ordered Gaelen. He gave her a push causing her to stumble, falling to the floor.

Her face was blanched, her teeth set. Her expression flinched as she used the injured left arm to push back to her feet. The distance wasn't far, but with a throbbing wound it probably felt like a mile to her.

"I'm a romantic at heart, so I'm going to let you die together. Well, almost together. I'll take her out first, Jace. Let you hold her as she dies, and then I'll kill you. I'd prefer it to be slow, but those police are supposedly on their way. Don't know what's holding them up. It's too early for the bakers to have the first batch of donuts ready for them." McTavish chuckled over his own words.

"Was that supposed to be wit?" Pel asked. "Because it lacked both the 'w' and the 't,' leaving you the self-centered ass you've always been. Though it's probably unfair to all mules to compare them to you."

"Still attempting a standup comedy routine? Help her settle in next to you. Nice and snug. Put your arm around her so she doesn't hit the floor when I kill her."

"Your bedside manner needs polishing, McTavish. How many patients fall asleep on your couch? Or are you busy priming them for whatever job you want them to pull off? Cars like that honey outside probably demanded three, maybe four jewelry stores hit," Pel said, though he did put his arm around Gaelen's waist to support her.

"You're tempting fate," she murmured.

"Angry man, careless man," he whispered back. "Duck when—"

"Stop mumbling over there," McTavish snapped and raised the stolen gun.

Just before he fired, Pel swung the cached weapon up in his left hand and pulled the trigger.

At the same time, a gun barked in Gaelen's right hand.

But McTavish wasn't down. He fired once, twice, the shots digging into the grand piano, and then the hammer fell on nothing just as another shot echoed from the entranceway, and Dr. Rowan McTavish dropped to the floor.

Gaelen attempted to rise, staggered, and put her hand out to steady herself on the grand's cover.

Pel watched in horror as drops of blood fell to the keys, scarlet against the ivory. Then she slid to the floor.

Chapter Fifteen

She slept for a week. Or so it seemed, but it was too much effort to leave the bed, particularly as Pel was there with her. Her shoulder still hurt, but the paramedics in the ambulance that had sat idling on the road while the county sheriff's team surrounded the house had given her a painkiller before taking her to the emergency room. She'd been lucky, the doctor treating her there claimed. McTavish's shot had been more than a graze but less than a puncture. She'd simply bled spectacularly because she hadn't stayed still after being shot. Her arm would need to be in a sling for over a month, and she was ordered to take it easy.

Which was impossible. There was too much to do.

Pel had ridden in the ambulance with her, but his words weren't concern over how she felt. They were a lecture.

"What the hell did you think you were doing?" he demanded.

"Saving your life?"

"Where'd you get the gun you fired?"

"It was your gun," she said wearily. "When McTavish pushed me toward the piano, I stumbled. He didn't realize I was near where your gun had stopped its skid when you kicked it away, so I grabbed it. Where did you get the one you fired?"

He'd grinned down at her. Took her right hand, running his thumb up and down it in a soothing gesture. "I'm paranoid, remember? I've also had a lot of time to think. Apparently, I can think like an insane maniac, because I figured if McTavish had tried to kill me while I was in the roadster all those years ago, he'd want to make a statement on his next try, too. That meant, as long as I didn't buy another vehicle like it, he'd kill me at the piano. When I bought both the baby for C.C.'s and the full-sized grand for the house, I made sure the piano benches had a lip that was deep enough to hide the underside of the seat. Then it was just buying smaller weapons and velcroing holsters beneath the benches. I had a backup gun at hand whether he made the attempt at C.C.'s or at the house. Satisfied?"

She'd sighed and closed her eyes. "I have a feeling you're much better at protecting yourself than I am at protecting you. Did either of us kill him?"

"No," he admitted. "We winged him. The kill honor goes to Cliff, who was outside waiting for his moment of glory. He insists the sheriff's department held him back. Something about being a civilian."

"So, while we didn't freeze, we both pulled our shots?"

"We both pulled our shots," Pel agreed. "Now stop talking. You need to rest."

"You're not injured at all, then?"

"Just my pride. Sleep."

What they had given her made that an excellent idea.

****

It was two weeks before anyone would let her begin wrapping things up at the deserted Desert Wynd office. Cliff had returned to LA, but it was to give his notice. He'd accepted her invitation to be partners at Firebird Investigations. "I really don't like LA," he said.

"And why is that?"

"Neither you nor Paprika Mendez live there."

Currently, Rika was in LA, though. Visions Records had lured her over to talk about a CD of her own plus being part of Nan Rawlins' tour after the holidays. The suggestion had been made by Jace Hastings, who turned down the chance to take the spot himself. They intended to release the song she'd sung for *Jace Hastings Alive and Kickin'* as a single to the music networks.

Storage boxes were waiting to be loaded with Desert Wynd case files, but to ensure that she didn't strain her healing arm, Pel had arranged for a temp to come in the next day to move the paperwork out of the file cabinets. The only thing she was allowed to do was go through Hank's office. A pile of emptied frames balanced on one of the visitors' chairs, the photos dropped in the trash. All except the one of Luke and herself. That one she'd put in her briefcase-sized purse.

A collection of cheap pens with the Desert Wynd logo on them waited to be picked up by someone from a homeless shelter. They were taking the stationery, as well. The sheets would work well for the children to draw on, according to the volunteer she'd talked to. Any generic office supplies were headed to the Firebird office.

When she pulled open the bottom right-hand drawer, she expected to find files on Hank's last cases, including the one for Rowan McTavish. There hadn't been one in the cabinet where she'd found it weeks ago, but the desk drawer held something unexpected. A large paper bag, the top rolled down to cover whatever was inside.

Cautious of what she might find, Gaelen left it in the drawer but unrolled the untidy scrunch Hank had created. Inside were bullets. Spent shells. Hundreds of them. Had he gathered them up after shooting practice at the range, intending to take them to a recycling place? She knew they were worth money, but it would take quite a few before their worth equaled the effort Hank would have put into taking them anywhere.

Still, curious about them, she took a few out. Turned them over in her hand. Something about them niggled at her. Then it hit her.

"Detective Valente, please," she requested when her call went through to the precinct. "Tell him it's Gaelen Shaw Wyndom calling."

When he came on the line, she smiled to herself. "I'm clearing out Desert Wynd and just found something I think you'll be very interested in seeing. Could you possibly come by the office? It's rather heavy, and I'm still recovering from a bullet wound."

"Would an hour work?"

"It works very well for me," she told him.

He was curious when he arrived, and she directed him to the lower drawer. "Hank's collection to be recycled," she explained.

"I'm not the right person to handle recycling bullet casings, Gaelen," he said. She was glad he'd begun calling her by her first name rather than 'Mrs. Wyndom.' She hadn't been Mrs. Wyndom in a long time.

"Look more closely at them," she suggested. "They remind you of anything?"

He looked clueless but pulled out his phone, took a picture of one, then enlarged the snapshot to study it more closely.

"I think you'll find the markings match those on the casings you have on quite a few unsolved cases. Including Luke's," she said.

Valente looked up, startled. "But that means—"

"That Hank Wyndom murdered his son."

When he continued to stare at her, she sighed. "I don't know what was in those documents that Luke saved to those flash drives, Detective, but he knew they were dangerous to have, and he was afraid of what Hank would do. Did you ever find the originals in any of the files here after McTavish murdered Hank?"

"No," he admitted. "You think he destroyed them?"

"I doubt it. Hank would have used them to blackmail the people who hired him to assassinate their associates. McTavish said that's why he'd killed Hank, because he tried to extract money to keep the not-so-good doctor's secrets. So somewhere is a storage unit full of files that are waiting to be found. I'm sure you can find them, though it will take a few calls and search warrants, even though Hank is dead."

"Shall I take these with me, then?"

"Please do," she said. "And if you don't mind rifling through that box of Hank's personal things, you should find the gun that likely fired them."

When Pel came to reclaim her, Gaelen smiled brightly at him. "Had a good day dealing with things here?" he asked. "You look as chipper as you did the day you walked into C.C.'s and told me you'd quit your job."

"I am as chipper. You know why? I solved Luke's murder *and* I found a key that looks very much like the one I have for my safety deposit box. As the bank Hank used is still open, shall we go see what's in it?"

"Always up for a treasure hunt with you, slick," he said.

She'd been to the bank enough times to no longer need to show Hank's death certificate or the will that surprisingly had indeed left everything he owned to her. Now she wondered if it had been his way of paying her back for killing Luke.

"I've got a key to try," she told the teller. "I just don't know the box number."

"Oh, we can find that, Mrs. Wyndom," they assured her and went off to collect the manager.

"We need to do something about that 'Mrs. Wyndom,' " Pel said. "I know it's Luke's name, but it's too associated with his father."

"I feel the same," Gaelen confessed, "but I haven't had the time to get to a lawyer to start paperwork on changing it."

"I've got an idea that would change it without seeing a lawyer."

"You do?"

"You've been working so hard I think you need a few days' vacation."

"Where did you have in mind?"

"Las Vegas," he said.

"No."

"Yes. I understand you're familiar with a wedding chapel there."

"No."

"The Gaelen Shaw I know likes vehicles that look like everyone else's, classic love songs, and performers who've seen better days."

"Jace Hastings is still in demand. It's simply that Jace Hastings demands to be left alone."

"But Pel Flannery doesn't," he countered. "And Gaelen Shaw likes traditional things, such as yellow gold engagement rings with modest diamonds."

She glanced to the one that now rested on the ring finger of her left hand. The one he'd given her when they dissolved the fake engagement and the real one had blossomed in its place. Yeah, she did like simple, traditional things.

As the bank clerk with the manager trailing behind her arrived, the topic was dropped, albeit temporarily.

"Right this way, Mrs. Wyndom," he said. "Got the second key right here." He held it up to prove he did.

She turned to Pel. "You're right about the name."

"I'm right about the trip and what to do on it, too."

"Your key, ma'am?" the manager requested.

But when he slid the drawer out and left them to go through it, Gaelen was stunned.

"It's money. *Lots* of money!"

"Hank's blood money? Paid to him as a hit man?"

Pel suggested.

"I can't keep money he received for killing people!"

"Then figure out what else to do with it."

She didn't have to think long. When she called the bank manager in and showed him the neat stacks, most of it in hundred- and five-hundred-dollar bills, he looked as astonished as she felt. "Can you tally this up and do an electronic transfer for me?"

"All we need are the routing and account numbers to do so."

She smiled up into Pel's amused face. "Give the man what he needs, Mr. Flannery. The Blue Marble Aid account numbers, if you please."

Rather than rattle them off—which she knew he could do from memory—he swept her into his arms and kissed her passionately. She was vaguely aware that the bank staff hustled off with the safety deposit drawer to count the proceeds, leaving them alone in the vault.

"I can't go off and get married in Las Vegas again, Pel. My mother, my grandmother, and Rika would kill me."

"We just don't tell them, and we'll get married twice. Ever since you finally agreed to be Mrs. Flannery, they've been having far too much fun planning a big wedding with C.C." No one had been surprised that C.C. felt neither Jace Hastings nor Pelham Flannery could marry the woman who brought him home to music without a lot of hoopla.

"But, Pel, we really should tell someone," she insisted.

"And we will," he promised. "When we leave

here, we'll swing by the cemetery and tell Luke."

She knew her eyes had turned watery when she had to blink them numerous times to see his lovely smile, gaze into his beautiful green eyes. "We'll tell Luke," she agreed.

Author's Note

I have a thing for men who work in music.

I hung out Friday evenings at a rock-and-roll station in my hometown during my senior year in high school. Well, I wasn't alone. There were usually three of us, all girls, one of whom was dating the disc jockey on the air in that time slot. Then I dated a disc jockey myself at a different station, who introduced me to another one who was new to the station, and I married the new guy. When we broke up, I ended up dating yet another one.

But then I also dated a trombone player who liked the same jazz music that I did, and subsequently married a man who swept me away with his touch on the ivories.

Yeah, I've got a thing for men who deal with music.

When I started writing *Ghost Notes*, I realized the moment C.C. Pelham walked onto my stage that I needed a record company. But I already had a record company that I'd created in another book, *Superstar*, where the hero's name just happened to be Paul Montgomery. When Pel confessed that he hadn't sung in a decade, I knew who we needed to call—Paul.

Now, I have to admit, I really doubt that someone who hasn't sung in ten years could get up and running quickly enough to knock 'em dead with a show tossed together in six days, but, hey, this is fiction. And Paul seemed to think Pel could pull it off, so that's what we did.

Part of the fun of writing stories with heroes who play music for a living is that I get to pick out the songs they might perform, and I had a Jace Hastings soundtrack to listen to while writing most of *Ghost Notes*. Actually, Pel Flannery—or rather, Jace Hastings—was born via numerous replayings of "Misty" as performed by Jason Gould, Barbra Streisand's son. If you're curious, I have a list of the songs with composers and the names of performers I listened to posted in the blog on my website: www.4TaleTellers.com.

The first critiques I got from fellow writers doubted that Jace Hastings could disappear in the modern world as Pel did. But it turned out that everything I'd had Pel do was on the nose. I found that out by reading *How to Disappear* by Frank M. Ahearn. Actually, I think it's too much trouble to even make the attempt. Pel had a pretty good reason to do so, though.

Hope you enjoyed your time with Pel and Gaelen. If you did, please leave a review at Amazon, Barnes and Noble online, or Goodreads.

And thanks for reading *Ghost Notes*!

~Beth Henderson

A word about the author...

Beth Henderson can't imagine writing without music playing. While she can't carry a tune—well, not one on key—she was hanging out at one of the local radio stations when a senior in high school, went on to marry a DJ and land a job behind the scenes in broadcasting herself. Later, she dated a musician who played the trombone, and married a composer/pianist.

It was during the second marriage that she turned what she was best at—spinning stories—into a career that is now closing on forty published novels, plus numerous novellas and short stories, though written under several different names. At least in her story worlds, music can mingle with her flights of fancy and dance the night away.

Visit her at www.4TaleTellers.com.

Thank you for purchasing
this publication of The Wild Rose Press, Inc.

For questions or more information
contact us at
info@thewildrosepress.com.

The Wild Rose Press, Inc.
www.thewildrosepress.com